ALL FOR THE CAUSE

Also by Gail Kittleson

Women of the Heartland Series

In Times Like These
With Each New Dawn
A Purpose True
&
Kiss Me Once Again
a Women of the Heartland story

and

In This Together
Catching Up With Daylight

ALL FOR THE CAUSE

a novel

GAIL KITTLESON

WordCrafts

All for the Cause is a work of fiction. All References to persons, places or events are fictitious or used fictitiously.

All for the Cause
Copyright © 2019
Gail Kittleson

Cover concept and design by David Warren.

All rights reserved. No part of this book may be reproduced, stored in a retrieval system, or transmitted in any form or by any means—electronic, mechanical, photocopy, recording or otherwise—without the prior written permission of the publisher. The only exception is brief quotations for review purposes.

Published by WordCrafts Press
Cody, Wyoming 82414
www.wordcrafts.net

Dedication

To my father-in-law Galen Kittleson, an Alamo Scout in the raid on the Japanese Prison Camp at Cabanatuan in January, 1945—and to my mother-in-law Darlene, who knitted for the troops, faithfully wrote letters, and waited for Galen at the war's end.

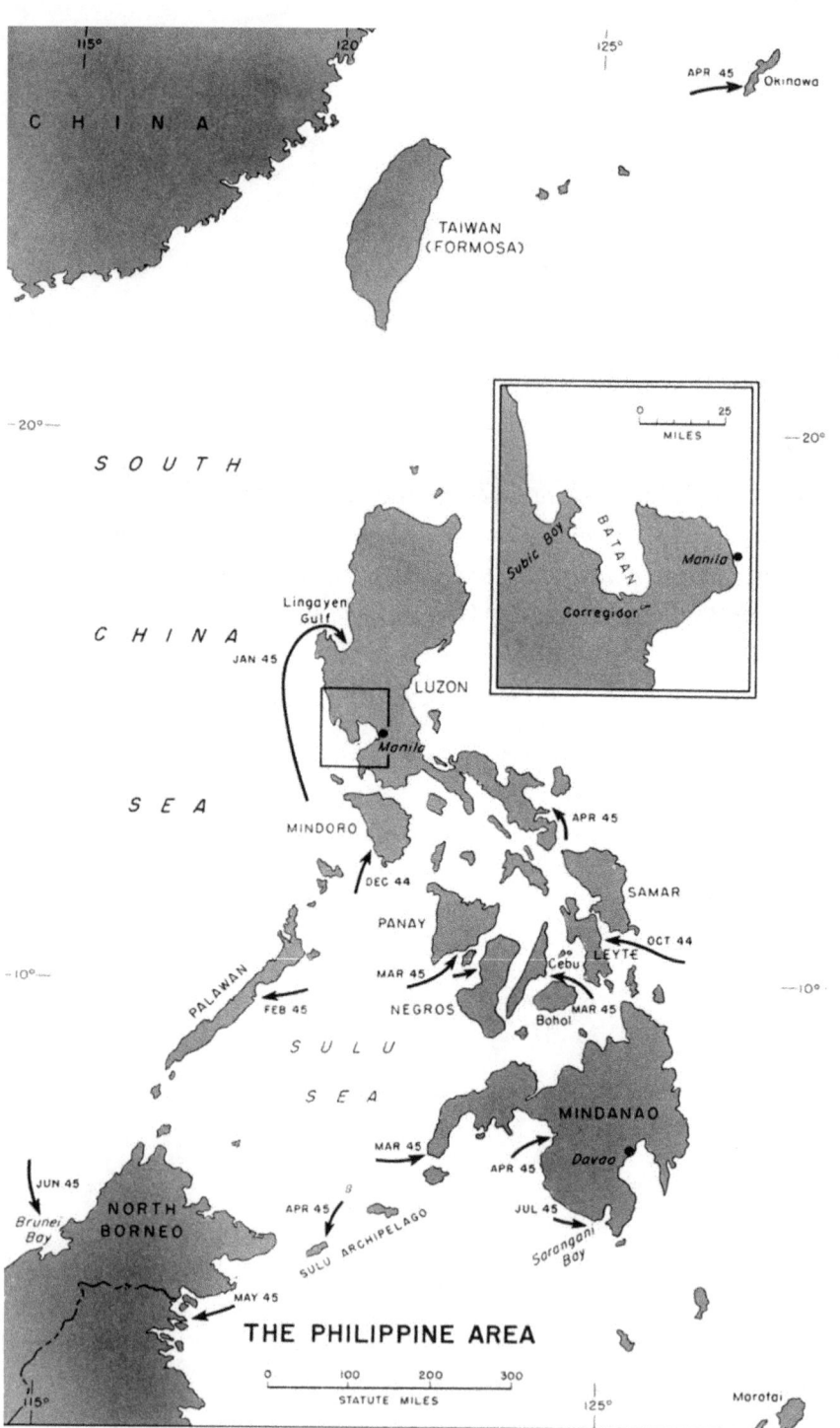

Chapter One

"What do you say, Lilly?"

About to bite into the vanilla ice cream cone Mr. Olsen handed her, Twila's five year-old niece Lilly spurted, "Shanku, Mister O."

Mr. Olsen glanced through the café's front window. "Dark clouds up north... Storm's a brewin'."

Through insistent static, the radio coughed out a message, and the locals in for morning coffee perked up ears.

> We all know that General MacArthur wisely declared Manila an open city after the December attacks that destroyed half of the bombers in his Far East Air Force at Clark Field. To avoid disaster, the General withdrew our forces from Luzon to the Bataan Peninsula and set up his headquarters on the island of Corregidor.
> In so doing, he bought time for 75,000 American troops in the Philippines and delayed the Japanese conquest four months, even while forfeiting aerial superiority. During this time, Malaya, Singapore, and the Indies have fallen to the Axis, but our forces on Bataan have held out.

All for the Cause

For a few seconds, the static won, so Mr. Olsen gritted his teeth and fiddled with the tuning dial.

Muttering broke out through the cafe. Then, as if in response, the newscaster's voice returned.

> *Harassed by constant artillery shelling, aerial bombardment, and disease, Filipino and American defenders can no longer resist the invader. The writing is on the wall.*
>
> *With regret, we announce General Wainwright's unconditional surrender of Allied forces in the Philippines. Upwards of 11,000 American soldiers have now fallen into enemy hands.*
>
> *Let us hark back to our President's Fireside Chat on December 9 of last year, when an estimated 62 million Americans tuned in:*
>
> *"Powerful and resourceful gangsters have banded together to make war upon the whole human race. challenge has now been flung at the United States of America. The Japanese have treacherously violated the longstanding peace between us. Many American soldiers and sailors have been killed by enemy action. American ships have been sunk; American airplanes have been destroyed.*
>
> *The Congress and the people of the United States have accepted that challenge. Together with other free peoples, we are now fighting to maintain our right to live among our*

world neighbors in freedom, in common decency, without fear of assault."

It goes without saying, pray for our boys. And that's how it is on May 6, 1942.

Distant thunder rolled as Mr. Olsen poured coffee for his customers, and comments crackled like popcorn.

"Surrender?"

"Unconditional, he said. Who woulda thought..."

"Sure ain't lookin' good."

"Sure hate to think of 'em bein' prisoners."

"Ain't Howard Hannam's son over there?"

"Yeah, and my brother's boy. Sure hope MacArthur keeps his promise to rescue them fellas."

While the men jawed about the news, Twila dabbed the ivory rim surrounding Lilly's lips. Her sister-in-law Sharon gave her a smile.

"Thank you for the treat, Aunt Twila. We're sure glad you work here at the café."

The twinkle in Lilly's eyes sent a wave of satisfaction through her—no better way to spend her tips. If only Dad could see how his little granddaughter had grown. Better write to him about her tonight—heaven knew nothing else newsworthy would be happening in Halberton.

"We'd better get going before the storm hits." Lilly clung to Twila's skirt as Sharon Brunner grasped her free hand.

"What a mess you've made—you got ice cream all over Aunt Twila's uniform."

"It's okay, I need to wash it anyhow."

"Come on, Lilly. It's about to rain—maybe Daddy'll come home early."

"Show Daddy my ice cream?"

"You can show him the part on your dress, at least."

"Give him a hug for me, please. We don't see him much these days." Twila gave Lilly a final kiss on the forehead.

"He's like a freight train. The lumberyard keeps him running." Sharon pulled at Lilly, whose smile highlighted the gap between her front teeth.

"Bye, Aunt Twira. Come shee us, okay?"

"You bet I will."

Mr. Olsen hailed her from the kitchen, so Twila snapped to.

"Marvin, I know you're busy with the crops, but Twila's been hanging around that Higgins boy, Ray's youngest. It started during the summer, when she had more free time."

Mom knew about Lonnie? Twila's cheeks burned. Thank heavens for the iron heat grate in her bedroom. Tiptoeing over creaky boards, she slipped to the cool wooden floor. With her ear plastered against the crossbars, Uncle Marvin's voice rose as if he stood right beside her.

"Them Higginses—rich as all-get-out, always thinkin' they're above the law. That Lonnie's a ne'er-do-well."

"If Don were here, things would be different. I hate to ask, but maybe you could…"

"Now Myra, the apple don't fall far from the tree."

"You've made me pay for my youthful sins so many times, you could line your old truck with gold."

"Well, you know Mama never found peace after…"

"I *know*." Her mother's shrillness made Twila wince.

"You made Margaret leave home, too."

Anger and regret laced Mom's tone. "My flirtation with the dancing world hurt everyone. You have no idea how that one stupid decision still haunts me."

What dire deed shadowed Mom's younger days? A cool breeze rustled the leaves outside Twila's open window, and in spite of the blackout, the kitchen light glowed down below. This must really be serious.

A twinge of regret meandered Twila's spine. Mom had realized her nocturnal habit all along, yet hadn't nagged at her once.

"Just so's you remember what you put us all through, Myra."

"Remember? Confound you, Marvin. Do you think I like not seeing Margaret?"

Except for the clock's ticking, silence reigned. When she spoke again, it was hard to make out her words.

"Rehashing this won't help Twila. With Don deployed, I don't know how I'll cope when she graduates."

"That gal comes by her spunk natur'ly, like her freckles. You wasn't quite sixteen when…"

"Oh, just go on about your business, I should've known better than to ask you."

Tick… tick…

"Aw, we'll think of somethin'. Just so's…"

Smash! Something shattered against the wall. Mom threw a dish at Uncle Marvin? Next, the screen door slammed, and the light went out.

Creeping to her window, Twila studied Uncle Marvin's trek to his dilapidated truck. The wind whipped dry leaves around him and seized his cap, so he raced down the alley to grab it. Back in his vehicle, he pumped the accelerator and sent murky exhaust drifting down the alley. Under duress, the old truck puttered west into the Iowa night.

Rain spattered the pane and slid drop by drop onto the windowsill. The cool dribble against her knuckles highlighted how eerie the house seemed with Dad gone.

Uncle Marvin barely missed a downpour, but not before he tasted Mom's wrath. Such a bitter tinge to her voice. When had she ever lashed out that way? And when had she asked anybody for help?

The rain turned into an onslaught. This afternoon, Mr. Olsen predicted, "Gonna be an early fall—already feel a chill in the mornings."

A sniffle wafted from below, and Twila lowered herself beside the grate again, but the kitchen swam in charcoal. Only intermittent sniffs interrupted the clock's steady ticking.

Though tempted to carry out her usual escape, she crawled into bed. One July evening, she'd even fled this prison in a hailstorm. The iced-over drainpipe made the going easier, and like always, Lonnie waited in the *Half Froze Bar's* smoky back room.

Her sigh stretched into a groan. Summer had lasted forever—hot, monotonous days at the café and working in the garden in the evenings. Then came the canning—the fruit cellar bulged with quart jars of everything from tomatoes to applesauce.

Even returning to school had been an improvement, although the football team was floundering, with its star quarterback and two linebackers gone off to war. At least basketball practice would start soon—something to look forward to.

By now, Lonnie would be playing pool. Under his *Wildroot*-sleeked hair, he'd nurse a pout, and his slouch would mirror Humphrey Bogart's.

Halberton's respectable folks labeled the *Half Froze* evil, and Dad would never have allowed her go in there. But what harm could there be in playing a little pool?

Ah well. Lonnie would be less disappointed tonight than Dad if she got in trouble. The thought of letting him down created an ache in her chest. The adventure of the forbidden bar faded as the cinematic image of ravaged Welsh homeland marched across her ceiling. *How Green Was My Valley*—what a movie! Since the theater owner's wife had been sick for a week in August, Twila volunteered to work the concessions and got to watch it three times.

Tonight, those Welsh hills seemed far more real than Halberton's nondescript farmland, and Huw Morgan's plaintive narrative replayed verbatim:

Everything I ever learnt as a small boy came from my father, and I never found anything he ever told me to be wrong or worthless. The simple lessons he taught me are as sharp and clear in my mind as if I had heard them only yesterday.

Dad was the soul of this family, too, and it had been almost two years since he left for the West Coast. He'd had no choice, really. The Army needed him for a training center, but his parting look still haunted her.

I'm going from my valley... Devastation tinged Huw's voice—but this was where the comparison ended. Huw cared so deeply about his home, but when she finally managed to leave this podunk town, she would feel no regret.

Was it this same longing that had lured Mom away? *You wasn't quite sixteen...* The flaking ceiling plaster gave no clues.

"What on earth did she do? Must be evidence around here somewhere."

But where? The wooden chest of drawers in Rodney's old room held only yellowed baby clothes. Why in the world did Mom keep all that stuff? What about her cedar chest? Maybe the secret lay deep in its mothballed recesses.

Another sniffle drifted from the kitchen. Mom never cried, even when Grandma Fowler died. Whatever troubled her right now must be worth a search, and tomorrow was Saturday—she'd be working overtime at the Hormel factory.

Tick... tick.

The window revealed not a single light burning in the whole block. For all that went on in this little burg, they might as well be living out in the country.

Mom finally climbed the stairs to her room. Then, as if someone flipped a heavenly switch, the rain ceased and the moon teased the earth from behind a cloud.

My flirtation with the dancing world...

Making a fist around her iron headboard, Twila vowed, "Even if I have to turn the house upside down, I *will* figure this out."

Chapter Two

In late October sunshine, Twila hurried to Rodney and Sharon's house to watch Lilly while Sharon helped her grandma with something. In the back yard, a high maple dropped a few recalcitrant dry leaves.

Before she could knock, Sharon opened the door, and a newspaper fell to the porch floor. Front page headlines blared,

MISS VICTORY SEARCH GIVEN BIG RESPONSE

"Miss Victory?"

"The Los Angeles Examiner has launched a search for the typical American war worker in all of the munitions factories out in California. See these photos?"

Sharon pointed out two workers poised at Rockwell hardness testing machines. With perfect victory rolls, they formed the picture of patriotism.

"This one, Audrey Tandy, works down the line from my sis. Just think, one of them could win the title, plus an all-expense-paid trip to Chicago to compete on a higher level, not to mention a thousand dollar savings bond."

"Wow! But who in right mind would want to leave California?"

Sharon caught her upper lip with her teeth. "A homesick girl like Nan—she's been gone six months already, and misses us all. I can read between the lines in her letters. Anyway, the *Examiner* will send the winner back afterward."

Lilly bounded up the steps and tackled Twila from behind "Guess what? My new teeth is growin' in, and my teacher says—"

"*Are* growing, honey." Sharon licked her finger and rubbed a smudge on Lilly's nose. "Aunt Twila will give you a bath tonight—don't fight her, all right?" She rolled her eyes. "If there ever was a tomboy, this one is it."

"Just like your aunt, huh? Okay, show me what you've been up to."

Lilly grabbed Twila's hand and pulled her toward the back fence. "I'm makin' a fort outta corn stalks, n' you can help me."

Twila stooped to enter Lilly's makeshift creation, but her imagination remained in beautiful southern California. Doing bit for the war in The Boeing Factory, did Nan and that lovely Audrey Tandy have any idea how lucky they were?

Autumn, 1942—the Bataan highlands

Delirium claimed Captain Burgmeier in this attack of fever. Throughout the sticky jungle night, PFC Stan Ford applied a cool, albeit filthy, handkerchief to his buddy's forehead. Knowing the fever's hold came and went at will, he waited while Cap spewed a trail of disconnected observations.

"Second Corps cut off… Japs took Mount Samat… we lost two entire divisions and a regiment… Sector H split… We need I Corps… replacements… rations dipped to two and a half ounces of rice per man now…"

"Cap, calm down."

"Fresh Nips… they never run out… routed three Philippine Army divisions… enemy at Trail eight… writing's on the wall… Colonel Doyle's withdrawn to Pantingan River…"

Trying to follow his train of thought made Stan's head ache. As an officer, Cap had been privy to the details of last days on Corregidor. No doubt, everything he referred to occurred, but the fever jumbled it all in the poor fellow's head. And for some reason, he needed to repeat everything ad nauseam.

"The 33rd Pennsylvania's isolated, enemy knows position... 31st under heavy air and artillery attack... San Vicente line...Trail 44 and Trail Two... wounded survivors... nurses out of meds."

Cap's monologue brought back the days of early April, 1942. In January, the Japs had already forced them to flee Manila and re-align to defend Corregidor. From there, they'd done everything humanly possible to thwart the enemy.

If only the supply ships could have made it through the Japanese blockade... If only this, if only that... Who could have imagined they'd be reduced to capitulating?

Inside the caves, soldiers suffered dengue fever, dysentery, or malaria, but the meds had run out long ago, despite a few successful airdrops. An unbearable odor permeated the area, the troops had run out of ammunition, and enemy shelling continued nonstop.

But surrender?

"General King... impossible choice... 78,000 men... pulled back to Binguangan River... Colonel Irwin... ditches full of dead and wounded...Wainwright beleaguered... desperate measures... retreat after retreat... General Bluemol..."

Confined on Corregidor, General Wainwright faced an impossible situation. General Sharp had been persuaded to lay down his arms, and was now attempting to convince Colonel Christie in Panay to do the same.

If even one commander refused, the enemy would resume offense and slaughter the 11,000 American soldiers on Corregidor.

Questions ran rampant—had General MacArthur agreed to this? Before he left for Australia under cover of darkness, had he approved giving up Corregidor and the southern islands they'd defended for so long?

Stan's stomach soured. Better starve than surrender. Others shared his sentiments, and word came that many of Colonel

Christie's men had vanished into the hills. Cloistered meetings took place, and pros and cons roiled in Stan's head.

Then, out stretching his legs, he heard someone reading. Sure enough, there was Captain Burgmeier staring out into the bay. Not reading... reciting something. Stan advanced close enough to hear.

I will arise and go now, and go to Innisfree,
And a small cabin build there, of clay and wattles made;
Nine bean-rows will I have there, a hive for the honey-bee,
And live alone in the bee-loud glade.

And I shall have some peace there, for peace comes dropping slow,
Dropping from the veils of the morning to where the cricket sings;
There midnight's all a glimmer, and noon a purple glow,
And evening full of the linnet's wings.

I will arise and go now, for always night and day
I hear lake water lapping with low sounds by the shore;
While I stand on the roadway, or on the pavements grey,
I hear it in the deep heart's core.

When Cap noticed Stan, he sauntered over. "Do you know the author?"

"William Butler Yeats, sir."

"Ah. I thought you'd remember. I'm leaving tonight. You're a Yeats man—want to come?" The captain issued his invitation and faded back toward the caves.

Confirmation flooded Stan. Anything was better than surrender

Now, a Filipino brought a gourd of fresh water and offered to sit with Cap. "You sleep. I watch."

Lying on a mat beside Carlos, Stan marveled at how the skeletal youth snored away in bliss. Exactly what everyone needed, but even now, Cap's continuous commentary echoed in his head.

"Decimated... incendiaries over the Alangan line... ordered to stand down, the whole battalion..."

He must've catalogued these specifics from radio messages on the sixth and seventh of April. He possessed that type of brain—perfect for his career, a professorship in literature.

His incessant focus on the surrender pulled Stan into analyzing the situation far too many times. Undoubtedly, some radioed orders never reached intended commanders. In other cases, the officers considered sick, weak men pitted against ridiculous odds and realized the generals lacked a clear picture of conditions on the ground.

So they chose to ignore orders. *Ignore orders...* Two years ago when he joined the Wisconsin National Guard, Stan would never have allowed for this possibility. Obedience to commanders was emphasized above all else. But he'd seen stupidity up close now, and ineptness corrupted by power.

Gradually, Cap quieted down. That Filipino must wield some native secret for inducing serenity.

Finally, an opportunity to catch a nap, but Stan's mind refused to shut down. The unnerving jungle quiet and occasional human movements outside this nipa hut kept him on the alert.

Besides, the questions in his head demanded answers. In those commanders' shoes, would he have obeyed, if compliance meant thousands more men would be killed?

Truth be told, General MacArthur, called to the Philippines out of retirement, had disobeyed orders by amassing the troops on Corregidor in the first place. Cap had described the Rainbow Plan that instructed MacArthur to relocate his men to the mountains on Bataan and await better-equipped reinforcements.

"That was time-honored, seek-the-highest-ground military wisdom." Cap's eyes glinted when he detailed this bit of recent history during one of his lucid periods. "And why did he decide to take on the Japs instead? He underestimated strength or overestimated ours."

What if General MacArthur had obeyed and led them all to higher ground? *What ifs* were the topic of many a midnight chat with Cap. If only they could have one now. Cap would turn each fact inside out, and like a master debater, reduce the situation to simple terms.

Following his logic often wore Stan out enough to sleep. But just before he did, Cap would inevitably add one of his pithy quotes to tie everything up.

Which one would he choose tonight? Maybe something from the ancients—let's see—Marcus Aurelius? "There is a dignity and proportion to be observed in performance of every act of life."

Peeking out at his buddy was a bad idea. One glimpse of Cap sunken into a fitful sleep, too far gone to display his inherent passion for words, sucked the life out of Stan.

Sleep remained a stranger.

"You're cooking supper? Thank you, Twila."

"Sure, Mom."

Myra Brunner's weary emerald eyes glinted in September sun coming through the kitchen window.

"You look so tired lately, and Mr. Olsen's only giving me a few hours a week at the café. Oh, I picked up the mail—you don't have to drop by the post office any more."

The ceiling bulb brought out rich claret highlights in her mom's hair, a shade darker than Twila's. For a moment, the tight wire drawn through her lips loosened.

Oops, better not be too nice or she'll know something's up.

"No letter from your dad today?"

"No, but there's one from Algona. That'd be Aunt Margaret, right?" Twila gestured to an envelope on the table.

"I hope it's nothing bad about your cousin Paul, although I doubt he could write from a Japanese prison camp."

"He's in prison?"

"Yes—he joined up before Pearl Harbor, and when his ship was sunk last May, he..." Myra picked up the letter but made no attempt to open it, so Twila tipped the conversation back to Aunt Margaret. No information had shown up in her dedicated search of the house, but maybe Mom would let something slip.

"You and Margaret must've been close growing up, but we never see her. I wouldn't even recognize Paul."

In the midst of tearing open the envelope, her mom hesitated. "Close? Not really. Your grandma had a way of driving wedges between us kids."

She never, ever mentioned Grandma.

"How?"

"What? Oh, I don't know. Your dad says she thrived on conflict, so we always ended up at each other's throats. That was one reason we…" She flipped through several sheets of stationery.

"Decided to stop with Rodney and me?"

"Mmm… something like that." Myra bit her lower lip. "Actually, you took so long making your appearance, we…" She studied the envelope. "Think I'll go read this on the couch. My feet are killing me. Thanks again for cleaning up the kitchen."

Against her better judgment, Twila tossed down her dishtowel and reached out. The letter squished between them, and Mom's eyes glimmered when she stepped back from the hug.

"With your Dad gone, I've been—"

"Overwhelmed?"

"You're so much better at words than me. I know he's only in California, but still…"

Twila retrieved her dishtowel and tackled a wet pan. "Only a year ago a submarine opened fire on that one town—"

"Elwood, north of Santa Barbara. They were aiming at an oil refinery. Your dad's farther north."

"But didn't one missile land inland on somebody's ranch?"

Her mom nodded.

"Wish we could've gone along with Dad, like Charlotte and her mom."

"They were supposed to need him for less than a year, to get the training started. With my job and you a sophomore, we thought it made more sense to—"

"Have me graduate here. But I miss Dad so much."

"He hates not being here for your senior year. I hate it, too."

"He told me your work's as important as his."

"He did?"

"In my birthday letter."

"That's right. It's November, and you turned eighteen last month. I can hardly believe it."

"You changed the subject. Dad said working at Hormel's is—"

"Anybody could do my job. We just happen to live close enough to Minnesota. He's training paratroopers—doesn't get any more vital than that."

"Well, those guys have to eat something, don't they?"

"And that something is SPAM." Her mother's rare chuckle triggered something inside.

"Tell me again why the military needed Dad?"

"After the Great War, his best buddy stayed in the service. His letter saying they needed men with weather balloon experience surprised us both." Her sigh drifted right into Twila's heart.

"He's never talked about what he experienced in France, but he would do anything to defeat Hitler. We knew Rodney could handle the lumberyard, and besides, your dad was born to serve. But you know all this, don't you?"

"Sort of, but everything happened so fast, and my head was filled with... I was so immature."

"Mmm." Mom grabbed her foot at the same time her stomach growled.

"Put your feet up. I'll bring you supper. Milk or water?"

"Tea, please. We still have a little, don't we? One small pleasure."

"You deserve a cup. Be there in a jiffy."

Chapter Three

Frigid wind drove between the storm windows—the early winter Mr. Olsen predicted had arrived a day after Twila's Halloween birthday. Before the war, streetlights or headlights flickered here and there, the café's hours had increased, and the Mercantile started staying open until eight.

But then came the blackout and so many other changes—rubber, gas, and sugar restrictions; no more hoods or full sleeves on dresses. The War Department Production Board encouraged the military look, allowing slacks for women, but the school still required dresses.

Since the Japanese controlled kapok production, the Navy called for milkweed floss for life vests. Twila's high school crew collected the fluffy white stuff from ditches and fencerows last summer, and won a county contest for the most bags.

The water kettle jiggled on the burner, so she poured Mom's tea and delivered a plate of reheated stew to the living room. Another letter from Aunt Margaret languished against the overstuffed chair, but Mom's hand fell slack. Dad's request in his latest letter came back full-force.

Your Mom wouldn't like me appealing to your sympathies—you're just like her, though you won't appreciate me saying so. She's carrying a heavy load and still keeping the books for the lumberyard. Anything you can do for her will make me proud.

Graying ginger-brown strands loosed from normal tight victory roll along Mom's temple. Setting the tray down jiggled the teacup and startled her awake.

"Don't know what's gotten into me. I fell asleep on the trip home tonight, even with Luella's motorized tongue. Her supervisor says she never shuts up."

"Never?" Twila sank into Dad's armchair and inhaled the tang of his pipe tobacco.

"Yum. You did something with the leftovers."

"I experimented."

"Whatever it is, I like it."

"Me, too. Mr. Olsen adds turmeric to his soups. It's his secret ingredient for a little pizzazz."

A wan grin crossed her mom's lips. "We can use some of that."

"Another letter from Aunt Margaret so soon?"

The twist of Mom's lips said more than words.

"Did she say anything more about Paul?"

"Just that she read about an Army nurse who escaped when Corregidor fell. Here's the gist of it:

They herded thousands toward some northern camp, sturdy Wisconsin, Iowa, and Michigan men whose ribs stood out like chicken bones. These GIs faced an insufferable trek through malarial jungles.

"Her last letter said Paul was one of them, right?"

"She's not sure he made it to land after the Japs sank his ship. He might have been picked up by... Otherwise..."

Her shudder was contagious. Drowning at sea—what could possibly be worse?

"She still sends a box to him every week. I should pack him one, too, and another for Butch."

"Two cousins over there—I can bake cookies tomorrow. We still have enough sugar, I think."

"Great—getting something from home must mean the world to those boys."

17

The howling wind interrupted the evening quiet. Then she said, "It's my fault you don't remember Paul."

The look in her eyes, as though she'd traveled too far away from the here and now, made Twila's neck itch. Funny, she'd always wanted to know more about Mom's side of the family, but right now, she wasn't so sure.

"Tell me again how a nice Wisconsin boy like you ended up in this sunny spot?" Recovered from his latest bout of Dengue fever, Cap needed some human interaction as he and Stan waited in a steep ravine for Carlos and some Filipinos.

Cap already knew the details of Stan's younger days backward and forward, but seemed never to tire of hearing them. "It's like a good book. Every time you read it, you find something rich that you'd overlooked."

To that, Stan shrugged. How many ways can you describe chopping down a tree? But he started in, covering everything from long days in the north woods hauling wood with his father and brothers, to his mother's determination to prepare him to attend college, to her fury when he signed up with the National Guard.

"That couldn't have been easy for you."

"Nope—the hurt in her eyes when I told her still comes to me out here. She's set on at least one of her sons escaping the lumbering life. Don't know if she'll ever forgive me."

"My folks took my draft notice in stride, but it helped that the army sent me to officers' training."

"Yeah."

"But your mother must have known you'd have been drafted eventually."

"Believe me, I reminded her, but she took no comfort in that."

"Umm, Poe used that theme in *The Raven*—refusing to accept the truth." Cap waited for agreement.

"If you say so, prof."

"All right, go on."

"You know about my unit's dead ends and delays, I'll skip that this time. And then, at long last, we arrived on Bataan."

"December of '41, right?"

Once Cap heard the tale for the umpteenth time, he'd be satisfied. Or would he? His mental lapses worried Stan. Only a doctor would be able to attribute these symptoms—Dengue, malaria, or some other tropical disease attacking his body?

From the beginning, everyone dumped water from empty gasoline drums, coconut hulls—anything that could hold liquid to breed mosquitoes. Those little tyrants carried all manner of ailments, and mosquito nets sure weren't foolproof.

As if to prove the origin of his ailment, Stan slapped a mosquito on his arm, leaving a bloody trail. "Bet I know something about the army that you don't."

"Bet you do, too."

"Word has it they sprayed Australian ponds with kerosene guns when an outrageous number of soldiers came down with Dengue last year. Wish they could do that here, but..."

Do what you can. How many times had Stan's dad said that? But right now, what he could do seemed paltry—stay close to the Filipinos and learn from them, keep watch on Cap, and recite stories.

"So, what was it like being a college teacher?"

Cap scratched his head. The draft had pulled him from instructing literature at a college. The Army's call came when he was halfway to his goal, immersed in words. Of course he longed for stories.

"All I ever wanted to do was teach."

About to ask another question, Stan opened his mouth, but Cap beat him to the punch.

"So, what did you think about all day while you worked out in the woods with your dad?

His first response was "Food." But that failed to satisfy Cap, who made him drill down deep. Interestingly enough, more stories unfolded. Supplying fodder for Cap to consider forced Stan to embellish his family history, until he began to believe some of the innovative details himself.

Hopefully Carlos would soon be back with the guerillas they'd joined. Sitting still drove him into cases of nerves, so Stan volunteered to stay with Cap. When Carlos returned, he took over for a while.

Carlos always had another story to tell. His tales of growing up in the big city overflowed with just the type of intrigue that satisfied Cap's endless hunger.

Chapter Four

"You have such good leadership qualities, Twila. The senior plague hit you hard, but at least basketball keeps you aboard."

"Yeah."

Mrs. Harmon brushed at a wayward hair. "Are you interested in teaching? I think home economics might suit you."

"I've never been real good with kids."

"Even little Lilly?"

"She's an exception. And leaders have to have followers, don't they?"

"Not always right away. Immature students perceive a natural leader as bossy and give them wide berth."

"That describes what happened after Coach Jenkins enlisted—our team really fell apart. I did my best, but nobody listened."

"But if you were the teacher, things would be different."

The 1939 Lane Bryant catalog behind Mrs. Harmon's desk announced a *SALE for STOUT WOMEN and MISSES*, and she noticed Twila glancing at it.

"My Dad always said a muscular build meant a strong woman."

"But the boys have always called me a *heavy Chevy*."

"Oh, pfft! What do they know? Don't you think these women out doing men's work need strength? This war has changed things for us in a good way, in my opinion?"

"Audrey Wells has joined the WAACS. And I heard recently that Kate Isaacs went over to England on her own."

"Isn't her husband there?"

21

"He's wounded, in some makeshift hospital in London. But knowing, Kate, she might've gone anyway. We always wondered what that girl would try next.

"The *Register* reported that another Iowa girl became a Women's Air Force Service Pilot. Did you see the *Life* magazine story about them?"

"Rodney showed me, and said I'd be a good candidate. They even fly the new B-29 Superfortresses. But if you could've seen the look on my mom's face when he mentioned me joining up..."

"She's already sacrificing so much. But right here in Halberton, Glenora Carson does a man's work in her brother's absence."

Mrs. Harmon scanned the deserted classroom. School let out for Christmas vacation today, but here she was, still working.

"A nurse from Cresco started working in airplanes years ago, and recruited other women. Before that, men assumed we lacked the constitution for flying, whatever that means."

When she tossed her head, her double chins jiggled, and Twila stifled a laugh.

"But Ellen Church proved her worth and still flies with the troops today. Others operated front line telephones back then, but now anything goes. It's a golden time for young women like you."

"Did you want to serve in the Great War?"

"I was already teaching, and when my husband came back, we started our family."

"Would you have become a teacher if you had a choice?"

"Goodness, yes—I *love* teaching. It's my God-given talent to help others in my own unique way, like your mom up at the factory." Mrs. Harmon rubbed her eraser. "Finding our niche may take time, but nothing fulfills us more."

"Thanks, ma'am." Twila picked up her books and headed out.

With only a few months of school left, the hallway seemed less confining. Beyond the principal's office, the trophy case displayed last year's basketball trophy—conference champs.

The glossy photograph of the team challenged her—during that season, she always found her place. Being a guard offered less glory than the forward's position, but blocking shots and rebounding made all the difference for the team.

Her *niche*. But how to do that now?

Aware of incredible blue sky on this winter day, and her long wool coat brushing her calves, she set out for home. Minutes later, an *a-oo-gah* almost knocked her out of her saddle shoes. Lonnie, with another practical joke.

Satisfied he'd gotten a rise out of her, he idled his fancy '39 Chevy's engine. She'd stopped accepting rides from him last fall, but he still shadowed her.

She shifted her books to her hip, and like the power riding the electrical wires overhead, a question popped out of her mouth. "Why aren't you in the service like everybody else?"

He sneered at her and revved the engine.

"Doesn't your family have to ration gas?"

"None o' your bizwacks." He narrowed his eyes. "So, what're *you* doin' for the war?"

"My Dad's a Great War veteran, but he volunteered again. If you had half his guts, you'd enlist."

In a flurry of dust, Lonnie took off. Maybe his dad, a banker, had used his influence with the war board.

The snow had melted enough this afternoon to create a pool of water where the sidewalk dipped, and by the time Mom got home, it would be a patch of ice. Twila grabbed a shovel from the shed and made a tunnel for the melt to flow down to the alley. In the dark, Mom could fall and break something.

Inside the house, she hung up her coat, and Great Grandma Brunner's flecked hall mirror beckoned her. Same old rusty curls and standout freckles, but she paused long enough to pose her question.

"So what's my talent?"

No answer, of course. Might as well start supper. A few scruffy spuds languished in the bin, a bit wizened by now. Why not surprise Mom for a change? Might be something in the fruit cellar.

Obsessed with preserving every food known to mankind, Mom spent every spare second in the garden. Canning season lasted through September, and they had enough stored away for years.

Green beans, carrots, peas, corn, and tomatoes—whole, diced, stewed, soup and juice—plus green tomato relish. Cucumber relish, corn relish, 40-gallon crocks of sauerkraut lined up like sentries along the wall, turnips and potatoes in burlap bags, and dried onions draped over thick crossbeam nails.

Mom accepted rationing the way she accepted everything else. She took each new announcement to heart and did her best with what they had.

But with more Hormel workers joining the armed forces and higher quotas passed down by the food production board, tensions escalated. A worker who rode the shuttle to work with her mentioned this at the café one day.

"Challenge after challenge all day long. I can't imagine how your mother deals with it all."

But Mom kept up with everything here, too—she deserved a good supper after another long day. Down the steep wooden steps, dank air rose, and cobwebs swayed like phantoms.

A mouse skittered across the floor, and the iron furnace, subdued until the last possible moment before the pipes froze every fall, crouched in a far corner. Any moment, it would belch forth a great groan, and heat would spew up to the kitchen through a giant metal pipe.

A stand of regal quart jars of corn brought inspiration. "Mom loves corn fritters—that's what I'll make. And maybe we'll open some peach jam for syrup."

But what was that down on that bottom shelf? Twila set the jar back to retrieve a cumbersome leather object. Back in the main room, in a swatch of light from a single high window, she perched on a rickety old chair.

Her fruitless search for information about Mom's past had been cast aside, but she'd never thought to look in this small, cold room. Who would store memorabilia down in this dungeon?

And why should this thick old scrapbook catch her eye now, when she wasn't even looking any more? But here it was.

The mildew on the cover tickled her nose as the book fell open to a tattered playbill.

Earl Carrol Follies—January 26, 1917

Come one, come all!
Noted contortionist
Myra Fowler
whose gravity-defying
movements intrigue the eye

...and confound the mind.

Twenty-six years ago. Mom would have been a teenager. The sketch beside the words showed a dancer with flaming auburn hair.

Mesmerized, Twila gawked in wonder. Finally, her breathless utterance broke into the basement gloom. "Mom."

The broken whisper crackled in the musty air. The young contortionist's limbs threaded her neck and abdomen in intricate twists, but a coffee-colored birthmark on her neck said more than the brittle black letters spelling out *M y r a F o w l e r*.

Mom's birthmark always had intrigued her, and at bedtime, she used to trace it with her finger. Her teeth tingled as two yellowed tickets floated onto the floor.

Snitches of past conversations suddenly made sense.

"People eye me askance, anyway."

"Aw, come on, Myra. You've surely proven yourself by now."

After Grandma Fowler's funeral, Pastor Jerrod said the prayer group would remember her, and out of earshot, Mom muttered,

"*Gossip about me* is more like it. 'Laugh and the world laughs with you, cry and you cry alone.'"

The old playbill cited Dallas, Texas. Had Mom joined this traveling troupe against Grandma Fowler's wishes—run away with them?

A sound from the back porch alerted Twila that supper wouldn't cook itself, so she set the book back on its shelf. A yellowed photograph floated out—two bright-eyed look-alikes—Aunt Margaret and Mom.

Reinserting the photo, she grabbed the corn and climbed the creaky stairs. This time, she didn't hurry at the thought of some bugaboo chasing her. She had just opened the bugaboo and looked right into its eyes.

Stan stumbled on a root and gave up the struggle—why not crawl? Steady rustling behind him heightened his sense of responsibility. Somehow, he'd become the leader.

It was crazy, three of them against hundreds of Japanese, but he refused any naysaying. One day's trek higher into the interior—that was the goal. Just one day, and after that, one day more.

Against all odds, he and Captain Burgmeier had aimed for the mainland in a rubber raft they found hidden along the shore last spring. Two-thirds of the distance to Bataan, enemy fire found them.

Diving under water, they made for the shoreline and scrambled up as continuing sprays of gunfire evidenced other escapees. Taking cover in towering, centuries-old jungle, they kept moving higher. So far, so good—they might have died in the raft.

Three days in, they had come across Carlos. That, too, had been fortuitous—three of them still alive. Going over the details of escape heartened him. They'd come this far—they could make it farther.

Back in those early days, a low whistle behind him signaled something amiss, and he had paused to consider next move. If only he knew how many soldiers had made it across the bay—and where they were right now.

One thing was certain: they could count on the Filipino guerillas hidden in the jungle. They hated the Japanese for heinous crimes against civilians—hated them more than the Americans did, most likely.

One mission filled his consciousness. The trio must locate some guerilla fighters in order to hit the enemy and gather intelligence.

A pungent odor wafted—this must be why Cap had halted. After a few tense minutes, animal grunts revealed the source; wild pigs.

Ruing the demise of his compass in forced swim, Stan waved the others on. He had no intention of stopping until they found some Filipinos who knew what they were doing.

Yes, months had passed since those tentative times. Now they had joined a Filipino band that knew the terrain and could sniff out the enemy. But rehearsing the beginning of long journey still brought comfort and hope—they'd been at large, unarmed in this wilderness, and alone.

But they'd found a certain amount of safety—right under the Japs' noses.

Chapter Five

Winter, 1942 Bataan

Carlos lived to relate to whoever showed up, and his tales about growing up in the Chavez Ravine of Los Angeles opened Stan's eyes to a different way of life. Fortunately, Cap continued to consume the young man's stories.

Once again, the three of them awaited word from a Filipino reconnaissance team that left in the wee hours. They often checked in with another guerilla group that had finagled a receiver able to bring in reports from the southern islands of the Philippines.

Hopefully the Filipino scouts would bring back word about Japanese build-up on the island of Leyte and in the Leyte Gulf. This would confirm other recent intelligence. If those reports were true, they could anticipate a lot of action on the island of Samar in the future.

While they waited, Carlos regaled them with details about his youth. Even though he was as American as either of them, his family and culture seemed foreign.

"My father came here from Mexico in the twenties to work the fields, and became a citizen two years later. He speaks English better than anybody in our barrio and says we were doing fine until the Navy decided to build the Reserve Armory in our section of Los Angeles.

"He made us all practice our English, and even though my older brother was a Zoot Suiter, my father made him stop wearing the over-sized jacket and baggy pegged-leg pants when the government announced the wartime fabric restrictions."

"Wait… wait. A Zoot? What's that?" Cap kept his voice low, but his inflection told Stan he would remain captivated for a good long while.

Carlos raised his eyebrows. "You've never heard of Chicanos who wear extra big suits and pork pie hats, a long watch chain, and thick-soled shoes?"

"I grew up a long, long way from Los Angeles, and there was a lot I never heard. Joining the Army broadened my sights, but I've still never heard of these Zooters."

"Zoot Suiters. It's a dress of our own, for us *pachucos,* my brother said. So I suppose you've never heard of Lalo Guerrero?"

"No."

"He's a singer—his music stood for *los pachucos.* Our community loves him like you love Bing Crosby. When the law started cracking down on our area, my father forbade my brother to sing Guerrero's songs. Nobody loves America more than my father—he said being called to work here saved his life.

"Of course, my brother obeyed him, but a lot of his friends listened to Lalo even more and kept wearing suits out in public—so what if the sailors mocked them? But after I left, my mother wrote that things got worse.

"A murder in Sleepy Lagoon caused a lot of trouble. The last I heard, seventeen young Chicanos were accused of killing a Latino named Diaz, but nobody really knew how he died. The case can only make things worse in the Chavez Ravine."

A lumberjack's son keeping company with a southern California boy named Carlos, and an Illinois native studying to be an English professor—what an unlikely trio they made. And no wonder Carlos had practically conquered the Filipino language. He already knew two languages before coming here, and could translate most of what the natives said.

Not that they spoke much—hand signals and head gestures

sufficed, with constant awareness of the enemy. But the natives taught Carlos new techniques with his knife—good men to have guarding your back.

Since Carlos had told this story before, Stan let his mind wander to the violent kicks and yells of four Japanese soldiers they'd recently run across on a trail. Caught by surprise, they all perished in the ensuing fight, but certainly left mark. Stan fingered a bruise on his left knee, still painful to the touch.

Their fighting style reminded him of the merciless guards and the captured GIs they'd seen on the trail to Camp O'Donnell last spring. Meeting up with those poor captured Americans revealed how lost he'd been at the time. He and Captain Burgmeier had whacked way up the mountain to Calumpit, not that far from San Fernando, and met Carlos on the way.

A bamboo forest gave them opportunity to observe the pitiful gaggle of soldiers still being marched toward the camp. Fifty or 60 miles of forced marching had taken its toll on men already ill and dazed by incessant shelling.

So many collapsed while they watched that Stan lost count. When one of them could no longer take a step and sprawled on the rocky earth, a guard came along and beat him with his baton. Then he kicked him again and again, all the while shrieking in Japanese.

Some of the phrases still rang out in Cap's nightmares. Probably meant something like, "You stupid American, get out of my way," or worse.

The thrust of a blade and a dying groan often followed the shrieking. That day, far too close to the trail for comfort, Cap fidgeted so much in the underbrush that Stan kept a hand on his shoulder.

Would he really have run out and attacked a guard, knowing he would expose them? Men had been known to crack under far less pressure.

As the days out in this jungle stretched into weeks and months, those images had magnified. To add to his worry, Cap showed more signs of confusion and instability. Pitted against illness, rank amounted to nothing.

Cap's philosophical nature kept his mind in the clouds a good share of the time, anyway. But lately, it seemed he lost contact with reality at times. Carlos often shot Stan a worried look after Cap said something peculiar.

Suddenly all bird chatter quieted, so the three of them automatically felt for knives. At last, a Filipino hurried down the trail, followed by the guerilla leader.

"Enemy close. We get 'em." The fire in his eyes communicated better than words. He hated the Japs—who knew what they had done to his wife and children?

Wait and watch, listen to the tremble in Cap's breathing and pray for him to make it through this one. Anxiety raked Stan's insides, but he held steady and swung into action exactly when he needed to. All the while, he visualized those dying Americans on the trail in the spring.

Had he handed over his weapons as ordered, he would have trodden that same mountainous path. But the night before the final surrender, Captain Burgmeier proposed an action that made more sense than sitting out the war in enemy hands.

Why not escape and hide out in the mountains?

But most men—those on that killing climb—did obey General Wainwright's orders. And they were his people as much as his family back in Wisconsin. Every day he aimed to make life miserable for captors.

Fury at inhuman treatment of the Americans fueled every stab Stan made at a Jap, every neck vertebrae he heard splinter. Every Nip he took out counted as progress in rescuing the surviving captives.

"Vengeance is mine, saith the Lord," once defined his concept of killing, but the war had changed things. Now, vengeance occurred *through* him, became his vocation. Conquering the enemy overtook him heart and soul, and he fought as if under a spell.

When this altercation ended, the entire Jap patrol lay dead. Carlos faded into the jungle as naturally as the guerillas, while Cap and Stan followed along at a slower pace. Long minutes later, everyone gathered in a hamlet of grass-roofed huts.

The leader approached Stan. "You captain?"

With a lop-sided grin, Cap stepped up. "Yeah, he's a captain. Carlos, help me introduce Captain Ford."

The leader nodded and held out his hand. "You good Captain." He gestured toward the others. "Teach us more fight like GIs."

At first, Stan wanted to slug Cap. Everyone knew that impersonating an officer got you court-martialed, but on second thought, maybe Cap knew what he was doing. These saboteurs respected American officers, and Cap knew his limitations when the fever held him in its clutches.

One of his quotes flashed before Stan. "'We are all ready to be savage in some cause. The difference between a good man and a bad one is the choice of the cause.' Philosophy 202, William James."

Cap nudged him in the back. This ragged band of sinewy men waited for his response. Crazy they would ask him for help when they knew so much more about the jungle. But what they sought was not jungle expertise—they wanted tactical guidance.

"All right." Stan squatted down, and the Filipino leader instantly understood the drawing motions he made on his knee.

"You men know these trails. Draw us a map."

Someone produced a bark scrap and a chewed-up pencil. Eager eyes stared at Stan, giving him a surprising sense of wellbeing. With a little strategic planning they might create even more troubles for the Jap patrols.

Strangely, at that very moment, he remembered something. According to his calculations, this must be Christmas Day.

One February day, Rodney sat out front in his truck when Twila exited the school building. She ran over, and he motioned her in.

"What's up?"

"Are you headed for the café?"

"Nope, tomorrow."

"Okay then, hop in. I want to show you something."

Turning a U-turn at the end of the street, Rodney headed west out of town. "One of our saws broke down. Gotta drive up to Austin for a part and thought you might want to ride along."

His grin reminded Twila how well he knew her—of course, she wanted a break from Halberton. They hadn't spent any time together lately, but if she dropped in at the lumberyard, he would have welcomed her.

Maybe it was partly her attitude. Everyone played an important role right now. Her meager offerings, going to school and working at the café, seemed paltry in comparison.

Her bit part in the senior play last fall made her feel the same way. The charade, with the hero a poor caricature of Roy Rogers in *The Carson City Kid*, starred Marilyn Mercer as Joby Madison, the gorgeous saloon singer who won Roy's heart.

But zooming down the road to Austin with Rodney was a treat. Twila tapped her toes on the floorboard as the truck rounded a wide S-curve.

Once Rodney straightened out the wheel near the Minnesota border, he turned his attention to her. "Not much left of high school, eh? I remember those days—hardly any of the guys in my class are still around."

His comment brought back the day he'd failed the physical because of a childhood bout with rheumatic fever. Good thing Dad had been here to remind him how important the lumber business was to the war effort.

In Austin's outskirts, Rodney checked his watch. "Gotta get back soon, and this part's on the other side of town. Would you mind taking this in to Mom while I pick it up?" He handed her a large manila envelope.

"Sure. What is it?"

"Oh, some business stuff—papers she needs to read. She might have time to look them over on her break."

He rolled to a stop at the Hormel plant's back entrance. "Go straight up the stairs. Mom works out in the factory, but maybe they'll let you see her."

The paved yard surprised Twila, but this huge area would be a mess without it when the rains came. A line of Hormel trucks lined up along a vast warehouse, and workers hurried in and out.

The distinct odor of slaughtered animals permeated the place, so she adjusted her breathing. Up a short flight of stairs, the low hum of machines and a buzz of voices led her through some double doors.

"Hello, Miss. What can I do for you?"

"I need to deliver this to my mother."

"And that would be Myra Brunner, sure as day." The woman's grin spread. "You're the spittin' image—probably heard that a million times. She's busy on the floor, so you'll have to wait."

"How long will it be?"

"Who knows? Sometimes she doesn't even take her break—been known to work through a full day without one."

"Could you give her this for me, then? Actually, it's from my brother—important papers she needs to read."

"You bet. I'll put it in her locker." The worker scribbled on a piece of paper and glanced up. "Ever been here before?"

"No."

"Want to see where your mother works?"

Twila nodded, so the woman led her down a long hallway to a row of windows looking down on the factory.

"See her? Over under that tin awning. She's walking the line to make sure everybody stays on track."

"They all look the same with those uniforms and green hairnets."

"Yeah, but your mom's got a patch on her shirt pocket—they're hard to come by. Not many people supervise two lines. Stay right here. I'll be back in a minute."

Focusing in on the awning clarified Mom's slim profile. She gestured with her hand a couple of times, and a worker nodded. Farther along, she wrote something on her notepad.

There must be at least forty women on those two lines, looking like so many mannequins in a department store window. Except hands stayed in constant motion. The woman returned.

"See her?"

"Yes, I found her." The double meaning moistened Twila's eyes. Even watching Mom seemed like trespassing.

Just before she left, her guide's eyes lit up. "I hear you're a senior this year?"

Twila nodded.

"We'd hire you in a flash. Your mom brags about you, you know. What a worker she is!"

Waiting on the outside stairs, Twila reflected. So much responsibility—no wonder Mom's feet ached at night and she spoke in fits and starts.

Then she remembered. Rodney had wanted to show her something. Now she understood…he had introduced her to Mom's other world.

Chapter Six

One day in April, Mr. Olsen finally trusted Twila to close the café. Well, sort of—he had no choice.

Early that afternoon, his wife Thelma heard that her mother hung on the verge of death down in Cedar Rapids. A customer offered his extra gas coupons, and they left around three before the supper crowd wandered in.

Monday was a slack evening because most folks ate leftovers from yesterday's big meal. And it wasn't close enough to the weekend for folks to be traveling through Halberton—two of the reasons Mr. Olsen thought Twila could handle this responsibility.

"Got meatloaf and baked potatoes in the oven, so all you have to do is take orders and serve. Plus take people's money and close up. Think you can manage?"

She most certainly did, but tried not to sound too confident. That had gotten her nowhere in similar situations, so she kept her reply short, "Yes, I believe so."

He scrutinized her as Thelma appeared at the door, nervous as all get-out. "Come on, Olsen—we've got to get on the road—it'll be dark before we know it."

With a heavy sigh and a few final warnings, he took off, but a few minutes later, poked his head back in. "If you have any trouble, run over to the Mercantile. They're open a half hour later than us, you know."

Yes, she knew. What did he think would happen, anyway—a modern-day Bonnie and Clyde appearing to rob the entire 15 dollars from the till? But Twila bit her tongue and waited until the Olsen's '36 burgundy Studebaker finally chugged south out of town.

About five o'clock, two single customers ordered the special. Then a couple she had never seen before parked out in front. An hour later, she locked all the doors and scrubbed the kitchen floor while the man and wife finished meal. Mr. Olsen specified both doors must be locked because "down on your knees like that, you wouldn't even know if somebody came in."

Twila planned to ask where the couple came from, but when she refilled coffee, they paid no attention to her. Even through hushed tones, the gist of conversation came through. Their son turned 18 in August, and his brother had joined the Navy after Pearl Harbor.

A phrase from the wife struck a chord. *If only Daniel could be spared.* Like Butch, deployed to North Africa. Even though he'd been so anxious to go and so confident, March news reports of the fight for the Mareth Line had sounded grim. They still hadn't heard exactly where he was—even that much information would help.

Every once in a while, he sent a postcard that lined up with Dad's on a string stretched across the glass doors of the kitchen cupboard. Each one brought a taste of Butch's exuberance:

Rode a camel with a buddy—the humps make it a little different from horse riding.

Closest buddy here got a care pkg yesterday and we ate the contents in five minutes.

The greasy burners and the oven door resisted her cleaning efforts as she kept peeking out at the couple in the dining room. The husband held his wife's hand now—they were in this together, like Dad and Mom. Wouldn't it be nice to end up with someone you could talk to about everything?

After they paid bill, she pulled the wide front shades for the night. Out by the curb, the man held the car door and his wife smiled up at him. Dad followed the same practice, and Mom often said,

"Manners matter, Twila. Your father's always courteous, no matter how much he has on his mind."

They talked about everything. No wonder thick letters to and from California helped keep the U.S. Postal Service in business.

Down the two-block Main Street, most businesses had closed already. A faint lamp still shone in the jewelry shop, veiled by black out drapes, but then, the Liberski family lived in the back. Otherwise, seven p.m. showed no sign of life.

Just then, Lonnie spun around the corner with a blonde sitting close. His arm lolled around her shoulder—probably thought driving with one hand made him look like a big man. Funny how she'd never noticed that when her shoulder had been involved.

With a huff, she cleaned up the strangers' table and discovered a quarter. What a generous tip—Twila wished more folks would stop by on way to somewhere else, since the locals rarely left even a nickel.

Still wondering where those customers hailed from, she pocketed the treasure and swept up the day's dust and crumbs. With the boss gone, her breath came easier. No one knew if she hit every corner or changed the water halfway through. She did change it, of course, but savored the sensation of being alone, being in charge.

Nobody asked, "You're sure you added sanitizer?"

The result of her labor—a sparkling clean floor—meant more this way. Mr. Olsen would inspect everything early in the morning and be pleased. But what really mattered was her own sense of satisfaction.

Ever since Mrs. Harmon mentioned following one's passion, that word had tantalized Twila. To be passionate meant giving something your all, but even though she gave her best and Mr. Olsen had increased her hours, no strong emotion accompanied her here at the cafe.

Could being in charge qualify as a passion? How could it fit into her desire to contribute more to the war effort? Hadn't Mrs. Harmon said something about growing into being a leader?

The image of Mom supervising all those workers arose. Wasn't that what Mom did, lead the people on the lines?

Twila smoothed Butch's class ring on the chain around her neck, recalling the fragile moment when he entrusted it to her before leaving for boot camp. He'd been packing his duffel bag when Mom and Dad took her over to say good-bye.

Uncle Marvin and Aunt Edna hovered over him, along with his two younger brothers and sister. But Butch radiated excitement—he couldn't wait to leave.

At one point, he drew her aside. "Hey there, Twi. How's my favorite cousin?"

She could barely answer.

"Hey, no tears now! I've seen enough for two lifetimes already. I wanted to ask if you'd mind watching over my ring while I'm gone?"

He set the golden treasure in her palm, and she closed her fingers around it. "I promise."

Memories from her first few weeks of high school engulfed her. She'd been so frightened and shy, but Butch always acknowledged her in the hallways. But in his first year at Iowa State, he'd signed up with the army.

"I'm in the Army now, Rod." Butch's voice had a lilt to it. "Leavin' on the early train for Burlington and on to Fort Leonard Wood—they're building that place for the likes of me."

"Wish I could go, too. Stay safe, now." Rodney's wet cheeks testified to his sincerity.

"Once they whip us country boys into shape, we'll be a force to be reckoned with."

Dad shooed them together like chickens for a photograph. He captured Butch in his smart new Navy uniform with Rodney and Twila flanking him, and that photo hung on the string with postcards.

No one had any idea that a year later they'd all be saying good-bye to Dad down at the depot—the most painful leave-taking of all. A group of friends gathered, and Rodney and Sharon brought three-year-old Lilly to see him off.

Lilly's silken hair provided the perfect spot for Twila to bury her face. But even at the conductor's last call, when Dad hurried down the wooden platform toward the door, Mom controlled her tears. Not long after that, she started working longer hours.

Now, the quiet café absorbed a heartfelt sigh. "Everyone's doing part except me. I just *have* to find some way to serve."

Yesterday's sermon went over her head until the pastor read several firsthand accounts of divine intervention during the Dunkirk evacuation. As she checked her list of closing duties on the counter, the tales sifted back.

"All of our lives, we've heard that prayer can change things. But our friends in England have learned firsthand the effectiveness of asking God for help. With entire army hemmed in by the Germans in the Battle of France, the whole nation bowed heads, and in amazing ways, the Almighty answered.

"You know the story, but it bears repeating. Using every available boat, public or private, the majority of trapped British, Belgian, and French soldiers made it back to England. Operation Dynamo, they called it, and dynamic, it surely was.

"We must heed this example of our Creator still at work through His people. Prime Minister Churchill called the entrapment a colossal military disaster, as 'the whole root and core and brain' of Britain's army seemed about to perish or be captured. But his idea to employ private citizens in the rescue made all the difference.

"Afterward, we all listened to his *We shall fight on the beaches* speech. Even the Prime Minister, not necessarily a man of faith, branded the rescue a miracle. And all because ordinary people stepped up to offer what they could.

"Private fishing boats sailed across the Channel with the Navy. Women banded together to prepare bandages, feed starving returnees, and aid the wounded. Everyday women and men—regular citizens like you and me made ordinary contributions to accomplish something extraordinary.

"We, too, throw in our lot with our boys over there, knitting sweaters and socks by the ton, sending packages and writing letters. Some of you take the place of younger men in fields and factories. All over our great nation, the winds of patriotism stir us to band together."

Suddenly, Twila realized she had never asked for help figuring out her passion. The shiny milkshake machine made its final, graduated wail when she turned the OFF switch. She sank into a leather booth and folded her hands like when she was a child, praying with Dad before bedtime.

Her whisper emerged hoarse. "I've been a poor follower the past few years, but..." A gaggle of erroneous choices paraded before her. All of that wasted time with Lonnie, lying to Mom, neglecting her schoolwork—what right did she have to pray?

"I do believe, though, and I want to help our troops. Please show me what I can do."

Irrevocably, when Carlos and Cap were resting, Stan was drawn back to fourth or fifth day in the climb to the highlands. Tonight, these memories invaded again while he kept watch.

They'd been making good progress—if they were going the right direction. But they never really knew for sure. Carlos hunkered down beside Stan a little off the trail, and behind them, Cap whispered, "What can you see?"

Carlos squinted. "The Bay. Sparkling." He held up his hand and mouthed, "Hear that?"

Ears like a lynx—in a few seconds Stan and Cap heard it too, a steady *swish*. But from which direction? This insular jungle made it difficult to ascertain distances. They might have glimpsed the bay, but in reality, it was days away.

Marching. Troops marching. The vibrations grew stronger, spiraling alarm through Stan. Lots and lots of men. He slipped down beyond the trail they'd hacked through the jungle and soundlessly crept toward the sound.

Soon, bursts of Japanese mingled with a few halting words of English. He waited...waited some more. It was all he could do to keep from swatting at flies the size of pencil erasers, but he controlled the urge.

The swishing grew closer. Closer. And then, within a few feet, GI uniforms tucked into frayed leather boots came into view. Those boots scraped against stone and tripped over roots. Higher, men with shoulder blades ridged under shirts fought to keep balance.

They'd held onto Bataan against impossible odds, even after the Japs repeatedly broke through the lines. Cursing the enemy, these captured soldiers remained steadfast. But now, defenseless, they could only moan.

Over sixty miles of brutal slopes all the way from Mariveles, in the south of Bataan, the Nips must have marched them. Several fell and endured rifle butts shoved into ribs.

Enemy curses resounded as sweat dripped down Stan's back. Driven like stunned animals to Camp O'Donnell, these GIs were his people.

Their downcast eyes and posture spelled disaster. It seemed impossible that General MacArthur had approved the surrender, but how do you fight when your supplies are cut off and men are already dying in droves?

A little later, Carlos and Cap sneaked behind him. Finally, the ghastly parade dwindled off into the jungle, and Stan started up a trail in the opposite direction. The others followed, but not five minutes later, Cap stumbled and fell against a tall acacia tree. Carlos dribbled a little water down his throat.

He squeezed his eyelids shut—that intense pain behind his eyes must have returned, worse even than that in his joints. This attack resembled the two he'd suffered during the night.

But they dared not stop, though Carlos whispered, "Did you notice his gums are bleeding now, and his nose."

"He's burning up."

"Yeah, but the fever might be gone soon, right?"

"Or it might last three more days"

"Let's pull him behind that stand of bamboo. Maybe with a little rest..." But they both knew rest would change nothing. The next minute, Cap's skin could turn cold and clammy, or he might hallucinate and cry out in terror.

"We've got to stay together, but also find help."

"*Si. Y esto es.*" He'd taught Stan a little Spanish, and this was something like, *and this is it...*

Carlos positioned his arms under Cap's left shoulder, and Stan did the same on his other side. Lugging buddy up the overgrown trail, his silent prayer floated up through the dense foliage canopy.

Please send help for Cap.

No immediate answer, but his silent cry still brought a measure of consolation. A few feet at a time, they dragged Cap along.

And then, he startled them by spouting, "*Unus pro omnibus, omnes pro uno...* Alexandre Dumas."

Carlos looked to Stan for an interpretation.

"*All for one, one for all....*"

"*Si,*" Carlos grinned. "He's still with us."

That period was as close to desperate as Stan had felt, and he couldn't seem to stop going over those days in his mind. Things were far better now, although Cap's bouts of fever never seemed to stop. In fact, they were growing more frequent.

Chapter Seven

Aware of a slow moving car on the street, Twila waited in the evening stillness. A few minutes later, a light flashed through the front window—that would be Honor Trimble, the town sheriff, making sure businesses had battened down for the night.

Talk about passion—even his name fit his occupation. He'd been at his post forever, and his steady plod through town testified to his determination to carry out the law.

Today's *Globe Gazette* lay on a table, so she carried it to the kitchen. Mr. Olsen didn't mind her taking it home for Mom to read—one small perk of working here.

To the rhythm of Honor tramping around the building, she locked up. He met her at the back door and touched his cap.

"Evenin', Twila. Workin' late tonight?"

"Yes, it's my first time to close."

He tried the doorknob. "Looks as if you done just fine." He sniffed. "Sure you shut everything off in there?"

"Yes."

"Good. What do you hear from your dad?"

"Not a lot. Sounds like he's really busy out there."

"Proud of him—we all are. Not many serve in two different wars, doncha know?"

"Yes."

"Your mother's doing her part, too. Have a good night, then." Honor's boots crunched down the alley, but he turned back a few seconds later as she started toward Main down the long side of the cafe.

"Awful dark between them buildings, ain't it? Better be careful. Jest never know what'll happen these days."

"Thanks, Honor." For some reason, a warning coming from him didn't bother her.

He set off again, and she followed the length of the cafe toward Main Street. The darkness grew so thick she could barely see where to walk, but this route got her home faster. Let's see; how far down was that old barrel, anyway?

Down Main Street, the stillness proclaimed no auto in sight—she might as well be out on a deserted country road. Between peaks and cupolas of tall old houses, bats swung from chimney to chimney like high wire artists.

Change came slowly to Halberton, but the electrical wires fit in now, when at first, they'd seemed so out of place.

At the post office, she turned the little dial to open the family box. Nothing today. Farther toward home, the idea of continuing like this until she married someone and became a mother haunted her.

Evening shadows narrowed her path through the back yard and the scent of early honeysuckle drifted from the neighbors' place. Inside the back porch, a strong smell assaulted her—something must've died in here.

"Probably a mouse found that poison Mom set out last week."

Too dark to check right now, so she went in and hung her coat on a hook—always the one next to Dad's. She brushed his sleeve and pictured him out in the California desert. In the kitchen, she dropped the newspaper on the table and drew the blackout curtains above the water pump.

Might as well pull the heavy drape to shut off the back hallway, too. She felt for the lamp on the shelf above the table and switched it on.

Just like that, the darkness became light. If only she could turn a light on inside herself. What was it Mrs. Harmon had said about everyone discovering own unique talent to help people—*niche*?

"Sure wish I knew what mine is." How did a person figure these things out?

"Dad, you know what you're supposed to be doing. So does Mom, and you're both making a big difference for the troops. But how can I know what I 'm supposed to do?"

She turned to clear off the table and the *Gazette's* headline story grabbed her in a stranglehold.

> Algona, Iowa: Prisoner of War camp to be constructed in late summer. This facility, required by the war department to house the growing number of prisoners taken in North Africa and elsewhere, will include a modern hospital.
>
> The camp will be built a distance from the city by Italian war prisoners. Camp Algona will be self-sufficient, surrounded by a double wire fence, and staffed by trained army guards. Citizens need not concern themselves over matters of safety.

The kitchen clock vied with Twila's heartbeat. Algona. Aunt Margaret lived there, about two and a half hours away, maybe more with the 35-mile-an-hour speed limit. She and her children were family—except they'd only met once, at Grandma Fowler's funeral.

What if things changed, and she and mom got together again? That seemed impossible, but just yesterday, Sharon and Rodney announced something new in family. In a few months, Lilly would have a new sister or brother.

Would they choose an *L* name for the new baby? But even more importantly, would Dad make it home for the birth?

Sometimes his letters helped her visualize parachute

training—sounded pretty dangerous, but so necessary. He called himself a tiny cog in an enormous wheel, but that was his nature, happy to work behind the scenes.

A mourning dove issued its lonesome call from the lilac bushes out back. Every night, Twila could count on this, but changes occurred for humans all the time. She read the article again and imagined that prison camp with its brand new hospital. The camp would be like a small city springing up overnight. If only the Army had chosen a closer location.

Minute after minute ticked away, and her thoughts whirled. Then something clicked inside.

Wouldn't the camp need workers? Her next thought made her ears hum—she could be one of them. She could almost see the walls of the camp going up, with those Italians cutting window frames and laying floorboards.

Could this already be the answer to her prayer?

At Mom's footfall on the back porch steps, she started up and hurried with supper. She also made a decision—not a word about this. No use getting Mom upset.

But she *would* leave the paper here, in plain sight.

Yet another night patrol. Mosquitoes buzzed Stan's ears, and thick jungle roots and branches made every attempt to foil this trek. If he wasn't tripping, Cap was. The two of them fell behind the others, but what could he do?

Cap had taken off his boots, soaked through after wading through a low place, and slung them over his shoulder. Now they flap-flapped against each other as he walked. Without them, it was only a matter of time before he injured a toe or his whole foot.

These intricate trails wound back and forth in such profusion that there was no use trying to keep track of direction. They were moving eastward, generally, but the paths meandered up and down. Taken altogether, they proceeded upward.

A screeching night bird lanced an ear-piercing cry. At least he hoped it was a bird—might just as easily be a Jap calling out his location to a patrol leader, or reporting that he could hear some fool GIs making a whole lot of noise.

Perspiration drooled down the back of Cap's neck, and the endless mosquitoes were enjoying a feast. Weariness became a living thing, a snake wrapping its body tighter and tighter around Stan's chest.

He'd always believed sleep would eventually come. Didn't every human being have to sleep sometime?

But for him, that time never seemed to arrive. If he slept, some Nips might sneak up on them, and then… Mostly, he accepted this, but seeing Cap or Carlos drop off into slumber at the slightest opportunity had begun to irritate him.

At times like this, he had to practice mind control. "It's all in your head," his dad used to say when he complained of aches or pains out in the forest.

"Think about something else. Picture the load we'll haul home tonight, and the new boots we'll be able to afford. Think how good you'll feel about putting in a hard day's work."

Advice from the Wisconsin forest came in handy out here in enemy territory on a pitch-black night with a Nip patrol waiting at any curve in the trail. And Stan embraced it—he could keep going. He *had* to.

Every time the Filipinos stopped, he at least closed his eyes. Mimicking sleep like this made an adjustment in his near-despair.

If he added up all the brief halts when a scout left to sniff out the terrain, there might be ten before dawn. Ten times ten minutes each—that meant he'd slept about an hour and a half.

Just then, Cap groaned. Stan reached for him through the darkness. His heartbeat pulsed in his ears, but at least Cap quieted at his touch. Then the brush stirred slightly, and Stan reached for his knife.

But like a jungle animal, Carlos's bright eyes glinted. "Keep it down, muchachos. We're almost on top of an enemy outpost. Been on trail all night."

"Are we attacking?"

Carlos gripped the bolo tied to his waist and whispered, "Not Cap. And we can't leave him alone. Stay here—I'll come for you when it's over."

He blinked and then was gone, a cat slinking into the gloom. Dense wet foliage brushed Stan's shoulder as he leaned toward Cap.

"Did you hear that?"

"What?"

"We've got orders to stay here until Carlos comes back."

Cap frowned. "But you're the leader."

"Yeah, right. And I say we do what he tells us."

Nothing could describe his relief when Cap gave no more argument and dropped to the earth. From the noise he made, he must be carving out a niche in thick jungle grass.

Something about being told to stay put brought a sense of relief. Carlos would never have suggested this if he hadn't felt position safe—relatively, of course. But beyond that, it had been a long time since anyone issued Stan an order. He had often chafed at that very thing, but not tonight.

In the dense darkness, he sank near the intermittent whisper of Cap's breathing and wiggled out a space for himself in the grass. Then he closed his eyes, let his shoulders loosen against the earth, and set himself to listen.

Not a sound from the direction where Carlos had disappeared. He waited, counted to fifty, and bent his ear again. Nothing. Cap's breathing deepened—good.

Then came the miracle. Stan drifted off.

The next thing he knew, a patchwork of jungle foliage created holes for the sun to shine through. He started up from his warm nest, aware that full daylight displayed location to anyone who happened along. A few feet away, someone moved through the tangled vines. Cap still slept, his clothes a veritable thorn patch.

Stan brushed his pants as he sought his knife—full of those tiny barbs, too.

But no matter. He must've conked out for several hours. For the first time in weeks, his eyes had stopped itching. Even as he readied his bolo to attack, a fresh realization came to him. He was still capable of sleep—he would survive.

That is, if Carlos or one of the Filipinos broke through the brush instead of an enemy soldier.

Chapter Eight

A single burning light bulb dangled from its braided cord on this end of the hospital ward. Scrunched beside a youth-sized bed, Twila held Lilly's plump little-girl fingers.

Too numb to form a rightful prayer, maybe her insistent "Help!" counted. Out in the hallway, a nurse and doctor chatted too loudly, sending chilblains down her arms.

"Don't know as I've ever seen so much swelling in a child this age. Could affect the little tyke's brain, or her eyes." The doctor lowered his voice. "Make sure you keep a close watch, and no visitors except close family."

A nurse entered, listened to Lilly's heart, and watched the clock as she grasped her wrist for a minute. Then she looked into Twila's eyes.

"I'm taking her vitals every half hour. We've gotten really busy, but this cherub needs someone to keep watch over her every second. Can you stay around?"

"I won't leave until her daddy gets back, ma'am. He's my brother. But can you tell me what happened?"

"She had a fall on the school playground. After school, she was walking home with an older child and they stopped to play on the monkey bars, they said." At a call from outside the room, she paused.

"Let me show you how to take her pulse. If there's any change in 20 minutes or you see signs of her waking, call me right away."

"What signs?"

"If her eyes twitch or she stirs even the slightest bit."

"All right."

The nurse guided Twila's fingertips to the pulse point on Lilly's wrist and told her when to start counting.

"What did you get?"

"A hundred and thirty."

"Me too. Still a little high, but it's regulating." She pointed to Lilly's chart. "When you take the next one, write it down right here."

A nod satisfied her, and Twila decided she liked this slim-as-a-reed nurse. The one who was here earlier made her feel like an intruder—she'd said only one thing. "Visiting hours end at seven, Miss."

Knowing she could help out heartened Twila. Heaven knew Mom would have a fit when she came, and Rodney and Sharon had hands full with the new baby being born.

So much business at the lumberyard right now, too. Who would ever have thought Iowa trees would be supplying builders in Chicago and Detroit?

Earlier today, a customer at the cafe said the Navy was transforming the *Greater Detroit* and the *Greater Buffalo,* the two largest excursion ships, into the USS Wolverine and USS Sable.

"Over a thousand workers for each one, can you imagine? 'S gonna take a lot of work to make them seaworthy instead of staying on the Great Lakes."

No one mentioned that Charlotte's parents were involved with that renovation, but the topic reminded Twila to answer Char's latest letter after work.

Then someone came in for a piece of pie and shared a letter they'd received from a relative, and the subject never returned to the ships.

From then on, what an afternoon it had been. Rodney had left work early to take Sharon to the hospital in Austin and asked Greta, Sharon's cousin, to notify the Brunners.

She'd run all the way to the café, and calming her enough to understand her garbled message presented the first challenge.

Customers gawked, but Greta finally spit out that Lilly had been taken to the hospital in Osage.

Twila's heart raced, and when Mr. Olsen said, "Go on, your family needs you," so did her feet, all the way home.

The hall clock joined in with Lilly's quiet breathing. At least it remained steady, but her eyes hadn't twitched. About forty minutes later, the slender nurse returned.

"Her pulse is down a couple more points. Good—that's progress. You must really love this chubby towhead."

"Oh, I do." Twila glanced down at Lilly. "Do you remember any more details about the accident?"

"Lilly was playing on the monkey bars with the child who walks home with her. Unfortunately, that unexpected rain shower this afternoon made the bars extra slick, so she fell. Must've hit her head on something.

"Luckily, a teacher saw her and called the doctor, who drove Lilly here. He said she's a bit of a daredevil."

For the first time in hours, a chuckle bubbled up. "She comes by it honestly. Risk-taking runs in our family."

"Well, these days, that's not all bad." The nurse hurried down the hall, leaving Twila plenty of time to reflect.

Her "stretch the limits" attitude had motivated her to contact the army prison camp when another article appeared in the paper. She'd nearly memorized the entire story.

> *Workers needed at Army Prisoner of War Camp now under construction. This self-contained, 275 acre facility will oversee thirty-four branch camps and house up to three thousand inmates at a time. The main headquarters near Algona will process German prisoners for three other camps in a four-state area. Italian prisoners, presently em-*

ployed to build a one hundred fifty bed, electrified hospital, will soon be set free. The prison stockade, surrounded by two rows of ten-foot high fencing, complete with guard towers, will be connected to the main headquarters by telephone lines.

Army personnel unable to serve in battle will act as guards, but the commissary, canteen, and hospital require civilian workers, including typists, stenographers, and other office personnel for processing POWs—upwards of 80 civilians in all.

All interested parties, inquire at Camp Algona, PO Box 62, Algona, Iowa.

The day she read the story, Twila could think of nothing else. Again, she left the newspaper on the kitchen table. Later, in her room, she wrote her letter of application and mailed it the next morning.

Within days, the camp responded with a letter and an application. For two days she debated. Should she ask Mom or not? Finally she decided they'd been doing so well, why rock the boat? Even if she applied, the camp he might not accept her.

A month had passed since she carefully penned in her information after searching out her birth certificate and some other papers while Mom was gone. The sense of adventure involved overshadowed her sense of guilt.

She'd mailed the application on August twentieth. The date had a nice ring, and when the letter dropped into the box in the post office lobby, satisfaction filled her. Even if she received no offer, she had made an effort. She had done her best.

Sitting here beside Lilly, she took stock. Sending that application was the kind of action that made teachers point out her impetuous nature throughout her school years. Last year, her literature teacher had urged them to apply what they were reading to everyday lives. Maybe she needed a little of Hamlet's so-called cowardice—or procrastination.

The puffy skin below Lilly's eyes and around her left temple launched alarm through Twila. What if...?

But that kind of thinking simply wouldn't do—she wouldn't allow it. As far as her application to Camp Algona, what was done was done. No amount of second thoughts could reverse it. Hours ago, her world revolved around the dilemma she would face if the camp offered her a job.

Then came her wild dash home after Greta raced into the café. She'd hardly entered the kitchen when their neighbor Shirley panted on the back steps, having heard the rumor about Lilly. It took a full minute to pacify her, just like Greta. Why couldn't people keep heads at times like this? Giving in to fear did no good.

At least Shirley had managed to relay an important message.

"Elmer's driving you to Osage. Sharon's about to pop, and Elmer was down at the lumberyard when Rodney got the news.

"Can't imagine why the Osage Hospital ain't good enough for your sister-in-law, but anyway, Elmer's waitin' for you out in the alley."

Half listening, Twila grabbed a dollar bill from the household stash in a pint jar behind the flour bin. No use explaining that Sharon might need a specialist who worked in Austin. Her heart was already in Osage with Lily.

She flung herself across the back yard and into the old bubbletop, and Elmer took over where Shirley left off. Sailing west out of town, gravel flew as he slammed his big boot down the accelerator.

Manure from his chicken coop spread all over the floorboards. Dust roiled through holes in them, and Twila sneezed and sneezed.

"Yer little niece was so cute, like an angel. The wife wasn't so pleased when they named her Lilly, doncha know? Why not Hyacinth or Rose, she said—oh yeah, or Daisy."

He paused, but Twila could think of nothing to say.

"That little gal was so much like you when you was little."

They careened around a corner so fast, Twila left fingermarks in the old leather seat.

"Kin still hear Lilly sing-songin' *Aunt Twiwa wuvs Wiwy*, with you pushin' her on the swing. Heard her clear t' our place."

His effusive commentary matched the stream of tobacco juice venturing down his chin. It was all Twila could do to hold her tongue—she hated the way he spoke of Lilly in the past tense, as if...

Seeing the hospital, a big white house on Fourth Street, brought relief. Elmer came to a jerking halt in front and she bounded out with a quick thank you.

The soul of kindness, he promised to drive Mom over when she came home from work, a generous offer with gas so rare. Shirley and Elmer might be the queen and king of blabber, but they were good neighbors.

Dad would say, "You take the bad with the good." Oh, how she wished he were here right now. Thinking of him brought up another memory that made her cheeks burn as she hurried up the hospital steps.

One night last fall, she had jumped from the front porch roof on her way to the *Half Froze* and startled Elmer nearly out of his wits. From the shadows beside his house, he blinked big-as-baseball eyes, and she held her finger to her lips.

"Shh! This is a surprise for Mom." He nodded, and she scooted toward the bar. But of course, he couldn't keep any secret, much less such a magnificent catapult.

When she breathed Lilly's name, the nurse at the front desk gestured to her bed where Rodney sat beside Lilly. The little girl's paleness took Twila's breath away, and the nurse cautioned them to keep voices low.

Rodney grabbed Twila in a bear hug. "I hated to leave Sharon there alone, but—"

"You can go to her now. I won't leave. You can pray just as hard while you're driving."

"Right." Worry crowded his forehead. "You'll pray, too?"

"The very best I know how."

"That's how we all do it." He touched Lilly's forehead. "I'll be back as soon as I can." He left to see if his second child had arrived yet.

Now the clock struck the half hour. Twila smoothed her finger over Lilly's hand and offered up another plea: *Oh dear God, help her to wake up.*

The evening dragged on, and with all the goings-on in the ward, she lost track of time. At one point, commotion broke out in the hallway. A man yelled orders, and a nauseating ether odor wafted through the doorway. Someone panted—a woman about to deliver a baby?

Another half hour ticked by, the nurse turned off the harsh light and shadows emerged. By now, Mom must be enduring Elmer's chatter on the trip down here.

"Oh, Dad. If only…" For him, the sun rose and set in Lilly's eyes, but it might take days for word to reach him.

Then Lilly's thumb jerked. Or had she imagined the movement? Twila rubbed her eyes and stared some more.

Someone in the next bed coughed. And then came another twitch.

Chapter Nine

As if they were made of crystal, Twila eased Lily's fingers on the scratchy sheet and raced out the door toward a chin-high countertop. Just then, the nurse hurried down the hall, so Twila waved to her to hurry.

"I think Lilly moved her thumb, ma'am."

Back with Lilly, the nurse's starched white cap stood out like a banner in the shadows. She held Lilly's hand for some time. Finally, her eyes brightened.

"I believe you're right, Miss. Would you mind going back to the desk? Push the black buzzer beside the phone. That will summon the doctor."

Twila could hardly breathe as she followed instructions. *Black button beside the phone...* Nothing happened, so she pushed it again.

A door opened and someone stumbled out of a nearby room. "What...?"

"Your nurse had me buzz you, sir. Quick, it's Lilly Brunner."

He sprinted down the hall. When she entered the ward, he bent over Lilly, and over his head the nurse mouthed two simple words. *Thank you.*

Not much later, Lilly's eyelids gave a slight, yet undeniable flicker. Then Mom walked in, so pale Twila's heart skipped a beat. She stood in the doorway with her hand to her throat.

Twila ran to her. "She's getting better. She's going to be okay." Trembling, her mom collapsed against her.

Around midnight, Rodney returned. Lilly had wakened

completely by then, so he told her about her new baby brother.

"His name's Luke, honey."

"Luke and Lilly…"

"Yes. Do you like it?"

Lilly nodded and clutched his hand.

When the doctor checked her again, he shook his head. "It looks like she's on the mend, but she'll need to stay under observation for a couple of days. If one of you wants to spend the night with her, that'll be fine."

Mom had clutched Rodney's hand the whole time, and her sharp intake of breath said more than words.

Twila spoke up. "I'll stay. You both have work tomorrow, and Mr. Olsen's wife can cover for me."

Rodney gave her a hug, "Are you sure?"

"Yes, I really want to."

"All right. Thanks a million, sis." He took Mom's elbow. "Come on, I'll drive you home."

When Lilly fell asleep, Twila dozed in the chair next to her bed, but sometime before dawn, a racket in the hall woke her.

Someone screamed, "No! No! They're going to—"

"Mrs. James, calm down now. The doctor is only trying to—"

"No! Get me out of here."

There was no ignoring the noise, so Twila peeked out at the nurse wrestling an injured woman to a wheeled gurney. A trail of blood led to the entrance door and splashed the woman's yellow shirt. Nearby, a younger woman, maybe the patient's daughter, wrung her hands.

"It was an accident. I'm sure it was…" She leaned against the wall repeating herself, but made no move to help. Glancing around for the doctor, Twila hurried toward them. Nowhere in sight. She raced for that black button and pushed it three times.

"Don't let them…" The woman's screams intensified, and the nurse had all she could do to maintain her hold, with the gurney moving underneath.

Instinctively, Twila grabbed one end and steadied the contraption. The nurse gained the upper hand, and the bleeding woman finally collapsed. Blood still gushed from her abdomen, but the nurse grabbed a towel and pressed it against the wound.

"Thanks." The nurse caught her breath as the doctor appeared, and Twila backed away.

Lilly still slept peacefully as she sank onto the chair next to her. It was almost as if she'd dreamed that scene. But half an hour later, the nurse slipped in to check Lilly. On her way out, she whispered, "I can't thank you enough for your help out there."

"Is the woman all right?"

"I think she'll make it. She's getting stitched up right now. Usually two of us are enough for night duty, but we've got two babies being born."

She took a deep breath. "What a night! You sure know how to keep your head about you. Have you ever thought of becoming a nurse?"

"Not really, Ma'am."

"Well, you'd make a good one, no doubt about that."

Just then, Rodney walked in, and as if sensing that, Lily wakened.

"Lilly, the doctor says you can go home tomorrow, and you get to stay with Grandma and Aunt Twila overnight. How would you like that?"

Lilly's eyes sparkled. "Can I go to school?"

"Not till next week." Rodney patted her hand as she yawned, and added, "Take another nap now. I'll be back tomorrow, okay?"

"Umm…" She fell asleep in an instant, and Rodney turned to Twila.

"I just had to check back in before work, Twi. Sure am glad you could stay with her. The nurse told me you've been a life saver. I don't know what we would've done otherwise."

"Don't they say, 'When it rains, it pours?'"

"That's for sure. I really missed Dad at the lumberyard this week. Will's a good man, but he's not—"

"He's not Dad."

"Yup."

By the time Rodney picked her up at noon the next day, Lilly seemed like her bubbly self again. Twila went to get the mail and when Mom came home, she lunged at a letter from California.

Fixing supper, Twila whistled Benny Goodman's new release, *Taking a Chance on Love*.

"Twila, your dad says..." She paused to read more. "Oh, I wonder how... He says maybe when the group they're training now gets..." She stalled again.

"Would you please read it all and then tell me what he wrote?" The hurt in her mother's eyes sent regret through her. Why couldn't she just bite her tongue?

"Sorry." Her mom retreated, like the turtles in the marsh south of Halberton when someone came upon them all of a sudden. Twila usually backed off, too.

But today, she tackled the silence. "I didn't mean to hurt your feelings, Mom, but when you read like that, I can't make heads or tails of it."

"All right. Sorry." After a full minute, she started over. "When this group they're training leaves for the Pacific, he might get a leave."

"Seriously?"

"Yes, and he might come home, even if it's only for a few days."

"When would that be?"

"He doesn't know for sure yet." Her mom scanned the yard through the window. "I almost hope it's not until after the first hard frost because I've let everything go all summer. Didn't do such a great job last year either—I'd hate for him to see the yard like this."

"We can get things back on track. At least the garden's weeded, and your flowerbed couldn't be prettier. Besides, everything will probably be covered in a foot of snow by the time Dad comes."

Her mom winced. She'd read something into her words, but what? Maybe she felt guilty putting the flowers ahead of the other outside work...

Mom hated conflict, so a person always had to guess what was going through her mind. It was hard to disagree with her, and having an honest talk took so much energy.

But then her mom perked up. "I have Saturday off. Maybe if we can trim the hedge and do some raking—haul the debris down to the river. Maybe we can borrow Rodney's truck."

"Sure. I don't have to work until two. We can start bright and early."

"Mmm... sounds good, honey." Her mom went back to reading the letter for the third time.

"He's slipping, Stan. I wish we could do something for him."

Carlos put his head in his hands.

"You and me both. The natives' medicine is the best we have right now."

"Hopefully they'll keep him alive until help comes." Carlos let out a long sigh. "It's just that..."

Stan might have finished his sentence for him, but waited.

"Who knows when that'll be, and this fever's taking him farther and farther down."

"Yeah. We just have to stay together."

"That's what my brother used to say to *mi padre* when he got on him about being a Zoot Suiter—we have to stay together. But sometimes I wonder if maybe one of us should try to get to the coast. Maybe there'd be a submarine. Better yet, a Jap headquarters is what we need. All we'd have to do is make off with radio, and—"

"A great plan, if there were twenty of us and we were armed. But I have a question. Why hasn't the fever gotten you yet?"

"Maybe 'cause I'm a dirty Mexican, like the sailors call us. Living like lowlifes makes us stronger." Carlos leaned back to study Stan. "But then, it hasn't gotten you, either."

The post office box opened with a twist, and a letter postmarked Algona, Iowa fell into Twila's hands. Her heart in her throat, she knelt on the airy foyer's chilly wooden floor and tore open the envelope.

One word stood out—*accepted*. A giddy wave swept her as a cold late October gust announced someone entering the building. She didn't even notice who it was until she caught a whiff of cherry pie.

That would be Honor Trimble, who had just eaten a piece at the café.

"Are you all right, Twila?" He peered down at her. "Got some news from your dad?"

"No. Oh yes, I'm perfectly fine, Sheriff. Great."

"Good. Well then, I'll be on my way. Gotta check on the creamery. Somebody said they smelled somethin' different down thataway..."

As he made his way out, Twila wished this moment could last forever, like in the movies. She reread the letter, written by a nurse named Alcott.

Despite the freezing wind from North Dakota, she reread the entire page on her way home. This nurse was the one who would interview her, the letter said. An interview—oh my goodness! The afternoon took on a dreamlike quality, as had an evening a few weeks ago in the Osage hospital.

Lily's first words when she awoke the second time were, "Auntie, where are we?"

She'd leaned in so close, the dry cracks on Lilly's lips seemed cavernous. But her clear blue eyes shone like diamonds—she was going to be all right for sure. The nasty nurse came in just then, but nothing could decrease the moment's joy.

Icy wind rustled the letter, and for a second, Twila considered detouring to the lumberyard. Rodney's eyes would spark at her news.

But she continued home. Soon, she would tell him and also explain how much his kindness had meant to her through the years. Her rush toward home evoked a parade of memories.

Months ago on graduation day, he had eased the pang of missing Dad. Outside the auditorium in line to shake hands with everyone, she hadn't noticed Rodney sneak up behind her. Between neighbors' and friends' greetings, he whispered in her ear.

"So proud of you, lil' sis. Dad would be busting his buttons about his little girl—you've always been his sweetheart."

When the crowd finally thinned, Rodney and Sharon walked Mom and Twila home. While they pushed Lilly and Luke on the playground swings, Twila sat with Mom.

"What would you like to do besides work at Olsen's, Twila?"

"I don't know."

All around Halberton at that time, spring was making its appearance. Pines added soft pale green growth and anthills erupted through sidewalk cracks. Rich purple and magenta lilacs blossomed on every block, and fragrance filled the park.

"Well, things take time. You'll figure it out."

Listening to passersby discussing the weather, the crops, and of course the war, it seemed impossible her school years could be over. Down the block, she could still see the school. Above the front doors, a workman had etched 1928 in the concrete.

From there to the shed housing balls and jump ropes, she knew every inch of the property, the burn barrel outside the back entrance, the jungle gym and swings. Ah, well. No use getting lumpy in the throat over a building.

"I hope you're right, Mom."

Back at home, she finished her ice cream and the special graduation cake Mom had baked and took Lily to the sink. "Hey, Lilly, gotta keep your good dress clean for church next Sunday."

"There she goes, seeing what needs to be done and doing it—Twila's always been like that, right Mom? I won't be surprised at whatever my little sister ends up doing."

Now, looking back to that day, the seeds of guidance showed in Rodney's words, and in her own personality. Those seemingly meager beginnings had only needed time to germinate, as Mrs.

Harmon said. Now, nearly half a year had passed and things were coming together—a *nurse* was going to interview her! What if she could help out in the hospital?

Imagining that interview and what Camp Algona's hospital would be like, she raced up the back stairs.

Chapter Ten

Mom was later than usual tonight, a perfect interval to get a head start on tomorrow's cleaning. While she worked, Twila mused over Camp Algona and the letter from Char she hadn't even noticed in her excitement. Char had mentioned classmate Millard Schott, a perpetual harassment all through school.

Millard's torments drove even deeper during junior high. Playing high school basketball increased Twila's confidence, but from the stands, Millard still reminded her that her physique left something to be desired.

He and his buddies kept it up in the hallways, but she followed Dad's advice to ignore them. Still, one taunt stuck. "Look at that heavy Chevy comin' down the hall."

True-blue Char lashed back at them more than once. "Twila could take any one of you down in a fair fight, but you'd be too chicken to face her!"

That made them hoot with laughter, and Dad's advice—*if you ignore stupidity, it'll go away*—carried Twila through. But then Pearl Harbor exploded the war right into Halberton, when Joe Lundene perished on the *Arizona*.

Twila barely knew him, since he was a senior when she entered high school, but everyone in the community felt this loss. The attack motivated many young men to join the Navy, and day-by-day, more empty desks appeared in study hall.

Most were seniors, but some begged parents to sign off for them to enlist early. Millard, held back in the third and seventh grades, was two years older than the rest of class, but still not eighteen. One day he failed to show up, and his younger brother said he'd joined the Navy.

A "blessed subtraction," someone said. But everyone noticed his empty seat—and the hallways were a lot quieter.

At graduation, the principal read Millard's name after everyone received diplomas, and Twila wished him well. He may have made life miserable for her, but now he could take that misery to the enemy. He might even become a hero.

Finagling the mop behind Dad's chair revealed record dust swirls—how long had it been since they'd cleaned back here? Probably the day before graduation, when Mom hit every corner of the house.

Over the summer, even more men joined the fight, and many girls already had jobs to do with the war. One took a male worker's place at Hormel's, another was making missiles at White's in Waterloo, and Mary Lou Simpson joined her cousin plaiting bomb heads in Alabama.

She invited Twila to come along—tempting but impossible. She'd chuckled at Twila's response.

"Are you kidding me? With Dad gone, I'll be lucky if Mom lets me get as far as Osage."

But graduation seemed long ago. Time had flown by, and finally, she could do her part. Yes, Algona was a distance away, but still in Iowa, at least.

Daylight turned to dusk. The teakettle whistled, so she sprinkled green tea into the strainer and filled the teapot. She'd already set everything out to make grilled cheese sandwiches as soon as mom got here. She read her acceptance letter once again.

"The camp wants me—they really want me!" She danced around the table. This was a hundred times more exciting than the day Mr. Olsen hired her.

Then she remembered—on graduation night, Mom had made her a promise. "Your dad and I will support you, whatever you decide to do for the war effort. You know that."

Now, the time had come to test that promise. She shook the mop over the porch railing and set the table, keeping her letter smack in the middle.

Within half an hour, Mom sat down and thumbed through the mail as the sandwiches grilled. Without a word, she set the bills in a pile—no letter from Dad today. Twila filled plates, but before they ate, she picked up her letter.

"I got this today, Mom. Back in July, I wrote to that new prisoner of war camp in Algona, and they sent an application. The reply came today. They've accepted me."

Her mom paled, but attempted a smile. "To do what?"

"I'm not sure, but a nurse wrote this letter, and is going to interview me."

"Mmm. Does Margaret know?"

"How would she? I've barely even met her."

Her mom jerked back as if she'd been struck. "Right." Her face whitened even more. "When would you start?"

"After the first of the year. Just think, maybe I'd be able to work in the hospital." A thrill overtook her, instigating a stream of words.

"I applied for anything they needed me for, office work, anything. But the application asked what I really liked to do, and—remember when Lilly got hurt?

"I loved being there with her. A couple of times, emergencies came up, and the nurse was so busy, she let me help out a little. I can't explain it, but that made me feel…"

"Go on. How did you feel?"

"She taught me to take Lilly's pulse, and in the middle of the night, a woman came in—she was bleeding everywhere. I only steadied the gurney for the nurse, but she said I had really helped a lot. I started to think, wouldn't this be a way to do my part?"

Her mom folded her fingers together as though 15 years had disappeared, Twila was a child again, and they were about to recite, "Here's the church, here's the steeple."

"I'm so excited." Twila grabbed her hands. "I… I even prayed about this. Remember that sermon about ordinary people doing bit at Dunkirk?"

The look that passed over her mother's face left her unsure. Maybe this would come to an unpleasant end. After all, she'd applied for this job behind Mom's back. She groaned—if only she could express her thoughts better.

After a long silence, she gave up and started to clear the table.

"Twila, sit back down." Her mom's sigh intertwined with the clock's ticking, and she returned to the table.

"You already have a place to stay in Algona."

"What?"

"I'll have to swallow my pride and admit Margaret was right. She wrote me a few months back and described the camp construction. She said they'd be needing civilian workers, and hinted that this might be a good option for you."

"She did?" Twila sank back into her chair.

"She even offered to let you live in Paul's room."

"She... Oh, my."

"At the time it didn't seem realistic, and I thought you'd be helping Sharon out when the baby came. But then Sharon's mom wrote that she could come and stay as long as they needed her. And after Lilly's accident, Rodney said her nurse told him you're a natural."

She gave a wan smile. "Why didn't I see this before? Was there ever a hurt animal you didn't try to nurse back to health? Remember the bedraggled robin you kept in the back porch until its wing mended?"

That forlorn bird and a myriad of other needy creatures... an abandoned kitten, a bedraggled puppy, even an abandoned baby mouse. Once, Char found a baby raccoon with a broken leg and brought it over, certain they could make the little fellow well again. Char's mom had refused to let her put it in the shed, so Dad built a little cage out behind the porch.

"Besides that, you've always liked to take charge and you usually figure out a way to make things work. That's a good quality in any occupation."

She drummed her fingers on the table and closed her eyes a second. "If you're certain you want to do this, I'll write Margaret to make sure she still has room. I wouldn't doubt she wants you to come since she's going to be working at the camp, too, and Harry's building for the army down at Camp Dodge for who knows how long."

Elbows on the table, she rested her head on her fists. "Margaret's so concerned about Paul, and another adult around the house might be a good thing for Benny and Diana." She let out a breath. "I'll write to her tonight."

How could this be happening? Twila could hardly believe her ears—she'd finally get to know the sister Mom hadn't seen for all these years, and her cousins. She leaped up and twirled around, and Mom shocked her by joining in.

When she pulled back, she held Twila's hands. "We've had a few hard times, you and I. But all-in-all, we've done pretty well since your Dad left, don't you think?"

"Yeah—and if this works out, I'll only be a few hours away."

"Why wouldn't it work out?"

"Well, this nurse may not like me—"

"Oh, she'll like you. Don't worry about that." Mom's sigh sounded weary, but not discouraged. She found a pen and her notebook.

"Things could be far worse. You might have signed up for the WAVES or something even more dangerous. Can't believe what some girls are doing these days. Flying big airplanes, making bombs—someone told me how dangerous it is for them to work with TNT."

A cloud dimmed her eyes to gray. "I'll write your Dad, too, although I know he won't object."

Here in simple kitchen, something powerful settled down. A fresh kind of understanding—maybe it was a blessing.

Myra rubbed her hands together. "Well, I've got my work cut out for me. I'd better get at it." She started for the living room, and Twila ran the dishwater.

All the while, she thought, *Even though Mom's so lonely for Dad, she's willing to let me go.*

From the living room, a newscaster launched into the evening news report.

> Allied planes have been raining a heavy assault on Japanese bases in the Marshall and Gilbert islands, and on the fourteenth, a torpedo narrowly missed the battleship USS Iowa, with our President aboard.
>
> He is en route to a conference in Tehran with Prime Minister Churchill and other Allied leaders. Thankfully, disaster was averted.
>
> In other news, the Allies have successfully raided a Vemor, Norway plant vital to enemy bomb-building ambitions.

When the report ended, Mom switched off the radio. After setting the kitchen to rights, Twila sat in Dad's armchair to write her reply to Nurse Alcott.

With both of them writing, a unique quietness prevailed this evening. Not everything had to be spoken out loud.

Chapter Eleven

In his usual straightforward manner, Uncle Marvin neglected to knock. His shuffle on the back steps alerted Twila, so she hurried to let him in. When she saw his load, she gave him leeway—he couldn't have knocked on the door if he had tried.

The unmistakable bulge of a plucked Thanksgiving turkey rose from an enamel roasting pan. He set his burden down on the wood box and wiped his forehead.

"Best o' the flock. With your dad gone, you 'n your mom deserve a good 'un."

"Thanks. Mom'll be really grateful."

He scratched under his cap. "Well, I'd better get goin'."

"Don't you want your pan?"

"I'll pick it up sometime."

"Would you like a cup of coffee? I've just baked some cookies, and we sent a box to Butch. Have you heard anything from him lately?"

"Not for a while." He peered around the porch as if looking for something. "Well, I got some more deliverin' to do."

Still he stood there, rubbing his calloused fingers together. Must be enough dirt in those deep cracks to plant a potato.

Expecting a final pronouncement before he backed out the doorway, Twila waited, but he took his time. She'd never known him to hurry, except that night when Mom threw china at him.

"Things goin' all right for you two here?"

"Yes. Mom's awful tired—she's been working lots of extra hours up at the plant."

"Well. Good then." He lowered his eyes and backed out, but wavered on the top step with the door open. "Be sure to keep this bird cool till morning."

"We will." At about twenty degrees out here, that would be no problem.

The peculiar set of her uncle's shoulders, one lower than the other, and the way his left leg bowed out a little as he headed to his truck caught her attention. A lot like Mom's.

Could he be double-jointed, too? Out of nowhere came the impossible image of Mom with her legs and arms wrapped like pretzels around her torso. Were Uncle Marvin and Aunt Margaret able to contort bodies, too?

Bracing in the cold air, she shut the back porch door. As far as she knew, he hadn't been here since last fall. Probably Mom's plea for help had left him with no idea how to proceed, and now, Thanksgiving gave him an opportunity to give them this turkey.

From the gaping neck hole, she pulled out the giblets. Better get these boiled with a cup of raisins and some walnuts for the dressing. Mom would be so tired when she got home.

Even though Sharon offered to bake the pies for tomorrow and Mom's widow friend was bringing scalloped corn, so much work lay ahead. By nine o'clock, peeled potatoes sat in salted water, the turkey lay in its roaster stuffed for baking, and homemade buns rested on the counter, glossy-topped in the lamplight. The house smelled of yeast and sage, melted butter and black pepper.

Dark circles under Mom's eyes testified to her exhaustion, so Twila offered to clean up the kitchen.

"Thanks. Your dad always enjoys stuffing the turkey—sure wish he could be here, especially with the new baby. I haven't held little Luke for a week now." Her voice softened. "But your dad hasn't even gotten to meet him yet."

"Go on up to bed, Mom. Sleep in tomorrow if you can—I'll get up early to put the turkey in the oven."

"You really want to?"

"Sure. Makes me feel grown-up—I think now I could make the whole dinner by myself. Well, except the gravy. Mine always has lumps."

"I'll show you how tomorrow." Myra faded into the living room as Twila shook the tablecloth over the porch railing. Such a crisp, clear night—her breath came sharp, but the air held promise.

Soon, she'd be in Algona. Who knew if she'd even get home for Thanksgiving next year? Something stirred out in the plowed garden, maybe a raccoon seeking one last kernel of sweet corn.

Down the alley, someone pulled a back door shut. Elmer and Shirley had buttoned up place for the night, and the only light came from a three-quarters moon outlining the lightning rods on the shed roof.

Not long before Grandpa Brunner died, on a similar night, Dad had taken her along when he went across town to check on him. With a storm brewing, they had to hurry, but the sensation of walking through town hand-in-hand to Grandpa's tiny house near the railroad tracks came back to her in full force.

Nothing special happened that night, but the memory made her miss Dad even more. He had a way of knowing what she needed, and that night, she'd felt so important being included.

The moon disappeared behind a cloud, and she sent up a prayer—this was getting to be a habit. Then she hurried inside to tidy the kitchen, but when she headed through the living room to go upstairs, Mom lay on the couch.

Normally, she could only fall asleep in her own bed. A little closer, at exactly the right moment, the moonlight strengthened, giving a clearer view.

Mom hadn't even bothered to pull the drapes, usually her first action when she entered a room. Twila leaned in to study her face. Such clear-cut cheekbones, a little up-turn at the end of her nose, a few freckles, and that birthmark.

As a child, she'd often asked about it, and Mom's answer varied.

"It says I'm me. It's been there since I was born. Pa said if it had been on my right foot, I'd be destined to travel. On my left, it would mean extra intelligence."

"So what does it mean on your neck?"

Mom laughed. "It's either the devil's signature or an angel's kiss, baby. Take your pick."

Both alternatives piqued Twila's overactive imagination, but when she rehearsed the conversation with Dad, he chuckled. "Lots of people have birthmarks. Nothing but an oversized freckle, kiddo." That put her curiosity to rest.

Mom shifted positions. The lift of her chin, even in sleep, showed determination. She was holding things together, doing her best for Dad.

Into the moonlight, Twila breathed her thoughts. "Even though you seem so far away sometimes, at least our longing for him binds us together."

Those weary emerald eyes shuttered open. "Wha…?"

"Come on, Mom. Let's get you up to bed."

December 1943

Crash. Thwack. Zrring… zriing! When all was said and done, Stan hoped the crashes and thwacks outnumbered the Nip bullets whizzing through the air. So far, that's how it had gone, but nine months into guerilla exploits was no time to get cocky.

Beside him, Cap smashed an enemy's temple with a rock. But from the left flank, the shooting continued. Panic needled Stan—where had Carlos gone? It had been a few minutes—or was it hours—since he'd spotted him among a new group of Filipinos that joined them a week ago.

Exuberant and carefree, Carlos knew how to obey, but still followed his own instincts. And with Cap fading in and out, responsibility for him weighed on Stan. If anything happened to that California lad…

Zrring... a bullet ricocheted close to his ear. He shook his head like a steer ridding himself of flies. Another shot dodged, but far too close for comfort.

Help us... help us now...

Cap scanned the side of Stan's head and grinned. "That one took a bite out of your helmet, man. I'm going to get him." He darted through a stand of bamboo before Stan could protest.

Before this new band of Filipinos came upon them, Cap had fallen into a depression, but now he rallied. A sour-smelling liquid the natives poured down his throat probably had a lot to do with this change, although last night Cap thrashed and screamed in his sleep again.

As usual, his subconscious had transported him back to the surrender on Corregidor, and Stan tried to talk him back into the present.

"General Lough's been cut off—this is terrible. Sir, what shall we do?"

"There, there. Calm down Cap. That was a long time ago, before the surrender." Cap stared at him wild-eyed, so Stan repeated himself.

"Surrender—what're you talking about?"

Stan added, "Our whole army surrendered back in May. But we're up in the mountains now, don't you remember?"

"You're crazy, man. That's fool's talk."

"No, it's the truth. You and I found that raft, the Japs shot at us, and we swam to shore. We found Carlos..."

"Carlos?" Cap stayed quit for a while after that—blessed silence. But then he spurted, "A fool thinks himself to be wise, but a wise man knows himself to be a fool."

"Shakespeare?"

"Right. You're a smart guy."

"But you're calling me a fool?"

Cap ignored the question, and threw more dire memories at Stan instead. Everything they'd done here would be wasted—they'd be allowing the Japs to kill so many more Filipinos if they surrendered—how could anyone even entertain the thought?

Eventually he tired of arguing, and after he fell asleep, the episode left Stan restless and wakeful. What had happened in Cap's brain to make him return to that time, to live in it for longer and longer periods? It was impossible to understand.

But right now, another member of this Jap patrol skulked toward him, unaware that he was being observed. Stan gripped his weapon tighter. This time, his bolo, recently sharpened by one of the guerillas, would serve his purpose well. The long, single-edged knife designed for breaking through dense foliage had become his favorite weapon.

True, the thing weighed more than his army knife, as Carlos pointed out. But the sturdy blade proved reliable no matter the target. The natives had taught all three of them to aim more accurately when they'd been out hunting a wild pig.

Even though he'd lost a lot of weight here, Stan wanted to maintain his strength, so the more pounds he lifted, the better. When no one was looking, he did exercises holding the bolo.

Come on, come on.

Like an obedient child, the young Japanese took a few more tentative steps. Stan aimed the bolo for his chest, and the sickening *whoosh* of the blade sent the enemy off into an Imperial Japanese version of glory.

Just before the impact, Stan looked away. The sound alone convinced him he'd hit his mark. Then came the thud. A Filipino ran ahead and stripped the victim of his weapons. Even seeing the native's hand brush the Nip's still-warm skin made Stan shudder, and for a split second, he allowed for human feeling.

The poor lad looked more like a boy than an adult. His fragile cheekbones, sprayed red now, reflected patchy midday sun.

"Sorry, but you chose the wrong side."

He couldn't recall when he took to addressing the men he felled... kind of like Cap quoting the classics to whomever he saw. The short address he gave the enemy allowed him to move on. That was the secret to survival out here—do what you have to do and take the next step. Leave the past behind.

He'd certainly been able to do that with the distant past. Traipsing through the Wisconsin forest with his brothers seemed more like a distant dream than an actual memory.

It took a few seconds to notice the absence of fighting around him. The stillness drove an uncomfortable wedge under his breastbone, something like the oppression on an August day in Wisconsin when the sky turned sickly green and a peculiar quiet fell over the land. Tornado season—stay on the alert.

A guerilla collected the other enemy weapons they had stashed in a pile. Then Cap appeared through a bamboo thatch. Noting the eerie look in his eyes, Stan spoke first.

"You accomplished your mission, I take it."

"Yep. Odysseus has returned home victorious."

"Right."

"We won this one. There ought to be a parade, with festive *carosas*, and painted water buffaloes bowing down to Saint Isidore, like in that one village we passed near. Remember?"

"Yeah, but they were giving thanks for the harvest, and it wasn't much of a celebration compared to before the war. Remember how the Filipinos explained the tradition?"

"Umm... patron saint of farmers..." Cap seemed lost in thought, but at least he'd moved past the surrender—must've have been about two weeks after they crossed over to Bataan that they heard faint music from that town... Started with a *P*, but Stan couldn't recall the name.

Then out of the blue, Cap said, "Virgil knew what he was talking about. 'Fortune favors the brave.'"

"But wouldn't you call the enemy brave, too?" Stan helped the Filipinos gather more weapons and once again, glanced around for Carlos. In his poor Tagalog, he asked one of the guerilas.

"Ahead, two-three guys. Meet you later, he say."

Like a stage play, the action all around him continued. Carlos, in watchful Filipino companionship, was safe. And for the moment, Cap seemed perfectly fine.

Oddly, the verdant jungle colors blended into a form of comfort. Like the north woods in his other life, this place had become home.

He studied the terrain until Cap slapped his shoulder. "Some day, we're all going to be heroes."

"But you only made me a captain, remember? If you'd told these guys I was a major, I'd be up for General by that *some day* you're talking about."

"Let's say we level ten more patrols in the next few days and keep it up till the war ends. When the command discovers how many Japs we took out up here, and how many American lives we potentially saved, they'll…"

Stan fell in behind him and the Filipinos. "You're nuttier than I thought, oh learned professor. And for once, I've got a quote for you. 'You can't build a reputation on what you are *going* to do.' Henry Ford. Not to mention my Grandpa Ford, who actually met old Henry back in the day."

Cap half turned. "You don't say? Were they related?"

The glint in his eyes tempted Stan to tell a whopper, but he declined. "Nope. I suppose you know this one, too: 'Whether you think you can or think you can't, you are absolutely right.'"

"What a memory you have. But I must alter your verb—it's *believe*, not *think*."

"Ah, I stand corrected. You're the professional here."

"If you think you can out-quote me, you'd better think again. If you *believe* you can, it's the same scenario."

This joking demeanor encouraged Stan—maybe Cap could recover some day. If only they could get him to medical help. But a few minutes later, he squinted off into the distance, and his left eye began to twitch, a sure sign of another feverish attack.

But for now, his cheery voice belied worry. "However, I'll give you this, Stanley Ford. You make a much better army officer than I do, and I wager you will make Major some day."

He was back in the present again, back in reality. But how long could it last?

Chapter Twelve

The blow stunned Twila. At first she felt no pain, just shock when something struck her head with no warning. For a stretch of time, her body seemed to float in mid-air. But this voice, she knew all too well, and the beery breath that accompanied it.

"There, Miss Smarty Pants, let's see if this helps you contribute to the war."

Heavy footsteps and a faint whistle drifted off as she sank to the snowy earth between the café and the newspaper office. In spite of Honor's warnings to take the long way around to Main Street, she'd chosen the shortcut again. What could it hurt?

Closing up the café had become a familiar routine. When Thelma stopped in the other day, she mentioned how nice it was to have Mr. Olsen home for supper once in a while.

"So glad you're here to help out. Otherwise, our kids hardly see dad."

Picturing Dad out in California might have generated a sharp reply, but Twila held her tongue. She could have described Mom on Christmas Day, hardly eating anything, and holding little Luke as though she'd never let him go. She looked so forlorn, and so did Rodney, watching her from across the room.

"Glad I can make things easier for them."

"But I hear you're leaving?"

"Yes. We all have to make sacrifices because of the war, don't we?"

Before closing down, she'd been humming the last song someone played on the jukebox. Finally, Mr. Olsen had broken down and ordered one. The move increased his younger customers, and almost made Twila want to stay longer.

Artie Shaw's version of *I'll be With You In Apple Blossom Time* had been playing, and the wistful tune stayed with her. If only Dad could come home, even for a short time.

Step by step through the darkness, she made her way toward Main. Once, she thought she heard something, but only the faint purr of a car sounded from the alley. She hurried a little, though it was hard to see in front of her.

Then *crash!* A blow to her head accompanied by a sharp tobacco smell, and she felt herself falling… falling. With nothing to grasp, she flailed her arms and then her head smacked into something cold and hard. Very, very hard.

For a moment the alleyway swirled before her, with only a pale sliver of moon in the night sky far above. She smelled the back room of the *Half-Froze* and heard rather than saw a sneer. But before she could cry out, the darkness swallowed her up.

January 1944

After another skirmish, Stan had no idea how long, something like a pole slid under his shoulders. Then native faces formed a ring above him. He lost track of where they'd been, or how a powerful fire in his left leg made it hard to focus.

Whoever stooped over him blurred in and out, and then someone lifted him, carried him, head and feet dangling. He blacked out and when his senses returned, he was stretched out in midair. His deliverers rarely spoke, but kept a steady pace. They were moving down the mountain—the sensation of descent came as clearly as the pain.

With a grimy finger, the man at his head forced his eyes open every once in a while and instructed, "Stay wake." Once, the bearers settled him to the earth and someone splashed cool water on his face.

Stay... This became Stan's prayer, and he rehearsed how he ended up in this circumstance. He'd been with Cap and Carlos. For a change, Cap, once again risen from the dead, had led the way. He'd been excited because the Filipinos had heard word from some native people they called Negritos.

Americans had been spotted along the coast, so they'd agreed do a little reconnaissance. If GIs had been spotted, that could only mean the time was near—the time to liberate the islands.

They defined an area the Filipinos has set up around the camp, and felt fairly confident within that perimeter. But yesterday—or was it the day before—they'd ventured outside the circle.

Quiet all day. No enemy encounters, but they kept talk to a minimum just in case. With the sun setting over the distant bay, they'd started back on the trail they'd hacked earlier in the morning. Stan recalled thinking that no matter what, he'd always remember this particular sunset's beauty, orange and persimmon against a silver blue sky.

Then with no warning, Cap reared back with his knife arched over his head. Stan reached for his bolo just before an otherworldly shriek sounded. He lost sight of Cap then, and the next thing he recalled was an excruciating weight crushing his knee.

Stay... gotta stay awake... stay awake. He put every effort into obeying, but along the way to wherever these men were taking him, the jungle walls faded into gray mush. His bearers' voices became so much bird chatter, and he entered another world.

"Wha... what?" A nipa roof above him, and a Filipino woman standing not too far away. Not much more than a girl, really—what was she doing over there? A metallic scrape resonated. Something was being stirred, and then someone else moved around in the enclosure. Stan fought for clarity. Where was he?

Lightning shot through his leg when he attempted to roll over. It took a while to realize that the next sound he heard was his own cry.

The girl startled and backed away. When he closed his eyes, she shuffled near again. Maybe she'd thought he was dead. That touch on his forehead, what was it?

"Fever... no break." She dabbed his face with coolness straight from heaven and at the same time, a putrid odor battered his senses, burned his nose. Before he could resist, the girl spooned something into his mouth. He choked, but she held his jaws shut until the fiery liquid traced down his throat and settled in a blaze just below his ribs.

His entire esophagus must be blistered.

But she brought water, and he gulped it down. Though the light in her limpid eyes drew him, he dipped back into another world smelling of pine and horseflesh, the world of his youth. In that world, his father led the way, and Stan learned to halter lead the family's big lumber steeds deep into Wisconsin forest to chop trees to haul to the sawmill.

When he reawakened, someone else attended him. He oriented himself. Across the room, an older woman sewed some fabric. She left her seat when he stirred, and the deep wrinkles on her face spread when she stood over him.

"Fever break—good... good. You gonna live, GI!"

He tried to speak, but she forced another dose of that vile liquid down his throat and narrowed her eyes. "Drink, doctor say."

Doctor? He wanted to ask what she meant, but she pulled his head back and shoved in another spoonful. When he started to cough, she covered his mouth with her hand and repeated her command. Then she slipped in another ghastly spoonful.

"Drink."

He obeyed, but not without sputtering at a taste more bitter than green gooseberries. The horrid stuff offset an inferno roaring in his leg. But then he slept, and when he woke later, the pain had lessened.

This time, the same woman brought a bowl of something else, a sort of broth. Spoonful by spoonful, its soothing mildness quieted the blaze in his throat. Relieved to be swallowing something besides that medicine, he could have wept with gratitude.

Words rose, but mastering his tongue took such effort. At long last, he managed a feeble "Thank you."

His nursemaid grasped his elbow and spoke through trembling lips. "Thanks *you*—come here, save my people."

Sleep returned, with short periods of wakefulness. In one of his lucid moments, he attempted to sit up, but flopped back in a dizzy swirl. The woman forced more of that liquid down him, and after more water, his raging thoughts funneled into succinct questions.

Where were Cap and Carlos? Would they come back for him? Yes, of course they would. The question was *when*? He set his mind on healing, as if he had anything to say about that, and tried once more to sit up.

This time he took it slower, and at the halfway point, he spied his left leg—still there, but swelled double. Wrapped in brown leaves, the joint resembled a rolled rubber life raft.

For a few seconds, he allowed himself to stare before gradually dropping his torso back onto the mat. The thing was huge. Men with beriberi blew up like this, and were unable to even roll from side to side.

A sick sensation washed over him. That much swelling could only mean infection.

"Help—please have mercy on me. I can't lose this leg, or I'll never get back to Cap and Carlos."

A light sprinkle dappled the hut's grass and bamboo covering. Tightly threaded together, the leaves of its nipa roof extended over the enclosure a couple of feet. Above the inner section ranged rows of dividers to strengthen the webbed construction—someone had worked hard to arrange them, providing some order in the midst of this chaos.

That steady dripping, his favorite sound, had always lulled him to sleep as a child, but not now. No, his questions made no allowance for rest.

What if they had to amputate his leg? Once more, he cried out for mercy.

After darkness fell and he'd consumed another great draught of that blessed broth, a nameless energy filled him. If it weren't for his leg, he would get up and seek Cap and Carlos and the guerilla group.

Evening brought deep silence punctuated by ever-present insects. After some time, glimmers of light radiated from the other end of this village or encampment. Those bright pinpoints advanced closer, ever closer. Japs?

Then a mellow voice outside the opening gave some orders—a little more of the local tongue made sense now. Something about the coast, he thought.

Two Filipinos entered the enclosure, and without meeting his eyes, attached bamboo poles to his mat and swung his weight onto shoulders. Hoisted up, his head nearly touched the rough wall.

They ducked through the opening, and from a distance, Stan's wizened nursemaid waved to him, then held her hands together at her lips as if in prayer.

Nothing to do but lie back and trust while his carriers carted him off. And hang on, for this ride promised to be precarious. Hating his dependence, he gritted his teeth—how quickly his options had shrunken.

How he slept on that makeshift stretcher, he couldn't have said, but when he woke, it was still night, or possibly the next night. He recalled being set on the ground a couple of times, drinking some water, and swallowing that awful concoction again.

Yes, it must be the next night. Now, the men set him on the earth again, in a sort of thicket. A distance away, a body of water reflected moonlight, and his carriers whispered back and forth. They gestured for him to lie still, and in an instant, were gone.

Were they the same men who had taken him from the hut? He had no idea.

He only knew an incessant throbbing in his knee, but the fierce burning had diminished. Being able to raise his head without feeling faint gave him hope.

Lie still... probably the only order he could obey at this point.

Night sounds filled the jungle, so unlike the Great Horned owl's cry back home. Peculiar, sometimes raucous calls lanced the darkness—animal, bird or human? A sense of helplessness overwhelmed him until one of Cap's quotes came to mind.

"'Nothing can bring you peace but yourself.' R.W. Emerson." Lying there helpless, Stan begged to differ. Weren't his own imaginings and questions and impatience destroying this night's tranquility?

When a head popped through the bamboo about eight inches from him, his heart thumped out of control. He looked again, and could hardly believe his eyes.

"Shh..."

No mistaking that familiar glint. Carlos kept his voice low. "Thought you might want to know what's going on. There's a sub coming for you—you're a VIP, man. Said they'd stow you away. So far, so good—no Japs in sight."

"But how did you get—"

"My L.A. training, remember? Street smarts." Carlos grinned, but bit his lip at a sound from beyond the thicket, toward the water. He waited until rooting and grunting evidenced a wild pig or some other animal hunting for grubs.

"You gotta get help for this leg, and soon. There's a hospital ship beyond the bay, and the sub's taking you to it." Carlos glanced around again before breaking into a wide grin. "When you're fit to run again, come back and rescue us."

A birdcall came from the right. He froze, hand on his knife. But within seconds, a friendly Filipino face appeared.

"What about Cap?"

"He's..." The rest of the reply became lost in whatever the Filipino told Carlos.

"Time to go. I'll take care of Cap." He gave Stan a thumbs up and faded into the jungle.

Lifted once again, Stan let out a long breath. Everything depended on…some would say destiny, but truly, it was these men. As the muscled Filipinos hurried downward, then swished through the sand, tears burned his eyes. They were risking lives to port him closer and closer to the bay.

Out of nowhere, a memory flashed from his little country church back home. Two days before he left with his Guard unit, the pastor pronounced a blessing over him.

"May you sense God wherever you go. He's always listening, and in one way or another, answers our pleas."

Under a shifty Southern Pacific moon, the Almighty was working through these humble men. Yes, and the same peace enfolded him as when he read the little Armed Services Prayer Book his church had sent with him.

Somehow these natives found the correct point, for two American sailors emerged from the shallows and pulled him into a PT boat. One of them surveyed his knee and gave him two pills with some canteen water.

He nearly wept—he wanted to touch uniforms, embrace them. But they disappeared, and he soon fell asleep again, until other voices roused him.

"Over there. Lift him onto here. Now down, a little more…"

The next thing he knew, a fresh salty breeze tickled his face. Nearby, a hatch creaked open, and handed from one team to another, he was lowered into utter darkness.

He'd always thought a sub's cramped quarters would drive him wild. But he barely had time to notice how tight things were before the ingredients of those pills took over.

The next time he came to, he rode in a small vessel that entered into a massive shadow hanging over glistening velvet water. Men slung him into some contraption that hoisted him higher, and others pulled in the line. Moonlight and salt spray melded around him.

"Gotcha." Sailors surrounded him, and one with a medic's patch started cutting off his pants. The luxury of a bunk, the unearthly scent of real coffee, a doctor and nurse unwrapping his leg—he must have entered one of those Hollywood films.

Everyone spoke as if he were superfluous.

"Somebody poured sulfa powder on this. Good sign. Proud flesh here. Give it a thorough scraping and prepare a big dose of penicillin—good thing that new supply just came in. If we got him soon enough, we can save his leg."

"Morphine before I scrape?"

The doctor must have nodded, because almost immediately, something burned into Stan's upper arm. A nurse presented a set of knives on a towel so clean it almost hurt his eyes. He dared not look into her face—so scrubbed, so earnest, so... American.

He needn't have worried, since he started off into that other world again. In a freezing onslaught, the big workhorses that dragged the lumber snorted and stamped hooves. He pulled thick leather straps tight around a bundle of fresh-cut timber and strained to hear what his dad called out.

"Come on, son—we'll have to leave the rest for the first thaw. All that matters now is getting home."

He dropped off for a few seconds, and then his father's words came again. "See those clouds in the northwest? A heavy snow's on its way, and with this wind, there'll be a blizzard. Gotta get home fast."

Chapter Thirteen

"No deep break in the skin. Good thing you brought her in right away, Honor." Doc adjusted his glasses. "Good thing you had your flashlight along, or she might've laid out there until morning."

"Just can't imagine how she fell, Doc. It was dark, but she's as sure-footed as anybody in town. And for this to happen just where that confounded pipe sticks out—looks planned to me."

The door banged and cold air swept Twila. Then Rodney's voice joined in. "What happened?"

"Wait a minute. Here's some blood up higher—oh, man. Somebody struck her—see, right here? Her head's been hit twice. Once on that pipe, down low, but there's another big lump near the crown—see? This blood's still wet."

"You think there was foul play?"

"'Peers to me somebody walloped her a good one, Honor. No doubt about it, and the angle points to somebody fairly tall."

Doc probed a bit more. "Not sure what he might've used—maybe a wooden baton—no, it'd take a cutting edge to leave this v-shape. Looks like it's time to get out your detective tools, Honor."

"But everybody likes... Who would've..."

Gradually, what everyone was saying began to make sense, although Twila failed to force her eyes open. What was she doing here, with Doc, Rodney, and Honor Trimble gathered around? Her head hurt something fierce. She raised her hand, but Doc held her wrist.

"Good, she's waking up."

"It's Rodney, sis. You had an accident on the way home from work. Just lie still now, and Doc'll take care of you." His tone relayed another unspoken message. They'd figure this out— he hadn't played those radio detective games in his youth for nothing.

A few seconds later, he started sleuthing. "Can you talk yet? Tell us what you remember."

"Tobac... cigarette smoke... whistling."

A door closed, and then a small hand squeezed hers. As Twila faded, Mom's shaky tremor became evident. "Oh Twila, honey. What happened?"

"We need to keep her quiet, Myra. That's the best medicine right now."

"Mom, do you have any idea who would want to hurt her?"

A bitter twinge entered Myra Brunner's voice. "I'll bet it's that good-for-nothing Lonnie Higgins. Twila threw him over months ago, but the Higgenses hold a grudge forever."

Honor cleared his throat. "Hmm... makes a lot of sense. I'll take that into consideration. See you later."

Pace... pace... pace... two sets of boots. Rodney was going along to help. A door opened and shut, and Twila's consciousness gave way.

"Finally opening those eyes? Thought you might sleep forever."

The unfamiliar voice contained a definite Southern twang. Stan shook himself awake and screwed up his courage to look down at his leg. It might not be there, he remembered that much. But two feet—ten toes—showed near the bottom of the bunk. *Whew*. He closed his eyes and rolled back to his pillow.

"That nurse sure is pretty, ain't she?"

Stan had been back in Wisconsin, re-living the day his older brother Raymond drove him down to Steven's Point to catch the troop train. His mother gushed tears the whole way, and he wished she'd stayed at home. Besides facing his own fears, he'd had to comfort her.

"I never thought you'd have to go. Maybe because we live so far up here in the woods, I thought they'd overlook you. And they might have, if..."

He kept repeating what Dad had already said. "It's better for me to go with my Guard unit now than be drafted. This way I'll get settled and trained before..."

On the train platform, she buried her face in the lapel of his wool coat and sobbed some more. Finally, Dad pulled her back and shook his hand.

"Stay safe, son. Write to your mother regular, you hear?"

"I will. Thanks, Dad."

When a nurse came to change his bandage, he understood his neighbor's earlier comments. He couldn't take his eyes away from her. She was probably thirty or so, but the line of her eyebrows, the curve of her jaw, her slim nose, her white hat and uniform—everything about her intrigued him. And her assessment of his leg gave him such hope.

"Good news—signs of infection are lessening every day. When we get to San Diego, you'll be transferred to a hospital, and it won't be long until you can start rehabilitation."

When she pulled his feet to the floor, sickness rose in his throat. He swallowed it down and set his mind.

"So today, young man, we'll see if you remember how to walk."

Surveying the tight space, she added. "No stairs for you yet, so we can't go up on deck, but you can practice going from here to... over there. That guy with the curly blonde hair is your destination. Are you game?"

"Yes, ma'am."

Finally. He'd wondered when this moment would come. Waited for it, longed for it. Pain still shot through his knee when he put weight on his foot, but he managed to avoid wretching in front of everyone.

One moment at a time, he told himself. This challenge could only be met one moment, one step at a time.

One... two... he swayed, but the nurse caught him. A helpless feeling enveloped him. When had he been reduced to leaning on a woman?

"That's all right. It's been weeks since you took a step. Start over now. One... two... three... four." Another collapse, but again, she was right there.

"Try it again. Two more steps and you'll be there."

Perspiration dripped down his back, but he made it. And then she helped him turn for the return trip. Only one swaying episode before he crashed on his bunk, panting like a dog.

The nurse tapped his shoulder with her fist. "That was great. Now drink some water and rest. "I'll be back in about half an hour, and we'll do it all over again."

"It's a date." Stan pasted on a grin to hide his grimace, and she saluted him.

Honor Trimble had never been inside the house before, as far as Twila knew. When she opened the door, he pulled at his mustache with a nervous forefinger.

"You're lookin' mighty good. Glad you healed so fast." He planted his feet on the kitchen threshold. Excitement tinged his eyes, and he wasted no time launching into his message.

"Wasn't a hard case to crack, I'll say that. Your assailant gave us plenty of clues."

"Good. Would you like to sit down, Honor?"

"Don't mind if I do. Got any coffee in that pot?"

"Sure. Just a minute."

"That fella left his shoe print, big as you please—matched perfect, if I do say so myself, right down to them little words carved in the sole. *Red Wing*... right good boots, at that. Soon's we got that clear, I saw him down to the station for the night, even though his daddy threw a blazin' fit."

He paused for a drink. "Your mama was right—it was Lonnie that hit you.

"'Course his daddy made a big fuss, but when I matched the print to Lonnie's shoe sitting right there in plain sight, well, what could he say? Then I revealed his fingerprint on the cigarette pack I found near where you fell, and...'"

Honor slurped again and wiped his mouth with his sleeve.

"It's rare to see old man Higgins with his trap shut, and I have to admit, I thor'ly enjoyed it."

He cleared his throat, and Twila gave him her best smile. "Thank you so much."

After he gulped the rest of his coffee, she refilled his cup. Good thing Mom made a little extra this morning, which was rare.

"What his daddy *did* say was, 'You threw away a cigarette package there?'

"The big kid just lowered his head. He knowed he was caught red-handed." Honor rolled his hat brim between his fingers. Thankfully Twila's head had healed enough to subdue the dull ache that troubled her yesterday, and she'd gotten dressed before Mom left for work.

A beautiful late December day beckoned her outdoors, but Doc gave her strict instructions not to leave the house. Then he said he'd stop by later today to see how she was doing.

"You were right about that side of the building being dangerous, Mr. Trimble. I should've listened to you."

"We all have to live and learn. That's the way of it. What matters is that Lonnie's learning his lesson too... 'least I sure do hope so. This ain't the first time he's been on the edge of the law, but nothin' ever got proved. Not till now."

Honor swallowed some more coffee. "That judge over in Osage gave him two choices—go to jail and face assault charges or enlist."

"Really?"

"Yep. Shoulda seen that boy's feet shift when he heard that. Almost lost his voice, he did. Ain't used t' bein' held accountable. No sirree."

"So he's going to basic training?"

"Yep, saw him board the train t' Fort Leonard Wood m'self. Yesterday mornin', bright n' early. His daddy didn't even bother to show up. It was just me n' his mother. Lonnie looked none to happy, but like I said, he's gotta learn."

After finishing his second cup, Honor settled his cap and advanced toward the back door. His shuffle hinted at pain in his hip.

"Uh huh. Learnin's what life's all about. Finally, the time comes even for a fella like Lonnie, spoilt as he is, t' grow up n' face the music. His daddy's money couldn't pull him outta trouble this time." He shook his head. "I'd sure hate t' be his sergeant, but then, he's got lots of tricks up his sleeve. He'll know 'zactly how to wear Lonnie down."

He turned before exiting down the porch steps. "I can count on you to inform your mama, can't I?"

"Absolutely."

Back in the house, Twila wrapped an afghan around her shoulders and sought Dad's chair. She still had trouble imagining Lonnie stalking her the other night. He'd been drinking, yes, but still—it wasn't like him to make a plan and follow through.

Picturing him submitting to Army discipline took even more imagination. Meanwhile, morning sunlight transformed a patch of the hardwood floor into gold. She ought to write a letter to Char—it'd been so long since she'd heard from her. Maybe she'd gotten sick or something.

But before she knew it, she was dozing.

Some time later, a rap on the back door startled her awake, and she scuttled out to answer it. One glimpse of a blonde victory roll made her gasp.

"Char! I... What are you doing home? I mean, how did you...?"

Her best friend's easy laugh paved the way for a sound hug. "Well, aren't you going to let me in? It's freezing out here."

"Yes, of course. Sure. I'm just so..."

"You were sleeping? In the middle of the morning?"

Heat swamped Twila's face. "Yeah. Normally I'd be at work, but—"

"I stopped in at the café, but saw you weren't there. Mr. Olsen was so busy, there was no chance to ask him where you were, so I..." She glanced at the clock. "We only have a few hours. Dad's gotta get back for work tomorrow, so we'll take the evening train. But I had to take this chance to see you."

"How about some tea? Oh, and take your coat off. Make yourself at home."

"Tea sounds great." Char draped her coat over a chair and scuttled over for another hug. "I've missed you so much. Never thought I'd get through Hamlet without some study sessions with you."

"But you did. Of course you did. So how did you get to come here today?"

"Dad had some business to attend to at the lawyer's, since Grandpa died last summer, you know. Mom didn't like me missing work, but one of my new friends said I deserved a break and offered to work overtime for me."

"That's a real friend. Now tell me about life in the big city. I try to picture you there, but—

"First of all, what are you doing here at home?"

Twila made the story as brief as possible and Char gasped, "Lonnie?"

"Never mind—I'm better. Now, on to big city life."

"Sure is different, but mostly, I like where we are. With night school and working, there's not a lot of time to explore. Oh..."

Char pulled a stack of letters from her purse. "It isn't that I haven't written, it's just that by the time I get home, the post office is always closed. So you can read these at your leisure. Speaking of that, you still look a little pale. That Lonnie—I always knew he was lazy, but this..."

"I guess he didn't take it well when I asked him why he hadn't enlisted yet."

"Well, if that isn't cat's meow—good for you! I'm so glad you came through it all right. Lonnie Higgins—I just never dreamed he'd have the gumption to do something like this."

"My sentiments exactly." They chuckled over the idea of him in boot camp, and then went on to another subject. And another.

After lunch, Char jumped up. "Oh, I have to go. I'd like to stay forever and ever, but maybe you can come and visit me?"

"Maybe, but I'll be even farther away soon. When the war's over, we can do all the things we used to talk about."

"Don't forget, okay? And don't you dare find a boyfriend before I do. We need to go to New York, ride on a Mississippi riverboat, visit California—we have so much to do together!"

Chapter Fourteen

The news blaring through the Madison train station reminded Stan that almost three years had passed since he left for basic training. His unit had been juggled around, he'd gotten sick and been assigned to San Francisco, and sailed in that merchant marine ship to the Philippines. Not long afterward came the portentous news of the Pearl Harbor attack.

Naval and air support from Pearl had been vital to General MacArthur's campaign. At that point, most of the planes, ships, and supplies were gone. The news had been difficult to comprehend, much less accept. Would the President send help from elsewhere? With troops stretched across North Africa, doubt burgeoned in the ranks.

Then came the Japanese assault on Bataan—months of nonstop bombing. Once Corregidor fell, a cavalcade of events followed, but he'd learned about them only through reading old newspapers while he recuperated. The rehabilitation wing of the hospital offered piles of worn copies, so he drank in the demoralizing details.

The British surrender of Hong Kong two weeks after Pearl, and devastating defeat in Singapore, which he'd heard about before the surrender in Corregidor, left a sour taste. This could only mean more Allies held captive by the Japanese.

The next months brought victories and defeats, from the battle of the Coral Sea in May to the victory at Midway in June. Those two led to the Guadalcanal Campaign in August. Nine American ships were lost in the Solomon Islands bombing—heavy cruisers, the Quincy, Vincennes, and Astoria sunk on August ninth, plus two destroyers and four transports.

In the October twelfth Columbus Day paper, more than two months afterward, the Navy finally admitted these losses. "A majority of the personnel were rescued," but the article also cited 'many casualties'.

Having been aboard several ships now, the thought of dying at sea sickened Stan. Cap's face rose before him, and he set the paper aside. Nearby, a fellow with his arm in a sling pored over the news too. When Stan stirred, he asked, "Where'd you serve?"

"The Pacific. And you?"

Keep your experiences to yourself, Private Ford—we've learned a great deal from interviewing you, but you never know who might be listening. Of course, plans are underway to invade the Philippines, and we wouldn't want to drop any hints to the enemy.

Heaven forbid any little slip would cause more suffering to the men still over there. By night, visions of them on the trail still visited Stan.

The other soldier seemed not to notice his hesitation. Besides that, he needed to talk—perfect. "I was at Buna, the Warren Front. The Japs were dug in, and Zeroes sank our supply ships before the battle even began."

He lifted his sling. "Wounded, but the scub typhus was what sent me home—had to show a fever above 102, and I guess I sure did."

"Is that like Dengue fever?"

"Dunno. Gives you the runs, eats your guts out, makes every step torture. Sure didn't want to come home, though—we gotta keep winnin' over there."

"Exactly."

"Spreadin' ourselves awful thin, doncha think? North Africa, Sicily, Italy... Think Churchill n' Roosevelt know what they're doin'?"

"I know what you mean. I sure hope so."

"Can't stop thinkin' of those fellas taken captive in the Philippines—wish I could go back and help out. When I get better, o' course."

A sudden wave of emotion engulfed Stan as he noted how drawn and pale the soldier looked. But he still would go back to the Pacific in a heartbeat.

He could identify. The hospital had seemed too clean, the rehabilitation room too fancy, the food too wholesome, the atmosphere too pleasant. How had he landed here, anyway? He still didn't even know exactly how he'd been wounded. But more than that, he had no clue why he hadn't died.

Since then, he'd slept in far too many locations to count. During the last few months, the ocean breeze helped him fall asleep at night. The hospital window opened to the west, and he'd come to count on its gentle salty *whoosh*.

The other thing he could count on was waking in a sweat some time later, certain an enemy patrol followed his trail. After slowing his breathing to a rhythmic calm, he would get up and take a slow walk down the hall.

This became a nightly ritual. One more exercise session for the day couldn't hurt.

In spite of the nightmares, he caught up on sleep and gained weight while putting everything he had into getting his leg to heal. The doctors said only time would complete the process, and warned him not to expect to walk as he once had. Ever. But he ignored that and put his heart into building up his muscles.

His soul, however, still crawled through the jungle with Carlos, Cap and the guerillas, always on the alert. One night, he could have sworn Cap lay a foot away from him, suffering one of his feverish fits. Between thrashing and moaning, he yelled out:

"Inferno down at Second Corps Headquarters... destroying the TNT and ammo... What have we come to?" His voice took on even more urgency: "Artillery barrage—don't you feel the earth rocking under our feet?"

Then he fell silent, but not for long. "It's a sign, I tell you. Seventy-seven years ago today, Robert E. Lee surrendered to Ulysses S..."

His forehead scrunched as if, kept inside, these thoughts would destroy him. "General Lee said, 'Nothing left to do... go see General Grant... rather die a thousand deaths.' Pure poetry, Stan, pure poetry. History's full of it. Wish I could've been there to hear him say that."

When Stan shook himself awake, the sense of Cap's presence loomed far too real. Instinctively, he reached out. But Cap had already vanished from this ward of recovering soldiers, leaving behind his essence—words. Memorized, pithy words that had survived the test of time, and had now taken up residence inside Stan.

What did Cap's appearance mean? Had he finally succumbed to the fever? Or was this hallucination simply a delayed consequence of his heavy sedation for surgery?

A month after that one, the doctor suggested a second surgery, which led to more range of motion. But even then, he refused to alter the recovery records.

"I'm doing pretty well, doc. Covering a lot of ground all on my own now. I want to get back into the fight."

"You have done remarkably well, Private Ford, better than I expected. But I doubt you'll ever be able to lay that cane aside. Muscles can rehabilitate, yet with the kind of inner damage your knee saw, full mobility is nearly impossible." His sigh showed he really cared.

"I'll be honest. I've never known anyone to completely overcome a knee injury this severe." He leaned forward and looked into Stan's eyes. "To have come as far as you have, I'd call a downright miracle. When you arrived, you presented quite the conundrum for our surgical team. The world out there is full of challenges, and you're an intelligent man. Why don't you find a different one to conquer now?"

Stan choked back words he knew he would regret. But as the doctor attended to another patient a few beds away, he muttered his rebuttal.

"Never give up the cane? How can anyone predict that?" Silently he vowed, "I *will* walk without it. I will. And I'll do a whole lot more than that.

GAIL KITTLESON

Late December sunshine flooded Nurse Alcott's office. "Before any prisoners arrive, we have a great deal of preparatory work to do, Miss Brunner. I assume you have secured housing?"

"Yes, with my aunt—she works here."

"That would be Margaret in the canteen—you surely resemble her. I'll let you know your exact starting date. You'll find your uniform in that small anteroom. Please try it on, along with your shoes, and let me know if any alterations are needed."

Through spectacles pushed up on her slender nose, she eyed Twila across the desk. Her nondescript brown hair formed a blunt line below her ear lobes and looked as though it had a mind of its own, curling here, waving elsewhere.

"Do you have any questions at this time?"

"Not that I can think of, ma'am." Then Twila noticed a worn copy of *LOOK* magazine on a shelf. She couldn't pull her eyes away, though she'd seen the October issue before.

"Something interests you?"

"Oh, sorry. I just noticed your magazine..."

"Umm... terrible situation. I have a few acquaintances serving over there right now."

"Oh my. You know somebody?"

"Yes, one of the 77 nurses ordered to evacuate in the Philippines was kidnapped by the Japanese last spring. I wish I could do something for her."

She knew someone in Bataan. Oh, wow! The story of the United States' surrender had been rehashed by Mr. Olsen's customers for weeks. Over 10,000 soldiers, sailors, and nurses in enemy hands.

"They've been held so long already..." Twila fumbled for something to say.

"Yes." Nurse Alcott shuffled some papers. "Well, then. I look forward to working with you, Miss Brunner. Please pull the door tight when you leave."

Leaving her to stare at a framed nursing license on the wall, Nurse Alcott strode out into the hall. The certificate proclaiming this woman a registered nurse mesmerized Twila. Like her starched white hat and spotless uniform, they declared her fit to contribute.

The same was true of the military nurse on the *LOOK* cover. From her cap to her nifty uniform, her image spelled perfection—and she surely had a certificate, too.

"What would it take to earn one of these?" Twila's tenuous whisper danced through the small, quiet room.

Her new adventure had begun, and her heart swelled with gratitude, but she wished she could start work right now. She tried on her uniform—*her* uniform.

The new leather shoes fit, but needed breaking in, so she walked out into the hallway. Then she caught herself—better get out of here before Nurse Alcott came back.

Snow piles formed long lines along Camp Algona's perimeter, and the cold air refreshed her as she walked to Aunt Margaret's building. After saying good-bye, she hurried to the train station, skirting ice patches along the way.

Doc's warning still rang in her ears, "Take it easy—no ice skating or sledding. Your noggin has been through quite a trauma."

The brisk wind blowing her scarf did nothing to dispel the warmth inside her. What would soldiers call this trip?

Reconnaissance for her upcoming mission. With 15 minutes to wait, she walked the length of Main Street, at least three times as long as Halberton's. Algona had the feel of a city, with enough stores to say you'd really gone shopping.

Even an ice cream shop—maybe she could bring her cousin Diana here for a treat some day. Last night, when Aunt Margaret showed her to Paul's room, Diana had sniffed. "I wanted to switch to this room when Paul left, but Mom wouldn't let me."

Twila let her comment go. "So he's a Hawkeye fan?"

Diana eyed the pennant hanging above her brother's desk. "Yeah." She fingered a couple of his trophies. "He's a big basketball hero here, and wanted to play for Iowa—be a Hawkeye, you know. He was homecoming king. Everybody worshipped him."

When Aunt Margaret called her, Diana left abruptly, but even her dubious welcome couldn't diminish Twila's excitement. A whole new life awaited her—far better pay than Mr. Olsen could offer, and work she looked forward to. What could be better?

When the stationmaster called her train, she chose a seat by a window. Passing through wintry countryside quieted her impatience. How many of these farm families had sent a son off to war?

In Waterloo, a mother and father had received death notices for all five of sons when the USS Juneau was sunk. Joe, Frank, Al, Matt and George—everyone at school could recite names.

Clackety-clack... more passengers boarded in Garner, including a soldier who sat right in front of her. Such a fresh haircut, and every stitch of his uniform was in place.

The devoted expression of that nurse on the magazine cover floated before Twila. Soon, she would return on this very same train. Soon she would be doing her part, too.

Chapter Fifteen

The three-day journey across the country left Stan stiff and sore, but he forced himself to get up and check out the other cars every half hour. The narrow aisles provided a perfect exercise area—without his cane.

Carlos would have a ball getting to know as many people as possible on each train car, and Cap would be all about hearing stories. Ever since that night he'd appeared to Stan in the hospital, his presence came through at the oddest points, always with a quote.

"'You must not fight too often with one enemy, or you will teach him all your art of war.' Napoleon Bonaparte said this. Have you heard it before? Or how about 'Just remember Pearl Harbor and fight on to victory.'"

Standing in a food line an hour north of Madison, a soldier passed by, and he was singing those exact words. Just a coincidence, but it brought up another scene from Grand Island, Nebraska, where women handed out sandwiches and coffee to everyone on the train.

Since Stan brought up the back of the line, one woman grasped his hand. "You're headed home?"

"Yeah. For a while, at least."

"Our two sons are in the Navy—one's on a submarine. Did you see any subs?"

He wavered, and the woman bit her lip. "Sorry, I shouldn't ask things like that."

"It's all right, ma'am. If it hadn't been for the sub that took me to a hospital ship, I might be buried in the Philippines by now. Maybe your son was one of my rescuers."

She swept away tears. "You never know. Get well, now. You've done your duty, son."

A great title for a book some day—*You Never Know.* Cap would be the one to write it, too—his quotes could take up half of the pages.

If he made it, that is.

Later, when all was dark and most people snored in seats, Cap revisited Stan in his sleep. Out on patrol, an ambush resulted in a Nip's hands around his neck, and he struggled for his life. That was when he woke up, paralyzed by a suffocating feeling.

A soldier in a nearby seat kept him from sprawling into the aisle and made light of the incident. But across Iowa and into Illinois, Stan forced himself to stay awake.

In the process, he heard so many snitches of war stories being passed on. By the time this was all over, they would be endless.

The announcer signaled the northbound train for home. At the same time, an insistent inner urging warned that *home* would never be the same.

On this last leg, he set his goals. Push-ups and pull-ups every night, build up his stamina out in the woods, and keep his stay as brief as possible. No one would understand, but that mattered little. Not with his buddies still in life-and-death danger out in the jungle.

At that point, one of Cap's quotes strengthened his resolve. "'He that respects himself is safe from others. He wears a coat of mail that none can pierce.' Henry Wadsworth Longfellow."

"Thanks, Cap." As Stan breathed this, another goal presented itself: get rid of this silly cane.

At the next stop before home, he got out for some coffee and left the cane near a bench in the waiting area. It had served him well, but maybe somebody else would have need of it.

All for the Cause

A fresh sense of purpose motivated Twila when she stepped off the train in Halberton. On her way home, she stopped in to see Mr. Olsen, who offered her ten cents more an hour to work until she left town.

"And you can close on Monday, Wednesday, and Friday. That'll give you more hours."

Later, Mom quietly listened to her descriptions of Aunt Margaret's house and family, Nurse Alcott and the camp.

"I'm glad you're getting to know Margaret and her family. I hope you know how proud I am." She straightened her shoulders. "We should look over your wardrobe, don't you think?"

That Saturday, the mercantile owner, a longtime family friend, exchanged yard goods for ration coupons and chorused the latest news.

"Didja hear we're bombin' German airplane factories? Ever since Murrow's 'Orchestrated Hell' broadcast on CBS, I've known we'd win. Have to do whatever's necessary, that's all there is to it. All that work Don's doing out in California—I'm behind him all the way."

Hunched near the radio the evening of the Edward R. Murrow broadcast he mentioned, Twila had pictured planes bombing Germany by night. Those bombs might have fallen on families of prisoners she would meet at Camp Algona.

The war chatter at the café grew thicker by the day.

"Have you heard about them blockbusters? Ten thousand pound bombs that blow up a whole block in one shot."

"What about them seven-man Lancaster crews flyin' into Berlin's eighty-eight defensive guns? Can you 'magine us havin' weapons like that back in the Great War?"

"They call them bombs cookies. D'ya know why?"

"No."

"Me neither." The elderly speaker's cackle echoed as he spit tobacco into a spittoon six feet away.

Twila dodged the streams as Mr. Olsen turned the radio up. "A month ago, Greek guerilla soldiers executed 78 German troops they'd held captive for months. In retaliation, the Nazis shot down every male 12 and older in Kalavryta on December 13th, more than a thousand souls. They also destroyed 28 small surrounding communities."

A town of a thousand—oh my. The blatant Nazi attack showed no mercy, and neither did Olsen's regulars.

That night, Twila dreamed of a Nazi chasing her through a cornfield. Harsh green leaves slashed her face, and then a long knife poised over her head. She woke with her heart pounding a loud staccato, and talked herself out of the nightmare.

"Twila Fae Brunner, the U.S. Eighth Corps has arrived in Europe. With General Eisenhower in command now, there's nothing to worry about."

On the December day when the General became the Allied Supreme Commander, Mr. Olsen celebrated by turning the radio even louder. He gave customers free coffee all morning, accompanied by his best salute.

"Good news, folks. The Huns have worn down the Brits, so they're lettin' our officers take over. Best thing I've heard in a while."

On Christmas Eve, Twila and Mom sat together with hot tea to await the President's Fireside Chat. Dad would be listening too, a comforting thought.

> "The American people have had every reason to know that this is a tough and destructive war. On my trip abroad, I talked with many military men who had faced our enemies in the field. These hardheaded realists testify to the strength and skill and resourcefulness of the enemy generals and men whom we must beat before final victory is won.

The war is now reaching he stage where we shall all have to look forward to large casualty lists... dead, wounded, and missing. War entails just that. There is no easy road to victory. And the end is not yet in sight."

Mom drained her cup. "So then, we'll keep doing what we have to. Right now, we need to have the best Christmas we can.

But nothing seemed normal, since Rodney and Sharon took the children to Sharon's parents for Christmas Eve. On Christmas day, Sharon lamented, "Luke will probably be a year old before Grandpa even gets to see him."

Finally, Lilly's plaintive question undid Mom's careful smile.

"Gramps isn't home yet?"

New Years day, 1944 passed with the usual fundraising dance. The town turned out, minus most of its young men. Twila danced with Honor, who moved mighty slow, and two of the girls from her class still left in town.

Every day, she watched the mail for a letter from Nurse Alcott, and every day, went home disappointed. Late January brought an unseasonable warm-up. The old-timers compared the weather change to the thermometer's fifty-degree fluctuation last January.

Then they delved back into memories from years past. "Member the winter of '36? Never seen so much snow. The train couldn't make it through the drifts."

"Yeah, I was over in Davenport then, and we had t' dig 'em out almost every day. Terrible winter, and we though it'd keep the drought away."

"Ha! But it come anyhow. That next summer was a blisterin' beast. Corn halfway to your knee by the Fourth, and two weeks later, even shorter."

"How'd we ever make it through them days, Herb?"

"Almost didn't, I tell ya..."

The bleak talk went on until Twila spent some of her own money playing the jukebox to drown it out. Normally, she met the new after-school influx of teenagers with ambivalence, but not today. Hopefully, some of them had change in pockets and wanted to hear the latest hits, too.

It was a rough week—no letter from Dad at all, so Mom's spirits drooped. Not a word from Char, either, and she'd read through the whole stack she'd brought. Ah well, better write to Paul and Butch—they had something to complain about.

A week later, her letter from Nurse Alcott arrived. In only a few weeks, she'd be in Algona. Time couldn't travel fast enough.

Chapter Sixteen

"Have you told your mother yet?" Mr. Ford thrust his pitchfork into a hay bale as Stan wiped his brow.

"I'd rather face enemy fire than Mom."

"No use letting her think you're home for good." His father's sigh swept the dusty haymow. "You know she's scared to lose you, don't you?"

"But it's not just me—everybody's sons are leaving these days. And Mom's got two older ones who'll be around here always."

"Don't make no difference t'her. Ron's gone, too, and she's always been partial to you two younger ones. Can't argue with a mother's love."

Below them, the cows and horses awaited feed. A wintry blast made the air crackle even inside the barn, and breath became a haze of white mist.

He'd been here for almost six months—that ought to make Mom happy. Those months seemed more like six years. He couldn't leave soon enough.

How could even a mother's love ignore the evil let loose on this earth? This whole time, two worlds had pulled at him and now, he had orders to another locale. But this next stint wouldn't last long, either. His mother would take to bed for a week if she had any inkling of his long-range plan.

As soon as he washed up for the noon meal, he told her about his call to Camp Algona. She took it like he'd expected.

"Haven't you given enough? You still have quite a limp."

"Hundreds of men are dying every day, and I'm only heading to Iowa. You ought to be glad I can still do something worthwhile."

She turned to her mixing bowl and something rose in him, defiant and strong. Enough of being pampered. He wished he were going a whole lot further, but at least this was a start.

One day, he'd ridden to Steven's Point with a friend and checked at the recruiting office for something he could still do. The recruiter gave him hope.

"Let me see," He looked through a file drawer. "There's a new prisoner of war camp in north central Iowa, built to house Germans captured in North Africa.

"We've already staffed the one at Fort McCoy, but this one still needs guards, especially men with deployment experience."

Stan's heartbeat quickened. Being a guard sounded manageable, maybe even challenging as long as there'd be no Japs. His nightmares provided plenty of them.

After almost a full year, his walk had nearly returned to normal. He'd built up his strength doing exercises in the barn, and marched in the woods with a heavy pack, but at times, his limp still showed up. It simply had to go.

"Would you like to apply?" The recruiter obviously hadn't noticed any limp.

On the spot, Stan filled out the information.

"You should hear within a couple of weeks. Then you'll need a fresh physical."

"Right."

His acceptance letter came on a Thursday. His local doctor okayed him for stateside service, so he told Dad he'd be leaving in a few days. This time, *he* could tell Mom.

Iowa—not an exciting destination, that's for sure. He'd crossed that little nondescript state several times with dad on trips to buy a saw blade or some other contrivance for the mill and had always been glad to return to these forested hills.

But at least he'd be doing a necessary job. All the while, though, his *other* family, trapped on Bataan, would still be waiting in misery. They meant as much to him as his relations here. Maybe more.

Mom saw her off, and neither of them shed tears. But her parting words roiled in Twila's head all the way.

"I'll miss you so much, but your Dad told me not to cry. I'm happy for you. I know how much you want to try out your wings."

Behind her, a blue-suited conductor scurried people along. In a field across from the depot, some children sledded down the only hill for miles.

"See them sailing along? It's almost like a sign. Your dad reminded me our job is to let you go, so you can fly." Her eyes flashed, and Twila thought they'd never shone so green.

"That's what my mother refused to do. She never let us go—never let anybody off the hook."

A cloud swept her eyes as the conductor called, "All aboard for parts west!"

Mom's quick kiss heated the backs of Twila's eyes. "Off with you, then. Don't forget to write, and if Margaret seems too strict, try to be patient."

Passengers boarded in Mason City, Clear Lake, Garner, and Wesley, and windswept fields swept along between towns. Dad, a poet at heart, would call them barren and deserted, waiting for the final spring thaw.

Hundreds of times, he'd woven a bedtime story full of suspense and pathos... "Held captive by snow and ice, unseen life teemed below the fertile black earth. Left over from last year's crop, it eagerly waited to transform into seedlings on the first warm days."

His eyes would twinkle as he continued. "The farmers wait, too, all set to attack those would-be seedlings with plows. Because they're *weeds*, Twila, *weeds!*"

On the word *weeds*, he tickled her or swung her high above his head and they both giggled.

The brown leather seat warmed her back and neck, and Twila closed her eyes. Dad gave her so many good memories—if any loneliness lay ahead, or trouble, she had only to call them up to transport her away.

Aunt Margaret and Benny, the twelve-year-old cousin she'd met when she visited, met her at the Algona station. Benny's big brown eyes and shy smile reminded her of Paul's graduation photograph on Aunt Margaret's mantel.

A couple of inches taller than Mom and a little rounder in the face, with a spotless gray dress that matched her eyes, Aunt Margaret carried a formidable air. No one could have missed the way she jerked Benny's arm when he gaped at a couple of young soldiers boarding the train.

Too strict... be patient.

Several families said good-bye to sons, brothers, and fathers. Benny grabbed Twila's suitcase as if to prove his manhood, and gave her a shy smile. She instantly fell for his freckles.

At home, Diana, the spitting image of her mother, but a foot shorter, had the table set for supper. Sometime during mealtime chat, Benny disappeared, and the evening war news sounded from the living room.

"He listens each night?"

"Like clockwork. Drives Mom crazy." Diana wiggled her eyebrows to punctuate her declaration, but Aunt Margaret simply shook her head. Twila dried the dishes, and the whole time, Diana muttered about Benny's childish ways.

"He usually dries, but Mom probably decided it wasn't worth the fight to unglue him from the radio. He'll use you if you let him."

But after she went upstairs, Aunt Margaret joined Twila at the table. "Don't believe everything Diana says. Half of it's pure malarkey." She offered no further explanation. "Do you have what you need upstairs?"

"Yes, it's perfect."

"I probably should have put some of Paul's things away, but I want everything to be the same when he comes home."

"Diana said she'd like to switch rooms."

"That has nothing to do with you coming. Twila just wants the opposite of whatever I decide." Aunt Margaret's lips formed a hard thin line, ending the conversation.

In the morning, they walked to work together, a little more than half a mile, and Twila waited in the hallway outside Nurse Alcott's office as the clock struck seven. She must have been waiting.

"Miss Brunner, welcome." The head nurse offered her hand. Her hairdo was just as it had been last time, only a little shorter, and her starched white cap as crisp.

"Prompt, I see—an essential quality in a nurse. Come in."

She pointed to the same oak chair Twila occupied on her first visit. "Please complete these papers." Nurse Alcott went to answer a knock, listened a moment and peered back in. "I'll be back shortly."

After filling out the information, Twila set the sheaf of papers down and scanned the room. Like treasured artwork, Nurse Alcott's license captured her again, so she rounded the desk to study it.

The University of Iowa
On the recommendation of the faculty of the
School of Nursing
And under the authority of the
Board of Regents
The University of Iowa
has conferred the degree of
Bachelor of Science in Nursing
Upon
Alice Lee McPherson
Who has honorably fulfilled all of the requirements
Prescribed by the University for this degree
Awarded at the University at Iowa City in the State of Iowa
This fourth day of February…

The phrases sounded so official, like the Good Housekeeping seal of approval. *Alice Lee McPherson.* So, Nurse Alcott must be married.

Fulfilled the requirements. Those words implied some very hard work. She ran her finger along the certificate, and suddenly, Mom seemed near. Had she ever wanted to become a nurse or teacher? She never spoke of such things. Maybe some evening Aunt Margaret would let something slip about history.

"Miss Brunner?"

Heat deluged Twila's face as she whirled around.

"You've finished?"

"Yes, Ma'am. I was—"

"Studying my nursing license?"

"Yes." Her stammer sounded hollow, but a faint smile touched the older woman's severe countenance.

"Now you can guess how old I must be. Would you like to study nursing some day?"

"Oh, yes. But right now, I don't see how my family could—"

"Afford it?" She opened a desk drawer and retrieved something. "If we really want something, we find a way, don't we? And your work here may be the first step."

Then she ordered, "Turn around."

After Twila made a circle, she pronounced her verdict. "The uniform suits you well. Did you have to make any alterations?"

"Only minor ones."

"Put your best foot forward, Miss Brunner. You never know what the future holds."

Chapter Seventeen

Learning the ins and outs of the hospital and meeting some co-workers made Twila's first month whiz by. Nurse Alcott explained her role—no direct prisoner contact.

Lunch in the dining hall provided a world of information, some true, some rumor, with no way to tell which was which. Some discussions involved turmoil among the guards. One of them even declared he sure wouldn't mind killing a Nazi on the side, Geneva Convention or not.

An officer took him to task, so he finished eating in a hurry. After he disappeared, the table buzzed about his outburst.

The next few days, Twila watched for him, but a guard said he'd been dismissed. The speaker, an earnest lieutenant, spoke of the need for more discipline and better quality soldiers.

"If only every guard were the caliber of the Post Exchange officer or the sergeant in charge of the POW cooks and the Officers' Club mess. They know what they're doing.

"The command ought to hold briefings so we can learn from those men. Don't get me wrong, I wouldn't want jobs supervising Germans, but three-fourths of us have barely been through boot camp."

Those first weeks, she typed and filed reports and did other office tasks until one day Nurse Alcott summoned her for a tour.

"Observe and listen. It's important to understand the nurses' duties. We'll limit ourselves to the American patients."

She opened the supply room and pointed out an anteroom

holding all medications. In the ward, another nurse had just shaved a man's leg and was cleaning an ulcerated wound. Around the oozing sore grew a forest of thick black hair.

Twila flashed back to a fishing trip when Dad cut himself on a wire and rolled up his trouser leg. Blood gushed out, and he directed her to bandage it with his torn shirttail.

"Miss Brunner, I'd like you to meet Edna. Edna, Miss Brunner."

This nurse had a shape like Mr. Olsen's wife—amply endowed and thick in the middle. She barely glanced up, but offered a helpful commentary as she scraped.

"See here—that's proud flesh. Can't let it take over."

A putrefying odor rose from the deep injury, but Twila steeled herself and squelched her questions. The intense sensation she'd experienced when she cared for Dad's leg claimed her. Something had to be done, and she was elected. Such satisfaction—to be needed and to answer the call.

But it was more than emotion. She could almost feel the cold steel of Edna's scalpel in her palm. She could have taken over, and would have relished the opportunity.

Besides teaching her to bait her own fishing hooks, Dad passed on another important skill. By the time she was ten, he boasted that nobody filleted a fish faster or better than his daughter. Flesh was flesh. If she set her mind to it, she could do whatever they asked of her here.

Strange. With Dad half a nation away, he seemed closer than ever.

"Over here. Bring more tape and gauze."

After two weeks of accompanying Edna on her afternoon rounds, watching her never grew old, and little by little, Edna allowed Twila to get in on the work. With each small task, her desire to do more increased.

"We've kept this wound bandaged for two days now, but we'll let it air for a while. In a few hours, we'll re-bandage it for the night.

First thing in the morning, I'll check it again—if you're not busy with something else, you can come along.

"See this redness?" She tapped the puffy outside edge with her forefinger. "We'll know it's healed when this area turns pale pink."

One more opportunity to add to her growing list in the little black notebook Nurse Alcott had supplied. Tonight, she'd review her notes and figure out the most efficient way of handling each case if she were in charge.

In the meantime, someone was always calling her to help at a moment's notice. Sometimes she wasn't sure where to look for what they wanted, but usually came up with the desired object.

As Nurse Alcott clarified this morning, "You probably realize you're our gopher, Miss Brunner. You'll hear more and more of *go for this, go for that*. Stay flexible and keep a positive attitude."

Flexible...

For a moment, a younger version of Mom contorted before an audience on a bleak Texas roadhouse stage. Twila shook off the image and quickly refocused.

Carlos accidentally ran into Cap, who let out a squawk. Stan had the urge to stuff his mouth with bamboo fronds.

He and Carlos held breath, expecting an attack any second. But a full minute passed... two, with only birdcalls and insect stirrings breaking the silence. They waited even longer before breathing relieved sighs. Once again, they'd been delivered.

But how many times could this occur? Over and over, Cap's verbosity had potentially compromised them—at times, he seemed to have lost all sense of dangerous situation.

Ten hours from home, Stan awoke in sweat, with that scene from last year like a living thing within him. No use dreaming these images would one day disappear. Maybe they *never* would—maybe as an old man, he'd still hear Cap's voice and tramp through the jungle every night..

At least this dream had a positive outcome, so he focused on that—*Deliverance.* Such a beautiful concept. If Cap were here, he'd have some prose or a poem to recite about it.

The train trip to Algona was almost over, and for once, he'd been able to sleep without a real nightmare. When the conductor called out the station, he grabbed his duffel bag and asked directions to the camp.

This March day offered little beauty or warmth, but when he set foot in town, he knew he'd been delivered once again. This time, he'd been saved from home; from Mom's hangdog expression, from her coddling.

She couldn't help it, he knew, but that made being there no less discomfiting. Her expectations rendered him helpless to simply be himself.

West of town, his first glimpse of the newly constructed buildings heartened him even more—somebody had planned out the camp well. He might be at one of many army bases in his varied history as a soldier.

He happily presented himself for service, answered questions and signed his name on numerous dotted lines. Typical army.

An hour later, he arranged his things near the corner bunk he claimed in the least-occupied barracks. The place still smelled of fresh-sawn lumber, and scents from the camp kitchen made his mouth water.

Out in the hallway, a worker sang an off-tune song while he swept the cement floor. Listening closer, Stan recognized a personalized version of "Over There."

Fitting—if he had anything to say about it, this would be just one short stop along the way *over there.*

Send the word over there...the Yanks are comin'...

Well, in Bataan, the Yanks had already come. Now they needed to get out.

"This was one of those jobs Mom gave me when I'd upset her." Twila made the comment one evening in late March as she worked through a mound of black walnuts with Aunt Margaret. They'd been cracking the hard brown shells for hours, it seemed.

"But it's something to do during long winter nights, eh?"

The *click* of metal hooks filled the kitchen. Margaret wiped her forehead with the back of her hand, leaving a charcoal-colored smudge. With her high forehead and cheekbones, her resemblance to Mom became clearer every day.

Yet sometimes the two women seemed as different as marigolds and tomato plants. Both added color and scent to a garden, but could never be mistaken for each other.

"I'm so glad you're here to help me pick through these—they'll soon be too old to be of any use. Don't know how I did everything around here without you."

"I don't mind. Keeping busy in the evenings does me good."

"My feelings exactly, although your work is probably a whole lot harder than what I do. Ordering supplies, unpacking boxes, and counting money become pretty routine after a while."

"Depends how you look at it. I rarely do anything really challenging—except when Nurse Alcott has a meeting or Edna's swamped. Don't you have to deal with prisoners all the time?"

"Yes, but they're so thrilled to have access to toiletries and tobacco, paper and ink and paint, they see coming to the canteen as a privilege. They can buy almost anything they need with the scrip they earn.

"I've been warned about some antagonism between the officers and enlisted men, but they reserve disagreements for the barracks or outdoors. The first commander put them in different compounds, but I think it would be better not to separate the two."

She gave a snide grin. "But then, nobody's asking me. Since the prisoners get paid eighty cents a day for work, they have plenty to spend, and my job is straightforward—keep the shelves stocked and a close eye on everything."

"So you do inventory? I had to help with that at the café."

"Yes—all it takes is a sense of order, so it's not hard. Besides, I used to do it at a grocery store in town."

"The prisoners work somewhere?"

"Most of them are helping farmers clear lumber off river bottom land. They don't mind hard work, but need quiet activities at night. I've heard some excited chatter about playing soccer when the activity field gets finished."

"You can understand what they say?"

"Some. Grandpa and Grandma Ritzmann still spoke German when I was growing up, so some phrases are coming back. Compared to the battlefield or our boys' prison camps, they've got it awfully good here."

Twila cracked a dozen walnuts into her bowl. When she looked up, Margaret was on her feet, staring at her.

"You're fast, and so happy to help out. Surprises me a little."

"Why?"

"I thought you'd be more like your mom, I guess. Although she always did have spunk—no one could keep up with her. When she was little, you never knew where you'd find her—in the hay loft, down by the creek catching tadpoles, or up on a mulberry tree branch, laughing down at you."

Margaret clicked her tongue behind her teeth without even a hint of a smile.

"What would remind you of her?"

"Not taking things seriously. Always looking for something just beyond your reach, and not holding a thought in your head for half a minute. You're a lot more settled than she ever was." Margaret threw a handful of picked nuts into a bowl. "Actually, Diana reminds me more of Myra than you do."

"Mom must've changed a lot since you've seen her, because her job takes a steady hand and common sense. Working in the wards pales in comparison to all of her responsibilities."

"What exactly does she do at that plant, anyway?" Margaret

cocked her head to the side. So she didn't even know that much—but how would she? She and mom had only exchanged a couple of letters.

"She's in charge of a whole section that makes SPAM. The army started calling up more men, and now she's a supervisor. Meeting the quota is a huge challenge, and people admire her."

"That's good to hear."

"She misses Dad so much. I'm glad her job keeps her busy, and she works a lot of overtime, too."

"Ah, your Dad, Myra's knight in shining armor. They turned out to be right for each other, but I'd never have believed it back in the day." Aunt Margaret got up to add more corncobs to the stove.

"That Benny—where is he when I need him? This is his job, but I'm not going to freeze to death."

Why wouldn't mom and dad have been good for each other? And why had Mom allowed her to come here, knowing she might learn more about the past?

The wood burner blasted heat, so she took off her sweater. Once, she wanted to know every detail of Mom's youth, especially about her dancing adventures, and Aunt Margaret could likely share a wealth of memories.

But lately, that desire had dissipated. Sometimes, the less a person knew, the better. She loosened the top button on her blouse. Why couldn't stoves regulate the heat better? As Mom would say, it was feast or famine.

"You know how your folks met, don't you?"

"Dad came to town after the war to help his uncle—"

"To help his uncle? Maybe that was part of it. But I think he met your mom in Waterloo first. She used to hitch rides down there at night." Margaret brushed back a stray hair. "You do know she ran off?"

She didn't wait for a reply. "I lost track of how many times she disappeared and Mama had to send Marvin or Kenneth after her. Funny thing is, I had the same urge to take off and never come back."

Something rumbled in the basement, and Aunt Margaret raised her eyebrows. "Just the pipes reminding us they exist. Deep down, I admired your mom and wished I was gutsy enough to take risks, although I never would have said that out loud."

"Why not?"

"Your grandma would have slapped me silly, that's why."

"Was Grandpa still alive then?"

Margaret shrugged. "Didn't make much difference. Do you remember him at all?"

"No, and I don't recall much about Grandma, either. We only visited a couple of times, and she'd become so weak and sick, she hardly knew we were there."

"Too weak to slap anyone?" Margaret chuckled. "One advantage of her illness, I guess. Anyway, that's all in the past. I've spent way too much time mulling it over—what good does it do?"

They picked in silence until Twila reached the bottom of her pile. Flames rose and fell in the old iron stove, and the temperature gradually modulated.

The clock ticked away several minutes. Then, before Twila could stop it, a different question rolled out. "Did Grandma slap Mom, too?"

"Ha! She picked favorites, and they certainly didn't represent the best of the bunch." Margaret stretched her back. "I'll be done in a minute. Want to start sifting through what we've finished?"

"Sure." Twila began the slow process of holding each nutmeat up to the light to make sure no sharp bits of shell remained. Mom had trained her well, but witnessing Dad get a shell fragment caught in his teeth instructed her even more.

"You'd be perfect at the canning factory down in Ackley—the picture of efficiency."

"That's what Nurse Alcott said about nursing, too. Sure did my heart good." Even now, the compliment warmed her, especially since the head nurse handed out praise so sparingly.

After Diana and Benny completed other chores, Margaret

cajoled them to help. When Benny complained five minutes later, Margaret reflected, "This is how we worked when I was growing up. Most of us, that is."

She launched a knowing glance at Twila. "All summer, on into October, when we made the last apple cider." She squinted at Benny. "You ought to thank your lucky stars for how easy you have things. And don't forget to fill the cob box before you go to bed."

Benny groaned, but she ignored him. "Apple cider—back breaking labor. My, what a job."

But Twila lingered at *most of us, that is.* Aunt Margaret meant Mom—had Grandma let her get by with laziness? You'd never know it by the way she tackled her job, plus all the work at home.

But now was no time to ask questions. She turned to Diana. "How did work go at the creamery?"

Diana rolled her eyes and pinched her nose. "I'm just glad I only have to work a couple hours."

"Does having the camp here increase the creamery's daily quota?"

"Yeah, so the boss couldn't be happier. The war's gonna make him rich. Sure wish he'd pass along some of his good fortune with a raise."

"That's right, think the worst about everything. You ought to be thankful you've got a job." Aunt Margaret's scowl put a damper on any further conversation.

Chapter Eighteen

Benny turned the radio up so high, it might have been sitting inside Twila's head as she wrote a letter at the kitchen table. But at least the news was good.

> This is the Allies' month to make advances against the enemy. Our air carrier aircraft have assaulted Truk, the main Japanese base in the central Pacific, forcing the Imperial Navy to withdraw.
> At the same time, 20,000 German Eighth Army troops trapped by the Red Army, have surrendered, and upwards of 50,000 of Hitler's infantrymen went down fighting.
> In the Marshall Islands, the Americans have captured a forward Japanese base by occupying Bikini Atoll.
> In France 70 French Resistance members on death row in Amiens Prison under Nazi occupation have escaped after Allied bombs damaged cell walls.
> In the north, Lake Tinnsjo's waters buried a ferry carrying essential ingredients for German atomic research

All for the Cause

facilities. Sunken by one Norwegian resistance fighter, this ferry represents a great loss to the German war machine.

In Greece, partisans sabotaged a railroad used by German troop trains, and a train plunged some 400 German soldiers to deaths.

Finally, the American Air Force in Great Britain has forced the enemy to use fighter planes to protect aircraft factories against a massive bomber attack. American Mustang escorter fighters have decimated enemy fighter strength.

The war is certainly not over, but this month, our boys in uniform have made great strides toward that end. All of you on the home front, keep your chins up and continue to support the war effort.

And now, in stateside news..."

Aunt Margaret stopped knitting long enough to switch off the radio, and Benny leaped up with a punch into the air. "Wow! Ain't it great? It's about time our boys are givin' 'em what-for.

"Wish there was more I could do. Me and Wendell helped clean up the back room at the oil station today. Hauled three wagonloads of scrap tin down to the collection center. Mr. Bellows told us the army uses it for fifty percent of manufacturing now—at least we can make a little difference."

"Just think, what you took might end up in the newest airplane." Twila couldn't help responding to his enthusiasm, despite her aunt's frown.

Benny wagged his head and was about to blurt out more, but his mother lashed out.

"Don't encourage him, Twila. He's nuts enough over those planes and ships already. Benny, I don't want you hanging around at that station. You know that already."

"What's wrong with the Viking, Mom? Just a bunch of old guys talkin', and Mr. Bellows can sure use the help."

"Old geezers gabbing about every battle from here to kingdom come, that's what's wrong with the Viking. And Mr. Bellows gets along just fine without you."

Benny turned so red that his freckles disappeared. But all he said was, "Aw Mom. You don't understand."

"Never you mind. We're *all* doing our part for the war effort. That's what a *real* family does." Her inflection niggled at Twila. Was that another veiled reference to Mom?

Benny shook two bushels of dry, scratchy cobs from the basement into the wood box before going to his room. Diana faded upstairs, and Aunt Margaret's sigh floated from the living room.

"I'm beat. Think I'll go up, too."

"I'll turn off the lights."

"Thanks. You're a real help."

An hour after the house quieted for the night, Twila still lay awake. Muffled clanking alerted her to a train gliding into the depot without sounding its horn. She'd gotten used to its noise, but stayed awake tonight, thinking about Aunt Margaret and Mom growing up. Maybe not knowing Grandma very well had been a good thing.

At steady shuffling out in the street, she went to the window… lines of human shadows marched along in silence. She pattered downstairs in her slippers to watch from the dining room.

Ranging from the depot two blocks away, rows of captives were guided toward the camp by American guards. An eerie uneasiness pervaded the night, and Aunt Margaret slipped up beside her. Her whisper made Twila shiver.

"Troops captured in North Africa—the office warned us they'd be coming soon. They've been held in Europe, but now we've inherited them. At least they don't let off captured S.S. officers here in town, but stop the train out in the country and march them through the fields.

"That way they have no knowledge of Algona's layout—they don't even realize a town is close by. They're experts in logistics, and would probably be the ones to attempt an escape. Hopefully, tactics like this quiet folks' fears."

"Are you afraid of them?"

"Not really, as long as the guards take job seriously."

"What was that about the oil station earlier? I got the impression it's dangerous."

"What Benny hears there will further his notions about becoming a fighter pilot. He's only twelve, but sees this war so romantically, even though he knows Paul's in constant danger. The B-12 means as much to Benny as food does to most people.

"Lucky for me, Harry's only in Des Moines. At least he can write Benny a quick letter if I need him to, or we can drive down there if he gets out of control.

"The idea of the war lasting until he comes of age makes me sick. Those poor British mothers, having this all start back in '39, and having to endure the bombing, too."

Aunt Margaret sighed. "I'd do anything to end this war."

Just like Mom, but Twila kept the comparison to herself. The shuffling faded, so she turned to go upstairs. Aunt Margaret didn't budge.

"Aren't you going back to bed?"

"In a while—no use lying there for hours. My mind comes alive at night."

"No! No! Let me go..." Stan woke to his own scream and leaped out of bed. He gathered his senses—his side of the barracks housed only one other guard, a quiet fellow at the far end. No movement down there… that guy must be hard of hearing.

The nightmare returned in living color… coming upon a Japanese patrol of several soldiers so suddenly, there'd been no time for weapons. His crew tackled the enemy like football players, and made easy work of them.

But one gave him a gift he could do without—a lasting vision of terrified eyes rimmed with pain. That dying stare sent him into a sweat as he sank back on his bunk and stared at nothing.

His heart finally quieted, but there was no use trying to sleep again. He slipped past his barracks mate, a trained MP. Snores from guards in the other room filled the hall. There must be at least 75 now, and more would arrive next week, to keep up with the mounting number of prisoners.

His side of the barracks would fill up, and then what would he do? In the hallway, a sign had been posted since he went to bed:

REMEMBER!
SHARE NO NEWS OF THE WAR
With Prisoners

Across the way, a few single lights shone in the prisoners' compound. A couple of disgruntled guards had been discussing the captured Germans this evening.

"They get the same rations as we do."

"Are you sure?"

"That's how the Geneva Convention lays it out, and from what I hear, the new commander believes in it heart and soul."

"Who is he?"

"Name's Lobdell. That's about all I've heard."

The image of captured GIs stumbling up that Philippine mountain trail toward Camp O'Donnell rose before Stan. They were headed to the gates of Hell—no Geneva Convention there. Even as he considered plight, he reigned in his thoughts—if he didn't be careful, he'd become like Cap, fixated on a certain period in the past.

Lobdell. Where had he heard that name before? Then he remembered. There'd been a Lobdell in National Guard training with him back in Wisconsin, with a tank battalion. What if he were related to this new commander?

The cold windowpane framed Stan's hand, and voices stretched toward him across the miles between here and Bataan—the dying cries of American captives along the trail, the groans of those still alive. The longing to help them grated inside him.

For tonight, he must be satisfied with limbering up his recalcitrant knee. Tomorrow, he'd push himself harder—he'd never regretting leaving that cane behind, but once in a while, that left knee still threatened to go out from under him.

Tomorrow night, he'd walk even longer if he woke up...*when* he woke up. And some day, he'd enter an office, perhaps down at Fort Des Moines, to request a transfer.

"You came back wounded?" The officer's incredulity would show as he eyed Stan up and down.

"Yes, sir. Had a couple of surgeries and now I'm fully recovered. I'm ready to go, sir." He'd stand straight, eyes steady, and the officer would read his file, glance back up and say,

"You sure look fit, and you already know the jungle. We're desperate for men like you. Let's get you back over there pronto, Private."

Section by section, the prisoners' barracks filled and Twila's workload increased. Most of the staff appreciated Rommel's defeated troops bringing own doctors.

Edna passed the word at lunch, since Nurse Alcott had kept Twila busy in the American ward all morning. She changed bandages, took temperatures, administered prepared medications, and charted every move she made.

A few days later, Nurse Alcott updated the staff. "We house both hard-core Nazis and anti-Nazis now, and may have to protect the friendly ones from the Reich's devotees. Also, our commander will be replaced this month. Hopefully, the new colonel will be able to diffuse some of animosity."

Edna filled the pause. "I'm glad the German doctors are working with ours, and the translators really know what they're doing, but can you explain the *Lagersprecher*?"

"He's the camp speaker, the go-between, to vent prisoner complaints."

"Complaints? Wonder who speaks for our prisoners over in German camps?"

Nurse Alcott handled the comment without a hitch. "Our job is to comply with the Geneva Convention and hope for the best for our soldiers."

A week later, the army transported another hundred and seventy-five prisoners from Camp Carson, Colorado to Algona. This time, they arrived in daylight. That morning, Nurse Alcott held another briefing.

"These men are en route to Iowa City, where the local authorities have set up the fairgrounds to house them. They'll only be here a couple of days, but we'll handle medical needs one-by-one."

A new recruit to the nursing staff, Mona Glant, joined Edna, and Nurse Alcott handed a clipboard to Twila. "You'll accompany me to keep records, Miss Brunner."

After the other two left, she lowered her voice. "This way, we can process these arrivals and still take care of our regular patients.

"No matter what we see, keep your head about you. I don't expect trouble, since doctors have already screened these prisoners."

One patient was so thin, he looked like he might break. Nurse Alcott read his statistics.

"French transit camp—50,000 prisoners. Moved to—oh, I wish they'd take more care."

She showed Twila some smudged writing. "Write down Rennes, France—that's all we have."

She sized up the prisoner, young, pale, unsteady on his feet and with some peculiar dry scabs on his ears. After a few pokes and prods, she pursed her lips.

"Assign him to Ward Six—in no shape to travel."

Contagious. How could she recognize disease so quickly? Later, she whispered to a doctor. "Here's one for quarantine. I can smell it."

The doctor led the gaunt prisoner away, and Twila swallowed her curiosity—what did she mean by *it?*

So many sets of eyes, as verdant green as Mom's, ocean blue or hazel, others the rich shade of Iowa soil. Many men were downcast, but a few stared directly at Nurse Alcott, communicating a variety of emotions, from relief to pain, to coldness. The empty ones bothered her most.

After processing 30 men, Nurse Alcott led Twila to the dining hall.

"Nothing like hot tea on a day like this." She put her feet up and closed her eyes a few moments before devouring an egg sandwich a staff member brought—must have special arrangements with the cook.

Twila ate hers in three bites and took another. "I almost feel guilty eating, those poor fellows look so starved."

"I know." Nurse Alcott grinned. "But I don't feel guilty enough to forego an egg sandwich."

"Would you mind if I rub my feet?"

"That's a great idea. I may rub mine, too."

Pop... pop... pop. Nurse Alcott stretched her neck.

"If I had the energy, we'd go sit outdoors. Fresh air and sunshine always revive me."

"It's a gorgeous day. I can't believe May's almost over."

"To tell you the truth, Miss Brunner, today brings back the Great War for me. Especially the smells."

"You served then? Where?"

"In France. I was just out of training, 22 years old, and we worked in tents near the front. At least you could step away for fresh air. But years afterward, scenes still haunt me—men vomiting black fluid, pleading for help—but we had nothing to offer besides morphine."

"Black fluid?"

"The plague took as many lives as the fighting. Next worse were the amputations—or maybe mental disturbances. Some men with battle fatigue stared off into nowhere—that troubled me a lot.

"But I learned so much about wound care and sterilization during that time. The head nurse held us to high standards, and showed us how to keep wounds irrigated with antiseptic liquid.

"One of our battlefield surgeons instigated the technique. He saved many limbs, though the soldiers still had to suffer during long recuperations. At least that war hurried along medical progress."

She tucked some stray hairs behind her ear, took off her glasses, and rubbed her eyes.

"That one man you said you smelled—what's wrong with him?"

"Did you notice a mild beer scent?"

Twila shook her head.

"You know how you can tell when someone has the flu by the peculiar scent? Tuberculosis is like that, with a yeasty smell—that's what the prisoner has. His cough gave it away, too."

"You had tuberculosis patients during the war?"

"Unfortunately, yes. At the end, we all thought... Really, Miss Brunner, riding the ship home, we believed we'd finished with war forever. Surely the nations would never allow such horror to replay. But now here we are again."

She slid on her glasses. "Considering all the fronts where we face enemies, I'm certain the worst is yet to come. That sounds bleak, I know. To you, what we see here must seem awfully mild?"

"Comparatively, yes. Most of the time, I'm grateful to still be useful right here on our own soil. The transport ships back and forth across the Atlantic felled more than one good nurse."

"Do you know a nurse from Cresco with the troops in Europe now?"

"Ellen Church. She's got more courage in her little finger than—" Nurse Alcott glanced at her watch. "I stand in awe of her. Another few hours and we'll have conquered the list. Tea makes us new women—the British nurses imparted that wisdom to me."

As Twila silently rehearsed her stories, Mom came front and center. Maybe someday she'd share what she'd been through, too.

But sharing involved a risk. These Great War tales had already taken up residence in her heart.

Chapter Nineteen

The next week Nurse Alcott visited one of the branch camps. As Twila left the dining hall, someone from the kitchen staff hailed her. "Would you mind delivering this tray to the prisoners' ward?"

Twila agreed and waited outside the door until a guard spotted her. A doctor beckoned him, so he gave her directions.

"First bed on the right. Set it on his table." He crossed the room and she approached the first bed.

"*Ich brauche dich, Frau.*" The patient flailed his arm and groaned. Should she leave the tray on the floor?

His volume increased, and another patient hollered, "*Verschloss ihn.*" *Shut him up.* Twenty feet away, the guard spoke with the doctor, and farther on, an orderly helped a patient walk.

Twila took a hesitant step. The prisoner lurched from his bed and grabbed her around the waist, yelling at the top of his lungs. *Frau*, she knew, and "*Beeile dich!*" He *needed her*?

With little chance to fight, she kicked the bed frame. The patient's sour breath mixed with strong soap and another vile odor. Some disease?

Then another smell overrode everything else, or was it a taste? A scene from a Great War story Nurse Alcott had shared flashed before Twila as the prisoner's grip prevented her escape.

"True fear became real to me on a late winter day. I'd run out of platinum needles for tetanus injections, and ran to a supply tent that appeared empty. I had to have those needles, but as I reached for a box, a man yelled, "I am dying, sister. Come to me."

"Then a hand grabbed my ankle. Somehow, I shook him off and ran out, but I never entered a supply tent alone again. I'd skimped on the rules because we were so busy. That day taught me fear, and the reasons behind the rules. If you ever taste fear, don't think—flee."

"*Beeile dich, mein frau...*" In the prisoner's clutches, Twila's mouth went dry. Her next thought frightened her more—when Nurse Alcott found out about this...

"*Stoppen sie es jetzt*—stop it right now." A shadow fell over the bed and someone strong loosened the prisoner's hold and pulled him away. Twila fell into a wooden chair and stared as the German wilted in a guard's iron grip.

Two orderlies raced up, so the guard released the prisoner and muttered. "You know where to take him."

She drew a breath and looked into earnest blue eyes.

"Are you all right, Miss?"

A second breath. Another. "Yes. Thank you."

Those incredible eyes, the color of a summer sky on a clear day, held her. Then the guard blinked and took a step back.

"You never know what to expect, but you handled it well."

She wasn't certain Nurse Alcott would agree, but his assessment bolstered her. He leaned forward a little.

"You look a little pale." He gestured toward the door, but something rooted Twila to the chair. A swatch of blond hair fell across the guard's forehead. He shoved it back and took her elbow.

"Sometimes it takes a bit to get your land legs back."

He led her down the hall. "Where—do you know where they took that patient?" She hated the tremble in her voice. Compared to Nurse Alcott's experiences, this was nothing.

"To a quiet room down the hall. The doc'll evaluate him."

"They won't punish him?"

"I doubt it. Our new commander wants to re-educate these guys rather than punish them. He's going to designate a whole department with that in mind."

A distance down the hall, he let go of her elbow and pointed to a chair. "Why don't you sit here to catch your breath? Take your time."

A few minutes in the cool quietness calmed her. Everything had turned out all right, yet Nurse Alcott's comments kept running through her mind.

The reason for the rules...

A few minutes later when Edna heard this story, she bobbed her head in commiseration. "I'd say you've learned a lesson. I've had to learn mine, too." She patted Twila's arm. "That kitchen worker should never have asked you, in my opinion. But don't worry about it. Happened on a good day, I'd say."

Twila tried to imagine Nurse Alcott's reaction—would she issue a sharp reprimand or lend a sympathetic ear?

Chapter Twenty

Leaving the young nurse to catch her breath, Stan hurried back to his post. Something about her reminded him of—who was it? Though visibly shaken by the altercation with that prisoner, she had still maintained control—no crying out, no tears.

He had put on a good show outwardly, but under the tight collar of his uniform, his neck sweltered. It had been a long, long time since he'd performed a rescue. Another thing—the victim had never been a woman.

At Camp Beauregard, he'd seen a few females in uniform, maybe because the camp became the hub of the Louisiana Maneuvers and more office workers were needed. In afternoon quiet, his thoughts reverted to the two imaginary countries the command had formed there: KOTMK (Kansas, Nebraska, Texas, Missouri, and Kentucky) versus ALMOT (Arkansas, Louisiana, Mississippi, Alabama and Tennessee.

In the maneuvers, KOTMK and ALMOT supposedly fought over Mississippi River navigation rights. Together, these two entities represented 400,000 US troops learning the ins and outs of war. A mind-boggling operation, the largest training of its kind ever, arranged to test conventional defenses against armored vehicles.

"Hey Stan, I'll be back in a few minutes." The call of the other guard on duty brought him back to the ward. He couldn't help but grin, recalling how he'd trained with the likes of George Patton for European warfare.

European. But then the army sent him to the Philippines with a tank battalion, in terrain far too mountainous for a tank to maneuver. Brilliant.

A doctor down the way hailed him, so he forsook his mental meanderings and hurried away. But on and off throughout the afternoon, that young redheaded nurse came to mind—who had he seen with that many freckles peppering her nose?

Back at Aunt Margaret's, a letter from home waited. Along with hometown news, Mom included something about Addie Bledsoe:

Addie's mother-in-law has remarried. Esther Tomey told me Sunday after church that George Miller and Bea Bledsoe tied the knot a few weeks ago. But then, I'm always behind on the goings-on around here.

At first I didn't know who Esther meant, but it seems George started calling Berthea Bea, and the name stuck. In January, she also became the new school secretary. I saw her in the Mercantile last weekend, and she'd lost quite a lot of weight.

With Harold now deployed and Addie gone to help Kate Isaacs in England, she must've been lonely out on the farm. Esther says Bea has a new lease on life.

Goes to show how second chances can change a person. That's your local gossip for the week.

Quiet, shy Addie went to England? Who would ever have imagined that? But nowadays, people were doing all sorts of things no one would ever have imagined.

Setting the letter aside to peel potatoes for supper, Twila thought about Addie the whole time. Was it Char who first wrote about Harold finally finding a way into the armed forces?

Addie and Kate must've stayed close over the years.

That thought carried Twila across the Atlantic. So many Americans stationed there—at lunch today, several guards talked about an upcoming invasion of France.

"It'll be brutal, but it has to be done. It's the only way we'll ever shut those Germans down."

Maybe Harold was one of the thousands preparing to invade France. Even someone from little Halberton, Iowa could make an enormous difference in this war.

She set the potatoes to boil and took some leftover roast beef from the cooling shelf in the back porch. Plenty of juices in the bottom of the pan, perfect for making gravy. Thanks to Mom, she could make some without lumps. She put the meat in a frying pan to reheat just as the back door banged and Benny bounced in.

"Hey, Twila—didja hear 'bout Hitler and Goring? They were standin' up on a high observation tower in Berlin and Hitler said he wants to do something to make the Berliners happy. Goring says, 'Well, why don't you jump off this thing?'"

"Mmm... where'd you hear that?"

"Somebody at school, an older guy. Don'tcha think it's funny?"

"Yeah."

"Did you get to see some Germans out there at the camp yet?"

"As a matter of fact, I did. But don't say a word about it, okay?"

"To Mom? You gotta be kidding. Can't say nothin' that don't make her mad."

He grabbed a few cookies and went into the living room to turn on the radio, even though the war reports wouldn't be on yet. She might have asked if she could help him with his homework, but his question took her straight back to that prisoner today. Boy, had she *ever* seen a German, far too close for comfort.

The week flew by with more prisoners arriving. In addition, the camp made preparations for a change of command. Rumors spread about the new commander; Twila forgot his name, something with an *L*.

She put the incident with the prisoner out of her mind, except when Nurse Alcott summoned her for one reason or another. Each time, she expected a dressing-down, and spent a few extra minutes reviewing the rules posted on the office door.

One day on her way to the cloakroom, she was perusing them again when the head nurse approached. She paused and glanced at the list.

"Reading the rules again, Miss Brunner?"

"Yes, ma'am."

"Word has it you've acted admirably."

"Admirably?"

"Come on in and I'll show you the report. Such quick thinking, and you never said a word about this."

"About...?"

She held out a yellow paper, and reading the first lines brought a chill.

"Oh, that. It happened when you were visiting the branch camp. At lunch, a civilian worker asked me if I'd mind delivering some food—"

Sharp eyes scrutinized her. "I assumed something like that must've occurred. So you agreed?"

"Yes."

"But it seems other people became involved, and one of them took note of your behavior."

"The prisoner?"

"No, a guard. He wrote you a commendation. Look down at the bottom."

The prisoner directed a calculated attack at Miss Brunner, but she handled the situation professionally and without undue emotion. She even showed concern that he might be punished for his inappropriate behavior.

Heat steamed Twila's face. "I—it really was nothing. It did shake me up a little, though."

"Would you be willing to work in the prisoner ward?"

"Why, of course."

"You wouldn't be frightened?"

"I don't think so, but I would be more careful, that's for sure."

"Do you know this guard?"

"I'd never seen him before, but would recognize him if I saw him now. He's the one who deserves a commendation. If he hadn't been there, I'm not sure what I would have done. Now I know what you mean by the taste of fear, and the reasons behind the rules."

For a long moment, Nurse Alcott studied her. "All right, then. I'm going to take you at your word and we'll leave it at that." She slipped the report into a manila file folder. "Miss Brunner, I believe you're perfect for this job."

"There's no work I'd rather be doing, ma'am."

That afternoon, she assisted Edna with a festering wound. When they finished, Edna patted her shoulder. "Thanks for the help. I don't know if it's all the reading you're doing or just a natural knack, but you usually know what I need before I ask."

That reminded Twila of her goal to read at least a chapter a night in the textbooks Nurse Alcott had lent her. And she ought to write Charlotte again, even though she hadn't answered her last letter. Strange.

Mashing the potatoes with a little cream and butter, she determined to write that letter tonight. But another engagement would come first, because Benny burst in from the living room with his geography book.

"Hey, Twi—our teacher gave us a nasty assignment. It's our last one, and counts for... I dunno, a lot of points. I sure do need help with this one."

Chapter Twenty-one

Late May brought flowers, and Aunt Margaret said they'd plant the rest of the garden on the weekend. Then a cold north wind played tricks on everyone, and her daffodils froze in place one night.

The next morning, Twila squatted beside the delicate, cheery flowers. Such a small occurrence in the midst of the war, and yet the way the fragile petals dissolved at her touch made her sad.

Later in the day, a guard loitered outside the gate when she passed through after work. She'd just reached up to tighten her headscarf before starting home. She nodded his way, and he fell in step with her.

"Miss Brunner, would you mind if I walked with you?"

Those blue eyes—she'd know them anywhere. A couple of times, her rescuer from the German patient had saluted her in the dining hall, but initiated no conversation. She'd wondered if they would ever talk again, and now, here he was.

"No. I mean, yes—It's all right."

"Private Stanley Ford at your service. Stan, if you don't mind."

"And I'm Twila. Thanks for taking care of me that day with the prisoner. I think I was too shaken up to say that at the time."

"Glad I could help." His smile highlighted a dimple in his left cheek.

"Do you go into town often?"

"Only when I get off duty a little early and there's a pretty girl I want to walk home." He matched his gait to hers and bent his head against the wind.

At the first crossing, an official black vehicle with a big white star painted on its side whooshed past.

"Always seems a little odd to be out in the ordinary world after a long stretch of duty. Do you feel that way, too?"

"The ordinary world? Does that even exist anymore?"

"Umm... I know what you mean. Back in Wisconsin, our nearest town has an S&L store like the one here. I'd feel at home in there if I had on my regular clothes."

"What would they be?"

"Jeans and my dirty old cloth cap with a pleat in the back. I gave my Mom strict orders not to mess with it—requires a certain amount of sweat and dirt to maintain its shape." He kept a straight face though his eyes twinkled.

"Will she obey?"

"I doubt it, but at least I tried."

They stopped for traffic on the main road and continued across a busy intersection toward Algona's south side. He seemed comfortable with silence, which stirred her curiosity.

"What's Wisconsin like?"

"Hillier than here, with pine stands everywhere up north. My family's been in lumber for three generations."

"Really? My brother runs the little town lumberyard my Grandpa started years ago."

"Where?"

"Halberton, Iowa, north of Waterloo and south of Austin, Minnesota."

"Wouldn't be surprised if some of our lumber ended up in his yard—before the war, that is. Now, I imagine he's sending every extra scrap to the shipyards, just like us. And your father?"

"He's training paratroopers in California right now."

"That would be interesting. Must've had some experience in the last war?"

Twila nodded.

"Wish I could've gone a little farther from home, but..."

Aware that many camp guards were unable to serve in the fighting force for one reason or another, Twila stifled her next question. Like Rodney, Stan must have had some physical setback, but they both looked healthy on the outside.

When they turned, the wind blew right in faces, but after some time, Stan answered her unspoken question.

"I spent the first years of the war in the Pacific, but got sent back to recuperate."

"You were wounded?"

"Yeah."

He said no more, so they crossed Main Street, where Mr. Plum waved from the doorway of the Diagonal Grocery. He often was out changing signs this time of day, and took time to greet her.

"Hello there, Miss. How's your aunt doing?"

"Fine, thank you." She waved back and turned her attention to Stan. "My cousin's somewhere out there in the Pacific with the Navy. We haven't heard anything from him for such a long time. Where did you serve?"

"The Philippines."

"Really? That's where Paul might be—if he made it to land when the Japs attacked his ship."

"It's possible. Lots of small islands there, and you never know where somebody might have swum ashore. I expect some families won't get word until the whole thing's over."

"The news said lots of men were captured. He could be one of them."

"Yeah."

"Wouldn't Aunt Margaret have heard if that were true?"

"Not necessarily."

Stan fell into silence, and more questions piqued her mind. Why hadn't he been captured? Had he been wounded and sent home before the surrender? But asking him didn't seem right, so she turned the conversation back to Camp Algona.

"What is it like being a guard?"

His voice came from far away. "I don't mind it, but being far away was easier, in a way. When you're so far from everything familiar, everybody knows *home* is an impossible dream."

"Were you ever on Tinian Island?"

"No, about 1,500 hundred miles east. Everything looks close on a map, but thousands of miles might separate one place from another. Even getting to a hospital ship took… actually I don't know how long."

"How were you…"

"Wounded?"

"Yes. I mean, it's none of my business, but…"

Stan slapped his leg and grinned. "That tells me the docs did a good job. You haven't noticed me limping?"

"No, not at all."

"This makes my day! The old wound doesn't affect me much any more."

"I'd never have guessed you'd been hurt. You look the picture of health."

His grin spread ear to ear, and that strong dimple winked at her. Sunlight struck his face when they turned a corner. "If you want to see my scars, I promise I'll think about it."

"That's all right. I see plenty of them already."

They walked in silence for a while longer, and at the next corner, she stalled.

"Thanks for the escort home. I live down this street with my aunt. My nephew Benny will be the only one home right now, and he's so fanatical about the war, he'll have a conniption fit if he sees a soldier close up."

A door slammed somewhere, and she restated her comment. "Actually, my aunt would be the one to have the fit. She tries to keep him clear of anything to do with the camp. She doesn't want to stir him up about the war any more than he already is."

"Where is she right now?"

"Still at the camp—she works in the prisoners' canteen."

"Tall, with sort of reddish hair?"

"That's her."

"I know who she is. Now I see the family resemblance, although I like your freckles better than hers."

Just banter, but his cheerfulness was catching. He glanced back toward camp.

"Well, then, it's time for me to employ my disappearing-into-the-jungle skills." He doffed his cap and flicked back the unruly shock of hair that dusted his sandy eyebrows.

"I'm still not used to having this much hair after having it butchered for so long. May have to get it chopped off again."

He made a slight bow. "Thanks for allowing me this pleasure, Miss Brunner. Until we meet again."

No limp at all as he turned and walked away—she checked that out before continuing home.

For weeks, people had been whispering about the Allies invading occupied France. Now everyone focused on the constant clouds and rain over there. Would General Eisenhower have to call off the invasion?

June first came and went, and newscasters still jubilated over the fall of Germany in the Crimea. They also set the stage for the fall of Rome, but had nothing to offer about the European front. The word around Camp Algona was that everything depended on the obstinate weather over the English Channel.

But mid-morning of June 6th, Twila dropped by the main office to deliver some reports and found the staff gathered around a radio in one corner. They hardly lifted heads at her knock, and when she entered, the woman who usually received the medical reports held out her hand without budging from her chair.

"We're tuned in to General Patton's speech to the troops—the invasion is on!" She volunteered this from the corner of her mouth in a conspiratorial whisper. "Stay a minute and listen if you want to."

All for the Cause

Even knowing Nurse Alcott had more work outlined for her, the sharp male voice coming over the wires drew Twila in. The man's bravado came through in his every word.

> *Men, all this stuff you hear about America not wanting to fight, wanting to stay out of the war, is a lot of bullshit. Americans love to fight. All real Americans love the sting and clash of battle. When you were kids, you all admired the champion marble shooter, the fastest runner, the big-league ball players and the toughest boxers. Americans love a winner and will not tolerate a loser. Americans play to win all the time. That's why Americans have never lost and will never lose a war. The very thought of losing is hateful to Americans. Battle is the most significant competition in which a man can indulge. It brings out all that is best and it removes all that is base...*

The stenographer glanced up and mouthed, "Did you need something else?"

Twila shook her head and backed away, but gradually. The General surely knew how to captivate an audience.

> *... the real hero is the man who fights even though he's scared. Some men will get over fright in a minute under fire, some take an hour, and for some it takes days. But the real man*

never lets his fear of death overpower his honor, his sense of duty to his country, and his innate manhood.

On her way back to the ward, the speech stuck with her. Clearly, General Patton had written it to put steel into his men who were about to risk lives for the cause.

At the same time, she hoped Benny escaped hearing it, or he'd be swooning over the swashbuckling leader for the next year. This was just the kind of thing Aunt Margaret tried to keep from him.

Innate manhood—if anybody was a man, it was Dad. When he fought in the Great War, surely he had known fear. How did he overcome it, especially when he was wounded? He never talked about that time, but maybe he would if she asked him.

She bet he'd admit to being afraid, but would the prisoners here? What about the SS officers, with utter devotion to leader? If they experienced no fear in battle, surely they might have when they'd been wounded or taken prisoner.

Or, as someone recently said in the dining room, were they so sated with propaganda—brainwashed, the guards called it—that normal human emotions failed them? Except anger, maybe. Didn't the *Fuhrer* rely on stirring up anger to recruit supporters?

That night, Benny fidgeted so much at the table that Aunt Margaret threatened to staple him to his chair to get through supper. In spite of her harsh admonition, he kept breaking out in chatter about the Channel crossing to the Normandy beaches. He simply couldn't keep his excitement inside.

"Didja hear 'bout the landing craft? They made..."

Aunt Margaret cut him off. "Benny, stop. We all realize the invasion's begun. I know it's impressive, but you don't have to repeat everything you hear word for word, all right?"

Diana elbowed him in the ribs. "For once, why don't you listen to mom? You're driving all of us crazy."

But nothing could calm him this evening. Even faster than

usual, he dashed through drying the dishes and raced to the radio. Diana shrugged off the reports and went to her friend Betty's house, while Aunt Margaret joined Twila and Benny around the radio.

Even she seemed mesmerized by the broadcaster's depiction of soldiers stuffed like sardines into landing craft designed especially for this mission. The wind and waves tossed them to and fro, seagulls accompanied the landing craft, and many soldiers were beset by nausea.

The newscaster outdid himself in bringing the scene to life—hoards of Allied planes in the skies, enemy guns strafing the beaches, and salt spray billowing all around.

Aunt Margaret's knitting needles couldn't have clicked faster as the three of them entered into the tension of approaching the French beachheads under enemy fire. Twila picked up her needles, too, to keep her hands busy.

Of course, Benny sat entranced, his eyes bulging with excitement. Afterward, he was effusive. His "Didja hear'?" resounded through the living room time and again. Twila only had to nod her head now and then. How could he ever get to sleep tonight?

Aunt Margaret commented only once. "This sounds inhuman—horrendous. I thought being in the Pacific was the worst, but now I'm glad Paul's there instead."

"Oh, man! I'd wanna be in on this, wouldn't you, Twila? Now we get to show them Germans what for." Benny punched the air with his fist. "Now we're on French soil, and they'll realize what we're made of!"

Aunt Margaret sighed and rubbed between her eyes. What could anyone say? Then an idea occurred to Twila.

"Come down in the basement with me for a minute, Benny."

"What for?"

"I need help finding something." On the way down, she added, "We need a big square to write on." After scrounging in several corners, he pulled out an old bulletin board.

"This is just the ticket."

He looked baffled as she shook the dust off in the back porch and told him to bring some pens and pencils, even crayons or chalk—whatever he could find. By the time he did, she'd spiffed up the bulletin board and set it on the table.

"Okay, now bring the F volume of the encyclopedia here—oh, and some straight pins."

Half an hour later, with Aunt Margaret's needles vying with the clock, that old board bore a sketch of France's north coast. Sitting back, Twila admired work.

"We did pretty well, don't you think? This is as complete as we can make it for now. Now, you write the names of the beaches where our guys have landed. Tomorrow, you can add more."

Face flushed and eyes alight, Benny would have continued all night. But Aunt Margaret shooed him up to bed.

"Aw, Mom—do I gotta go at ten? Even on this big day? For the love of Mike..."

Aunt Margaret's sigh sailed the room. "Do I *have* to go at ten... and who is Mike, anyway? There'll be more news tomorrow. Didn't the announcer say we have a fierce fight on our hands, with those blasted French hedgerows blocking our troops and providing cover for the enemy?

"Ah, heck. Why didn't General Eisenhower set the invasion for a Friday instead of a Tuesday?"

Twila helped out. "You know the answer—the weather in the English Channel. Tomorrow, the newspaper at the library may have a more detailed map you can copy after school. Then we'll transfer the details to ours. Make sure you jot down all the names of the towns."

After he went upstairs, Margaret turned to her. "What'll I ever do with him? And Diana's supposed to be home by now. I'll have to wait up for her—might as well get my nightgown on. Before you have children, think long and hard." She started up the stairs.

"I'm in no hurry at all." Her response produced a wry grin, so she added, "If you want me to, I'll wait up for Diana."

All for the Cause

"No thanks. She's my cross to bear."

From a special bulletin reported by John Snagge of the BBC at midday today, June 6, 1944.

'D' Day has come. Early this morning the Allies began the assault on the northwestern face of what Hitler calls his European Fortress. The first official news came just after half-past nine when Supreme Headquarters of the Allied Expeditionary Force—usually called SHAEF from its initials—issued Communique number one.

I share it with you in its entirety: 'Under the command of General Eisenhower, Allied Naval Forces supported by strong Air Forces, began landing this morning on the Northern coast of France.'

It was announced a little later that General Montgomery is in command of the Army group carrying out the assault. The Army group includes British, Canadian and United States Forces.

General Eisenhower has issued an order of the day addressed to each individual of the Allied Expeditionary Force.

'Your task will not be an easy one. Your enemy is well trained, well equipped and battle-hardened. He will

fight savagely. But this is the year 1944. The tide has turned. The free men of the world are marching together to victory.

I have full confidence in your courage, devotion to duty, and skill in battle. We will accept nothing less than full victory. Good luck, and let us all beseech the blessing of Almighty God upon this great and noble undertaking.'

This order was distributed to assault elements after embarkation. Appropriate commanders throughout the Allied Expeditionary Force read it to troops.

And so we also commend these words to you. We here in America join General Eisenhower and our boys in heartfelt prayer for victory in Europe.

The officer laid aside the paper he'd just read and addressed the guards gathered in the dining hall. "Gentlemen, we wanted to update you concerning our troops in harm's way.

"I am sure we all agree with these sentiments and lend our support to our expeditionary forces. At the same time, we must emphasize the need for utmost secrecy about this invasion here in the camp. As you know, our prisoners have no access to news from the outside, and this must continue.

"Thank you for the work you are doing here. We can expect more prisoners to be arriving, and will continue to add to and support our staff."

"*Work we're doing*, my foot!" Leaving the meeting, Stan couldn't help muttering. The command meant well, but to someone who knew what it meant to face a ruthless enemy, his words rang hollow.

All for the Cause

What those GI's faced in Normandy went far beyond work.

At least the Allies were making progress—that was good news. But Stan's next thought brought consternation. What had he heard lately about the situation in the Philippines? Close to nothing.

With such a strong focus on securing Europe, how could General MacArthur ever amass enough resources to save his men in captivity? He said he would return; made a solemn promise. But at this rate, would any Americans still be alive when he finally did?

The prisoner roll increased even more, and Stan told Twila he'd been assigned to orient the latest group of new guards. Just before the new commander arrived on the twelfth, the whole camp was in a flurry. One day, Nurse Alcott passed around copies of the Geneva Convention and beamed as she described the new commander's wishes.

"Colonel Lobdell is requiring all staff to read this in full, for a better vision of our goals. I'll give you two days. Report to me when you've finished."

At lunch, a guard said that office workers had spent half the previous night mimeographing the copies. "Things are gonna be different around here. I don't think much gets past this new Colonel. Either we shape up or ship out, as they say."

Back at home, the garden never ceased to need weeding, so Twila plunged in during the evenings, with Diana fuming along behind her. Benny pulled too, with constant chatter about the day's news.

Aunt Margaret weeded like a madwoman, but also supervised.

"If you'd pull weeds as fast as you talk, Benny, we'd be done in ten minutes." Quite the mismatched team, they razed the latest crop of smart weeds, plantain, and chickweed in record time.

"Green beans are almost as disgusting as peas. They're the worst vegetables ever!"

Aunt Margaret shushed Diana. "Hey, remember who created them."

If only she could ignore her instead of egging her on. At first, Twila thought summer vacation would quiet things down, but she already wished school would start soon, and it was only late June.

Snap, snap, snap. Four sets of fingers waged war on a pile of beans. A robin chortled from the maple tree, and a cardinal retorted from the neighbor's old burr oak that towered above every other specimen in the block.

Dad's voice sounded in her head. "See the little fringe of bristles around the cup of this acorn? They're burrs—that's why they call this tree a burr oak."

They spent so much time outdoors together, and he often explained natural wonders. At times like this, he might have been right here beside her. She cherished the sensation until Aunt Margaret broke the spell.

"We'll soon have this batch boiling in the canner. Thank goodness for pressure canners—the water bath method took even longer, and definitely gave us a bath."

Someone whistled from down the street, a fresh sound on this sweltering afternoon. Soon, the rhythm became clear—*bum bum bum, b-bum bum bum, b-bum bum bum bum bum ... pause... bum b-bum bum bum bum.* Twila couldn't quite make out the tune, since the whistler employed more gusto than musical sense.

Yesterday as she left the building after work, she'd bumped into Stan and invited him over, but he gave a non-committal reply. Maybe she asked him too many questions about the war.

Diana, Aunt Margaret, and Benny sat in a semi-circle facing her, with backs to the alley. The whistling grew closer, and when someone emerged from the line of lilacs along the back fence, Twila waved a handful of string beans.

Stan had come, after all. He spotted her and ambled over.

"Just like our prisoners. Never any rest for the wicked."

Aunt Margaret bristled. "I know it's the Sabbath, but we worked at the fundraiser all day yesterday, so this is the only chance we have to—"

"What a great carnival you folks put on—you sure know how to do fundraisers around here." Stan leaned on the clothesline pole. His jovial smile tempered the defensive cut of her reaction.

"Oh, were you there? I didn't see you."

"Nope—I volunteered to work so the younger guards could spend hard-earned money. They brought back rave reviews."

He pulled up a chair next to Benny, grabbed some beans and started snapping off ends. "How've you been, buddy? Haven't seen you in a coon's age."

"Didja hear our boys are liberatin' Cherbourg? Almost a thousand soldiers have landed, not countin' more'n 20,000 airborne troops and 1,500 tanks. Besides that, Lightning Joe Collins has got 4,000 fighter planes and 4,500 bombers in the skies. Altogether, there's over 12,000 vehicles in France right now—ain't it somethin'?"

"Wow. Quite the offensive, I'd say. Where do you get all of your figures?"

"The paper said four British parachute divisions have landed between Cherbourg and Le Havre. That's four times the amount the Nazis landed on Crete."

He took a quick breath, so Stan had a chance to jump in. "And Hitler has taken command of his forces in France—what do you think that means?"

"Must be runnin' scared?"

"Exactly. But he's got four field marshals under him who don't like to lose, so it's still going to be quite a fight. And then there's the weather—a bad storm blew into the Channel on June 19th and wrecked a lot of our supplies on the mulberry docks our engineers made. Did you hear that?"

"No, but we'll still win. General Bradley'll find a way." Benny studied Stan. "You believe we will, don't you?"

"Yes. Absolutely."

"Why d'ya think so?"

"Because we have to."

Missing something in Stan's reply, Benny flashed ahead. "And we're gonna win in Saipan, too. Those da—"

He winced at his mother's severe look. "Them Japs might as well surrender, 'cause they don't got no hope with our boys after them. My brother's in the Navy, y' know, and—"

"Don't *have* any hope." Margaret's interruption momentarily silenced him, so Stan seized his opportunity.

"Been listening to the radio again, eh? Just keep this in mind: the word *surrender* doesn't translate into the Japanese language. They'll only give up when emperor orders them to, and I doubt that'll happen real soon."

"Didja ever see any Japs? Ever shoot any?"

On the edge of his seat, Benny waited. But Stan paled. He leaned back and stared down the alley, and the life seemed to drain out of him, Aunt Margaret sucked in her breath.

Stillness mushroomed, except for the steady *snap-snap-snap*. Margaret and Diana scowled at Benny, whose forehead developed more furrows than a field of corn.

But Twila feasted her eyes on the thickness of Stan's biceps under his shirt. Something was bothering him now, but he certainly had a way with people. Even when Aunt Margaret interpreted his greeting in the worst possible way, as if he were chiding them for working on Sunday, he knew exactly how to appease her.

Finally, he blinked and turned his attention back to Benny. "I have seen some. Way too close-up, and they made quite an impression on me. They may be smaller than most of us, but they're mighty devoted to cause. We'll have to keep at them until the bitter end."

A house wren skittered along the pump handle to her nest in the wooden house hanging from a young maple. From there, the little chanter put her all into her song.

In the shade along the slatted side fence, sparrows searched for seeds in the grass. Under Margaret's reproachful gaze, Benny snapped beans like crazy. Diana even stopped cracking her gum—blessed relief. The heat turned oppressive, and moments dragged like hours.

When Twila tried to catch Stan's eye, he seemed intrigued by the handful of beans he held. His shoulders slumped, and his eyes were veiled.

Chapter Twenty-two

Thinking back over the afternoon, Twila had to give Aunt Margaret credit. Just when the tension was about to make everyone burst, she made a suggestion.

"Sure is hot out here. Why don't you and Stan go inside and make some lemonade, Twila? I could use some right now, and the committee sent some lemons home with me last night." She raised her eyebrows meaningfully.

"Yes, a lemonade would sure hit the spot for me right now. How about you, Benny?"

Before he could answer, Twila set down the bowl in her lap and lurched out of her chair. Without a word, Stan followed her, and in the kitchen, she touched his cold hand.

"Sorry about Benny. He has no idea—"

"Of course not. It amazes me how even one simple word can bring everything back—always catches me off-guard."

"You handled it well. Benny thinks you walk on water, you know."

"Yeah. He sees our troops as invincible. I used to believe that, too. Well, come to think of it, I practically did walk on water once." His wink shot relief through her, and he leaned against the cupboard.

"The ship I was on took some fire, and my aim for the lifeboat left something to be desired. That salt water mixed with oil was nothing like the taffy we used to pull back home every October."

Aware of a thick line of perspiration riding his temples, Twila squeezed his hand. In spite of the heat, his skin felt like ice.

The clock's regular *tick-tock* backed the rhythm Stan made

tapping his toe on the floor. He pulled on his upper lip with his teeth, and twice, started to say something.

Action seemed the best course, so she pulled the lemon squeezer from the cupboard. "Do you have any experience squeezing lemons?"

He ran his fingers over the glass, but stayed quiet as she found a pitcher and dipped a cup into the sugar bin. *Carry on as if everything is normal...* interesting that Nurse Alcott had given that instruction just the other day.

"Yesterday, Mr. Plum slipped us an extra sack of sugar. Sure glad he's a family friend. I suppose he ordered extra in for the carnival."

By the time she filled a pitcher with water, Stan's re-established dimple informed her he'd fully returned from wherever the war had taken him. So did his next quip.

"Making lemonade out of lemons—that's what we do best." He grabbed a knife and sliced one in two. His chuckle sounded almost normal.

"What a lucky guy I am, getting to spend an afternoon away from camp. If I hadn't taken that hit to the knee, who knows where I'd be right now?"

His sapphire eyes declared his earnestness, and by the time he carried the tray to the back yard, the ridges gutting his forehead had disappeared. He set everyone at ease by kidding around with Benny and giving him some Filipino cities to look up at the library. Then he suggested they toss a football, and Benny's face shone like the sun.

Later, when Twila walked Stan partway home, he thanked her.

"I know I left you for a while there, but you didn't panic. I sure do appreciate that."

Squeezing his hand again seemed the only thing to do. On the walk back to Aunt Margaret's, she pondered the way a situation that seemed disastrous could turn out just fine. After all, hadn't she met Stan when a prisoner attacked her?

The Fourth of July dawned hot and muggy. With the morning off, Stan cleaned his small corner of the world and caught up on his letter writing.

What to say to his mother? Always a dilemma, but he decided to describe the barracks and a couple of the guys he'd gotten to know. Then he asked if she'd heard from Ron... sure had been a while since he had.

Various guards had been in and out all morning. Now several of them were discussing the fight for Cherbourg, a vital port in Northwest France.

"Don't you wonder sometimes? All those docks our engineers set up and so much ammunition destroyed, not to mention the supplies. If God's really on our side, why would He allow that storm to sweep in at just the wrong time?"

The guard aimed his question at no one in particular, and lying on his bunk feigning sleep, Stan didn't recognize who answered.

"It's a tough question. Bradley had planned to push south, but from what I've read, the devastation forced him to ration ammunition and take Cherbourg first. No doubt about it, we have to have a port, since all the artificial ones are gone. Must be awful for the engineers who set them up."

A third man offered his opinion. "I read that the losses put them down to three days' supply of ammo. Not much to go on. It's easy to second-guess, but..."

Easy to second-guess... Really? Stan might beg to differ. Second-guessing—wasn't that the greedy thief that kept robbing him of sleep?

Every night, some new question flaunted itself when he closed his eyes: *Why didn't you hear that Japanese patrol coming? How could they have caught you so off-guard. Were you daydreaming?*

Bree.. .bree.. .bree.. A sudden emergency siren blasted through the barracks and propelled him from his bunk.

"All hands on deck for an emergency. Guards, report to the duty officer immediately."

All for the Cause

After another miserable night, he'd been dozing after lunch, half-hearing the other guards discuss the European front. Now, everyone hurried to relace boots. Good thing he'd left his on.

He dashed down the hall toward the prisoners' compound, where the shrill *bree... bree... bree* continued. Along the way the most talkative of his barracks mates caught up with him.

"Think some of those SS guys decided to rebel, since it's the Fourth of July?"

Why even try to answer his pant? They'd find out soon enough.

"I was goin' to the..."

From the admin building, officers descended on the compound and started barking orders. One of them nodded to Stan and the others who skidded up behind him.

"You three come with me to secure the east perimeter."

They all fell in behind him, but curiosity overwhelmed one. "What's happened?"

"Without turning, the officer spat out, "There's been an escape. Make sure you have your weapons ready." They ran for the fence, where he turned to Stan. "Take somebody and go that way."

He gestured to the other two guards. "Come with me. Check for security all the way around. If you find a breach, commence a search."

Like clockwork, Stan's jungle instincts kicked in. Thankfully, the officer took the mouthy guy with him, and his partner knew how to keep his trap shut.

The fence line ran parallel to the north-south road where there were bound to be culverts. Made sense that a Nip... oops... a German might be skulking in one of them.

"Sure you don't want to come along to the town picnic? It's the best we could do this year, with no fireworks allowed."

"Stan said he'd pick me up a little later for the prisoners' band concert. I've heard they're pretty good."

"I hear them practicing sometimes. Maybe by next summer, they'll be playing in the band shell at the park. If they're still here, that is. According to Benny, we'll dispose of our enemies long before then."

She loaded Diana and Benny with potato salad, chicken, and pies for the picnic, and shooed them ahead of her.

Last night, Benny had one of his wild ideas. He declared this national holiday a perfect opportunity for Nazi parachutists to wipe out Algona and free all the prisoners.

"And then what? Every farmer in Kossuth County would get his shotgun, and every sheriff for miles around."

The loathing in Diane's voice startled Twila. Sure, the idea seemed far-fetched, but strange things did keep happening. At lunch the other day someone mentioned Allied pilots spotting "foo fighters"—flying objects they couldn't identify.

"Benny, would you please stop saying ridiculous things like that?" Aunt Margaret seemed at the breaking point lately.

Diana pounced again. "The Germans are busy fighting over in Europe. Do you really think they give a hoot about us?"

Benny slammed his fist into his other hand and went to bed an hour early. Diana fumed about his stupidity again, and when she went upstairs, Aunt Margaret held her forehead.

"Honestly, I didn't used to be this grouchy, but they're pushing me too far. Harry would be able to talk him out of these ideas."

"Do you have any idea how long he'll be in Des Moines?"

"No. He's making good money, but sometimes it seems like Benny's really falling apart."

Glad to have the house to herself, Twila wandered the rooms after everyone left. Heavy burgundy draperies covered the parlor's leaded windows, and Harry inherited a set of velvet furniture from his parents, so every corner was filled.

But the couches didn't compare with the comfort Mom's old furniture offered—oh, for an evening in Dad's big overstuffed chair.

Margaret and Harry's wedding photograph was centered on

the mantel. Young and vibrant, they might have just stepped off a dance floor. Harry had recently returned from the Great War, Margaret said, and she'd gotten a permanent wave. A friend loaned her a dress for wedding at Trinity Lutheran.

When Margaret met Harry, he'd worked as a carpenter and she'd found her first job with the Red Ball Transportation Company. After they married, an Algona businessman offered Harry a partnership in his contracting company, so they moved.

No wedding photograph graced the mantel back home. Mom told her once that she and Dad said vows before a Justice of the Peace somewhere over by the Mississippi River.

The front door opened and Aunt Margaret took a step in, noticed her, and gasped. "Oh, I thought you'd be gone by now."

"Stan's a little late. Did you forget something?"

"Gotta keep Benny and his friends busy so they don't sneak off to stare at the prisoners. Wish the camp was farther from town, but we need the depot too often."

Returning with a baseball bat and ball, she paused. "If I'd sent Benny back, he would've loitered."

"You know him so well. You and Harry have done a good job."

"Sometimes I wonder." She paused with her hand on the doorknob. "The years have helped me understand what Mother went through."

"Really?"

"Her mother never was the same after Mother's brother died in the Great War. And Dad—he gambled away everything he ever earned."

"Mom never mentioned that."

"She might not have realized what was going on—she was that much younger. Marvin wised me up when I was begging for a new school dress. He took me aside and said I'd better be happy with what I had.

"One night, he and Kenneth followed Dad to a bar out in the country where men bet on the Chicago horse and dog races. A guy from the city followed a route through all these rural areas and collected the money.

"Makes me sick to think of Dad forking over whatever he'd made shoveling coal for the railroad or whatever other job he could pick up. I suppose mother never knew if he'd come back from the bar rich or broke—or not at all."

Normally, Margaret would have yelled at anyone who held the door open on such a hot day. But she didn't seem to notice the heat radiating in.

"And then Myra took off with those dancers and scared the wits out of us. One day, she just vanished. I know they made her lots of empty promises, but—"

"What happened then?"

"We searched everywhere, but she was long gone. After a few weeks, they dumped her in some Podunk Southern Missouri town when she caught pneumonia. The local sheriff wired word about her, and Kenneth drove mother to pick her up from some kind folks who took her in."

"Who did you say Kenneth is?"

"You don't... Oh. Sorry. He was our older brother."

Was...?

"Mother had never been out of the county before that trip, and I don't think she ever crossed the county line again. I couldn't believe it when she got in Kenneth's car and they drove off."

"So she must have really cared?"

"For Myra? Yes—as much as she could care for anybody." Aunt Margaret's expression darkened and she pressed the baseball bat into her toes.

"Kenneth was maybe two years older than Marvin with a family of his own. His wife and two little boys lived a few miles from us, and he worked for the gas company. He raised Herefords, and I think he helped out landlord on his farm, too.

"Years later, Marvin told me that Kenneth helped with the mortgage payments on our farm—you know that's where Marvin lives now, right?"

In spite of the heat, she seemed in no hurry to leave, but Twila fought a strong desire to flee. The way it was going, this story could only get worse.

Chapter Twenty-three

"I wonder why Mom never mentioned she had a brother named Kenneth."

"Not surprising—those were horrible days. He had just bought his first car when they went off to get Myra."

"She came home all right?"

"Things got even more complicated. On the way back, they'd almost driven through Ottumwa when Kenneth…" Margaret leaned against the doorjamb and squeezed her eyes shut.

"He was changing a tire when a vehicle whizzed by—an egg truck, of all things. Your mom saw the whole thing, of course, but I never heard her breathe a word about it."

Her sigh swept the room. "The truck swerved and the impact killed Kenneth outright. When the sheriff told us, we didn't know what to do. They were hours away, Myra was so sick, and Mother couldn't drive.

"Marvin was always a nervous wreck anyhow, but he almost lost his mind that day. He had to go with the Sheriff to tell Kenneth's wife. Later, I found him out…" Her voice cracked. "It was a miserably humid day, and he'd gone out to the barn. He was pounding his fist bloody on a stall divider."

Margaret's sharp intake of breath matched the sinking sensation in Twila's stomach. What an impossible mess—Mom must have felt so guilty. A sense of hopeless sadness hung here in the living room as if the accident happened this morning.

"Of course, Myra blamed herself. The truth is, we all did. Nobody ever said that out loud, though." She angled her head in thought. "Well, Marvin might have.

"After the funeral, Mother commanded us never to mention Kenneth or the accident again. We stood there sobbing when she faced us. 'Get this out of your systems right now, do you hear?'

"Glorietta left home soon after that and we never heard from her again. She'd been taking care of the younger ones for years, and I suppose she just…"

"Glorietta?"

"Mmm… your mom must not've mentioned her, either. She's the second-born, between Kenneth and Marvin."

"Oh." The heat seemed more oppressive by the second. "Have you ever tried to find her?"

"Better to leave some things alone. I do think of her sometimes, and hope she found happiness."

"What about Kenneth's wife?"

"She remarried and had more children. But the anger seethed in the rest of us, except the two littlest ones."

"Littlest?"

"Oh my. You don't know about them, either. There were seven of us altogether."

"A stranger brought Grandma and Mom home?"

"No. That's where your dad came in. Maybe Marvin told him. He hitched a ride and drove the car back.

"Even after Myra got well, Mother wouldn't allow her to leave home. Mother was so cantankerous, it was hard to… and then she got downright mean.

"One day while I was at school, some county workers came and took Rhoda and Albert away. Marvin vowed to get them back someday, but then he had a family of his own.

"After graduation, I took off for Mason City. Living in that house had become a nightmare."

The doorknob might have shattered in her iron grip. "Myra wouldn't let me near her."

"Did she go back to school?"

"Not for quite a while. Mother treated her like fine china and viewed your Dad as an enemy. I don't know how Don managed, but he stuck with your mom through it all—must've been true love.

"I left just in time to see Charles Lindbergh at the dedication of the Mason City airport. Harry lived in the same boarding house where I found a room, and took me out to the big doings that day.

"That was our first date. Finally something good had come along."

"Then Dad and Mom—"

"They eloped about a year later, and your dad's little boy... Rodney must've been about five or six by then, and he'd already lost his mother."

A rock lodged in Twila's chest. *Your dad's little boy... lost his mother...*

"Mother never forgave your folks, but then, she never forgave anyone." She wiped her forehead. "Didn't mean to go on and on. I'd better hurry up."

The closed door left Twila stunned. Rodney was born before Dad married Mom? The news zigzagged through her heart. She had to get some air. In the back yard, two squirrels chased each other around a tree, scrabbling off chunks of bark, and she circled the garden as childhood memories surged through her mind.

Rodney never pushed her away when his friends came over. In the tree house Dad built, she was everybody's little sister. He'd stood up for her all through school years, and never missed a basketball game. How many times had his encouraging cheers during a tension-filled game brought calmness to her?

"Nothing has changed. Rodney's your brother, just like always.." Yet even as she said these words, a mysterious space opened up inside her.

The clock couldn't lie—Stan was almost an hour late. Maybe

he'd taken a nap or something, since he had the day off. But still, this wasn't like him.

Twila leafed through a dilapidated issue of *Look* magazine with pictures of a clinic in Rochester, Minnesota. Some photographer had snapped a patient with his head bandaged, sitting on the roof of the Hotel Kahler, near the clinic.

Although his eyes appeared to be covered, he held some reading material in his hands. Two phrases stood out. "...in hope of health" and "...one sick man among many."

Another photo advertised:

Rooms for 50 cents.
We cater to the clinic's poorer patients

Other ads showed hotels charging five dollars a day. An impossible price—could the clinic workers rent one of those cheaper rooms?

But what Aunt Margaret had just told her overwhelmed any other considerations. It was impossible to ignore what an unhappy person Grandma Fowler had been, and Grandpa, too. Yet what a house full of children they'd produced.

But the idea that Mom wasn't Rodney's real mother meant that he was her half brother. The revelation reverberated through her head. Margaret must think Dad and Mom had told her, but no one ever mentioned it, and they all shared the same last name.

As she smoothed her fingers back and forth over the sofa's ribbing, this new insight settled. Finally, certain things fell into place, random comments over the years, including an evening discussion that wafted to her bedroom through the grate.

"I've been through this before, Myra, watched everything fall apart, and I'm telling you, I won't let it happen. You're a fine mother, even if you don't think so. Rodney and Twila deserve a good home, and we're going to keep working at it."

She must've been about six then, and Rodney in junior high. His profile hovered before her now as if he sat across the room.

He shared Dad's distinctive upturned nose, dark hair and eyes, plus his walk.

But not a freckle graced his face, nor any hint of Mom's coloring. Why hadn't she ever noticed this before?

Had Dad's first wife died? Or did *watched everything fall apart* mean she left him and Rodney?

"Who could have guessed..." Her whisper filled the silent room on this oppressive afternoon.

A shiver ran through her, in spite of the heat. Where was Stan, anyway?

She switched to a worn issue of *Life* magazine with Rosalind Russell on the cover, in a striped blouse. Nothing glamorous about her playing the famed Amelia Earhart in *Flight for Freedom*. Here, the actress might have been next-door neighbor instead of a luscious actress in Fred MacMurray's arms.

Next came an advertisement for *The Under-Pup*, a Joe Pasternak Production featuring a new actress named Gloria Jean. Robert Cummings played a football star, and Beulah Bondi a "chilly old maid with a reserve like The Federal Bank." What a great description.

Some other advertisements caught Twila's eye—Marineland in Florida, an amazing attraction featuring two hundred species of fish in two open-air tanks. Until now, the article said, sea creatures had only been displayed in separate tanks.

In one photograph, a macaw perched on a visitor's shoulder—a young woman with one of those new short hair-dos Mona had risked a couple of weeks ago. Her bangs lay flat and straight, but the girl in the photograph wore hers rolled under.

On the back cover, a chipper young woman with two chrysanthemums in her lap sat with her male friend. Perfect shoes, beautiful legs, and the key to it all, the *Real Silk Hosiery* ad declared—pure resilient silk clinging wrinkle-free to her legs.

Superlatively fine dyes, the best obtainable, gives your ankles an easy-to-look-at 'million dollar look' in any crowd.

All for the Cause

At the model's feet knelt an adoring football player sporting the number 33. The advertisement offered the easy, shop-at-home method:

—if no Realsilk representative is calling on you regularly, do this: Get your phone book. Turn to R. Find Real Silk Hosiery Mills. Phone the local sales office in Indianapolis, Ind, or dial from the list of numbers in other cities. Chicago, Franklin 0797; Denver, Tabor 6926; Minneapolis, Geneva 2152, Seattle, Elliott 7768—

The issue was more than four years old, but the closest office seemed to be in Minneapolis. Twila imagined someone knocking at the door and opening a briefcase full of hosiery samples.

Would she spend some of her savings on real silk stockings? Mona told her you couldn't find a pair from here to Chicago, where they were still rare.

Thanks to the war.

Finally, she threw down the magazine and went out in back. The garden looked just like Mom's, and now she shouldered all that work alone. Today would be perfect for helping her catch up with the weeding.

Which brought her right back to Dad and Mom's story. Even though she'd been so impetuous, Dad chose her to be Rodney's mother, and she'd managed to put the past behind her. But how had she ever come to peace about Kenneth's death?

The string beans were ready to pick again, and clean-smelling tomato vines bore golf-ball sized fruit. She rubbed a geranium leaf between her thumb and finger. Such a variety of smells and sights in this simple back yard.

All the while, the startling new information replayed—an older brother and sister Mom never mentioned, plus two younger siblings. They'd be her aunts and uncles. Sunshine through the maple and oak trees rendered everything mottled and flecked.

Just like life.

But one thing hadn't changed. Dad and Mom loved each other and had made a good home for her and Rodney.

Just then, a short, squat soldier strode down the sidewalk, paused and lifted the gate latch. So muscular—his arms were like tree boughs.

He caught sight of her and yelled, "You must be Twila?"

Her heart thump-thumped.

"A couple of prisoners escaped. The whole camp's on alert, but I work in the motor pool, so we're off today. Stan sent me to let you know he couldn't come."

"Okay, thanks. Some prisoners escaped?"

"Yeah, the whole world's out lookin' for 'em, even the FBI." He looked around. "Where can they hide in this flat country?"

"Do you know where Stan is now?"

"Posted outside the second POW compound."

She thanked him and went inside for a glass of water. Dad and Mom had given her such good Fourth of July memories— always a red, white, and blue cake to go with the ice cream Dad churned after a fried chicken and potato salad dinner.

From the time she was little, they let her stay up late to see the fireworks down by the river. Rodney went off with his friends and Dad helped light the display while she snuggled with Mom on a blanket in the town park.

The Fourth of July—this was no day to sit around alone. Why not walk out to the camp and try to find Stan? The exercise would do her good, and a listening ear was exactly what she needed.

Chapter Twenty-four

"You have this holiday off, Miss Brunner. Can't keep yourself away from this wonderful place?"

Twila wished she could disappear into thin air when Nurse Alcott spotted her near the hospital. Under those all-knowing eyes, her brain failed. If only she could think of a handy excuse.

"I suppose you've heard about the escape—quite the excitement around here. And you might be on the look-out for a certain guard? I haven't seen him today."

"Do you think anybody would mind if I talked to him for a minute?"

"Probably not, if you can locate him. Most officers are concentrating on the escapees." She grabbed Twila's elbow and scrutinized her. "But remember to keep your dreams in mind."

"Oh I will. No need to worry about that, ma'am."

On the way to the compound, Twila stumbled on one of the doctors in a canvas lounge chair, reading. She pretended not to see him, though ignoring the growing sunburn on his bare shoulders wasn't easy.

Stan's eyes lit up when he spotted her near the prisoners' compound. "Hey, Iowa girl. I've got a half hour break in five minutes—can you wait?"

A building's shady side gave her a different view of the camp. This would be how the prisoners saw things, she imagined. Soon Stan appeared.

"Sorry I couldn't make it to fetch you earlier. I hoped you'd figure something went wrong."

"Yes, so I decided to come over."

"Glad you did. Want to go with me to retrieve my supper? Brown bags today—even the cooks are getting some time off."

"But you're not."

"With good reason. I'll tell you about it in a minute."

Chatter echoed from the exercise field, where some prisoners played soccer. At the same time, laughter wafted from a town league baseball game in the other direction.

Stan chose a spot under a tree, and while he wolfed down three sandwiches, Twila's news poured out. By the time she stopped, he'd topped them off with an apple and two cookies.

"Wow, that sure is a revelation. How do you feel about it?"

"I'm not sure. Better just getting it out."

"Yeah. Sounds like your mom was a spunky one back in the day."

He folded his sack into a perfect rectangle and slipped it into his pocket. "They want these brought back to use again."

He rested his back against the tree and stretched out his legs. "Sometimes it's good to finally know the facts, even if they're slow in coming. Maybe it did your aunt good to get it all out, too."

"I think so. I hope so."

"It's always better to know the truth, even though it's not necessarily easier. But sometimes people's memories hurt so much they keep that stuff quiet. I suppose it seems simpler, but in the long run, it might not be. My family has its share of secrets, believe me."

"Really?"

"Oh yeah. I had an uncle who got mad when the lawyer read my Grandpa's will. So mad, he tramped off into the north woods. No one ever heard from him again."

"Really, he vanished?"

"Uncle Mort was his name—became a mountain man of sorts. The woods swallowed him up, which isn't hard to imagine if you've seen them. Sometimes when I'm out, I imagine him walking up to me—he's a big old scruffy guy with a long beard.

"He sees my nose and high forehead and notices how big my hands are. Then he says, "You must be my brother's son.""

His chuckle invited her to join in, but then he turned sober. "I see a million unspoken secrets in these prisoners, a million troubles hidden away. Can you imagine being so far from everything familiar, knowing your homeland will be completely different when, or if, you ever return?

"Sometimes the quieter ones stare east through the fence. I can't help but think of all the hopes and dreams and sorrows locked away in hearts."

"You see them a lot more than I do, but I do think about them. It's as if real lives are out of reach right now. I'd think it would get them down."

"I'm sure it does. But who can they trust?" Stan stood and flexed his shoulders. "Want to walk a little?"

She fell in step. "That's why I've decided to be a lawyer, to defend people who don't stand a chance. Seeing the way Colonel Lobdell follows the Golden Rule inspires me."

"It would be great to make a difference. Sounds like you've thought this all through."

"Believe me, I've had plenty of time. And you want to help people heal. That's noble." He twined his fingers through hers. "Our dreams go together pretty well, don't you think?"

The sunshine intensified, but a sense of comfort pervaded Twila. Nobody listened better than Stan, or with more understanding, and it was clear that what he just asked required no answer.

"We both want to make a difference—that's what I mean. Sometimes, I think people might give up because of the war."

"That's for sure. I think Mom must have felt that way." They turned back toward the compound. "Just so you know, I'd never tell what I just told you to anyone else."

His sigh served as answer enough. On the tin roof of a shed outside the compound, sunshine created a sparkling sight, and even in the afternoon heat, a bird chirped somewhere.

Agitated calls from the activity field seemed out of place. "*Achtung! Schneller!*"

"The war will end. It *will*. And then we'll be free to follow our dreams." Stan scanned the playing field. "At least we still *have* dreams. Knowing where I'm headed gives me a good feeling."

"The one thing that bothers me about my dream is the cost. Mom's working fulltime to keep the household together while Dad's gone. I don't want to give her one more worry."

"You save your pay, don't you?"

"Every penny, and I have some money from working at the café back home, but that might not be—"

"I don't know how much law school costs, but if the GI Bill gives me two years, I figure my savings will cover the rest."

The soccer game ended as they approached the compound, and Stan halted just outside the door. Twila decided to tease him a little.

"For your information, Nurse Alcott saw me here and mentioned you. That was as good as giving me her blessing."

"Surprising—she acts like your guard dog."

"I like to think she's looking out for me."

His shrug left the matter up in the air. It would take more than this incident to convince him.

"It's been a different kind of Fourth for us—not quite what I intended."

"That's okay."

He wiped his hand over his forehead. "About your dreams…if you're careful and take advantage of every opportunity, you'll find a way."

He sounded so fervent that she had to believe. But then he released her hand and stiffened.

"Well, I'd better get back to work." An ominous light flickered in his eyes, and reading it proved impossible.

All for the Cause

Mid-July, but the cement-block building offered more protection from the heat. Twila was assisting Edna with a patient's bath when a messenger raced in and whispered something to the guard, who fled down the hall.

The messenger, a soldier she'd seen at lunch, took over the watch, but tension etched his face. Something must have gone haywire in one of the prisoner compounds. At the noon meal, rumors wafted like dandelion fluff, but no one seemed to know exactly what occurred.

Nurse Alcott became even more tight-lipped than normal. Later, Twila asked Stan when they passed in the hall. He'd been awfully distant lately, but stopped long enough to tell her he'd walk her home if he could.

He failed to show, but halfway home, panted up behind.

"Crazy day."

"We heard some scuttlebutt in the dining hall, but I never know what to believe."

"Last week's new prisoners were captured mostly at the port of Cherbourg, and they're really different from Rommel's Afrika-Korps. The Korps has far more officers, and they're much more committed to Nazism than the run-of-the-mill soldier.

"Some of these new fellows are still teenagers, and others look 40 or over. It appears Hitler's scraping the bottom of the barrel. I helped march this group up from Hobarton, and not one of them sang marching songs or showed any morale. Another thing—they wore several kinds of uniforms."

"They're not all German?"

"Right. Nine are even sailors, and a bunch have been conscripted from other countries, even Russia. Today, some of them contacted our German interpreter in Compound Two. He said they asked to be transferred to another camp because of the strong Nazi sentiment here. They're afraid for lives."

They crossed to Aunt Margaret's street. "Colonel Lobdell's put us on high alert, and prisoners keep coming forward to say they're in danger.

"Besides that, the SS officers resisted going on work detail, because they see themselves as higher than the rest of the prisoners. Have you heard how the colonel handled that?"

"Tell me."

"He's downright brilliant. He gave them a week of bread and water, with fewer and fewer ingredients going into the bread toward the end of the week. That did the trick.

"He also made sure the last men to cooperate put in a full day's hard labor before they sat down to a good meal." Stan's dimple flashed. "The way to a man's heart really is through his stomach."

"You think so?"

"The colonel proved it. But we're still in pretty good shape, better than some other camps. A few have even experienced forced suicides."

"What do you mean?"

"Hard-core Nazis are true believers who hate everything the United States stands for. They bluster and threaten prisoners who dare to acknowledge anything good about America. The most harmless comment about how tasty the food is can get a prisoner in trouble with the SS guys.

"Major Blaine thought our advances in Normandy would convince them Hitler's not invincible, but some seem beyond persuading. They've been trained since childhood to fight to the death, and were trained to silence complaints against the Reich."

"Can you picture American soldiers turning on each other in a prison camp?"

Stan blanched. *Wrong question to ask.*

Finally, he replied.

"No. Never. This kind of Nazi devotion is more like a religion. We're loyal to our country, but don't see President Roosevelt as a god. Some SS officers actually worship Hitler, like the Japanese with emperor."

In the distance, Benny came racing toward them, but Stan backed off. "I'd better get back—got double watch tonight. I'm betting Benny wants to talk about the Battle of Ancona. Tell him I had to go, all right?"

He kept backing up, but made a megaphone with his hands. "Tell him to look up Agugliano and Offagna, and I'll talk to him soon."

Benny's pout evidenced his disappointment, but when he heard Stan's instructions, he headed straight for the library. Twila turned to scan Stan's disappearing figure. Benny would believe anything he said. Diana liked him, too, and so did Aunt Margaret.

But what was going on with him lately? This afternoon he seemed as friendly as always, but the next time she saw him, he might avoid her. Everyone said women were more complicated than men, but she might beg to differ.

A few days after all the July Fourth excitement a letter from Mom waited on the kitchen table. That meant Diana must've gotten home early from the creamery. Twila tore it open, and one sentence immediately stood out:

"Your Dad is coming home. I'm not sure when, but probably in December. He'll travel by train, and has two weeks off. I'll let you know when I find out more."

Her whoop brought Diana and her friend Betty from the living room. For once, Diana looked genuinely concerned about something besides her latest heartthrob.

"What is it, cousin of mine?"

"My dad gets to come home for a visit. Oh, I can't wait."

"Seriously? I'm glad mine's still away. Mom's tough to deal with, but Dad makes me feel even more guilty."

Twila almost said, "Well, sometimes a little guilt can be a good thing," but thought better of it. Diana danced off with Betty, a vivacious girl who could pass for Lana Turner's daughter.

Their giggles filled the living room, since Aunt Margaret wasn't home. "Did you see how red Peggy White's face turned today when

Vick asked her to borrow a pencil? Can you imagine how long her summer will be, way out on that dairy farm?"

"Yeah, my mom says her folks got married late, so they're practically like grandparents. Besides that, Peggy has to go to that little church where breathing's a sin. Bet she doesn't even know the facts of life yet."

Such trivia—you'd think they didn't even realize a war was going on. Twila took her letter up to her room to savor the good news.

The dining hall offered a way to get to know a variety of workers, since the shifts kept changing. On this mid-November day, an older guard named Captain Arnold was talking when Twila slid onto a wooden bench with Edna.

"This whole year, the weather's been crazy. That January thaw had all the trees budding. Then a big ice storm destroyed a lot of timberland in Louisiana and Texas. February led to a soaking March, and in April, the Mississippi flooded so bad in St. Louis and over by Keokuk. Who knows what'll happen next?"

Another guard spoke up. "It's not just here, either. Hailstorms took out a lot of fruit in California, and Georgia's peaches froze. Then those three hurricanes out east this fall killed 400 people." He shook his head. "Seems worse than any year I can recall."

Someone else offered dismal outlook. "My folks live along the east coast; guess there were actually more hurricanes than three. Grandpa says maybe it's the earth reacting to all the destruction."

"Yeah, who knows how many forests and jungles the bombs have wrecked, and then there's all the sunken ships. Can you imagine how much oil has been spilled?"

Edna folded her napkin and caught Twila's eye. "You think those things affect the weather? Guess we can't do much to solve any of that, can we?"

"True. When we stick our heads outdoors, it's still going to be more than ten degrees below zero." Captain Arnold shuddered.

"But that's normal here—it's winter."

He reared a quizzical brow. "You're from here?"

Edna nodded. "I've lived here my whole life." She nodded to Twila and added, "So has Twila."

"My sympathies to you. Glad I get to go home to North Carolina—we get snow sometime, but nothing like this cold. Bone chilling." He took some more bites of his meal.

"Thanks for all your work, ladies. You have a lot to do with boosting morale around here, along with the Colonel's changes."

"We just do our jobs, Captain."

"But with such kindness, madam. Your attitudes make all the difference to men just back from Hades. Believe me, more than one has told me so."

He jerked his head toward the table across the way. "That's why Captain Lobdell makes use of that German chaplain. And why he has us escort him to some other camps by the Mississippi, in North Dakota, and way up in northern Minnesota."

The fire in another worker's eyes matched his irritated tone. "And allow him to wear his German uniform—isn't that going a step too far?"

"Put yourself in the prisoners' places—that chaplain understands what the enemy soldiers have been through. Some of them haven't heard from families since we started bombing German cities, or even longer. They have no idea if parents or wives and children are alive or dead."

"No skin off my back."

"Stop to think a minute. We've even bombed some of medieval cities."

"Only because the Luftwaffe hit Great Britain like they did, and the bombing's probably not done yet." The riled-up guard stuck his chin out. Twila took an instant dislike to him, but the captain's controlled reply calmed him down.

"I'm just saying that some of these prisoners have no idea if they even have a home left to go back to. That'd be tough on anybody."

He downed the rest of his coffee. "By the way, this chaplain has a pretty amazing story.

"He belonged to a church in the Old Country disfavored by the Nazis, and frequented a Christian youth organization with enemy ties. The Gestapo arrested him time and again, but he held to his convictions.

"Finally, the Reich gave him a chance to redeem himself by serving with the Afrika-Korps. After his capture, he was brought here and when he offered his chaplain services to the command, the answer was *yes*."

Edna butted in. "Wow—I had no idea. He told you all this?"

"Some of it, but Colonel Lobdell let us know his thinking about him, too. Makes sense to me—he's downright brilliant, in my opinion.

"He realized how valuable it was to have someone fluent in both English and German to help communicate with the prisoners. Someone who'd experienced the same propaganda they did back when this all started."

Edna half stood. "The chaplain seems so courteous when he visits the wards."

"Yeah—guess you could say he's a sheep in wolf's clothing. He's even been a help to us Americans posted here—helped us see what it'd be like to have a mad man take over your country."

With no small effort, Edna navigated her way from the long bench. "I doubt I'd have the guts to stand up to something like that."

One of the guards who hadn't said a word finally spoke up. "Ma'am, some people think FDR's a madman."

Giving him a look as cold as hoarfrost, Edna shooed Twila ahead of her, and they deposited trays on the intake counter and hurried off.

A guard held the door for them, and outside in the hallway Edna whispered, "That didn't even deserve an answer. But Captain Arnold—he would send my daughter into a faint. All of that coal black hair and his way with people."

Her sideways glance struck Twila as comical. "But you didn't seem all that impressed."

"I barely know him. Besides, my Dad might come home any day now. He's been gone for over two years, so I can't stop thinking about him wrapping his arms around me."

"That's great. How far away do you live?"

"About two hours. Mom misses him something awful, even though she works full time."

"Glad my Horace is a plain old farmer, with emphasis on *old*. Born too early for the Great War and too late for this one. He gets a bit down in the mouth about that at times, but I remind him *as goes the farm, so goes the nation*."

At the door to the American ward, she patted Twila's shoulder. "Sure hope your dad makes it home."

Chapter Twenty-five

The dream lasted forever, and encompassed so many details that Stan could hardly get his bearings when he woke. Trying to shake off the memories only strengthened them.

This one took him back to the first two days, when he and Cap scrambled up a killing mountain trail. That day, they came upon Carlos huddled in a ravine. He shrank under a Ylang-Ylang tree, attempting to make himself invisible.

But then he realized the intruders weren't Japanese, raised his palm, and crawled out. His hands and wrists looked like raw meat.

"How did you break away by yourself?"

"Street smarts, I guess."

"But this is the jungle."

"Yeah, but so is L.A."

From the moment they met in May of '42, Carlos fit right in as the three of them got turned around and re-crossed the trail. They'd seen nothing of natives yet, and nothing of the Japs.

During a break, Carlos muttered, "General Wainwright could die in captivity as well as anybody—Nip commanders could care less about his rank. So could mosquitoes and malaria."

Cap swatted an insect. "My guess is, they march our guys all the way to San Fernando in Pampanga Province, then ship them to O'Donnell by cattle car. I think they might separate out the generals, though."

Stan remained silent, though he disagreed with Carlos. Better save his energy—still plenty of walking ahead.

But with each step upward, he defined his argument: without a doubt, the enemy would care about the General's position. If they needed a hostage to exchange, a general would come in handy.

Later, Carlos nodded off, and when Cap could barely keep his eyes open, Stan nudged him. "I'll take watch, go ahead and sleep a couple of hours."

Cap complied, and Stan settled in. Amazing how some men could slip off into dreamland as if they were out on an afternoon picnic. For the umpteenth time, he analyzed the Allies' dire circumstances in the Philippines.

If only the government had given General MacArthur the money to build a defense force, but in '35, they'd sent him here with obsolete weapons and very little money. To shake Washington up, he finally resigned his Army commission, but stayed here with 13,000 troops to train Filipino regulars and reservists. What sense would it make to send them all home?

But soon, Japan became enamored with dominating all of Asia. In '41, Washington placed the Philippine army on active duty and sent National Guard units to aid. Having never seen combat duty, Stan had thought, "Between Wisconsin forests and this Louisiana swampland, how could I be better trained?"

In retrospect, his faulty reasoning brought a grin. Neither lumbering nor military maneuvers could have prepared him for this.

Something stirred in a thick tangle of vines. He relaxed only when a couple of birds jawed at each other.

Coming to the rescue of a renowned General... there was such bravado at first. But little more than a month after his unit arrived, Japanese bombers attacked Pearl Harbor.

At the same time, they wiped out all but a third of America's air power here, too. The men's high hopes faded, and by December 10th, Imperial troops invaded these islands. Americans evacuated Manila and withdrew into the Bataan peninsula and the little island of Corregidor off Bataan's tip.

Despite Washington's promise, no aid was forthcoming, since

by then the U.S. was at war with Germany, too. Still, he and his buddies held off the enemy with knives and entrenching tools when ammunition ran out.

Then on March 17, President Roosevelt ordered General MacArthur to evacuate, leaving General Wainwright to command the Army Forces in the Far East. But what was he to do with starving soldiers and no ammunition or supplies?

Beside Stan, Cap jolted awake. "All right, your turn."

He murmured a musical rhyme: *"I am a stranger here, within a foreign land; My home is far away, upon a golden strand, Ambassador to be of realms beyond the sea, I'm here on business for my King!"*

A woman named Cassel wrote the words, he said, and he reverted to the tune often. "I heard it in a Presbyterian church one time. I was visiting this girl, and..."

His energy made Stan think better of his plan. "Let's wake Carlos and keep moving." So they struggled on through twilight.

Carlos was always willing to move ahead, but Cap's good intentions wore down easily. The tubers they found, along with some porridge provided by a native in a small nipa hut, were far from enough, and his stomach issued violent growls.

"You must have ravenous creatures living down there."

"Yeah." Cap's grin seemed off somehow, and Stan determined to search out a wild pig. But roasting it out here scared him to death. The three of them already stank bad enough for the Japs to sniff them out, but if they saw smoke or smelled meat cooking...

He'd heard the Nips marched on a daily ration of one ball of rice sprinkled with fish powder. His own stomach was giving him fits, but keeping up morale was vital. Was it worth risking a fire?

He took a step and his boot sank into what looked like a long trench. The three of them stared, and then Cap fell to his knees and started digging with his hands.

After mere seconds, he pulled fingers from the earth—a human hand. His face turned the sickly greenish-yellow of the sky just before a tornado hurtled down.

"Oh God! Oh God!" His cry sent alarm through Stan, and Carlos knelt beside Cap.

They kept digging. An arm... a torso. Bile rose in Stan's throat—an American G.I. Then another, and another... hapless bodies, already cold.

One by one, he eased the small metal rectangles from fallen GI's necks.

No Geneva Convention here. Interrupted by stands of bamboo, the rude graves went on and on. A few bodies here, another one a few yards farther, and then unburied bodies left to rot, ravaged by wild animals. American soldiers with limbs torn off.

Fourteen dog tags in his hand—a mass in his throat.

Should they follow the marchers all the way to San Fernando? But then what? Surely, Imperial forces would cut them off.

No, they must fight back the best they could, which meant sabotage. Stan led the way at right angles to the fallen, and Cap and Carlos followed.

Gradually, a plan formulated. Find some Filipino guerillas. Create a team to strike by night, over and over and over.

He gathered his comrades. "Gotta keep going. We can't let these animals win."

The next thing he knew, someone was shaking him by the shoulder. "Stan! Hey, wake up. You've been dreamin' again. Where were you?"

The barracks wall shone in moonlight from the window. One of the guards bunking nearby stood over him with a concerned look.

"I don't know what you went through over there—must've been awful. But everything's all right now. You're safe."

It took a full minute to reorient.

"You okay now?" The other guard peered at him in the shadowy room.

Finally getting his meaning, Stan shook his head. "Yeah, I'm all right."

But something the guard had said gnawed at his gut. *Everything's all right now.* No, it wasn't, and it wouldn't be until Cap and Carlos and the rest of the captives on Bataan came home.

The hours sped by as Twila finished her Thursday afternoon work and walked home. On the kitchen table, another letter from Mom awaited her. Reading without taking off her coat, the second paragraph stopped her short.

I have some really bad news. I saw Charlotte's grandmother at the store. She said Char contracted a terrible disease, something starting with a P.

Poliomyletis? Nurse Alcott had briefed the staff on its symptoms the other day. Fever, headache, sore throat, vomiting, stiffness in the arms and legs...

But not Char. Char never got sick.

The doctors placed her in a rectangular wooden box that covered her entire body except her head. All day and night, a nurse stayed there to crank a handle in order to stimulate her muscles.

I hate to break this to you, bur even though the doctors did all they could, Charlotte died last week. Her parents held her funeral where they live now.

The letter fell into Twila's lap and a sob welled up in her throat. Charlotte, so healthy, so full of life, so energetic... How could she have caught such a terrible sickness? Crawling into bed tempted Twila. How could she take this in?

But just then the back door slammed. Benny would already be looking for her. He'd probably need help with his homework, and Aunt Margaret would be hungry when she got here.

With a heavy heart, Twila tucked the letter under her pillow and descended the stairs. She made stew and encouraged Benny.

Motivated by the map they'd made, he'd drawn a larger one on butcher paper, including England and the Channel.

That one, he posted above the radio. He kept a pencil handy to circle battle locations during each night's newscast, and proudly pointed out the names of French towns, from *Barfleur* in the west all the way to *Etretat*.

Last night after he ran over to Wendell's, Aunt Margaret lamented, "This just isn't right for him being so focused on the war, but what can I do about it?"

"I can't think of anything—you can't change the news, right? Maybe he'll become a history teacher some day."

But nothing she said lightened her aunt's mood and thankfully, nobody started a conversation after supper. The newscaster relayed nothing dramatic this evening, which was a blessing.

Picturing poor Charlotte lying in that box for hours on end, Twila retired early and wept into her pillow. Could she think and speak up to the end? Had her parents been able to visit her? Most of all, did that nurse talk with her, even if Char couldn't answer?

All writing back-and-forth, the way they compared notes on Hamlet, the plans they'd made to travel together, seemed so trivial now. Mom's letter contained more dreary news, too—another Halberton soldier had gone missing.

Sleep was impossible, and her alarm clock showed four o'clock the last time she looked. Somehow, she got through the next day, and that night, a radio announcement nearly drove Benny through the ceiling—the failed plot to assassinate Adolph Hitler.

"Why couldn't they make it work? What's the matter with them guys, anyhow?"

"*Those* guys." Aunt Margaret swiped her forehead. "Things don't always work out, Benny. That's just the way it is." She gave Twila one of her looks, and after he went to bed, she expressed her true feelings.

"Why can't somebody just stick a knife in Hitler's back?" She dropped her head into her hands. "If Benny knew half of the thoughts in my head, he'd die of shock."

She waited up for Diana again, and Twila was almost asleep when a shout echoed. "A lot *you* know about it. You're so busy with your job and everything else, you don't even care."

Aunt Margaret's cool retort: "Then I'm in good company, since you don't care, either. You've got a dad sacrificing for the war and a brother fighting the Japs, but all that matters is *you*."

"How would you know?"

Then came a stinging slap, feet pounding on the stairs, a door slamming.

Surely Benny heard it all. In the morning, granite silence pervaded the kitchen, so Twila chatted with him and wished him a good day.

"Oh yeah. With all this stuff I have to do?" He held out a list of chores long enough to occupy him for hours. At times like this, there wasn't much she could say.

At midmorning, Nurse Alcott summoned the workers. "There was a report of a failed attempt on Hitler's life on July 20th. Some of our prisoners would welcome this, but it would send others into a rage. Our job is to be sure no word leaks to them."

In August, news came of the instigators' so-called trials and public hangings. Edna expressed everyone's dismay. "Never thought I'd feel sorry for Germans being brought to justice."

The second weekend of the month, Aunt Margaret confined Diana to the house for two weeks after her latest offense. But she broke out when a traveling carnival came to town. Aunt Margaret caught her in the balloon shoots and dragged her home.

Twila stayed at the carnival with Benny as long as possible, and when they tiptoed in, all was quiet.

But the month also brought good news, borne by Benny. He was waiting for her on the top step one day after work.

"Didja hear? The Americans are holding Tinian Island. Took almost a week, but now they've liberated Florence, too. We're gonna land in southern France next, and before September, I betcha they'll liberate Paris."

He grabbed her hand. "Just you wait and see if it don't happen. Gotta make sure Wendell knows about this."

"All right, but be back in half an hour, okay? When your mom comes home, she'll want to see you in the garden." At such an awkward age but still hungry for signs of love, Benny accepted a quick hug before taking off.

All summer, he trumpeted the latest news about baseball. He bemoaned the new rubber-less balls major league teams had to use due to the rubber shortage.

"Know what the Spalding Company puts in 'em now?"

Twila shook her head.

"Some gummy juice from the balata plant—that's why so many games were shut-outs last season. The ball's so dead, even the best hitters can't get no power on it."

Still, he listened to games whenever he got a chance. That wasn't often, because his chores started in the morning. The games weren't all at night anymore, to accommodate the many listeners who worked night shifts.

When the radio announcer mentioned the World Series, Benny went wild. One September afternoon, he met Twila on the street as she walked home.

"The Seventh Army Air Force team at Hickam Field has a former major-leaguer at almost every position. Joe DiMaggio's in the outfield—he's a Hall of Famer, still playin' over in Hawaii."

"My dad really likes Joe. I haven't heard much about him lately."

"The Navy got tired of losin' to his team, so the Pacific Fleet commander ordered the Navy's best players back to Hawaii. That's Admiral Nimitz—he's bringin' in players from all over the world for the '44 Service World Series."

At home, he flashed the Des Moines Register. "They're callin' this "the *real* World Series."

"Where'd you get that paper?" They hadn't even noticed Aunt Margaret come in, but her scowl got attention.

"Wendell's Grandpa. I'm just readin' it and takin' it back."

Twila knew Rodney would be listening to every game he could, so she wrote him to send Benny a letter. He did, even though they'd never met.

After each of the 11 games, Benny wrote to him, and faithful as late September frost, Rodney replied. Benny read his letters out loud. Rodney took the time to discuss the fine points of each game. One ended in a tie, the Navy won eight, and the Army claimed two victories. But those losses didn't matter to Benny.

After mailing his letter following the final game, he boasted, "I'm an Army man, no matter what. Don't know why, 'zactly, since Paul's in the Navy. Maybe it was them guys stormin' the beach and crawlin' through the hedgerows in France. Didja know Joe gave up a $43,750 salary for $50 a month from the Army?"

He held up his fist. "Attaway, Joe—Army all the way! Rodney says maybe someday, you'll tour the U.S. and if you get close to Iowa, he'll take me to see you."

Aunt Margaret hailed this new correspondence a miracle. "If I hadn't seen this with my own eyes, I wouldn't believe it. I'd have to hogtie him if that were a school assignment. I ought to talk to his teacher and see if his letters to Rodney can count for English class."

She scrunched her forehead. "The series has been good for the guards, too. Gives them something different to think about. Sure hope it's doing the same for the GIs."

She was thinking of Paul. Twila recognized all the signs—puckers in her brow, a glint in her eyes, and her tight fists.

"If they can get near a radio, that is."

Chapter Twenty-six

"Must be the moon," another guard muttered to Stan. "Three prisoners injured in one day."

"The moon?"

The other fellow shrugged. "Somebody said more weird things happen when it's full."

Something to consider. Had Cap's symptoms incapacitated him more when the moon was full? Stan had been much more aware of the moon's phases in Bataan, but never thought they might correlate with Cap's ups and downs.

Ah well, whatever happened today in the prisoners' compound couldn't hold a candle to what he'd relived in the night. Weariness dogged him, so he skipped the evening meal and retreated to his corner.

He dusted a film off his little chest of drawers and rearranged his belongings. This small space at the far end of the barracks supplied far more serenity than he'd claimed since he left Bataan.

When he'd been so far away, he'd longed for Wisconsin and home like everybody else. But after a few days back, home had quickly lost its appeal. He'd itched to get away. Mom's constant attempts to fill every moment accounted for some of his restlessness. Clearly, he'd gotten used to the isolation of the jungle.

Take rest; a field that has rested gives a beautiful crop. Ovid

Cap's crooked grin appeared before him. Since they'd always needed rest over there, he quoted this one often.

Stan's sigh wafted over the long room filled with eight other men writing letters or getting ready for bed. Still six empty bunks, but with all these new occupants, he'd become afraid to fall asleep, knowing he might awaken them all later.

Lately, he'd noticed prairie dogs all around the camp. At least one of them always stood at attention and swiveled its head every few seconds for signs of danger. Not much different than the way he'd lived on Bataan.

After the rest of his barracks-mates slept, someone passed through the dimly lit hallway. Maybe he'd been in battle too, and found it better to walk the halls than struggle to sleep.

After the other nightwalker disappeared, Stan put on some socks and began his trek. Midway down the hall, he worked on his stretches. The left leg was getting stronger by the day. Remembering that Twila hadn't noticed a limp at all, he grinned into the obscure hallway mirror.

His most frequent happy thought centered on Twila. She didn't have to talk all the time, and had an idea where she was going. Besides that, she made no effort to control what the wind did to her hair. Still thinking about her, he completed his regimen and added another couple of rounds.

One of these days, he should seek her out again. No hurry, since nothing could come of getting to know her anyway. He still had places to go and other work to do—faraway places and grim work.

After chow the next morning, he took a walk down the main road before reporting in. Something had niggled him ever since he read about Camp Algona's new commander. The newspaper article about him emphasized his belief in showing fairness to men who'd killed Americans in North Africa, even some who still maintained devotion to Hitler.

Then another guard, an MP named Mark, overheard rumors that some elitists from the *Afrika-Korps* planned to go on strike on Hitler's birthday. When Stan asked how he knew, he said he knew enough of the language to comprehend.

Then he fumed, "Over my dead body they'll go on strike."

The conversation transported Stan back to Bataan—there, the captured Americans received no special favors, if they had survived the grueling march to Camp O'Donnell. He visualized a gun butt coming down on a GI's head, spewing blood from the victim's ear.

Go on strike? Who did these Hitlerites think they were?

Mark mentioned his regret that he hadn't yet done overseas duty, and asked about Stan's. A scant outline seemed plenty to share—why discuss in the daylight what haunted him by night?

Turning back toward the camp, the promise of cooler weather arrived on a breeze. Saying good-bye to Iowa's humidity brought relief, and the crisp morning held a hint of winter. His thoughts veered back to justice. He looked forward to meeting the Colonel, but harbored some questions.

Having the prisoners eat meat every day and chicken every Sunday might be going a bit *too* far. They were given the same number of calories as the guards, and also enjoyed black bread baked by own bakers, along with noodles, macaroni, spaghetti, peas, beans, and other non-rationed food

Although all prisoner mail was read by a staff member, at least they could hear from home. The rules also allowed them to read German newspapers they received.

A car with a red cross on the door puttered through the gates.

The Red Cross—he'd seen them here before, inspecting the 50-bed wards and watching out for the Germans' well-being. This raised the ire of some of the guards, especially those with family members overseas.

When certain prisoners arrived with terrible mouth sores and swollen lips and jaws, dentists and doctors attended to them. Word had it that previous wardens in European holding camps had different ideas than Colonel Lobdell, and encouraged guards to beat German POWs.

The sad state of mouths came from having teeth torn out to remove gold fillings. This version of justice was understandable, considering the Luftwaffe's relentless bombing of England all these years.

Fairness took a beating in the light of war's brutal premise—an eye for an eye, a tooth for a tooth. Stan stood staring out over acres of farm fields in the process of harvest.

Truth be told, the Filipinos, who detested the Japanese, had once fought against American soldiers. Decades ago, another war had led to the United States buying country, Puerto Rico, and Guam from Spain, but native Filipinos had revolted at having a new ruler. Naturally, a fight had resulted.

The Philippine-American war lasted three years and took a quarter of a million lives. Probably many Filipinos would have liked to yank teeth from the Americans' mouths, too. At least in '35, the United States allowed for them to form a commonwealth, but now, foreigners once again ravaged homeland.

"Hey! You all right, Ford? Looks like you're a million miles away." Hopefully, Mark entertained no idea of playing nursemaid. All the more reason to go back to the front as soon as possible.

"Yeah, just taking my morning constitutional."

"I just heard the Marines have attacked in Peleliu. It's such a tiny island, I'm not sure why it's so important."

Stan fell in with him. "Peleliu may be small, but it's only five hundred miles east of the Philippines, and a big garrison of Japanese troops has an airfield there. As long as the enemy controls that island, they can threaten any attempt General MacArthur makes to re-take the Philippines.

"We gained control of the Marshall Islands back in February, and moved to the Marianas. It took until July to secure Saipan, and until the end of August for Tinian and Guam. In order to free the Philippines, we have to keep moving west."

"I ought to know, but where are they, anyhow?"

A fair question. A few years ago, Stan couldn't have pointed the islands out on a map, either. His answer, "In the South China Sea, basically between Australia and China," satisfied Mark for now.

"So that's why MacArthur went to Australia when the Japs invaded. I suppose I learned all of this in school, but…" He looked at his watch. "Well, it's almost time for us to get in there."

Just before they did, he asked, "What were we doing in the Philippines in the first place?"

This question would take a while. The history was mighty complicated, and not worth being late.

"It goes way back to the Spanish-American War at the turn of the century, and the Treaty of Paris. Maybe there's a history book around here somewhere.

"But the long and short of it is, General MacArthur has been in the Philippines as a military advisor since '37. He loves the country, and I'm sure he'll keep his promise to return."

"We've still got a lot of men over there, right?"

"Yeah, held prisoner. Re-taking what we lost is eating up a lot of time because the Japanese are putting up an awful defense. They believe they're superior to the Filipinos and have a right to rule the islands."

"This battle the Marines are fighting right now—in Pel—however you pronounce it. How long do you think it'll take to drive the Japs out? Maybe it won't be so hard now, since we've already beat them a few times?" Mark ducked through the doorway and waited for Stan.

"That'll only make them fight harder. They see things differently than we do. They worship emperor and will fight to the death for him."

"That's bad news."

"Sure is. We can count on it taking longer than we think. It always does."

Hurrying to the outfitting room for his equipment, Stan realized his hands were shaking. Even talking about the Philippines had such a powerful effect on him—he ought to know better.

In the shadowy corner where the weapons were organized, he filled his ammunition pouch with bullets and slung his M-1 rifle over his shoulder. When he straightened, there stood Cap, easing in and out of the filmy light like a ghost.

Hardly surprised, Stan waited. Most of the other guards left the room, but for some reason, Cap took his time this morning.

When his words finally came, he issued them with long pauses.

"Dripping water... hollows out stone, not through... force but through... perseverance." No need to cite which ancient wise man wrote this. He knew Stan could have finished the quote for him—Ovid again.

As quickly as he appeared, Cap dissolved into a sea of dust motes, and Stan hurried out. But as he fell in with the others coming on duty, he could scarcely get his breath.

If only Cap would give me some warning... What a laugh!

He shook off the experience and manned his post. All he knew was that he had to get back over there... back to Cap and Carlos. *Had* to.

Standing at the stove to stir corn cooking in a big pot went faster with the evening news in the background. Punctuated by Benny's exclamations, "Yes!" for the positive points and "Aw, Gee!" for the negative, Twila could hardly imagine a broadcast without his commentary.

> Patton's Third Army has halted as supplies are stretched to the breaking point. If ever those of us here in the States should realize that our efforts are essential to victory in Europe, it should be now. Without supplies, even the best general with the most ardent troops cannot move forward.
>
> In the Pacific, Japanese positions on Luzon in the Philippines have come

under intense Allied aerial assault. A massive fleet of carrier-based U.S. warplanes has begun aiming brutal fire at enemy bases in the prelude to General MacArthur's return to re-take the islands.

Meanwhile, in spite of pre-landing Naval bombardment, our Marines are meeting fierce Japanese resistance on the island of Peleliu. Enemy forces are using the rocky terrain, complete with underground caves connecting to various parts of the island, to advantage.

The U.S. Army's Eighty-First Infantry Division managed to secure Angaur and Ulithi, also in the Palaus, relatively quickly. Now, members of the 321st and 323rd Regiments are coming to the aid of the 1st Marine Division.

Hard-pressed at a site known as Bloody Nose Ridge, the Marines will soon be joined from the west by the men of the 81st. The goal is to envelop enemy positions on all sides and eventually dislodge them completely.

And that is how things stand this evening, September 23, 1944.

Benny flew into the kitchen and slipped on the wet floor. "It's the Army to the rescue. Bet them Marines ain't likin' this one bit, havin' to ask the infantry for help. I gotta go tell Wendell, 'cause he's an army man, too. Can I, Mom? I'll come right back."

"Doesn't Wendell listen to the news himself?"

"Yeah, but sometimes he don't get what's goin' on, ya know? And he don't have no—"

Aunt Margaret gave her pot another stir. "He doesn't have any..."

"Doesn't have any brother over there, neither." Another mistake, but she let it pass. "Our guys just gotta get back there n' get Paul outta that prison."

At Margaret's visible wince, Twila bite her lip. For weeks, she'd been asking how long the Navy could label a sailor "missing in action."

"So, can I go?"

"*May I.* All right, go. Be back in 15 minutes."

Benny raced out as she and Twila spooned the last of the sweet corn into jars and set them in the canner. They'd conquered this last picking in record time. Luckily, a farmer friend of the family picked it for them and left a full gunnysack on the shady side of the back porch sometime today.

The sooner they got at this laborious task, the better, so Twila started right in, and begged help from Diana and Benny when they got home from school. The three of them had every ear husked and cleaned by the time Aunt Margaret arrived.

As they cut the kernels from the ears, Benny dropped his knife so many times that she assigned him to cob duty. Hauling several heavy pails full to the shed and spreading them on screens set up on sawhorses kept him occupied.

After he went outdoors, Diana started in. "I *hate* doing this—there's corn in my hair, on my face..."

"And on ours, too. But are we griping about it? Just keep cutting."

But she couldn't, so her complaining netted her another job, far worse, in Twila's opinion. Cleaning up a corn canning mess was no fun at all. After she washed and dried the bowls, pans and utensils, Diana headed for the living room, but Aunt Margaret stopped her.

"You're not finished yet. You need to scrub the back porch, and by the time you're done, all the corn should be boiling, so you can tackle this floor."

"But they're so sticky—I can't walk without my shoes squeaking."

"Exactly. That's why they need to be scrubbed, and why I can guarantee it'll take several pails of hot water and more than one rinsing." With kernels flying in all directions and all the tracking in and out, the clean-up task topped them all, and Twila sympathized. If only Diana had kept quiet.

With everyone hard at work, Aunt Margaret adopted a cheerful mood. "We ought to have seventy quarts after tonight and be ready for winter."

Mom was probably preserving the last pickings from the garden, too, even though the fruit cellar hadn't fully emptied from last fall. Maybe Sharon was helping her—hopefully.

The last time Twila noticed, Aunt Margaret's fruit cellar looked about as full. Victory gardens sounded idyllic, but led to so much work.

Chapter Twenty-seven

How to phrase his request? As the long day progressed, Stan wrote his letter to Colonel Lobdell over and over in his head.

"I feel the need to return to combat because..."
"As tensions mount around the coming Philippine invasion, my heart tells me..."
"I find I can no longer remain in a job that could as easily be filled by a civilian, when..."
"As time has passed since my return from duty in the Pacific, I have been..."

Mentally, he tore up sheet after sheet of stationery. Nothing seemed to hit quite the right note for such important communication. All the while, he tamped down his urge to march into the Colonel's office and plead his case verbally.

No, no, no. Only a letter requesting a meeting would work. But how to write it? All afternoon he noodled various approaches... where was Cap when he really needed him?

This evening, he would accomplish the feat, no matter what. His determination kept him seeking just the right words, but just as his shift was ending, all hell broke lose. Another escape? The SS prisoners revolting again? Who knew?

In the end, his shift remained on duty an extra two hours while replacements attended to whatever had gone haywire. The cook held dinner for them, and sixteen ravenous guards made quick work of it in the dining hall.

By the time he made it to his corner haven, Stan was beat. Maybe he'd take a little nap before getting to his one goal for the evening.

"Know what Rutherford B Hayes said to Alexander Graham Bell after he invented the telephone?"

"I have no idea. What?"

"'That's an amazing invention, but who would ever want to use one of them?' Did you realize Bell never allowed one in his work area because he thought it would distract him?"

Cap's lackadaisical chuckle turned into a deep-throated laugh...then a cackle. His face yellowed and transformed—then hundreds of slanted eyes developed out of nowhere, and mocked Stan.

Sneering lips revealed sets of brown teeth. Gun butts smashed Stan's shoulder and hip, enemy screams assaulted his ears.

"March... march... keep moving, G.I.!"

A thunderous roar sounded overhead. Closer, Japanese gunners aimed weapons at him. He ran through impossible jungle... faster, faster.

"Hey, buddy. Wake up." Some guards shook him and whispered to each other. The lights were still on...he must've fallen asleep early.

"It's another nightmare—I heard he fought in the Philippines."

"Oh yeah? Must've been bad."

Two concerned brows hovered over Stan and forced him to swallow down his terror. Not again...this was two nights in a row he'd disturbed his closest neighbors.

"Sorry, fellas. I... I'll try not to let this happen..."

"It's all right. Go back to sleep now."

They slipped away and he sank back onto his pillow. "But it *will* happen again, and this stuff is getting worse. What am I going to do?"

Muttering to himself would do no good. After the others fell asleep, he started walking. But the shadowy nighttime silence brought no comfort, and menacing figures seemed to rise from the corners, or between the glass panes and window frames.

"No." He slumped against the cold wall. "You *are not* losing your mind. You just need to get back over there."

The cool plaster eased the heat roaring through him, and a puzzle piece slipped into place. He'd socialized with Twila lately as if he were a free man; as if he had a right to chart his course. He'd even mentioned going to law school.

What had he been thinking? How could he have forgotten Cap and Carlos? They might never be free again, along with so many other GIs.

The cool hallway brought a shiver, but he relished the discomfort. He had it way too easy here, fed and coddled as if the armistice were already signed. Dinner ran a little late, and he'd eaten as though he'd been suffering want.

Everything around this place was a distraction. He'd let Twila distract him, too. His goal shone as clear as the moon over the harvested Iowa fields in the distance. He must seek that goal; must *do* something to reach it.

It was now or never. Back in his cubbyhole, he grabbed his flashlight. Then he took some paper and a pen back to the hallway, sank against the wall and wrote his letter requesting a meeting with Colonel Lobdell.

Straightforward phrases, honest words—the unvarnished truth. Without re-reading it, he addressed and sealed the envelope, walked down the hallway and slipped it into the inter-office slot.

He returned to bed satisfied that he'd done what he could. Yet one burning question taunted him: would the Colonel understand?

"Benny, why aren't you in bed?" Twila shuffled down to the living room, where her cousin sat bunched up in the corner of the sofa with his arms around his legs.

"Can't sleep."

"Neither can I. What's keeping you awake?"

"I can't help believin' Paul's already dead." He buried his face in the quilt he'd wrapped around himself. His eyes widened as he glanced up the stairs. "If Mom heard me say that, she'd kill me."

Twila wrapped her bathrobe tighter, grabbed an afghan, and joined him. "Why do you think he couldn't still be alive?"

"The Japs're so mean—if he did swim to shore and ended up in a prison camp, he wouldn't be able to stand bein' cooped up like that. He woulda tried to escape, and the Japs woulda killed him."

"You really think he would have tried to escape, even if lots of other GIs were there with him?"

"Yeah. It'd be like when he was runnin' passes for the football team, or gettin' the ball to the basket in basketball. He just wouldn't settle for makin' a play halfway, y'know?"

"I do know—at least sort of. I wasn't a great player, but it was hard to let anybody get by me with the ball."

"You were a guard?"

"Yep."

"What a lousy deal. You never got to shoot!"

"True, but I kept the other team's forwards from scoring. Sometimes, I was able to stop a really good player's shot. That always made me feel good, and in a way, my part had the same effect as if I'd scored."

"Hmm. Paul played good defense, too, but scoring was what he did best. Girls' rules woulda driven him crazy."

"I imagine so. But Dad always told me, "If your forwards don't get the ball, they can't shoot, so your job is to steal it whenever you can. A stolen ball takes the chance to score from the opposition and gives it to your forwards."

"Makes sense. Workin' behind the scenes. That's what I hafta do, y'know." He peered up the stairs again. "Mom don't know it, but me and Wendell—" He slapped his hand over his mouth.

"What did you do?"

"Oh, just hauled more stuff to the garage."

"Every action we take helps, even if we think it's insignificant. That's what Dad wrote me when I felt like I couldn't do much for the war effort."

"Maybe someday I'll meet your dad, when he comes back." Benny's eyes lighted for the first time tonight. "That reminds me of them Japanese balloons. My teacher said—"

"What do you mean?"

"Didn't you hear? The Japs launched more'n 6,000 hydrogen balloons on westerly winds—toward us! You didn't know that?"

"No, tell me more."

"Only 300 made it, but one detonated out in Oregon."

"Wow—did it hurt anybody?"

"Yeah. A woman and five kids. Killed 'em."

"Benny!"

"It's true. They was out for a picnic or somethin'." His eyes flashed fire. "I *hate* them blasted Japs! Maybe Stan was right—they'll never quit. Wendell's dad told us they've got a new operation now, called Operation Sho-Go. Have you heard about it?"

"No."

"It means victory in Japanese. Man—even with all the planes and ships we've destroyed in the Leyte Gulf, they won't quit. And seventeen of our air carriers just launched a massive attack on Okinawa—I just don't get it. Why don't the Japs just give up?"

No immediate response came. How could he not hate them? Right now she might hate them, too. For a moment, she felt like Aunt Margaret. With all the complexities of this war, how could a boy like Benny grow up to be a normal human being?

Sitting there in the quiet darkness, Twila leaned her head back, thankful that he seemed to accept her lack of words. And then he asked, "Wish Stan could help us find Paul. D'ya think he could?"

"I don't think so. He's just one soldier, and he's been back here for quite some time."

"Ain't seen him for so long…are you n' him mad at each other?'

"Mad? Not at all. It's just that we've both been awfully busy."

That was true. But she'd wondered about Stan too. Seemed like they rarely crossed paths these days, and when they did, he always hurried off somewhere. She'd begun to think maybe he…

Before she could formulate anything else to say, Benny's head slipped sideways. The next thing she knew, he'd fallen against her arm and was snoring.

At least she'd distracted him from thinking about Paul for a while. It was hard to say anything encouraging on that topic, because no one knew a thing.

Aunt Margaret refused to discuss him at all, but still sent his weekly box of cookies and wrote him letters. When a neighbor stopped in last Saturday and asked if they'd heard anything, she just looked away.

He suggested she contact the Red Cross, and even offered to ask for her, but she shook her head. "No thanks. Lots of families haven't heard from sons."

"But that's what the Red Cross is for, Margaret. Why don't you let me—"

"We'll hear when we hear, and that's all there is to it." She folded her arms.

Subject closed. What could anyone say to that?

The wind turned wild, and had a heyday puffing around in the chimney. Twila tucked a pillow under Benny's head and luxuriated in the thick bathrobe that arrived early for her birthday. The card said, "From Mom and Dad, with love. You're growing into a lovely woman."

Soft, thick chenille in her favorite color, daffodil yellow—this was something a wealthy woman would wear, or a movie star. She'd seen robes just like this advertised in the JC Penney winter catalog, but never imagined owning one.

But then, this past year overflowed with all kinds of surprises she'd never imagined. And now, according to Mom's letter, Dad was coming home.

Her yawn collapsed into Benny's deep breathing, and she eased his head to the sofa's arm. Then she covered him with an afghan and stretched out on the other end.

Who would ever have thought she'd be sharing a sofa with her little cousin? If only Aunt Margaret would hear something about Paul.

Chapter Twenty-eight

Three days had passed since Stan mailed his letter. News broadcasts overflowed with references to the nightmare the marines were facing in Peleliu. Every report made his jitters worse. What if we failed to take that little island?

Thousands had already died in the attempt, while those American prisoners on Bataan still awaited deliverance. In condition, every single day made a difference.

Once again, his shift had been kept overtime, and the evening report blared over the guards' late meal. This wait was harder than slashing through the jungle—he'd even lost his appetite lately.

The way things were going in the theater, everything pointed to an invasion from the south. Would the Army even need infiltrators in the north—in Bataan?

Hearing the newscasters analyze the situation made his plate of scalloped potatoes and ham even less inviting.

> On the South Pacific Island of Peleliu, a helmeted Japanese skull calls attention to a warning sign ("Danger! Move Fast"). Finally, the campaign seems to be coming to an end, but at such great loss!
>
> The First Marine Division landed here on September 15, despite indications that the purpose of this campaign—to

protect General MacArthur's flank in the Philippines invasion—might no longer be necessary. Marine commanders expected only a few days of battle, but instead, faced bloody combat.

Complicated by coral cliffs and caves, the fighting has continued much longer than anyone perceived. Reinforcements have been sent more than once, and while a final casualty count is still forthcoming, U.S. forces have suffered thousands of losses.

In Europe, our boys prepare for a knockdown, drag-out fight along the Siegfried Line, and anxiety increases. France may have been liberated and the Allies may have crossed into German territory, but General Montgomery's push through Holland resulted in dismal failure, plus the destruction of the British Eighth Army.

The Luftwaffe may have lost much of power, but from all appearances, the Nazis still stand determined to counter our progress into the motherland.

Needless to say, we still face plenty of challenges on the continent. We can predict victory on both fronts, but how long that winding road will stretch remains a well-obscured mystery.

With another long night to look forward to, Stan took his time walking back to the barracks. Might as well write a couple of letters before going to bed—maybe that would wear out his brain.

In light from the hallway, he spied something white on his bed. He picked up an envelope with his name and no return address. He switched on his lamp and several lines of neat, angular handwriting greeted him.

He could scarcely believe his eyes—Colonel Lobdell had answered his letter himself. Stan sank to his bed.

The reply shot hope through him. "I have received your request and would be happy to discuss these matters. Meet me in my office on October 15th at 3 p.m."

Three days away. The next day while he surveyed prisoners playing soccer, Stan organized his appeal. The most logical route would be to join General MacArthur's men training in Australia.

But recently Raymond had written to him about the Ninety-eighth infantry, a group of big farmer types thus far denied battle. Someone with a relative in the unit told Raymond they'd been assigned to Ranger training in New Guinea.

The news quickened Stan's heartbeat. Surely General Kruger was fine-tuning them for clandestine work, hopefully in Bataan.

Raymond's letter also included the first information about Ron for months. He had to chuckle at Ray's description.

"Guess they got Ron's number during basic, and sent him to demolition school. He's a sapper. The last I heard, he was headed to the Seigfried Line—watch out, Hitler."

A sapper, one of the most dangerous of all Army jobs, but ideal for scrappy kid brother. Stan closed his eyes and visualized Ron skulking through enemy territory ahead of the other GIs, scoping out the dangers and removing obstacles in way.

Last month, General Eisenhower's three army groups had reached the German border with forces and firepower superior to the enemy's. But gasoline and ammunition shortages, plus dug-in German troops along the Siegfried Line made for slow going.

All along the line, Hitler had ordered pillboxes, gun emplacements, tank traps, and other obstacles. These ranged the line through countryside and cities alike, often right in the heart of a city in order to stymie the Allied advance. To make matters worse, the American assault was coming during the wet season.

Nobody had to describe that to Stan, except that in Europe, the downpours would be bone chilling at this time of year. Ron would manage, but what a miserable assignment he'd landed.

The sapper blew buildings to smithereens, crawled under fortifications to set dynamite charges or fought hand-to-hand. With an absolutely necessary mission promising a high casualty rate, these soldiers were called *pioneers* for good reason.

Without mobility and counter-mobility operations, plus ability to fight when necessary, infantry attacks would be stymied before they started. His little brother, the child who refused to accept the word, "No," had found his niche.

During training, Cap had described mission perfectly. "They engineer a way through by doing whatever it takes to destroy enemy strongpoints. They construct roads and bridges and impede enemy advances by laying minefields, building defense fortifications, or blowing bridges to halt enemy movement."

Always the one to suggest a new way to build a snow fort, Ron was perfect for this work. His creations boasted complicated tunnels and lasted longer than anyone else's when the spring thaw came.

People always said he and Ron could pass for twins, they were so close in age. But Ron was such a wiry kid—he could find his way through any forest tangle, and made playing hide-and-seek a memorable challenge.

Thinking how hard it used to be to keep up with him, Stan chuckled again. No doubt, Ron had told Mom he was assigned to drive a general around.

If Raymond knew what Ron was doing, then dad did, too. He had to be proud. Ron was the son most like him. And, though Stan hated to admit it, maybe he was the one most like Mom. He could always sit still long enough to read or study, unlike Ron.

He also had shown a bent for debating, but with Ron, she knew there was no use trying to win an argument. Maybe this had something to do with how much his choices disappointed her.

Stan set Colonel Lobdell's letter on his shelf. He'd never been as tough-minded as Ron. If Colonel Lobdell said no, what would he do?

Later, he lay in bed imagining meeting.

"I'm as fit as when I enlisted, and my memories are still so vivid, I could lead troops straight to Camp O'Donnell or Cabanatuan, where I've heard the remaining prisoners from the death march have now been moved."

He could imagine the Colonel pursing his lips. "You follow this pretty closely, eh? Tell me—do you have nightmares about your time down there?"

"At times, but they wouldn't keep me from doing my job."

"What was the fighting like?"

"Hand-to-hand the last months. We used whatever we could—mostly knives and bolos."

"And you would like me to forward this request further?"

"If possible, sir."

"How about your parents? Do they know about your plans?"

"Not yet. But I'm 22, and my father would understand."

"I applaud your patriotism and appreciate your spirit. If I were young again, I'd feel the same way." The Colonel would drum his fingers on his desk. "But with all you have been through, I think you've already done your duty."

Sweat broke out on Stan's forehead in spite of the building's coolness. He made fists of his hands.

No—the conversation simply couldn't end this way. Colonel Lobdell just had to understand.

On the 15th, Stan arrived ten minutes early and waited outside the Colonel's office. Each tick of the clock made his mouth dryer, but he commandeered his shaking knees as the Colonel arrived right on time and ushered him in.

"Take a seat, Private." He opened a file folder and thumbed through the pages while he spoke.

"I understand you still have buddies over there?'

"Yes, sir."

"It's understandable you would want to return, especially with some stories from POW camps filtering through already. I imagine we'll hear plenty more once this is all over."

He read for a full minute. "No wife or children?"

"No, sir."

"You have a brother serving in Europe, I see. Oh, my. He's a sapper." He peered at Stan over the folder and waited. When Stan remained silent, he continued. "How is your work going here?"

"It's fine."

"But you prefer returning to the fight?"

"I know I could be contributing so much more, sir."

The Colonel thumbed through his file again. "You have quite a history already—infantry and mechanic trained, expert marksman. Your unit headed to Europe, but got turned around after training in Louisiana." He squinted at Stan.

"Did you ever meet Patton?"

"No sir, although his unit trained down there, too."

"How about General MacArthur?"

"No, sir. But we knew he only left Bataan because the President ordered him to."

"Indeed, he's quite the old warrior. I heard that when someone asked what would become of his four year-old son, he replied, 'He is a soldier's son.'" The Colonel closed the file and laced his fingers.

"Still, I can't imagine him boarding his family on PT boats in the middle of the night, right under the enemy's nose."

"It is difficult, sir."

"So you were on Corregidor, taken prisoner and escaped, is that correct?"

Tightness strapped Stan's chest, but he took a deep breath to ward it off. The Colonel was after more specifics than he'd reckoned.

"It was such a confusing time, sir. We never imagined a full surrender, and I doubt that General MacArthur authorized..."

He cleared his throat and began again.

"When the rumors of surrendering to the enemy multiplied, it was hard to believe. But finally we had to, and stories of the way the Japs brutalized the Filipinos ran rampant. No one trusted them in the least.

"One night, a captain who had instructed us during my training in California told me he'd decided to follow the example of some other officers. They had already made it across the bay, he said. Knowing this officer's patriotism and wisdom, it didn't take me long to join him.

"He was the last person I would expect to disobey orders, but what he suggested made sense. What good could we do in captivity?

"A few hours later, we found a skiff and took off from Corregidor. By then, the rumors had proven true—General Wainwright had surrendered, and the enemy was about to herd our unit to a camp."

"You weren't discovered?"

"We were, but both of us knew how to swim, and there were others escaping, too. I guess the enemy gave up on us and went after somebody else. Once we hit land, we made for the hills."

"You must have trusted this captain without question."

Stan rubbed his hands together. "Yes. Back in California, he'd shared packages from his family with us. He was an ROTC instructor on his campus. He'd almost earned a full professorship."

"Is that right?" Colonel Lobdell put his elbows on his desk as though he had all the time in the world.

"We knew there were natives hostile to the enemy up in the hills, and after two days of scrabbling through the jungle, we picked up another American. A few days later, we found some guerillas—or they found us, and from then on, we did what we could to harass the Japs."

"Mmm..." The Colonel shook his head. "Our men held captive over there; do you have any information about them?"

A lump the size of a thick steak threatened, so Stan cleared his throat. "We saw some of them, sir, on the way up the mountain, or what was left of them. We happened to cross the trail they were climbing.

"They were in terrible condition. We witnessed Japanese officers beating and shooting men too weak to stand upright." He cleared his throat again. "Some had already died on the trail—we found bodies.

"Cabanatuan is about a hundred miles north of Manila. The distance and elevation would test anyone, but these men were already sick and malnourished."

Colonel Lobdell arched an eyebrow.

"Later, we found out that General Wainwright, General King and other officers were taken to Tarlac prison camp, but by August, Filipino scouts told us that had been emptied. Word had it they boarded a Jap ship. More recently, I've heard that the O'Donnell prisoners were being transferred to Cabanatuan."

Colonel Lobdell rubbed his forehead. When he looked up, his eyes glinted, but he said nothing. People passed in the hall, and voices came from another office. When he spoke, his voice had lowered.

"So you actually witnessed our men being marched toward the camps?"

"We did, sir. We were lost at the time, but once we found some guerilla fighters who knew the country better, they helped us draw maps and we figured out where we'd been."

"How long was it until you were wounded?"

"About ten months, sir."

"You managed that long in the jungle? Impressive. But then you were wounded, and someone saved your leg?"

"Yes, sir—the concoctions the natives gave me were revolting, but they must have worked." Even the memory made Stan wince. "As for getting me off the island, there are lots of little coves, so our forces were still making clandestine runs in and out after the surrender."

"A PT boat hauled you to a hospital ship?"

"Sir, I was in no shape to notice details. I do recall a submarine being involved, and some of the coves are narrow and deep enough to handle one."

"So you recuperated aboard ship, and then in a hospital?"

"Yes, sir. After a couple of surgeries."

"It's your knee, correct?"

"My left one."

"I assume you spent some time at home?"

"Yes, sir."

"Then you came here, and now you want to go back."

"That's right."

"I can understand." The Colonel crossed over to the window. "My hat is off to you for your bravery in the line of duty."

Heat razed Stan's neck and face. If only the Colonel knew his cowardice in other areas.

"For the record, I know a couple of those captive officers personally. What a shame. Such a waste."

The clock marked a minute… more. Colonel Lobdell kept staring outside. Finally, he turned and scrutinized Stan.

"Well, then." He returned to his desk and scribbled something on a piece of paper. "Take this to our doctors and be sure to explain about your injury—surgeries, everything. I wouldn't want to be responsible for your demise."

They locked eyes for a long moment.

"In the meantime, I'll make some connections. As soon as I get the medical go-ahead, we'll start the paperwork. I appreciate your intensity, Private Ford. From what we're hearing, the invasion will begin in the next few months."

Quelling his urge to lurch from his chair and shout, "Hurray!" Stan stayed in place. Nothing like a show of emotion to change the Colonel's mind.

Colonel Lobdell still took his time. "If the Army does call you back in, I'd like you to do one thing, if it's possible."

"Sir? Of course..."

"I'd like to know how it goes for you. By the time you return, we might have closed up this camp, and I'll be back home in Nebraska. But I'm pretty sure your quest will keep me up nights. Would you drop me a line and tell me about your mission?"

"Why, yes. I—"

"Here. I'll write down our address, just in case."

He scribbled for half a minute and handed Stan another note.

"Keep in mind that I have no idea if unfilled slots exist. This is a complicated business, and I imagine General Krueger, down in New Guinea, has his fingers in every single decision."

He saluted and offered his hand. "Good luck, son. I'll let you know as soon as I get word."

Chapter Twenty-nine

"So you finally made it down here." Clear blue eyes greeted Twila as she lined up pieces of chocolate cake on a tray in the USO kitchen.

"Finally?"

"I've been waiting." The dimple in Stan's left cheek stood out. "Well, to be honest, I've only been here three times, but I always watch for you."

"I'm on a mission for my aunt. See that sparkly young chick carrying the apple cider pitcher?"

"The one in the bright red dress? The one busy flirting with that captain? Wow—that girl really knows how to bat her eyes, doesn't she?"

"Um hm—you said it. She's my niece, sweet 16 but thinks she's 23. Name's Diana, and my aunt sent me as her chaperone. If you promise to keep an eye on her, I might dance with you later."

"Offering me a payback, are you?"

"Whatever works."

With a grin, Stan backed away to let her pass to the refreshment table. Seconds later, three soldiers descended on the cake, and, she soon discovered, on her.

"New around here, aren't you?"

She shook her head, and another fellow chimed in. "I've seen you out at the camp, haven't I? Are you a nurse?"

"Sorry, I haven't noticed you."

He didn't skip a beat. "That's all right, I noticed *you*. Come on, let's have a dance, sweetheart."

The third soldier, sporting a military police patch, watched them go, but wasted no time following. They'd only danced half a minute when he latched onto her hand.

"Can't trust this guy. You'll be safe with me, I'm an MP."

As he swept her onto the floor, a local band continued "There'll be blue birds over the white cliffs of Dover..."

"So, where are you from?"

"Here—Iowa. And you?"

"Virginia hill country. Never saw such plain land in all my life. How do you stand it?"

"Maybe that's why they call this the plains. Are you insulting my home?"

"Nah, but don't you ever hanker for some hills and valleys?"

"I'm too busy. If you're pining for your home so much, maybe they need to find you more work at the camp."

His raised eyebrows made her chuckle. He launched into his rendition of why Dover, England had never seen a blue bird and never would... but who cared?

Another cake eater tapped his shoulder, and Twila found herself in a third set of arms.

"You look good in them polka-dots, Miss."

"Why thank you. Too bad the army can't come up with something more interesting for your uniforms."

This guy was from Michigan, unable to enlist because of a bad accident with a horse when he was young. "Wrecked my back, but it sure makes me feel good to be doin' something for the cause."

When the song ended, he led her back to the refreshments. "Wonderful cake—did you make it?"

"No, that was the fine women of Algona. And it looks like I'd better go cut some more."

At first, she couldn't find Diana. Then she spotted her with a lanky, blond-haired fellow in the far corner and gave a relieved sigh. Stan looked genuinely interested in what she was saying. What a great guy—she'd been missing him, and tonight he seemed like his old self again.

Not much later, he caught her eye and grinned as if to say, "I'm taking you up on your challenge."

Two trays of cake later, he sidled up beside her. "I delivered your charge into the hands of the shyest guy here. If Albert gets the nerve to ask her to dance, I'll be shocked. But she won't be surprised. I set her up to help the poor fella. Told her he's been through a lot, which he has, and that he needs extra attention, which he does."

"Thank you."

He leaned closer. "*Don't Sit Under the Apple Tree With Anyone Else But Me* is our dance."

The low decorated lights reflected in his eyes, and a trill of disappointment enveloped her. She would have been happy to dance with him right now.

But instead, he helped her carry pitchers and trays. Chatting made the evening go faster, and by the time song started, she knew a lot more about him. He had older brothers working with his dad in Wisconsin, and a younger one who'd enlisted.

Stan even shared a little about his service. "Being overseas showed me you can adjust to anything. When my orders came for this place, I'd have liked something closer to the front, but now I'm inclined to think coming here was part of a long-range plan."

"Really?"

He picked up a heavy apple cider jug. "Yes. Mind if I help you pour?"

Fifty cups later, she asked, "Don't you want to be out on the dance floor?"

"I'm glad to do K.P." When he set the cider down, his eyes held hers. "There's only one girl I'm interested in dancing with."

Her heart lurched, and he glanced around. "We could dance this one, but I see Diana's gotten bored with Albert. Another guard is headed her way, and I have my doubts about him. Gotta keep my end of our bargain."

He disappeared into the crowd. A gaggle of soldiers trooped through the door, and Twila hurried back to the kitchen for more sandwiches. Some of these recruits looked like they just graduated from high school, or hadn't yet—probably home on first leave.

She couldn't help noticing one in particular. Tall and muscular, he looked a lot like Butch. Maybe a local girl was offering refreshments to him and his buddies somewhere in Europe. Maybe he was dancing with some cute girl...

A few minutes later, Diana appeared. "Stan said you need me. What for?"

"We're almost out of sandwiches. Make as many as you can, and thanks. Having fun?"

"Yeah. Who'd ever have thought all these guys would show here?"

"You never know. I used to feel so hopeless in Halberton, but the war turned things around—it led me here."

Diana put on a pout. "But I can't *date* any of them. My folks are the meanest parents in the world."

"They let you come tonight, didn't they? At least you can *look*, and practice making conversation. In two years, you'll be dating all you want. But don't you have any other ideas about your future?"

"Like working my fingers to the bone? You know what Mom did before the war? She worked for a grocer; did inventory hours on end. That's not for me, and I don't want to be a secretary or teach a bunch of snotty-faced little kids all day."

"What would you like to do?"

"Maybe be a pilot, if the war's still on. I heard about a woman who's going to fly P-39 Airacobras to Alaska for the Russians."

"Seriously? You're starting to sound like Benny."

"What an insult! I only know about those planes because a guy in our class did a report on them. Anyway, wouldn't it be something to fly a plane all the way to Alaska?"

"Sure would, but a girl would have to go to flight school, right?"

"Yeah, and she'd have to graduate from high school first. I get your meaning."

All for the Cause

Twila shoved another loaf of bread her way. "Here, make some more. And pretty soon, it'll be time to call it a night."

"You're a great gal, Twila, the best I know, but any day, I could get called back to the Pacific.' Stan made a fist at himself in the bathroom mirror. "That's what you should have said last night. But what *did* you say? Thanks for dancing with me, that's what."

He spread shaving cream on his face to the tune of a quote from Cap—the guy was relentless.

Fortune favors the brave…

"Brave—yeah, that's me. Courageous about fighting the Japs, but quavering like a 13-year-old with his first girl."

Giving himself another fierce look, he finished shaving and gave him himself another talking-to. "It's no good to keep her in the dark. You're going to tell her the next time you see her. Got that?"

He nodded, but the next second, doubts invaded. He had to admit that this girl had claimed a place in his heart. That dance with her last night—he never should have let it happen.

The band had slowed down so much at the end, and having her so close, right there in his arms—not a good idea at all. Maybe those members of churches who believed dancing was a sin were right.

All night long his nerves had been on edge, but he made it through the day somehow. But then in the dining room, the radio blasted a story that stopped him short.

> What a summer 1944 has been—our boys have driven the enemy out of Saipan, Guam, and Tinian. Still engaged in battle for Peleliu, each day they come closer to victory.
>
> Looks like it's time for General Mac—'I shall return!' to liberate the Philippines. We're kept in the dark

about the details for good reason, I'm sure. But make no mistake, we will never forget those held captive on Bataan.

A long pause led to the newscaster making an announcement:

Ladies and Gentlemen, a fresh report has just crossed our desk. We interrupt our prescribed broadcast to bring you the latest war news bulletin.
Today, troops from General Krueger's Sixth Army have landed on the island of Leyte in the southern Philippines, with General MacArthur watching from the light cruiser USS Nashville. Later, he arrived off the beach under sporadic mortar fire.
When his whaleboat grounded in knee-deep water, the General requested a landing craft, but the beach master was unable to provide one.
Undaunted, General MacArthur waded ashore and read the following prepared speech.

Some papers rustled over the airwaves. Sweat dripped down Stan's back. He could picture that wade to shore, hear the lap of the waves, and see the water sparkling.

More rustling—a spurt of static—Stan gritted his teeth. This fool radio had better not stop working now.

"*People of the Philippines: I have returned. By the grace of Almighty*

All for the Cause

God our forces stand again on Philippine soil—soil consecrated in the blood of our two peoples. We have come dedicated and committed to the task of destroying every vestige of enemy control over your daily lives, and of restoring upon a foundation of indestructible strength, the liberties of your people."

And that's the way it is on this twentieth day of October, 1944. Pray for the liberation of the Philippines and our brave soldiers held in enemy prison camps there.

The invasion was practically underway. Stan dropped his fork. The meatloaf and mashed potatoes he'd been so hungry for swarmed before his eyes. While he fought for control, others at his table placed bets on how long it would take MacArthur to liberate the islands.

"He's kept Australia safe—that's one down. I wager a month will do it."

"That's what we thought when our boys crossed the Channel, too, but look what a tangle they got into before they finally took Cherbourg. Now the same thing's happening with the sweep into Germany. Some sweep... it's more like a shuffle."

An officer added, "Battles are like mountains seen from a distance. They're usually far higher than they appear. When we get closer, we get a better idea how high they are. But when we climb them, it still takes longer than we expect."

Visions of destroyed Imperial Navy ships in the Leyte harbor inundated Stan. By the time this was all over, there'd be nothing left of the islands. He got up and walked outdoors to calm his nerves.

A month—no, longer than that. Three months? Six? The General had arrived, but that was only the beginning.

Who could guess how much time and blood it would take to rout the Japs from secure hiding places? Along the side of the building he halted and slapped his hands on the framework.

Come on, Colonel Lobdell... hurry it up!

It wasn't the Colonel, he knew. It was the Army, which was far worse. When did its wheels ever work efficiently, much less fast? Steeling himself for a disquieting evening, he headed for the barracks.

He'd never known so much impatience about anything. How much longer would he have to wait? Better take a long run tonight and use up all this extra energy.

"Miss Brunner, would you mind stopping by my office after your shift?"

A summons to the office... had she somehow failed in her duties? For the rest of the mild October afternoon, Twila pondered.

In the end, Nurse Alcott arrived late and asked only a few routine questions. She was *checking up to see how you're doing*, she said.

"Have you noticed any adverse effects from watching that surgery the other day? It was enough to make even an experienced nurse squeamish."

"No, ma'am."

"Would you mind dressing prisoners' wounds with Edna tomorrow?"

"I'm glad to help."

Nurse Alcott wasn't one to waste precious time, so this brief interview left Twila puzzled. Watching the surgery had been the highlight of the week—why should it have troubled her?

Viewing all those layers of muscle and tissue opened up to the air made what she read in the textbooks come alive. Besides that, she hadn't been asked to do anything particularly upsetting.

On the walk home, the past few months paraded before her. Compared to her mundane life back in Halberton, she'd come alive, too—before, she felt as if she life were passing her by. Now, she was *living* it.

Hopefully, things would continue like this. Every day brought a new challenge, and always there was something to learn. She paused on a street corner, breathing in the cool fall air. She'd always liked seasonal changes, especially this one.

So much good had come her way since that spring night she sent up her simple prayer for guidance. Seemed a long time ago already, even though only a year and a half had passed.

Work here at the camp excited her, and at home, things were going well. Benny had found a niche in her heart, and sometimes Diana almost seemed like a younger sister.

One night last summer, when Aunt Margaret had to stay late at work, Wendell came to listen to the news with Benny. The midsummer weed crop beckoned, and Diana followed her outside without being asked. For the first time, they had a good talk.

When they finished, an enormous pile of weeds languished on the burn pile. Washing up at the pump, Twila sprayed Diana with cold water. Diana returned the favor, and they chased each other around the yard.

Aunt Margaret's face was a study when she found them on the ground, laughing so hard they gasped for air. After that, Diana's nasty looks dwindled, though she still glared at Margaret and Benny.

A driver beeped his horn at a cross street, and Twila waved—he worked at the camp. This town seemed more and more like home, but sometimes she wondered about Aunt Margaret, like the day Diana peeled a big dishpan full of apples and was about to throw the peelings on the rubbish heap.

"Diana Valentine, you're throwing away half of the good part. Do you think we can just go and buy applesauce this winter?"

"Do you want us eating worms?"

"You don't throw out a whole apple because of a worm hole!"

Diana threw up her hands. "I can't do anything right."

A wall of silence transformed the rest of the afternoon into misery. *Had* Diana ever pleased her mother?

Something unique happened at the camp during late summer, too. The prisoners picked tons of sweet corn and peas for local farmers and canning factories—in fact, they saved Minnesota's pea harvest. But they refused to eat corn. They called it "food for swine."

Shock filled the staff. Not eat sweet corn, such a delicacy here? Yes, Stan said, in Germany farmers only fed corn to swine. The incident riled the Americans and a guard described the situation in the dining hall.

"Can you believe the Colonel backed down? It's a cultural thing, he said, not worth fighting over. The prisoners keep eating plain old potatoes like always, and we get more sweet corn. Not a bad deal, eh?"

"When we finish bombing the motherland, these fellows might be so hungry, they'll beg for an ear of sweet corn. But you're right, the Colonel knows when to pass on a fight."

The other guard grinned. "Yeah—show your strength only when necessary."

Benny had taught her what was and wasn't worth fighting over, too. For his first eighth grade assignment, he wrote an essay about the war that his teacher refused to accept.

According to him, "We have to describe something without naming it. Then we read our work out loud and the class tries to guess what we wrote about."

"So what did you choose?"

"The Norden Bombsight. Nothing's more important to the Air Force. But Miss Braley said most of the class couldn't possibly guess what I was describing.

"She said I needed to choose something ordinary that we see around home every day. I told her I made a model of the bombsight up in my room, and I look at it every single day."

He huffed and puffed when Margaret said he needed to cooperate with Miss Braley. "I'm not gonna. There's a war on and here we are, wasting time on silly stuff."

All for the Cause

"Did you tell her that?"

"Yeah, and she got pretty mad. Said she was going to discuss this with you and give me an F, but my report was better'n everybody else's. I mean, Lorraine described a comb, and only wrote half a page. Richard Akers picked his little brother's old red wagon—how dumb is that?"

"You do not use that word in this house." Aunt Margaret's sigh swept the back porch steps. "Oh, where is your father when I need him?'

Later, Twila suggested having Benny talk with Harry over the phone. His teacher dug her heels in, so Aunt Margaret agreed, and Benny came home from talk smiling. Harry had suggested he change his subject to aluminum foil.

"I'm gonna explain how people line baking pans and wrap stuff like cookies in it, but the military uses it for important stuff like electrical capacitors. Didja know foil can double as insulation and anti-radar chaff?"

"I had no idea—in fact, I don't know what you mean by *chaff*."

"It's stuff in the air that keeps the Germans from siting your plane. Pilots on bombing missions drop tin foil as a radar shield."

After he went to bed, Aunt Margaret reached into the brandy cabinet. "When Harry does come home, I'm taking a long vacation."

"You deserve one. But you won in the end—remember that."

"Maybe, except now Benny knows where I work. That scares me to pieces."

And so autumn had begun. Frost started nipping the maple leaves, and the ever-changing round of heat and cold, summer and winter, struck a melancholy chord as Twila started supper.

Diana brought the mail. "You've got two letters today. Gotta go over to Betty's for a while. See you later."

Mom's handwriting, black ink against a white envelope, spoke carefulness. The first letter conveyed a message from Dad—he'd been temporarily sent to Fort Vancouver.

"He's living on Officers' Row and rooming with an Army Air

Corps clerk. He described how Jeep carriers transport airplanes to the Far East from the airfield there, and says he often passes General Wainwright's office. Since the General was taken prisoner on Bataan, rescuing those poor GI's is all people out there can talk about."

Her second letter broke Twila's heart.

Marvin and Edna got word last week that Butch was wounded in France and taken to an army hospital. I wish that were all, but today, they learned he died a few days later, and the army buried him in France.

"No! First Char, and now Butch?"

The funeral is on the twelfth, the day before Butch's birthday. I'm enclosing bus fare to come home. Margaret will want to know, and tell her I hope she decides to come.

The paper floated to the floor, and Twila buried her face in her hands. Her whisper sounded loud in her ears. "Butch just can't be gone." But the harsh truth stared back at her in Mom's handwriting.

...buried him in France..."

Telling Aunt Margaret was going to be pure agony.

Chapter Thirty

"Never did hear that old balcony creak like this before." Tobias Strait scratched his head, and Archie Zaborski craned his neck.

"Hopefully, your forebears did arithmetic when they built this steeple. Mine were still in Slovakia then."

"Don't know as I'd wanna sit up there today, m'self. Downright rickety, I say."

A mild breeze carried comments to an endless line of relatives and friends waiting in front of the church. Speaking in whispers, women clutched purses. Their husbands stood beside them, stoic in the face of this grim reality.

The pain in Mom's crestfallen face struck Twila when she stepped off the train last night. When they met Aunt Margaret, Diana and Benny at the depot this morning, Mom and Aunt Margaret embraced each other. They'd stuck close ever since.

Finally, the pastor held up his hands for quiet, and a spit-shined black Monroe Funeral Services hearse delivered its load to eight pallbearers. Everyone knew Butch had been buried across the ocean, but those eight young men still showed great care. After they took seats in the first pew on the left, Marvin's family started toward the front of the church.

Their ascent instigated a fresh outbreak of weeping. Friends and neighbors sobbed for this native son who would never again enter this church—not for his wedding, his own children's baptisms, or Sunday services.

Beside Marvin and Edna, children lined the first pew. Next, Aunt

Margaret and Mom trekked down the aisle. Behind Rodney and Sharon, who held tow-headed baby Luke, Twila fell in step. From Rodney's arms, Lilly's plaintive question rent the still air.

"Where's Butch?"

"Shh."

She veered toward Twila, who was glad for the company. She took Lilly to the pew behind Rodney and Sharon and buried her face in the mild flowery scent of Lilly's hair. Small comfort. How could she explain so Lilly could comprehend?

In the next pew, Char's grandmother sat alone. Had she even been able to attend Char's funeral?

The choir chorused, *Blest be the tie that binds our hearts in Christian love...*

Could Butch hear them? Was what they sang true—a tie bound him to everyone from the next world?

Mom's letter said he died in a high casualty firefight to liberate a small French town, and last night, Uncle Marvin confirmed that fact. As if it made any difference—knowing he fell with his comrades provided little consolation.

As more and more people gathered in the farmhouse, Uncle Marvin kept saying maybe someday they'd bring Butch home. Mom had been so jittery that Twila felt uneasy too. After all, this was the house where she'd grown up, where she'd returned after Kenneth died.

Rodney was talking with Butch's brothers, so the visit stretched into half an hour. Somehow, Mom survived, and Aunt Edna hugged her just before they left.

"Thanks for coming, Myra. I've been meaning to..."

Marvin, as stoic as a fence post, repeated, "...bring him home... so he can rest in peace..." as Twila shook his hand. Finally outside, she drew in the fresh pre-winter air in tandem with Mom.

Bring him home—simple words with such powerful meaning. Having Butch at rest in the town cemetery would mean a lot, but they'd still miss his quick wit and kindness for the rest of lives.

All for the Cause

His class ring, wrapped in white embroidery floss, weighed on Twila's finger. When she'd offered it to the family last night, Uncle Marvin refused.

"He wanted you to keep it."

As the service began, Lilly fiddled with the ring. "Today, Halberton says goodbye to its second son to die for the cause of freedom. Mark these words—we will never forget."

Years of Decoration Days with purple iris sprays and lilac bouquets paraded through Twila's mind. Of course they'd never forget—how could they?

Within minutes, Lilly's relaxed breathing declared that she'd fallen asleep. The scripture reading led into *There's a Land That is Fairer Than Day.*

A lump kept Twila from singing, but the words flooded her.

...the Father waits over the shore... prepare us a dwelling place there... in the sweet by and by...

The pastor's booming voice filled the sanctuary with Butch's obituary. Then he spoke of eternal hope beyond this veil of tears.

Hope—that's what we need, but what does it mean?

A shuttered breath from the pew ahead of them alerted Twila. Next to Aunt Margaret, Diana narrowed her eyes, and Benny, up to his ears in a starched white shirt, stiffened. The next moment, Mom bent over double and Aunt Margaret pulled her out of the pew.

Stumbling over Diana and Benny, the duo made it into the aisle. Mom's Sunday shoes barely touched the oaken floorboards, and terror rode her features.

Magnetized, Twila picked up Lilly's sleeping form and left by the other aisle. Most onlookers still craned necks the other direction, hoping for another sight of Myra Brunner, the town recluse.

Who cared what they thought, anyway? Twila knew only that she must follow. Holding Lilly tight, she navigated the stairs. Thankfully, at the bottom, she could turn right or left, hidden by a floor-length velvet drape that separated the Sunday school rooms.

In a back corner, she eased to the cool floor as Mom's anguish swept every inch of the dark basement. She trembled at the sound—unearthly, and so unlike her mother.

"There, now." Could that soothing tone be coming from Aunt Margaret? If only she could comfort Diana and Benny like this.

With only the clock's *tick-tock* for accompaniment, Mom's voice sounded hollow, like it came from a cave. "Kenneth... Mama..."

"I know." Margaret's groan echoed Mom's.

"Awful d-days..."

"I don't know how any of us made it through."

"After... after you left..."

"I knew it would make things worse for you, but I had to get out. Can you ever forgive me?"

"Forgive *you*?" Mom's voice splintered.

"I knew Mother would turn her weapons on you when we were gone." Margaret's voice broke, too. "Blaming you was wrong, but losing Kenneth almost..."

An avalanche of fresh sobs. When they finally subsided, Margaret started again. "Everything got so out of control, and Marvin just couldn't shut up. Drove me crazy."

"Mother never..."

"Forgave you? Forgiveness was beyond her, don't you think?"

"But the little ones. They shouldn't have had to pay."

"They got out of there—we were all broken and miserable—especially Mother. Leaving may have meant deliverance to them."

"Do you... know?"

"No. But we could try to find out."

"You think so?"

"Marvin probably still has the address somewhere. When this is all over, why don't we ask him? Then maybe we could put this to rest, especially now, with Butch..."

"I couldn't ask him."

"Someday we can. Together."

"I've been thinking about Paul so much lately. Have you heard anything yet?"

"Oh..." With a guttural moan, Aunt Margaret collapsed. Such an anguished cry—Twila prayed Lilly wouldn't waken, and she slept blissfully on.

It was Mom's turn to pat Margaret's back and whisper comforting words.

"How can it take so long for them to...?"

"I don't know, but I'd rather not get another letter." Margaret's voice shattered into more sobs.

"I'm so sorry..."

At last, between gasps, Margaret managed, "I can't imagine him not coming home. That just can't happen. I couldn't bear it. He's always been my..." She wept again.

Finally, the two women quieted. The terrible truth was out. What was left to say? Upstairs, the organist pumped out the opening strains of a hymn. Twila cowered as Mom and Aunt Margaret shuffled across the cement floor toward the stairway.

With them on the first step... the second, she dared to draw a full breath. Then Lilly stirred.

Please... just another few minutes...

Shuffling sounded from above as people took seats. Still, Twila shrank back, as if to keep this experience close... She'd just witnessed something monumental—things could never be the same as they had been after this. She'd overheard a holy conversation.

Carrying Lilly up, step by step, a realization hit. Maybe this tortured scene had something to do with that illusive word *hope*.

```
     Two days ago, German forces barri-
caded two hundred Dutch citizens from
a city called Heusden in the town hall
and blew up the building. If we thought
our enemy would be less fearsome in
retreat, we were mistaken.
     After the massive German surrender at
```

Aachen on October 21, we all breathed easier—surely this meant the war would end soon. But determined to thwart the Allied advance into Germany, our enemy has heavily reinforced the Siegfried Line.

One encouraging note: one of the Luftwaffe's best ace pilots is no more. Major Walter Nowotny recently crashed over his homeland.

On the home front, President Franklin Roosevelt has won his fourth consecutive term as U.S. president. Yesterday told the tale at polls all across the nation. Would we break with tradition and re-elect FDR? Now we know the answer.

"I'm so sick of the news, I could scream!" Aunt Margaret dropped a glass she was drying, and Twila squatted to help pick up the shards. Two weeks had passed since Butch's funeral, and for some reason, Aunt Margaret had become even more tense these past few days.

"I know. Hearing about our victories makes me think things should calm down. Somebody at work said the way things are going, the war ought to be over by Christmas, but it sure doesn't look that way."

Someone knocked at the back door, and Aunt Margaret hurried into the back porch. She let a man in, and conversation vied with Benny and Wendell zooming homemade Spitfires through the living room.

Then Margaret peeked her head back into the kitchen. "Twila, would you mind running up to my room for my billfold? I think it's on my dresser."

All for the Cause

Ducking through a major dogfight over London, Twila ran upstairs and opened Aunt Margaret's door. She'd only been in here once, so she turned on a small lamp just inside the door. No need to worry—the blackout curtains were already drawn.

No billfold on the dresser, so she moved to the nightstand. She ran her hand over the top, and something fluttered down—a sheet of paper that landed face-up. Holding it for a second revealed a brief, typewritten message.

```
October 20, 1944
Mr. and Mrs. Harry Valentine
   Your son, Ensign Paul R. Valentine,
has now been missing in action in the
Pacific Theater for over one year. De-
spite all attempts, we have been un-
able to locate him.
   With gratitude for his faithful ser-
vice and sorrow for your loss, the U.S.
Navy regrets to inform you that Ensign
Valentine's status has been altered to
Presumed Dead.
```

Tears burned Twila's eyes as the paper fell from her hands. October twentieth... this must have arrived right after the funeral. Trembling, she lifted it again and scanned the message.

No mistaking its meaning. *Paul Valentine... Presumed Dead.*

With the telltale letter back on Aunt Margaret's nightstand, she finally spotted the billfold on a corner table. Sick at heart, she switched off the lamp and delivered the billfold to her aunt.

Thankfully, her visitor had a gift for chatter, so she raced to finish the dishes and hung the towels to dry. But Aunt Margaret came back in before she could leave.

"That was a friend of Harry's from the American Legion. Just had to make a donation, since they're sending Christmas packages to our boys. Thanks for finishing the dishes. Guess I'll go write to Paul."

A cold chill traced Twila's shoulders—did this mean Aunt Margaret didn't believe the Navy? A few minutes later when she entered the living room, Aunt Margaret gave Benny instructions for tomorrow morning. She tossed a few in for Wendell, too, and paused when Twila started upstairs.

"No news for you tonight? And no checkers?"

"No, thanks. I'm extra tired. Think I'll read a little and go to bed early." She retreated to her room and sat on the bed. All around her hung vestiges of the cousin she'd barely met—Paul's Hawkeye pennants on the wall, his letter jacket in the closet.

She opened the door and smoothed her fingers down the white leather sleeve. He was so young, Margaret and Harry's firstborn, and he'd been Margaret's favorite... that seemed obvious. And now she simply could not accept the news that he had died.

"If only I could talk this over with Stan." It had been a long time since she'd wanted to sneak out of the house at night, but right now, that didn't seem like such a bad idea.

Chapter Thirty-one

"Private Ford and Private Cobb, stop by before you go to lunch."

Stan joined the logistics officer with a guard he'd seen only a few times.

"You've been assigned to bring back some prisoners from the Waverly camp tomorrow—one of you to each truck. You'll return by evening and there will be only one stop on the way home, with bathroom privileges.

"We're a little short-handed right now, with all of the surrenders in Europe, but the driver will also be armed. Any questions?"

The other guard spoke up. "Should we take extra ammunition?"

"I don't think that will be called for—these prisoners have been exemplary for three months at present worksite in Waverly. Oh, I forgot—we'll send lunches along for the return trip. You'll take up your normal duties here on Wednesday."

During the midday meal, Stan considered. Should he be glad for this day of reprieve from watching and waiting for a call to Colonel Lobdell's office? He wasn't sure, but it still hadn't been a full week since meeting, awfully fast to have heard back from the command.

On the other hand, he'd be so disgusted if he missed the summons and had to wait another twenty-four hours. The way he saw it, each day diminished his chances, but at the same time, his determination to be a part of the liberation increased.

Either way, he had no choice, so at four a.m., he and Cobb boarded a truck bound for Waverly, a county seat about a hundred and twenty miles away. If Stan had wanted to listen to a radio en route, he wasn't short-changed, since the driver seemed to know more about the war than some commentators.

"Got a brother named Herb, back from the Navy. When his ship was torpedoed, he got some bad burns, but somehow, he made it home. Says we've come a long way since '41, when we only had one escort carrier and seven fleet carriers. Guess they was out on maneuvers when the Japs hit Pearl.

"Good thing, 'cause they fought in the Coral Sea and Midway. That's why we won, and since then, they've built what they call Essex-class carriers that launch raids far into enemy territory—17 of 'em. They're attackin' Jap bases in the Pacific, Herb says, 'n they're buildin' another one right now.

"Plus that, we've got over three thousand airplanes, and a bunch of supply ships from the west coast all the way to the theater. He swears we're gonna win, but it'll take some time."

The pride in his voice carried over the engine's roar. Every now and then, Stan interjected a comment.

"Sounds as if your brother really keeps up with things. He must have some solid connections."

"Oh, yeah. He's got buddies in California—gets letters every week. Besides that, some of 'em come see him when they're back here on leave."

He switched topics, and explained what had kept the Waverly site's prisoners occupied during the past few months.

"They've been split into three shifts. Been buildin' an elevator in the town of Plainfield a little ways down the road. The town's wooden one burned down in August, so it's been tough for them farmers to haul grain.

"A company out of Nebraska contracted to build one made of cement, and our prisoners been working 'round the clock. I hear they finished in nine days—how 'bout that?"

"Great—sounds like hard work to me." They passed a road sign that included mileage to the Mississippi River. "At least we're not headed to Plainfield Wisconsin. That'd be another six hours."

The driver shifted down for a curve. "These monsters are somethin' else to drive—really don't need all this power here. But for them soldiers in Europe with steep mountains along the way, this here's the Army's workhorse."

After passing through Mason City, he speeded up, and Stan learned more than he'd ever wanted to know about a deuce and a half. In fact, he already knew it all from his training, but it made sense to let this fellow drone on and on.

"She can haul 5,000 pounds—two short tons. That's how they named her. Each axle's got its own differential, so on hilly ground, you can get power to all three sets of wheels."

He took up a good share of the second hour glorying in this vehicle, with the engine's roar filling the pauses. Passing through Osage, the turn-off for Halberton caught Stan's eye.

Wonder how Twila's doing today? Probably that head nurse has her running.

At Charles City, they turned southeast, and just after sunrise, lumbered to a stop at a YMCA camp south of Waverly. Stretching cramped legs was the first priority.

Situated near the little town of Janesville, another town with a namesake in Wisconsin, this temporary camp was much smaller and far more primitive—not that different from boot camp. Rows of prisoner tents surrounded an outdoor kitchen. Small cabins for the guards and latrines rounded out the perimeter.

"Need some breakfast?" A friendly local hailed Stan from his farm truck.

"I wouldn't mind. Do you know the cook?"

"Yah." His reply sounded as German as any prisoner in Camp Algona. He left for a few minutes and returned with a steaming bowl of oatmeal swimming in cream and butter.

"Thanks. You live around here?"

"Yah. Name's Shipp. In September, they hired me to haul the prisoners up to the canning company. Back and forth, morning and night for the twelve-hour shifts. They say this was a record year—packed almost two hundred thousand cases of corn."

"What else do you haul?"

"Cream cans to the Washington Creamery—we pick 'em up from all the farms around here, and I drop a few here every morning. Always somebody who needs me to move something. It's a good living Are you from Iowa?"

"No, Wisconsin."

"Did you do any overseas duty?"

"Yeah, in the Pacific."

"Things are heatin' up there again, they say."

"So I hear. Do you know anybody serving?"

"Four sons—two Navy, two Army. Two in the Pacific, two in Europe—they don't take brothers all together any more, since we lost the Sullivan brothers."

He stared at the prisoners forming a line at the gate. "When I see these fellas, I keep thinking what if one of my boys gets captured. Maybe somebody over there'll do a good deed for them."

"I imagine you listen to the news from everywhere."

"The missus, she's tied to the radio, and always writin' another letter."

"And you haul German prisoners around..."

The man spat to the side and reached into his overall pocket for a kerchief. "It's a crazy world. I heard about a fella from down by Clarinda whose brother's in one of these camps."

"There's probably more than one family like that."

Just then a little boy ran up and yelled, "Papa, will John come with us today?"

"Not today, son. This soldier's come to take him back to Algona." The lad ran off again.

"He likes to ride with you?"

"Yah. I expect you know we have strict orders not to talk with the prisoners, but this one named John speaks good English. My youngest—he can't help talkin' to him.

"At the canning factory, people from town waited outside the door at quitting time some days. They were just hoping to have a word with them and practice the language."

He kicked at some frozen clods of earth. "Most of us around here, we still speak German. Our grandparents came direct from the old country.

"My father is having a time of it, with two grandsons fighting over there. He just shakes his head when he hears we're bombin' the southern cities now. That's where our people are from. But what's got to be has got to be."

"Mmm..." No easy answer occurred to Stan. At least *Ford* was an English name, so his family had no similar challenges.

He finished off the oatmeal and handed the trucker the bowl. "Thank you kindly, sir. I hope your sons come back safe."

Just then the little boy raced up. "Look, Papa. John gave me a gift." He opened his fingers to reveal German Army wings and a swastika from the prisoner's uniform.

"Can I keep 'em, Papa? John says he'll write to us when he gets back home."

The farmer cocked his head and studied Stan. He seemed to be waiting for him to say one way or the other.

"John must think a lot of you, son. Just keep them to yourself." The boy pocketed his treasures, and his father rustled his hair.

"Prob'ly thankful he had somebody to talk to. Must get awful lonely for his family."

"I would say so."

Stan sat in the back, so the trip home was louder and rougher. With the prisoners caught up in own thoughts, he considered that little boy's grandfather having *a time of it*. Must be difficult to realize his own people were fighting the United States.

Such a complicated war—his pondering soon led to picturing Twila at work in the American ward, and eventually gave way to the rhythm of the wheels on the pavement.

Thankfully, Cap kept his distance on this stint. After an hour, prisoners' heads bobbed, and the truck box filled with snores. Sitting next to the tailgate, where a prisoner would have to plow through him in order to escape, Stan allowed himself to doze.

The morning after Twila learned about Paul, Aunt Margaret plunged ahead as usual. A bracing November wind allowed for only brief conversation on the walk to work. That was a relief—less opportunity to let last night's discovery slip.

The whole day, she looked for Stan, but by three o'clock, had almost given up. Maybe his shift had changed—with so many new prisoners this fall, that often happened.

About this time, Nurse Alcott bustled her way "One of the men needs an emergency appendectomy. Would you like to assist me?"

Tamping down a thrill, Twila kept her reply short. "Yes, ma'am."

"There'll be—this will get messy. You're sure you can handle that?"

A doctor whizzed by as she nodded. Nurse Alcott seemed lost in thought for a few seconds, but then gave a curt order. "Follow me. I'll show you how to wash up. Once we get underway, do exactly as I say."

No time to wonder where Edna was or why she hadn't been tapped for this duty. A surge of energy enveloped Twila at the prospect of learning something new.

Observing the surgery from about six feet away, she only wished she could be closer. With the officer administering ether, the doctor and Nurse Alcott worked in such harmony, they might have practiced the procedure a few minutes ago.

In the end, only used scalpels and other instruments came her way, to place in the *To Be Sterilized* bin. The rest of the time, a remarkable, life-saving operation took place before her eyes.

When the surgeon said, "See this section? If we had waited much longer, the tissue would have burst, and this guard would have been in big trouble."

Straining to see, she controlled her curiosity. How could he tell the appendix would have burst?

After they left the surgical theater and cleaned up, Nurse Alcott returned to the ward with her. The whole way, she asked questions.

"What did you think?"

"That was so interesting. I wish I could have been closer."

"Really? Nothing bothered you?"

"No. It was so exciting to see the way you three worked together. But I would like to know how the surgeon realized the appendix was about to burst."

"An excellent question, Miss Brunner. I believe he would say the coloration and signs of strain on the tissues. I have another book I could lend you, with some pictures of symptoms that might help."

"Oh, good. Shall I stop by for it this afternoon?"

"Yes. In fact, I'll put it on the shelf outside my door, in case I'm not in. What about the initial cutting? Did you notice anything in particular?"

"I couldn't see much, really. But I did notice how you were right there with the sponge, even before the doctor asked."

"Mmm. You are quite observant." Nurse Alcott rubbed her hands together, always a sign that a conversation was at an end, so Twila tucked away several more questions.

"Well then. Continue with your work—you'll have to hustle to finish up."

"I don't mind staying late. Seeing the surgery was worth it."

Nurse Alcott's expression was impossible to read, a mix of puzzlement and pleasure and... But Twila tucked away her curiosity. Between her boss and Aunt Margaret, she was getting plenty of practice at figuring out reactions.

Leaving the building half an hour later than normal, she added the nursing book to her satchel. She put on her coat and scarf in the cloakroom and looked around for Stan. Not a trace, so she started home.

These late fall days grew shorter and shorter—it would be dark by the time she reached home. Hopefully Benny had filled the cob bin, and maybe this would be the night Aunt Margaret decided noses were red enough to start up the kitchen stove.

All alone in Halberton, Mom would wait a while longer, no doubt. She'd just put on another sweater and load another quilt onto her bed.

"Hey there!" The stride of a guard leaving the storage area attracted Twila's attention.

"Stan, is that you?"

"Who goes there, Florence Nightingale?" In a few moments, he stood an arm's length away.

"Exactly. I feel a little like Florence; actually got to watch a surgery today. What do you think of that?"

"That's great—what was it like?"

"I wasn't close enough to see everything, but it went well."

"Did the guy leave without an organ?"

"Yes, it was an appendectomy."

"Ouch! I haven't seen you since you went back home. Sure was sorry to hear about your cousin."

"Thanks. I was going to tell you before I left, but couldn't find you."

"Guess I've been pretty busy." His pause made her wonder, but then he went on. "Today, I got to travel cross-country in a deuce and a half for five hours. We picked up a couple loads of prisoners who've been working at the Marshall Canning factory and some other jobs over by Waverly."

"Really? Halberton would have been just north of the route you took."

"I saw the sign and thought of you." Another pause. "After all that sitting, I sure do need a walk—mind if I come along?"

"Perfect. I need to ask you something."

They fell in step and he said, "Ask away."

"All right. Would the Navy ever send a family a *Presumed Dead* letter if there was any chance the sailor was still alive?"

"Whoo boy. I hate to say never, but the chances are as close to never as I can imagine. Hopefully this isn't about Paul?"

"It is, but don't breathe a word about it, all right?"

"My lips are sealed. How did you find out?"

"By accident. Aunt Margaret sent me up to her room to get something last night, and a paper fell from her nightstand. When I picked it up—"

"You read it."

"You make it sound so wrong."

"Didn't mean to. I probably would have done the same thing if the part I saw intrigued me. That's just human nature—we're curious creatures."

"I guess so."

"You don't need to feel badly—maybe you were supposed to find out." He allowed time for her sigh. "So the letter said Paul is presumed dead now?"

No answer needed. Stan stopped and grabbed her elbow. "Wow... two of your cousins—I'm really sorry to hear this."

Walking in silence for a while, Twila swallowed her tears and relished his quiet understanding. He seemed to sense that silence might be the best thing right now. A block before Aunt Margaret's, he pulled her aside.

"Your aunt has no idea that you know?"

"No, and I dread going home. She acts as if everything's just fine. Last night, she even wrote Paul another letter."

"Whoo boy. This is rough."

"I'm not good at hiding things. Pretending has always been hard for me."

"Why do you say that?"

"My bit part in our high school play made it pretty clear." She stepped up the pace as a raw wind homed in on them.

"Well, maybe a diversion would help, at least for this evening."

"What do you mean?"

"You could invite a guest to eat with you, and he—or she—could stay around until after the evening news. He could engage Benny and you could join in. By that time, he could leave and you could slip off to bed. The way I see it, your aunt wouldn't suspect a thing."

In spite of the cold, she chuckled. "And maybe if that guest would let his teeth chatter, Aunt Margaret would realize it's freezing in the house. Maybe she'd break down and start a fire in the stove. Seeing a suffering soldier, she might bend that far."

"You haven't had a fire yet?"

"No, she's like Mom. A certain amount of suffering is required every fall before you dip into the fuel supply. It's our family rule."

"Interesting. I suppose growing up in the Depression has something to do with that. Guess we grew up with so much wood handy that my folks never saw it that way.

"Anyhow, I might be able to arrange for my teeth to chatter a couple of times. That is, if I were invited to a certain residence for the evening."

"How are you at peeling potatoes?"

"I'd say I do a better job of that than squeezing lemons."

"Well, then, I'd say we're in business."

Chapter Thirty-two

Benny burst through the kitchen door and stopped short. "Stan? What're you doin' here?"

"K.P. Your cousin's got me working my fingers off." Stan wiped his forehead with the back of his hand, sending a stream of potato water down his nose.

"Wow! Are you stayin' for supper?"

When Stan nodded, Benny turned back towards the door. "Oh wow! I'm gonna go get Wendell. We gotta show you some stuff."

He vanished quicker than he entered. In the living room, Diana and Betty half-practiced Latin declensions between wild giggles. Aunt Margaret still hadn't come home.

By the time Benny returned with a panting Wendell, the potatoes were boiling and Twila had floured some minute steaks to fry.

Stan only had time to mouth, "See you later," as the boys descended. In the midst of a flurry of war questions, he let them drag him up to Benny's room.

Half an hour later Aunt Margaret appeared, looking even more haggard than usual. Keeping her coat on, she looked around. "Where's Benny?"

"Upstairs. Wendell's up there with him. I hope you don't mind, but Stan walked me home, so Benny's got him up there with his maps."

"Oh. Well, I didn't have anything special out for supper, but if you want him to stay..."

"I thought we could make a package of minute steak go around. Is that all right?"

"Sure. I'm starving." She peeked into the living room. "Wonders never cease—those two must have low averages to bring up. Who'd have imagined them studying Latin?"

She hung her coat on a hook. "I'll set the table. Let's see, you've got the potatoes on, and we have bread and butter. How about some corn?"

"Sure, that sounds good."

She disappeared down the cellar steps, and before she came back up, Wendell raced through with a, "Late for supper—Mom'll be mad."

In the midst of a serious discussion of the invasion in Leyte, Stan and Benny sat down at the table, and Twila cast a grateful look Stan's way. He must've heard Aunt Margaret's voice and lured Benny to the kitchen.

When Aunt Margaret emerged from the cavernous basement, he asked about her day. Although she rarely said a word on that subject, she handed the jar of corn to Twila, sank into a chair and started talking.

"We had some excitement when some of the prisoners returned from Waverly. After three months away, you can imagine they were glad to be back in the commissary, with so many things to buy.

"Guess the camp at Waverly's a lot smaller, and they had to go without. Never sold so much pipe tobacco or paper in one afternoon before."

Seeing Benny gape, she caught herself, but it was too late.

"Them guys get tobacco?"

"*Those* guys. Yes." She threaded her fingers together and glanced at Stan, who blew on his hands and rubbed them together.

"Would you like me to light the stove? It's like the one my folks have. Dad wrote that he had to start ours up two weeks ago when that cold spell came through."

Aunt Margaret's eyebrows shot up. She let a few seconds pass before surveying Twila. "Does anybody else think it's cold in here?"

"Yeah, freezing!" The chorus from the living room matched Benny's exclamation.

"Oh, all right. I guess it's about time. Go ahead."

Up in a flash, Stan did her bidding, with Benny at his side. Before they went to the basement, Stan raised his eyebrows at Twila, as if to say, "Where there's a will, there's a way."

Benny begged him for a round of checkers after supper, and he agreed, but only when Diana agreed to dry the dishes in his stead.

"Did you hear that, Benny? A real man doesn't mind offering to help." Benny shrugged and ran for the checkers.

Soon, Stan called Aunt Margaret in. "We need you to referee," Such a peaceful evening. Studying must have transformed Diana. For once, she neglected to complain about her lot in the kitchen.

When the news came on, she and Twila joined the others, and toward the end, the newscaster cited continued fierce fighting and dire death tolls in Peleliu. Aunt Margaret set an even faster pace than normal for her knitting needles, and Twila focused on the checker match.

But when she saw Stan to the back door a while later, he whispered, "Oh man. You could've knocked her over with a feather when those death tolls came on."

"What can we do?"

He shrugged. "I don't know. Everybody has to face the truth in own time, I guess. But if you need to talk some more, just let me know."

He touched her chin with his fingertip and was gone.

Had he been away from his corner of the barracks for several days? True, sixteen hours had passed since he left this morning, but it seemed much longer. Lying in his bunk, Stan basked in the thought that Twila had been looking for him.

Even though the Colonel might summon him tomorrow and he could be leaving any day, he'd enjoyed tonight so much. But recalling Margaret's severe expression during the news broadcast made him shudder.

Twila had shot him a look right then. She'd noticed, too, but the children hadn't. Margaret turned so pale, she looked as though she might fall apart any second.

How could she avoid the truth much longer? And didn't her husband deserve to know about Paul? As he tossed this around in his head, one of Cap's quotes brought clarity.

"A lie can travel halfway around the world while the truth is putting on its shoes." Weeks had passed since he'd lanced one of these pithy statements. This one came from Charles Spurgeon... he'd begun to quote preachers now.

A couple of bunks over, some guards were deep into a poker game. Their hoots and hollers made great cover for his ponderings, and for chastising himself again.

He'd spent so many hours with Twila tonight, but hadn't told her a thing about his plans. Worse, when she saw him to the back door, he said thanks for the meal, but another message had been on the tip of his tongue.

He'd wanted to lean close and whisper, "If we were alone, I might take some calculated action to show you how much you mean to me."

"Like?"

"Like hold you close... hear your heart beat close to mine..."

"But Aunt Margaret might come out." She would have scrunched her nose, and he'd have replied, "Right. But the next time we're together, all bets are off, my little Iowa girl."

Now, he fumed at himself. What was the matter with him? If he left for the war, where would that leave her? So easy to tout his penchant for justice, but wasn't it unfair to lead her on? He never should have gone over to her aunt's place, never should've gotten involved with Benny.

He wanted to be a lawyer. Right... he'd be all about the truth. It was easy to think other people—like Aunt Margaret—should face it, but a lot harder when you had your own facts to face.

The fact was, Cap, Carlos, and so many other GIs might never have the opportunity to get to know a girl again, to date and marry someone. In light of situation, how could he even think to seek a young woman's attentions?

But even now, the tingle that traced his spine when he touched Twila's chin reverberated.

Nearly four weeks since he'd met with the Colonel, and still no word. Stan splashed his face with cold water and stared at his bloodshot eyes. He should've known that quiet visitation from Cap after he came home from supper at Twila's would lead to a miserable night.

Nights was more like it. The other day, he'd seen her in the hallway and chatted for a couple of minutes. She'd said that as far as she knew, nothing had changed with her aunt.

Right there in the hallway, he could have told her he was waiting for word. He wouldn't have had to lay out all the details, but at least she would know.

In his honest moments, he knew he'd fallen for her. But at the same time, if he had his way, he'd soon be headed for the South Pacific. That certainty strummed just below his breastbone. In his mind these two realities could not fit together. He had to stop living two lives, that was all.

Since that day, he'd managed to avoid her. If he broached the topic of leaving, she was too sharp—she would read his emotions about her. It wouldn't be fair to let that happen.

But the more he stayed away, the more he wanted to see her. Her companionship—her easy laughter and composure—had become a craving. For the 40th time, he determined to tell her he might be deploying.

"Just keep it brief… stick with the facts. Then say you have to get somewhere right away. Maybe right after work today, you can catch her when she's walking home."

He secured his weapon and ammunition and started making his rounds. Step by step, he'd make it through this day.

Maybe he'd see Twila and find the courage to tell her. Maybe he wouldn't. Whatever the outcome, nothing could make him lose more sleep than he already was.

A morning haze gradually lifted, but a few stormy-looking clouds hung over the camp. It wasn't too early for the first snowfall.

About an hour into the morning, another guard approached from the main compound and waved him over. "Are you Private Ford?"

"Yes."

"You're wanted right away in Colonel Lobdell's office." He held his hand out for the rifle, but Stan just stood there.

"Did you hear me? I'm taking over for you."

As if waking from a hard sleep, Stan nodded. "Yeah. Thanks."

With his M-1 in his replacement's hands, he untied his ammo vest and handed it over. After the guard walked away, he still stood there.

The moments you wait for stalk up on you. Often, they arrive when you least expect them. They shock you. You can barely take them in. He'd known this for a along time and experienced it before, but *this* time was different.

Covering the distance to the Colonel's office, he moved in slow motion—the road, the official vehicle headed out the gate, the stop sign—everything seemed larger than life. He'd wanted this summons, longed for the outcome.

But now, it would almost be easier not to know. What if he simply walked away from camp and disappeared? Stan shook himself. Never before had he even thought of going AWOL.

Sunlight blinked through intermittent clouds. The cool November breeze defied his jacket. These things he would remember, no matter how this meeting turned out, since one way or the other, his whole life would change.

As if to mark the momentous occasion, one of Cap's quotes sashayed on an air current. But something seemed peculiar. This time, there was no sense of him hovering nearby.

To improve the golden moment of opportunity, and catch the good

that is within our reach, is the great art of life. William Samuel Johnson
Within our reach...

If the Colonel had good news—if the Army wanted him—this particular golden moment could not be improved. It would be as golden as a moment can get. But if they rejected him? Well, he would have to deal with that somehow.

Outside the building, he filled his lungs and exhaled. Did so again. He simply had to expect the best.

Chapter Thirty-three

"Mail call!" Diana bounced into the living room and handed Twila two letters.

"Thanks."

"Looks like one's from overseas. Are you two-timing Stan or something?"

Since Butch's funeral, Diana had been a little easier to live with. Twila had no idea if Aunt Margaret had told her and Benny about Paul, but doubted it. One of them would have said something. She might be a professional at hiding her emotions, but neither of her children had inherited that ability.

One of the letters showed Mom's handwriting, and the other was from a guy in the class ahead of her in school. "Stan and I are friends—good friends. And just because someone writes me a letter doesn't mean we're in love, you know."

"But why would anybody write if he weren't interested in you?"

"Maybe because he's lonely?"

Diana stuck out her tongue and made a face that was easy to ignore. The guy who wrote this letter had never been close, but it seemed wise to withhold his identity for a while.

Scanning a magazine, Diana hung around while Twila opened the letters and read one. But finally the suspense got to her. "So who is this guy? Somebody from your high school class?"

"Older than that. You ought to be concerned—he's robbing the cradle."

"Oh, come on." Diana swung her legs over the side of a chair, with a beleaguered expression. She tried so hard to be grown up, but her childish impatience oozed out all over.

"Just tell me. Pretty please?"

She really was a cute girl, but her wheedling tone would drive anyone over the edge.

"I'll do better than that. I'll read you what he wrote." Diana's shocked look brought some satisfaction.

"Hey, Twi. Your mom gave me your new address, and we've got some down time while we travel. Riding in the back of this lorry, as the British call trucks, gets awful old. But it beats marching.

I heard about your new job. Can't mention specific stuff here, but it sure sounds like a challenge.

Not much news here that I can write about, but I sure do miss everybody. Take care of yourself and watch out for the bad guys.

"He doesn't sound real interesting."

"He's out on a mission. What's he supposed to write about, the latest dance step? I'm impressed that he even found paper and a pencil."

"Yeah, well..."

"Since he wrote me, I bet he doesn't have a girlfriend. Mail call without letters would be terrible for guys like that, don't you think?"

"Hmm... maybe so."

A while later, Twila added, "Oh well, he's probably too old for you, anyhow."

Diana rolled the magazine she'd been pretending to read, though Aunt Margaret hated her doing that. "Maybe he's got a buddy I could write to."

"Why don't you ask him? I can send your letter along with my next one."

Doubt crisscrossed Diana's face. "But what will I write?"

"About your friends, about school—anything. I don't think he'd really care. He just wants somebody to remember he's out there."

Several times since September, Diana had said she hated her

English class; hated writing. This would be a stretch for her, but maybe she would make the supreme effort.

"Private, I have received word for you this morning. No doubt you have been waiting anxiously."

Clasping his hands on the sides of his chair, Stan nodded.

"There's so much going on in connection with this invasion. I hate to disappoint you, but…"

If a heart could plummet to the depths of the earth, Stan's did. Heat rose from the back of his neck, and a drum rolled in his stomach.

"There is no possibility of you joining the Rangers, since they'll be entering from the south. This may occur even before the army could transport you there."

Was the Colonel enjoying this torture? He picked up a piece of paper as if to re-read something. Meanwhile, Stan scarcely dared breathe.

"But others are being sent into the island from the north. This is all top secret, but it sounds like the area where you were brought out to the hospital ship."

"Yes, sir." Stan's harsh croak sent him into a spin. He must not lose control… *must* not.

"Therefore, the army has need of you—they're going to fly you to California. You're scheduled on a flight out of Fort Des Moines on Tuesday." The Colonel shoved his chair back.

"This means the Army really desires your services, Private."

After his first full breath since entering the room, Stan bit his lip. He ought to be asking intelligent questions right now, but his brain had turned to mush.

"Next Tuesday?" That was all he could manage.

"Yes. They expect you on the coast by Friday, and these cross-country flights can take days. You'll likely be stopping at several bases along the way."

"Yes. Yes, sir."

They were *flying* him to California?

"Our shuttle might be going down the day before. I'll find out and let you know. Now, get some good sleep before then. I thought you might want to call your family to let them know?"

"Yes. I should call my brother."

"If you know his number and would like to talk with him right now, I need to be gone for a few minutes. You can use my phone—when you lift the receiver, our operator will take care of you."

He picked up a large manila envelope and stood.

Still stunned, Stan didn't think to rise until the Colonel stopped near him and held out his hand.

"Sorry, sir. I..."

"You've been waiting on pins and needles. I understand. May God go with you, son." He crossed the room, and with his hand on the doorknob, offered one more wish. "And Private, I do hope you are able to reunite with your buddies."

> November 20, 1944
> To the staff of Camp Algona.
>
> Another wartime Thanksgiving is upon us, and as this week begins, I wish to share some sentiments for this national holiday.
>
> When President Lincoln established this day of giving thanks, our nation was embroiled in the Civil War. It behooves us to recall the situation back then. Households were torn apart by opposing beliefs and by the deaths of young men. Across state lines, people battled it out. We can hardly imagine brother fighting against brother, cousin versus cousin.

Nearly one hundred years ago our nation turned upon itself in violence—and some areas still have not recovered. Now, we face threats from outside, from enemies intent on destroying the cultures of countries long our allies, so those of opposing opinions on other matters fight side-by-side.

Already, we grieve the loss of sons and daughters in this war. But in the midst of loss, our hearts remain stalwart, because our cause is just. Here on the home front, we continue to do whatever we can to strengthen our forces and ensure victory.

So on this Thanksgiving, let me convey my gratitude for all the work you so faithfully carry out here at Camp Algona. All of our efforts are in support of our troops. All of our desires focus on victory on every front.

Despite our struggles and losses, may each of you experience a heightened awareness of our many blessings this year. Here in the United States of America, we cherish our freedoms and stand behind our young men risking lives for the cause of freedom.

Aunt Margaret and Twila skittered across the street before an oncoming milk truck. "So many trucks out early in the morning—if we waited for every one, we'd be late."

That might be true, but if one hit them, they'd become patients instead of workers. Used to her Aunt's daring pace, Twila held her tongue.

"By the way, I saw Stan yesterday. He stopped by and asked about you... said he hadn't seen you all day."

"Mmm..."

"I invited him over for Thanksgiving. Hope you don't mind."

"No, that's okay."

"He makes such a big difference with Benny—seems almost like family." She cleared her throat. "I only work until noon on Thanksgiving, but it won't be much of a holiday without having somebody over."

"Harry won't be able to come home?"

"I doubt it. His last letter said they're working double shifts until the snow flies."

"I don't know how she did it, but Nurse Alcott has me off the whole day."

Leaving Aunt Margaret at the prison compound, Twila hurried along. She'd never arrived before Nurse Alcott, but maybe someday...

As she was about to enter the hospital, someone waved at her. Was that Stan?

"Hey! You've been hard to find the last couple of days."

She shrugged. "I've been following my usual routine. How about you?"

He ducked his head in the wind, and she pulled him into the entryway. "There, that's better."

"I've been... Nothing has been normal for me since..." He worked his lips. "Twila, I need to tell you something."

The hall clock showed five minutes before seven, and a familiar figure in a white uniform and nurses' cap turned toward them.

Stan noticed too. "It's *her*. How about at noon right outside the... um... the guardhouse?"

"Okay. I'll be there unless an emergency comes up. If so, could you walk me home?"

"Yeah. Sure." He looked flustered and backed out.

Why would Nurse Alcott intimidate him? Twila went through the inner doors just in time to say good-morning.

Chapter Thirty-four

"Miss Brunner, when you get your coat off, come into my office for a minute, please. I've received some news that might interest you."

A few minutes later, Twila took the same seat where she'd first been interviewed. Could that be less than a year ago? So much had happened since then, she felt like a different person.

Her boss wasted no time. "Six months ago, the Dean of the University of Iowa nursing department requested that I watch out for promising young women desiring nurses' training."

Sunlight highlighted her severe white cap. In a pause full of mystery, she pushed up her glasses and surveyed Twila. But she was used to this... she often caught Nurse Alcott studying her.

"Our Surgeon General, Dr. Thomas Parran, called a meeting advocating on-the-job nursing training for individuals who cannot leave present posts. That report is what I have received.

"In addition, the Nurse Training Act has been amended to include federal subsidies for emergency university training courses. With the amount of wounded returning from the war and many nurses still overseas, we will soon experience a great shortage.

The army has set up temporary hospitals all over the nation, including one in southeast Iowa."

She folded her hands. "The war is not over, but it will be, and we must be ready as our boys filter back. There's only one way to make that happen."

Nurse Alcott thumbed through a file before handing it over the desk. "I would like you to read this."

A little voice whispered, *Things are about to change forever. Are you sure you're ready?*

Nurse Alcott squinted as if witnessing her inner exchange. Someone knocked at the door and she said, "I'll be back momentarily." She pushed back her chair and left the office.

The first page quickened Twila's pulse even more.

University of Iowa Spring Schedule
Department of Nursing Education

Introduction to Nursing, Fundamentals of Biology, Fundamentals of Chemistry, Biology lab, Reporting and Scheduling...

The nursing certificate beamed down from the wall as Twila took a deep breath. Seemed only yesterday when she first saw it, but things had changed so much—could she really earn one like it?

Maybe she was feeling something like soldiers felt before a battle—no comparison in many ways, but they knew that the time was upon them. And so did she. Something radical was about to occur.

The other night when Stan came for dinner, Benny had bubbled over about the Maginot line face-off.

"The army's increased production of the Sherman tank, so we'll win quicker. They weld pieces of steel together instead of casting the entire tank and waiting for it to dry. Makes the tank stronger. I just wish the Philippines were flatter, so Shermans could go there, too."

"Yeah. But wishes don't always become reality."

No, not always. But sometimes, they did.

When Nurse Alcott returned, she was ready.

"Well, then. Can you imagine entering this program?"

"Yes, Ma'am. I liked high school biology, but I'm not sure about chemistry..."

"Liking a subject is quite unnecessary. Only the determination to succeed is required." She took her seat. "If the opportunity arose, could you commit to this course of study?"

"There's nothing I'd like better, but I'm not sure about the cost."

"If you really mean what you said, that will work itself out. The university has created an intensive course—no less work, but far less time and money involved. You would begin in January and work through the summer and fall. Counting your experience here, you would earn your nursing certificate by December of next year."

"By December of 1945?"

"You may not realize the extent of your training here. Nursing students rarely observe surgery until second year, for example."

Observe surgery? So the other day had been...

"You would live in the dormitory, but many Iowa City women with deployed husbands seek household help. Would you be interested?"

"Why, yes."

"I know one family that needs a student immediately. Their grandmother left for war work last year, and they are a well-behaved lot."

Nurse Alcott's eyes took on the same faraway look Twila noticed the day she'd described her work in the Great War.

"The father leads a unit in the European Theater. With a nursing position of her own, three children under the age of ten and a victory garden, my daughter-in-law hardly knows where to turn."

"Your..."

"Yes. She would understand your study load, as well." Nurse Alcott settled back.

"I... I would need to speak with my parents. You did say January?"

"Yes. Sleep on this. If you bring a phone number tomorrow, we can call your parents."

"Okay. Yes." Twila scooted forward. "You may have to help me out of this chair, Ma'am. I'm not sure my legs will hold me."

"Oh, *pfft*! They'll hold you. You just think they won't."

"So you'll be leaving next week. Tuesday?"

Stan nodded. If he stuck to the plan he'd made in front of the mirror this morning, he'd get this over with quickly. "I can hardly believe they're going to fly me to the coast. The train has always been good enough before."

"They must believe you have a lot to offer." The emerald in Twila's eyes grew deeper. "And I'm sure they're not mistaken."

"I don't know about that. But I do have some experience, and they obviously want me there right away. I'm sure Benny has kept you updated on what's going on in the Philippines."

"Oh yes. You can count on that. I could describe the squish of General MacArthur's boots as he walked ashore." Her laugh filled the small space.

Even in this storage room, the only convenient place he could think of for a quick chat, Twila looked gorgeous. But no. That kind of thinking would never do.

"Have you told your family?"

"I called the store down the road from my folks' place and left word for my brother. Someone will take him the message, and he'll call me back tomorrow. Better for him to break the news to Mom than me."

"She'll really be upset, won't she?"

"For sure. But then, the war has lots of folks upset." Stan shuffled his feet. "Thanks for meeting me here. It's not the most likely place for a rendezvous."

"But it works. I've often wondered what the inside of this building looks like, and now I know."

"Like almost every other building here—same old pukey green army paint, bare walls..."

"Yes, but here I am in the guards' storeroom. You never know what a day might bring." She sniffed. "Smells like Dad's hunting stuff in here. Anyway, this is what you've been wanting, so I'm glad for you."

Right now. This is when you make your exit.

The inner urging played in Stan's ears, but his feet remained glued in place. Besides, Twila kept talking. What was that she just said—something about nursing school? He focused in again.

"Nurse Alcott gave me overnight to consider. What do you think?" She angled her head as if awaiting his response.

"Nursing school—that's what you really want, isn't it?"

"Yes, but January is so soon. I never dreamed—"

"*This* January? And when would you be finished?"

Her puzzled expression troubled him. Had she already told him and he hadn't heard?

"Sounds impossible, I know, but by next Christmas, I'd have my certificate. She said I've had a lot of training here already, and the Surgeon General has shortened the course—"

"I knew she had plans for you. She's been training you all long."

"I guess you're right. She says there's a big nurse shortage, and with all the soldiers coming back it will only get worse."

Something in her tone touched a deep place, but words failed him.

"So much has happened so fast, Stan. First Charlotte, then Butch. Paul now, and this. "

"Any progress with your aunt?"

"I don't think so, but she buttons up her emotions, so I really don't know. Hearing about this opportunity the same day you get your news—doesn't that seem like a lot at once?"

"Yeah, I agree. War either slows things to a turtle's pace, or makes them move so fast we can't keep up." His determination to keep this short flew out the window, and he wanted to say, "But one thing will stay the same, no matter what."

Instead, he blurted, "So Margaret hasn't told you—hasn't told anyone—about that letter?"

"Not that I know of. She's as sharp-tongued as ever with Diana and Benny, and acts as if nothing has changed."

"What a conundrum. I wish I could do something."

"I don't know what will have to happen for her to…"Twila glanced at her watch. "Oops, Nurse Alcott may take back her offer if I'm late to work."

"We wouldn't want that to happen, would we?"

She shook her head and remained silent, but her eyes communicated something more. What was it? Helplessness inundated Stan. He ought to say something soothing. No, he ought to say, "See you later," and get back to his own duty.

"Thanks for telling me, Stan. Aunt Margaret said she invited you for dinner Thursday, but you must have a lot to do before you leave. If it doesn't work out, we'll understand."

"They're trying to find my replacement, and want me to train him. So I don't know, but I hope I can still come."

She fidgeted with an ammo vest brushing her arm.

"I mean, I should say good-bye to Benny…"

She studied the floor for a moment. "Of course." Then, she turned toward the door. "Good-bye, Stan."

The outer door shut before he could move a muscle. While he stood frozen in place, she had left

All of his reactions coalesced into one cutting truth. She hadn't even said she'd miss him.

Aunt Margaret left a note that she'd had to leave early for work, so Twila enjoyed choosing her own pace. Her mind whirled with all the recent events. She'd talked with Rodney at the lumberyard yesterday morning, and he promised to have Mom call her over the noon hour.

Since he already explained the details, Mom had sounded less shocked than she'd imagined. She only asked one question, "Is this what you really want?"

"I really do want to be a nurse, but I never dreamed it would happen so soon."

"Your dad and I are behind you, you know that. He would say an opportunity like this might come only once in a lifetime, and you should take advantage of it. I'm so glad you were in the right place."

"Have you heard any more about him coming home?"

"No, but wouldn't that be wonderful?"

Twila agreed, and after they hung up, she stared at the wall phone wishing she could call again. She hadn't even asked about Lilly and Luke.

Ah, well. Nothing a couple of letters couldn't remedy. She walked back to the ward, where things seemed too quiet to match the frenetic activity in her mind. She would soon be leaving this place, but much sooner, Stan would, too.

She'd grown so used to him being around camp, and when he came over the other night, he'd brightened everyone, even Diana. They would really miss him tomorrow, but he had so much else to think about now.

Last night, she had told Aunt Margaret she'd stuff the turkey and put it in the oven. Seemed like more than a year since Uncle Marvin brought last year's feast to the back porch. Now, Aunt Margaret's farmer friend had supplied one just as big, and it, too, waited in her back porch to be stuffed.

Making dressing was always fun. When stirring with the wooden spoon became too hard, Mom taught her to use her hands, like making mud pies when she was young.

After dinner, she set about tearing up the bread crusts they'd been saving for weeks. There was plenty of time, and this would be one thing they wouldn't have to do tomorrow.

Aunt Margaret had come home extra late and the rest of the evening, she acted so peculiar. She didn't seem to mind Diana going over to Betty's after supper, and even though there was a lot to do to prepare for tomorrow, she played a few rounds of checkers with Benny.

They continued right through the news, and for the first time since Twila could remember, Margaret's knitting needles lay silent the entire evening. Just one more oddity to ponder—at this point, nothing seemed normal.

But the strangest thing was the way Stan acted in the storage room earlier. Their conversation left her baffled. He acted as if they'd never danced together at the U.S.O., never shared so many walks and talks. Could he have put everything out of his mind already?

Just when she'd begun to see him as more than a friend and hoping they would... Suddenly, she wished she could talk about him with Mom. She'd mentioned him in her letters, but now, he was going off to fight.

The prospect of nursing school excited her, but so much had been left unsaid with Stan. Crumbling the last of the dry crusts into Aunt Margaret's massive mixing bowl, Twila gave a long sigh.

It was the war again. Nothing worked out the way you thought it would. This thought brought Nurse Alcott's words back.

"...*promising young women desiring nurses' training."*

Stan had been right about her. She'd had everything planned out, down to a job to earn spending money when she enrolled down in Iowa City. Taking care of her grandchildren, no less!

He surely could read people, but during talk, she'd had such a struggle reading him. Some of the time, he didn't even seem to be listening.

After talking with Mom yesterday she had made her commitment to Nurse Alcott. It was too late to turn back, and she really didn't want to. Only one thing to do—set her mind on this new adventure.

In the living room, the news had ended and Benny seemed relatively quiet. Twila turned her thoughts to Aunt Margaret—when would she tell Harry and the children about Paul?

Suddenly Benny yelled, "Whoo-hoo! I beat you fair and square. You gotta admit it, Mom."

An odd silence followed. Twila peeked around the corner, but could she believe what her eyes told her? Aunt Margaret was hugging Benny.

Chapter Thirty-five

Thanksgiving morning, and Twila couldn't believe what her alarm clock proclaimed. How could she have slept till seven-thirty? She hurried down to get the turkey in the oven, and found a note on the kitchen counter.

"Something came up. They need me at the camp after all, and I'm letting D and B sleep. We'll have to eat later, so maybe you could put the turkey in the oven around noon. Hate to leave you with all the work, but you'll have help. See you later."

Not a sound came from upstairs. She had the downstairs to herself, and there was nothing she couldn't handle here.

Eight o'clock came and the table was set with the best china from the buffet. By nine, the smell of onions melding with sage, melted butter, and eggs filled the kitchen. Soon, she'd mix in the bread crusts, and could hardly wait to scoop the mixture into the turkey.

By nine-thirty, she'd peeled and quartered the potatoes, and had jars of corn and green beans waiting to be opened and cooked. Aunt Margaret must have filled the stove before she left, and it was about ready for Benny to get more corncobs.

Strange he would still be asleep... Diana was no surprise, but Benny? Ah well, this was his chance. Might as well let him snooze some more.

But by nine forty-five, she knew something must be wrong. Maybe he was sick. She went upstairs with a glass of water in hand and knocked on Benny's door. Knocked a little louder. Opened it and peeked in.

His bed lay empty. His shoes were gone. Downstairs again, she searched for his coat and boots. Why hadn't she noticed they were gone? Diana's weren't here either. What in the world? Taking three stairs at a time, she checked Diana's room. Empty.

Retracing her steps, she pondered whether Margaret had mentioned anything last night that she'd forgotten, but came up short.

For a few minutes, she wandered the house, glancing out a window in every direction. Then, she threw on her jacket and a scarf. She had to find out what was going on.

The worker at the commissary was not much help. "Margaret? Why, they asked me to work for her a week ago. Somethin' she had planned. Let me see, what was it—maybe she had to go see her husband. Somethin' like that. I'm just glad for the work—she hardly ever needs a replacement."

The only other person Twila could think to ask was Nurse Alcott, who would think her daffy for coming in today—or that she was looking for Stan. But this mystery was too much, on top of all the week's upheaval.

Up to her elbows with patient reports, Nurse Alcott sucked in her cheeks when Twila presented her quandary. "Margaret? I..." she stopped. "Are you all alone at the house, then?"

"Yes. Benny and Diana are gone too. This is so strange. I can't imagine how I didn't hear anything when they got up. I wouldn't have bothered you but..."

"There's not a fundraiser today or anything like that?"

Twila thought she glimpsed the ghost of a smile, but Nurse Alcott immediately turned sober again. "Maybe all the goings-on lately have made you overtired, and you slept so soundly that..."

No help here, either.

"I imagine by the time you get back, they'll be home, and wondering where you are."

With nowhere else to turn, Twila started back—this was so

frustrating. She wanted to stomp her feet, but what good would that do?

Half running, she made it a quick trip, and loping along the back sidewalk, she heard voices. They were coming from the kitchen. Not Aunt Margaret's or Diana's. Not Benny's.

On the middle stair, the porch door swung open and long arms swept her up. That scent—aftershave and tobacco—there was nothing else like it on earth.

"Daddy! It's you—you're home!"

He hauled her in and Mom threw her arms around them both.

"I... You're here! What...? Where is...?"

"Margaret took the children down to see Harry on the early train. She said she'd keep you up late last night so you wouldn't suspect. We wanted to surprise you."

"She was really acting strange, but I didn't... I can't believe they sneaked out like this."

"She wrote me a letter about Paul last week."

Twila leaned against Dad.

"Yes, it was about a week ago, and then we had a telephone conversation. It's all so sad—so hard for her. Harry knows, but she wanted them to tell Benny and Diana together."

Mom pulled her to the table. "You'd better sit down. I know it's been hard with Margaret. She's—"

Dad broke in. "You're looking great, Tiger. I knew you'd be grown into a woman, but to see you..." He blinked fast and pulled out his handkerchief.

"You're home for good?"

"Yup. What a long haul this has been, but I doubt General Eisenhower himself could get me away now." He pulled her close again. "You've been such a faithful writer, and I can't thank you enough. We thought..."

He pulled Myra in, too.

"Your mother knew you couldn't get off for the weekend, so when I rolled in Tuesday night, we figured the next best thing would be to come here." He squeezed Mom's hand. "That is, once she got over the shock of seeing me."

"Having Thanksgiving dinner with you—couldn't ask for more than that. Margaret told me she invited somebody from the camp."

"Stan. He's the guy I wrote you about, from Wisconsin. But now he's being redeployed to the Philippines—leaving on Tuesday. So I don't know if he'll be able come or not."

"A soldier stuck in a POW camp on Thanksgiving? I'm betting he'll show up." Dad's chuckle undid Twila, and she burst into tears.

"Maybe we've surprised you too much." He handed her his handkerchief. "This was clean when we boarded the early train, and there's something about shared tears."

"Let me make you some tea." Mom bustled around as if they were at home.

When Twila caught her breath, another realization hit. "You gave up Thanksgiving with Rodney and Sharon and...?"

"Not so fast. How do you know that?"

"Well, I..."

"They'll be along in a few hours. You didn't put the turkey in yet, did you?"

Mom added, "Rodney said his car could use a good long drive and it would do them all good to get out of town for a day."

"You don't mean it. They're coming, too?"

"Have I ever pulled your leg about something really important?" Dad's grin showed a morning's growth along his jaw. "Rod hasn't had a break since I left, so I asked Harm to watch over things at the lumberyard for a couple of days. Like your Mom says, this'll do them all good."

All Twila could do was take a deep breath.

"And this Stan fellow will get to meet our whole crew." The twinkle in Dad's eyes teased her, and the tea calmed her down. But Mom was all a-bustle.

"We'd better get the turkey in, don't you think?"

Twila shook her head and Dad sprang into action. In five minutes, the bird was stuffed and settled in to bake.

"What's left to do? The table looks great, but Don, could you find some extra chairs?" Mom turned to Twila. "You've got the main things done already, and I brought the pie."

"On the train?"

"Why not?" Dad grinned. "I boxed it up so well, it *had* to get here in one piece."

"Six pieces..."

"Twelve, if you want to be picky... you made pumpkin and apple, remember?" He turned to Twila. "Your mother had me box up half the kitchen. We did say we're staying till Saturday, didn't we? Think you can find a place for everyone to sleep?"

Finally, Twila relaxed enough to giggle. What a Thanksgiving this would be!

The voice on the other end of the telephone line came in garbled, like someone speaking from a deep hole. Stan kept saying, "Raymond? Ray, is that you?"

"Stan?"

"Yes. It's hard to hear you. Is there a storm up there?"

"Storm... yeah. A bad one... midnight... fallen trees..."

"Sorry. Probably wasn't easy getting down to the crossroads to call me back."

"Broke down... had to take... Old Cherry..."

"You rode her down?" Sitting in the administrative office, Stan shook his head. Must be some storm. Raymond sure had been determined to talk with him if he'd ridden one of Dad's old draft horses a half mile to the nearest phone.

But there was so much static on the line, they might not accomplish much. In a way, he was relieved—he wouldn't have so much explaining to do.

He could picture poor Raymond, battered by wind and rain,

standing at the wall phone in Harkle's country store. Around him, uneven shelves groaned with the bare necessities—beans, flour, batteries, overalls...

"Yeah. I've been called back..." The connection crackled and Stan jerked the phone away from his ear. "...into the service, bro."

"What?"

"The Army's called me back in. I'm leaving on Tuesday. Not enough time to get home."

"Leavin' for where?"

"The Pacific." The less they knew, the better, for Mom's sake.

"You don't say..." Suddenly the line cleared, and Raymond could have been standing two feet away. "You can't come home before you leave?"

"No, I only have three days."

"Sure you're not stayin' there t' say good-bye to some girl?"

"How did you know? I do have a good friend here—a girl." Stan couldn't have said what came over him, but he blurted, "I think she might be the one for me, Ray."

"Better do somethin' about that before you leave."

"Nah, if something happens to me, she'd be—"

"Listen to me. This might be your only chance, and it might be hers, too. Tell her how you feel."

"I..." The crackling reappeared. Better get off the line before lightning struck and burned down Harkle's store. What would that lumbering community do without it?

"Tell Mom and Dad..." Stan felt pretty sure his "I love them" got lost somewhere between here and northern Wisconsin.

But then Ray's voice came through again. "I'll send you the..." More static. " You'll need a... send it right away."

"What?"

A distorted, "Take care of yourself, little brother," came through. At least that's how Stan interpreted. From then on, static reigned, until a sharp click told him Ray had hung up the receiver.

Listen to me.

In the wee hours this morning, he thought he'd wrestled through this one, and in the end, decided not to go over to the Valentine's today. But Ray's words kept intruding.

Might be your only chance...

The powers that be had arranged schedules to give each guard a two-hour break, but Stan forfeited his. Might as well let some other guy go see his family or have some free time. This meant he'd work more than twelve hours straight, from five to five, but maybe then he'd be able to sleep tonight.

Truth be told, he doubted it. Right now, Cap had slipped into silence, and Ray seemed to have taken his place as the advice-giver.

Tell her how you feel.

Stan shrugged off the insistent voice and turned his attention to the rest of garbled conversation. What could Ray be going to send? Maybe some kind of lucky piece—maybe that old rabbit's foot he used to carry.

Before he left the first time, he showed Ray where all his treasures were. Oh well, whatever it was wouldn't get here in time anyway.

Just this weekend left, and the cook was roasting turkeys for the guards—the aroma already wafted from the kitchen. For a moment, Stan imagined the homey scene across town. Benny would be hauling up cobs from the basement, Twila and her aunt cooking and setting the table.

Their conversation yesterday was in no way ideal—what had he been thinking, telling her his big news in the storage room? No, it was the day before. He'd been in such a state, he'd lost track of time.

Today wasn't much of an improvement, after another lousy night. He strained to call up what Twila had said in that brief encounter. Something about being glad for him, and she told him what Nurse Alcott had just sprung on her.

Now that he thought about it, she really didn't seem herself at all. She'd been carrying quite a load lately—finding her aunt's letter from the Navy would be tough for anybody.

He rubbed his forehead—had her eyes glinted when he first mentioned returning to active duty? He'd been so caught up in his own thoughts, he couldn't remember a thing, and either way, he had to get back to work. He gave himself a talking to.

"That's the last place you need to go. She didn't even say she'd miss you."

At a nearby desk, one of the workers shot him a puzzled look. Hadn't he ever heard anyone talk to himself before?

Only three more days—he had avoided Twila before, and he could do it again.

Crash... He barely stayed upright as he ran headlong into—oh, no. It couldn't be.

Colonel Lobdell.

Stan's face fired as the realization struck. The Colonel had been talking to another man, tall with dark hair. Both of them brushed themselves off. He had produced a domino effect. He held his breath as the Colonel peered at him.

"Private Ford? Is that you?"

"I'm afraid it is, sir. So sorry. I was..." Stan clipped his heels and saluted.

"Are you all right?"

"Yes, sir. But your glasses, sir."

The Colonel readjusted the wires. "There. Do I look presentable?"

"Yes. Sir, I apologize."

"Not that many guards are so excited to get to duty, Private." The Colonel's eyes showed only kindness, and the civilian grinned and launched a quip.

"Nice to run into you, Private..."

"Ford." Something about this fellow's eyes put him at ease.

The Colonel explained, "This is the man I was telling you about, Don. You and I remember the kind of action he's seen. Do you think we'd have volunteered to go back to the trenches if we'd been sent home from France wounded?"

"Not likely."

"Wait—you *were* wounded. No long-range effects, I hope?"

"Nothing that kept me from serving in this war. Same as you, I expect."

Colonel Lobdell stepped back. "Well, Private Ford is as eager to get back to the Philippines as he is to get to guard duty on time." He addressed Stan again. "Were you able to speak with your family, Private?"

"Yes, sir. Just now, in fact. They're having a bad storm, so the phone service left something to be desired, but at least I got my message across."

The Colonel pulled on his upper lip with his teeth. "You have another brother serving, is that right?"

"In Europe. Yes, sir."

"Mmm. Families have it awfully hard these days. God bless you all."

Stan saluted and walked away at a much more dignified pace. At the door, he glanced back at that other fellow. It almost seemed as if he'd met him before. Something about his mouth, the way he smiled…

Chapter Thirty-six

Such a wild day—Twila could hardly take in the fact that everyone had come. Lilly claimed her from the moment she bounced out of the car when Rodney pulled up to the curb.

"Aunt Twila!" She threw herself full force into Twila's arms and hung on for dear life.

Just then, Dad ambled up from his walk around town and yelled, "There she is! How's Grandpa's girl?" Lilly took off to be swooped up by Grandpa.

Then Sharon brought forth Lukey, whose cherub smile and big blue eyes made Twila never want to let him go. He squirmed when she held him close and kissed his silken hair. Soon he'd be running around, too.

In the hustle getting everyone and everything they brought into the house, her emotions ran wild. They'd come to see her. They'd left everything and traveled all this way. The train tickets; the gasoline. It all seemed impossible.

And Aunt Margaret, down in Des Moines—what a time for family. Imagining Benny absorbing the news about Paul was heartbreaking, but Sharon's urgent question grabbed Twila's attention.

"We've been in the car so long, everyone really needs a walk. Is there a playground anywhere near? The afternoon's warm enough for some exercise, don't you think?"

"Didn't we pass one on the way in?" Dad glanced at Twila.

"Yes, just a couple of blocks away. I can take them."

"I'll come along."

"I think Lukey needs to be changed first... where's the diaper bag?"

"Let me do that. You've been stuck inside with them all morning."

The changing only took a couple of minutes, and as she and Luke joined Dad and Lilly out front, Mom waved them off.

"Take your time. Sharon and I are watching the turkey."

The sun glimmered down as Lily ran ahead and Dad chased her. Her family, all of them, here on Thanksgiving Day. What could be better?

Nurse Alcott knew all about this, she was sure. That almost-smile she gave this morning—yes, Aunt Margaret had set everything up with her.

But something still niggled at Twila. Someone was missing. If only Stan would come over.

At the park, she transferred Luke to Dad and caught Lilly when she whooshed down the tall metal slide.

"Why, you big girl! That's a tall slide, but you're not afraid."

"Whee!" Lilly slid right into her arms.

"Oh my goodness. I can hardly lift you any more!"

"Mama says I growed a lot."

"You certainly have. But you're still my Lilly."

Fierce and unrestrained, Lilly's hug lasted only seconds before she ran off to the next toy.

After half an hour, Dad looked at his watch. "Time to go home now. Time for naps."

"Not me, just Lukey."

"We'll let your Daddy decide." Lilly skipped ahead, and Dad hoisted Luke to his shoulder.

"Great to be out, isn't it? It's a lot warmer in California, but I was prepared for anything... not unheard of for us to have snow and ice by now."

"Right." Twila touched his hand. "I'm still pinching myself—you're really, truly home."

"I'm pinching myself, too. My orders came down so fast, I barely had time to call Rodney." He pulled her to his side. "But here I am."

"I'm so glad. This'll make it easier to leave for the university." Twila hesitated. "Can't believe I just said that... it's too new, too. I assume Mom told you all about it."

"What an opportunity for you. I'm more than proud of you—you must've impressed this Nurse Alcott. We want to meet her before we leave."

Up ahead, Lilly stopped at the corner, and he called, "Look both ways. Is anything coming?"

She shook her head and darted ahead. Meanwhile, Lukey had fallen asleep.

"Now, what about this Stan fellow? Your mom told me a little, but not enough to satisfy my curiosity."

All of the past few days' emotions welled up, and Twila burst into tears. In the back yard now, she pulled out Dad's handkerchief.

"Here. Let's sit on the steps for a while."

"It's just..." She wiped her nose. "I can't seem to grasp everything all at once. It's too much to take in."

"Is something going on with Stan that we haven't heard about?"

"No. Not really." She sniffed. "That's just it. I don't *know*. The other day when he told me he was leaving, he... It seemed like he'd already left."

"Do I ever understand that, Tiger. That's exactly what we all have to do. As soon as we get our orders, we start getting our heads ready for what's coming, and honestly, it *is* as if we've already left. Your mom went through that with me.

"I sure didn't mean to hurt her, but I knew what I had to do would take everything I had, so days before I left, my head, and maybe my heart, too, were already in California. I guess it's the way we're wired as soldiers."

Was that why Stan hadn't mentioned anything about missing her?

"I remember thinking, 'the less I say, the better.' If I show too many of my real feelings, I'll never be able to leave. Don't know if that makes any sense?"

"Yes, kind of." Sitting there with such wonderful smells emanating from the kitchen, Twila's stomach growled and Luke sank into sleep in Grandpa's arms.

"That's my girl—a good old-fashioned appetite."

"But..." Her voice sank into a whisper. "What if Stan doesn't come, Daddy? What if I never know..."

"That's a hard one. What time did you invite him over?"

"I don't know. Aunt Margaret asked him."

"Would you think I was interfering if I..." He tapped his free hand on Lukey's solid little back. "I have a sneaking suspicion I met your Stan when I went over to meet the commander."

"What do you mean?"

"When we first got here, I walked around town, and when I saw Colonel Lobdell's name on the Camp sign, I had to go in. I knew a Lobdell in France during the war. He was a junior officer, not even in my unit, but we ended up together a couple of times.

"So, you know me, I showed my Army ID at the gate and they let me in. When I found the Colonel, he surprised me. 'Is that you, Brunner?' he asked, and held out his hand."

Dad shrugged. "You never know how much folks will remember, but being stuck together in dire straits makes it harder to forget people. We started talking about old times right there in the hallway, and that's when—by any chance, is Stan's last name *Ford*?"

"Yes."

"A young man in a guard's uniform—blond hair—came out of the office next door and was in an awful hurry. Ran into the Colonel and nearly knocked me over, too. Pretty muscular guy?"

She nodded. "It's not like Stan to run into anybody, but..."

"He'd just gotten a phone call from his family. That can be pretty rough. But he... Well, in my opinion, he looked like something else was bothering him."

Twila stared out at the burn pile. Dad had met Stan? What else was going to happen?

"Maybe it was you."

"Dad…"

"Look. I've been the old guy around young soldiers for two years. Lots of troubling stuff going on for them, and I learned to smell when somebody needed a friendly ear.

"What did you say when Stan told you he was leaving?"

"I… I don't remember. Miss Alcott had just told me about the new nursing course, so I told him about that. But Stan didn't even say he'd miss me. We both had to hurry back to work and…"

"Did you say you'd miss him? That you'd write?"

"No, but…"

"Sounds to me like a conversation that ended too soon."

"Maybe."

Sunlight played across Lukey's fine golden hair and dappled Twila's arm. From inside they heard Mom say, "They're just outside talking. Otherwise everything's ready."

Dad put his arm around Twila and lowered his voice. "What do you say we drive over to the camp and see if we can find him?"

"I don't know. He might think…

"Let me tell you something. Those young soldiers in training… nine times out of ten, what troubled them was something they'd said or hadn't said before they left home. Not a good way to go into battle.

"How about it? If we find him, good—we'll re-issue his invitation and he can choose one way or the other. If we don't, find him we'll just let it be."

She hardly had time before he was inside, depositing Lukey in someone's arms and getting Rodney's keys. And then she was in Rodney's car, with Dad at the wheel.

The dream that started this morning seemed to go on and on. Here she was, bouncing through Algona on the way to see Stan. The closer they came to the camp, the tighter she clutched the door handle.

And the harder she prayed. *If this is going to make Stan feel worse, please don't allow us to find him.*

Rodney tossed Lukey so high, Twila's heart flip-flopped, but each time, the little fellow giggled so much, everyone had to join in. Then he begged his daddy for more.

Everyone lounged in the living room after way too much to eat. Lilly sat beside Twila, twisting and turning her necklace, and a few feet away, Stan and Dad discussed the war. Mom, on Twila's other side, whispered, "He gets along so well with Rod and your dad."

Twila could only smile and nod—one more event to store away in her heart, on this day when nothing seemed real. But what was real had surfaced when she and Dad watched Stan coming from the prison compound.

He was about to cross the street when they stopped at the intersection. With his head down, he looked so deep in thought, she grabbed Dad's arm.

"Let's just let him go on. He has so much on his mind."

But Dad gave the horn a slight push, and hearing the *beep*, Stan glanced up. When he recognized her, he hurried over to her window.

"Hey, Twi. What's...?" His expression radiated apprehension mixed with concern. Then he saw Dad and his face flushed. He took a step back, but she reached out for him.

"This is my dad, Stan. He said maybe you met earlier."

Stan shook his head. "Oh boy, did we ever."

Leaving the car idling, Dad rounded the front and shook his hand. "We didn't get a formal introduction, but you left your impression on me." His grin did the trick, and Stan laughed.

"I'm not in the habit of running people down, especially my commander, sir."

His sideways grin to her, the way he came closer, the touch of his hand on hers, was *real*. When she sighed, his forehead wrinkled, and the concern in his eyes unwound her trepidation.

"These things happen. And what's happening right now over at our place—Twila's, that is—is a big turkey dinner with all the trimmings. We'd sure like to have you join us."

Stan studied him for a moment and turned to Twila, waiting.

"I wasn't sure Aunt Margaret gave you the exact time..."

He blushed. "Well, I wasn't..."

Dad grabbed his elbow. "That settles it. In you go."

The whole way home, he plied Stan with questions, and there hadn't been any quiet since. During the meal, Stan's hand brushed hers a couple of times, but with all the commotion, they had no chance to exchange a private word.

After the meal, Lilly ran in circles and Lukey's wild giggles prompted Sharon's warning. "Rod, we'll never be able to get them to sleep tonight."

"Maybe we should all take another walk to get everything digested. It won't be dark for another hour."

"Yes, yes! The park! Come on, Lukey—here's your hat." Lilly made the decision for them all.

Chapter Thirty-seven

Falling behind everyone else happened naturally. In Grandpa's arms, Lilly finally gave in to sleep, and Rodney carried an already snoring baby Luke. Twila's mom followed close behind them with Sharon.

A few steps back, with Twila here beside him, the day's light began to fade, and the peacefulness settling over the town seeped into Stan. How had his thinking become so muddled? He might easily have missed out on this, might have spent the rest of the day in his cubbyhole, alone.

"The other day..." Twila began at the same time as he did. They laughed and he offered, "Okay, you go first."

"The other day, too much happened all at once, and it seemed impossible to comprehend everything."

"I know what you mean. In that storage room, I don't know what happened. I couldn't keep everything straight."

"I meant to ask; I suppose you have no idea how long you'll be gone?"

"No way of knowing, but it's going to take some time to retake the Islands, and then there's Japan itself. Nobody believes we'll end this thing without invading there."

A breeze blew up and turned Twila's hair into a red whirlwind.

Time stopped—she might be on the cover of a magazine. His desire for her grew, but so did a nervous grinding in his gut that declared he must've been crazy to come tonight.

It was a wonderful dinner, and so interesting to talk with Mr.

Brunner, but now came the hard part. Why would a girl like Twila want to wait for a guy like him?

They were near Margaret's house now, and everyone else went inside. He and Twila slowed steps, and she studied his face. He longed to smooth away the lines between her eyes, but what right did he have?

It was easy for Ray, miles away, to tell him to express his feelings, but how could he possibly make everything clear? He made an attempt, but his tongue went AWOL.

The next thing he knew, Twila had pulled him to the side of the house. "Stan, are you okay?"

"Yeah. I'm just afraid you..." He glanced heavenward. "Oh, why is it so hard to...?"

"We're friends, aren't we?" She laid her hand on his chest, sending a thrill through him.

"Yeah. Yes." He straightened his shoulders.

"Good. At least I'm thinking that's a good thing?"

"Yeah." Was that all he could say? Cap would be aghast at his pathetic use of the English language. He cleared his throat as the western sky flamed behind Twila.

"I've been thinking it was unfair to tell you this. But then my brother said just the opposite, so I—

"Tell me what?"

He stood there without a word, hating himself for his fear, but she persisted. "Whatever it is, I'd rather know. I would think you'd have realized that about me by now."

"Sorry, I've been..." In the time it took for a deep breath, her eyes darkened into the shade of primeval forest.

Something about that transformation touched a deep place in him, and he sputtered, "You're the girl for me, Twila. The only one."

With those words choked out between them, her eyes widened. The grinding in his gut increased, but now he couldn't stop. "I hate to ask you to wait for me..." Helplessly, he threw up his arms. "But will you?"

Wordlessly, she tapped his shoulders and pushed him back into the shadows under the eaves. Some twigs forked his scalp.

Her slight giggle confused him, turned his muscles into wax.

"You look like you're posing for some nature photographer." She reached up to brush his brow, inducing that tingling again. "Except it's almost nighttime, and you're frowning."

His voice turned into a crow's rasp. "I have to know, Twila. Will you wait for me?"

"I might, if you show me how much you care." With an impish grin, she pushed him even deeper into the bush, so he steadied himself on a branch.

That twinkle in her eyes—was she enjoying teasing him? Her upturned lips issued an invitation, and she had never looked so inviting. For this moment, nothing else mattered—nothing in the whole world.

After Thanksgiving weekend—in fact, the day Stan left—the weather turned cold. In a constant influx of new prisoners, Nurse Alcott increased Twila's duties, along with her hours. With so much activity, she almost forgot Dad was back home now.

But every corner of the camp reminded her of Stan. Several times, she thought she spied him walking down the hall. Even the guardhouse, where they'd had that last meeting, reminded her of its tender resolution.

What a precious memory, evening walk, even though Stan had such a struggle expressing himself. Seeing him unsure and vulnerable only endeared him more. She'd had to work all weekend, but he came to see her one more time the night before he left.

While she sanitized instruments, she recalled last meeting. He certainly gave her plenty to remember. She'd never pictured him as the type to throw a pebble at her bedroom window, but he did.

At first she thought the wind was playing tricks with a branch, but then came another *plink*. When she spied him in the yard, she hurried down and urged him inside. His hands were icy, so she pulled a chair by the stove and made tea.

"You could catch a bad cold."

"Some things are worth whatever risk they take." He held his hands out near the stove. "And seeing you one more time is one."

His fingers still felt cold when he laced them through hers.

"Where are your gloves?"

"Packed away—sure won't need them where I'm going."

"I was lying there lamenting how busy we were today, with no chance to see you."

"Me too. Colonel Lobdell wanted to talk again—he sure is interested in the Philippines. And then I had lots of paperwork to attend to—it's always that way with the Army.

"When I got to my bunk, I knew there'd be no sleep without seeing you again." He swung into a chair, propelling her along.

"Hey, don't close those beautiful green eyes on me—no tears tonight. I'm memorizing exact shade, so when I look out at the ocean or the jungle, I'll see you—and believe me, I'll be looking at one or the other all the time."

"That's romantic, Stan. For me, it'll be easy to find your baby blues right up in the sky."

He inhaled his tea, and when she poured him another cup, he pulled her onto his lap again.

"Benny keeps asking about you. Is it okay to tell him where you're headed?"

"Yes, but no more than that. How are they all doing, now that the truth is out?"

"Sounds strange, but better, I think. Everyone seems subdued, although Benny says he still believes there's a chance Paul might come home some day."

"And there is. Stranger things have happened."

"Margaret says Harry is coming home for Christmas. From then on, they might need him down in Des Moines now and then, but he won't have to live there any more. That's a good thing, and I'll be gone, so they can get back to normal... well, sort of."

"Oh—would you give this to Benny for me?" Stan pulled some papers from his coat pocket and unfolded one. "I've worked out a code you both can memorize, so when I write about what I'm doing, you'll understand way more information than the censors think."

"Oh, let me see. House means island. Trees means enemy. Porcupine means prisoners. Wow, you dreamed up a whole page. He'll be so excited to see this."

"And on the back, I wrote a silly sentence—can you make sense of it?"

"Never enjoy waffles greater under igloos not ever after... What on earth?"

"Focus on the first letter of every word."

"N...e...w...g...u...i...n...—oh, New Guinea!"

"Yeah. Tell Benny to be on the lookout for clues like that. Hopefully, the time it takes to interpret what I send will help keep him out of Margaret's hair. Would you mind sending my notes on to him?"

"Not at all. He'll think he's the luckiest boy in the world to get all this insider information."

"Mmm... good. But I didn't come to talk about him."

"No?"

"Haven't you heard that talk is cheap? How about some action?" He bent his head to give her another kiss to remember, and the smell of his aftershave inundated her.

"You're sure you really want to marry me?"

"Absolutely. I only wish we could say 'I do' tomorrow."

"But what if you see Ginger Rogers again and she tells you she's available?"

"You sure are a dreamer."

"When do you think we'll see each other again?"

"No man in his right mind would try to answer that. But one thing is for sure, this will all come to an end in Japan.

"Our forces still have a long way to go in Europe, too. I hate thinking of Ron taking the brunt of the Germans' defenses right now—such a tough fight. But Japan will hold out even longer. Whatever we can do to wear them down before then can only shorten the time."

"What did you say Ron's job is?"

"He's a sapper. That's a combat engineer, one of the forward soldiers who clears mine fields before advancing troops. They go in before the main body to make a path through whatever blocks the way—tanks, buildings, fortifications, guns.

"Hopefully he'll survive. He could always run twice as fast as me, and he has a lot of running to do right now." Stan got to his feet, sweeping her up with him.

"One day it'll be over and they'll send us all home. There'll be so much mopping up to do all over the globe. What a challenge, but I imagine Ike's up for it."

He reached for her hands. "Ask me what I'm going to do when I get back."

"What?"

"I'll ask you to marry me proper, down on my knees, with a diamond ring in my hand."

Deep creases formed between his eyes. If earnest looks carried guarantees, she had one in spades.

"But for now, I brought you this." He rummaged in his pocket for something and pulled out a narrow gold band with a ruby heart in the center.

"My grandpa gave this to grandma a long time ago, and she told me to save it for the right girl. Her mother came from a rich family, so she gave one to each of us boys, but I like this one best. It says you have my heart."

Speechless, she fingered the stone.

"When I get home, I'll find you a diamond and show up at your door."

"But what if... What if I'm at some hospital a long way from Wisconsin?

"Like I said before, you're the only girl for me. I'll find you."

She nestled closer. "I don't think that will be necessary."

"At least now you and your folks know my intentions."

"Have you told your parents?"

"I'll mail them a letter before I board the ship. First, I had to be sure you wanted me."

He sounded so sincere—had he really thought she might refuse him? But her question was lost as Stan broke into song, right there in the kitchen. His voice, low and sincere, was not much more than a whisper.

"Woman needs man
And man must have his mate..."

"*As Time Goes By*... I love that song. Didn't know you could sing."

"Whatever it takes to convince you." He chuckled. "Guess I didn't tell you that Mom pushed me onto a local stage when I was little, just in case her plans for college didn't work out."

"You're full of surprises, Stanford L. Ford."

"Can you imagine naming an innocent baby that?"

"Sounds dignified."

"That's what my mom must've thought."

Recalling the touch of his lips, Twila carefully removed the instruments from the sanitizer and set them in positions on trays, ready for the doctors.

Ah... Those kisses. She could count the ones they'd shared on one hand, but each one gave her something to cherish. And Stan's promises were solid ground to stake the future on.

She tapped her pocket, with his latest letter tucked inside.

Tonight, she would write him another letter, memorize the code he left, and go over it with Benny.

Then she'd trace the route Stan said the ship would take. Most of all, she would pray with her fingers touching Bataan.

Chapter Thirty-eight

"Yes sir." Outside the HQ building window, a spritely California wind tossed towering palm fronds like chaff. Once again, an officer surveyed Stan's file and held his future in his hands.

"Your latest physical, done at Camp Algona; is that one of our POW camps?"

"Yes, sir."

"You were a guard there... mmm... not for long. Why did you leave?"

"Sir, I knew I had more to offer the Army elsewhere."

"How is that?"

"Well, I... from the time I spent in the Philippines. I know what to expect, and I'm ready."

"Mmm... Looks like you were there from fall of '41 through '43?" The officer rubbed his temple, and Stan could see he expected no answer. Instead, he studied the nameplate on the desk that separated them—Major Franken.

The officer looked up and blurted, "And you're ready for what?"

"Whatever assignment I receive, sir."

"What was the hardest part of your time in the islands?" He scanned a report. "I see you were wounded—was that the worst of it?"

"Leaving my buddies behind was the hardest, sir."

The officer showed no sign he had heard, and something niggled the base of Stan's neck. What if the Army changed course and someone decided he could be used here to greater effect? Perhaps someone fighting a bad headache.

His next thought sickened him. What if they said they couldn't use him after all? What if they sent him home?

"Ever heard of the Rangers?"

"Yes, sir."

"They're as essential to victory now as the Green Mountain men were to General Washington."

"Fort Ticonderoga. Yes, sir."

"At ease, Private. Shall we turn this into a friendly conversation?"

"Yes, s…"

The officer hid a smile. "Old habits die hard. At least you don't need any breaking in to Army protocol." He swiveled to a wall map of Southeast Asia.

"Now then. On September third, the U.S. Joint Chiefs authorized the Leyte Invasion, and on the third of this month, acknowledged that an attack on Luzon will follow. Perhaps you've followed the checkered dialogue between Washington and General MacArthur?"

Whoo boy… he certainly had. But it made sense to keep his reply neutral.

"I know Admiral Nimitz argued for seizing Formosa instead of the Philippines. Depending which newspaper article you read, General MacArthur is either a saint or a bugaboo."

"Exactly. At the very least, he's become a thorn in FDR's side, but Admiral Nimitz lacked the General's eloquence. That made all the difference, when it came down to it."

Another good time to remain silent. All that mattered was retaking the islands and freeing those captives.

"The Philippine government perceives they've been lied to, which is understandable. And General MacArthur did make Quezon a promise to return." Major Franken rubbed his temple again.

"For whatever reasons, mostly political, in my opinion, our forces in Australia are training toward the Philippines rather than Formosa. Our orders are to take not just Leyte, but Luzon as well."

He leaned forward in his chair. "And this, Private Ford, is why your experience interests us so much." He grappled on the bookcase for his pointer.

When he turned away, Stan wiped his soaking palms on his pants and took his first deep breath since entering the office.

"Here's how it's supposed to go. Admiral Halsey's Third Fleet, in the form of Vice Admiral Kincaid's Seventh, will shield General Kruger's Sixth Army going ashore. General MacArthur swears that six weeks will suffice for us to overcome the Jap garrison, but you know how such prognostications go.

"You may also realize the Chiefs were slow to accept MacArthur's analysis that Luzon's central plain would make a better staging area for attacking Japan than Formosa. They had viable points, but the logistical realities brought them around.

"For one thing, an attack on Formosa would require fighter strips and anchorages in the central and southern Philippines. But no one can deny the enemy's positions at present." He moved the pointer from spot to spot before giving a hearty sigh.

"I personally believe we're in for the fight of our lives on Luzon. Makes no sense that Japan would let go of this territory easily.

"With that in mind, and considering the terrain and autumn rains, the Luzon invasion scheduled for December may not take place on time. But our task force will go in sooner. That's another reason we felt your availability came at just the right time.

"Success demands making contact with our officers displaced in the north. I needn't explain how much the intel they've obtained will help our main body of troops. But they need what we can provide, also—radios and other supplies."

Heat razed Stan's neck. *The north.* Just where he longed to be.

"All of this is why I'm turning you over to a commander who served in the Philippines long before the Japanese invaded. He has direct contact with General Kruger, whose guerilla forces have been training for this invasion for some time. Some fine Midwestern boys among them, I might add.

"When we received your information from Colonel... what was

his name?" He glanced through the file again. "Lobdell... yes. We could hardly have hoped for a man with your qualifications."

Stan's heart went wild but he determined to restrain his emotions.

The Major leaned back in his chair. "Our informants in Manila send steady intel concerning the north coast, so this commander will know how to slip in where you can do the most good. Or the most damage, I should say." The officer closed Stan's file and stood.

"Report to him in Building Six. Any questions?"

"No sir."

Major Franken saluted him. "Room 17 down the first hall to your right. And good luck to you."

Dizzy with this news, Stan hurried out into a glorious California day. How to describe this pulsing in his chest? Not that different from the way he'd felt with Twila the other night... the closest he could come was *joy*. Pointedly, Cap added his benediction.

"Be sure you put your feet in the right place. Then stand firm. Abraham Lincoln."

"You nailed it this time, old buddy. No matter what happens, I know I'm headed to the right place. I just hope you're still there." Stan straightened his shoulders and hurried on to Building Six.

Tall black oak groves created silhouettes against a hazy January sky. The *clank-clank* of the Waterloo-Cedar Falls and Northern train matched Mom's breathing. With Dad off fetching coffee, she turned quiet.

In Cedar Rapids, they would say good-bye when Twila switched to the Cedar Rapids and Iowa City Interurban. She'd told them she'd be fine on her own, but they insisted on coming this far, and she was glad.

Her thoughts ran between Lilly, who cried when she said good-bye, and Stan. It had been almost five weeks since his last letter—he must have arrived in the islands by now.

Last night, Dad reassured her. "He'll have to store up his letters. Wouldn't be surprised if one day you get several all at once."

An air of unreality accompanied this trip. Last year at this time, she hadn't even moved to Camp Algona. How could she already be heading off into her dream?

The train rounded a curve and Mom turned her way. "As soon as you leave, I know I'll think of all kinds of things I should have said."

"Me, too... but one I don't want to forget. Thank you for being such a good mom, even when I wasn't the most grateful daughter."

"We did the best we could, both of us. We made it through."

"Did you know about me slipping out right from the start?"

"I've always heard every sound in the house, honey. I heard even more after your dad left. But at the time, I knew the more I fussed, the more you'd want to go."

"You did the right thing. I'm glad you stuck by me, Mom."

"Of course. Sometimes, though, I wished I could explain how a guy like Lonnie wasn't good enough for you."

"I still don't know why he attracted me."

"He was older, for one thing. Your dad was gone, too, and you've always been so close. My dad left..." Her eyes darkened. "In a different way. But even if he hadn't, I'd still have wanted something new and different."

She stared out at fields and farmhouses flying by. "I imagine Margaret filled you in on my antics?"

"She told me Grandma made it rough for you all to grow up."

"Mmm... must be so hard for her right now. Losing Paul, and now Diana... what exactly did she do?"

"Communicated with one of the German prisoners. I think she might have met him last fall out at her friend's house in the country when he helped with the harvest."

"And she's been writing to him?"

"Yes. I'm not sure how she managed to have her letters delivered, but..."

"Oh, if we want something badly enough, we can always find a way."

"That's for sure—like escaping through from a second story window in the middle of a hailstorm."

What a perfect way to pass this trip, sharing a chuckle with Mom.

"Margaret took it so personally, but Harry said to remember this is her only daughter."

"I hope she can. She always took everything on herself. We were on the brink of starvation half the time—Marvin remembers when our folks lost the farm during the Depression, but Mother finally scraped enough together to buy it back from the bank.

"She took in sewing, cleaned for people in town, and made sure Margaret and the older ones found jobs. Margaret worked harder than anybody, I think. I imagine she felt as though she could never do enough."

No use dredging this all up again—*let sleeping dogs lie*. This past year, those dogs had done a lot of barking, but Mom deserved peace.

"The past can gouge your eyes out if you let it."

"I hope you don't let it, Mom."

"No, not any more. Do you think I should write to Margaret about Diana?"

"It couldn't hurt."

Dad popped in with two cups of coffee. "Want one, Twila?"

"No thanks, I'm fine."

"If the next train's on time, we'll get home by dark, and by then, you'll be all settled in." He and mom sipped as the train clattered on.

"By the way, I saw Lonnie Higgins yesterday."

Mom gave him a sour look.

"He's home on leave, and the uniform does wonders. He actually stood up straight."

"Better you running into him than me."

"I thought about burning his ears, but Honor figures that freezing up at Camp Ripley took the sass out of him for good. His infantry unit's being shipped to Europe. Guess we know what that means.

"I wouldn't wish that on anybody—even Lonnie." But imagining him with a relentless Army sergeant did produce a grin.

Mom's eyes glinted. "I'm glad you didn't hide yourself away after that. That's what I did. Now I realize how much I missed."

Dad wrapped his arm around her. "But you came through it, hon. Time heals all." He glanced out as the train slowed. "Almost there—you haven't changed your mind, have you?"

His eyes told Twila he already knew her answer. This adventure would launch her into a whole new world, and she was ready.

People scurried about on the platform, and she enfolded Mom's free hand. Some things a person holds dear forever.

Chapter Thirty-nine

*T*hings have gotten worse with Diana—it seems she went a little farther than writing letters with that prisoner. Margaret is beside herself. On the telephone the other day, she wailed, 'Our own daughter, a traitor! How could Harry and I have raised a traitor?'

I reminded her Diana was only following an adolescent whim. But in Margaret's eyes, it's black-and-white and there's no room for any other considerations.

Then she said, "And to do this right after we found out about Paul... I can hardly believe she would stoop this low."

It's easy for me to see this is about Diana's immaturity and short-sightedness, not betraying her country, but for Margaret, what she did stands in direct opposition to everything Paul died for.

It's so hard to offer her any comfort. I don't think she can accept any, at least not right now.

I'm really glad you aren't living there now. Can you imagine how hard this has to be for Benny? But at least Harry is at home, so he has somebody to talk to.

Actually, they may not have told him any of the details. That would be like my side of the family. We've always swept as much as we could under the rug and hoped it would magically disappear.

I didn't mean to spend so long on this, and sure hope it can all get worked out. Margaret mentioned the law might even get involved, I hope not, for Diana's sake. After all, she's grieving too. I could never say that to Margaret, of course.

From your first letter, it sounds as if you've got your feet on solid *ground there. What a great start, to have friendly classmates and a job waiting for you. What I see between the lines is a very busy daughter, but you can handle this.*

Like your dad said to me a little while ago, 'Twila's a go-getter.'

He's spending most days at the lumberyard, and a couple of times, has sent Rodney home. Sharon is thrilled to have him catch up on things there, and says Lukey follows him all around the house.

He's grown inches every time I see him. Inches taller, and inches around—such a roly-poly child. Ah well, he'll grow out of that once warm weather comes.

Charlotte's grandmother stopped by the other day and said to wish you well. She brought over some photographs, so I'm enclosing them. Char was always such a good friend. I know you must still miss her.

Time to go to bed, so I'll close by saying we couldn't be more proud of you.

Love,
Mom

"Wonder what else Diana did?" Twila muttered to herself as she set the letter down on her dresser and checked the time. Still an hour left before Mrs. Alcott—Adriane—expected her. Probably about the amount of time it would take to brush up on the bone structure chapter for tomorrow's test.

But the photos arrested her—she and Char on the day she moved away with her parents. Seemed like forever ago. Char on her graduation day, and then beside a huge lighted Christmas tree in a massive building, maybe at the USO?

Char was as real now as she'd ever been. It seemed she might walk through the door any moment, healthy and so alive. After Stan left Camp Algona, it was like this, too. She half-expected him around every corner. That's probably how Aunt Margaret felt about Paul, and Uncle Marvin about Butch.

In one way, time and distance changed nothing. Char's smile came to her just the other day when the Alcott's playful puppy jumped up into her lap. Char would have loved cuddling with him as much as the children did.

And today, when a write-up of this semester's costs appeared in her mailbox, she could hear Stan saying everything would work out. He'd been right. Between her salary and the government tuition grant, she had nothing to worry about.

Holding that list in her hand, he'd seemed so close, so real, even though he was thousands of miles away by now. Nothing to worry about, true; but plenty to pray about.

December 16, 1944

"That's our plane, the C-46 Commando over there. Pretty safe, I'd say. These workhorses have been flying over the Hump to supply American and Nationalist Chinese forces for three years now."

Stan's commander shouldered his gear. "With overloads, monsoons, miserable airstrips and the Himalayas to face, our pilot probably thinks he's landed a dream job this time.

"Might as well get a move on. There's just twenty of us, but they'll be loading up some Wright engines for replacement parts and that pile of stretchers over there, too."

What a difference from his last journey to the South Pacific. For one thing, they were scheduled to land in little more than twenty-four hours. Waiting outside the plane, Stan chatted with an older civilian worker waiting to load.

Or so he thought. He realized how wrong he was when the fellow said, "This'll be my eightieth wartime flight to pilot. Our total westbound lift has gone up from five-hundred tons to sixteen hundred during the past year."

"How long have you been flying?"

"Started before you were born, I expect. I've flown just about every model, starting with biplanes. In '43, they called me into the

Air Transport Command out of retirement. Not too many pilots can say they miss grandchildren."

One of Stan's crew overheard and muttered, "Talk about experienced..."

The pilot gave a wry grin. "I'm an old-timer, all right, although anything can happen to anybody at any time. But from the time I saw a biplane land at an airport in Indiana, I knew flying was the life for me."

"How old were you?"

"I don't remember. I became a mechanic, and a few years after the war, somebody told me about the Navy's first flight to Hawaii in a seaplane. That was John Rodgers and his crew—I knew I'd discovered my hero. And I also knew I'd never be happy till I got my license."

"I had to work hard. When I re-enlisted, my commander appreciated maturity, I guess. And the rest, well...

"On this flight, we'll stop in Hawaii and proceed to Port Moresby, New Guinea. That's thirteen hundred miles north of Brisbane, so we'll cut off a chunk of flying time without even trying. But seven thousand miles is still seven thousand miles."

He joined the inspection crew, and no one asked any more questions, but during the flight, Stan overheard a couple of men describing the flight he'd mentioned.

"Nobody had flown two thousand miles before that, and even twenty-five hundred was unheard of. Lindbergh hadn't crossed the Atlantic yet, either. But Rodgers and another seaplane headed out, and the other one had troubles early on. Rodgers kept going, but ran out of gas near Oahu.

Stan got out his writing paper and recorded this story for Benny. He'd send it to Twila in his next letter.

A man named Rodgers glided the biplane to the ocean, and a search boat found him and his crew nine days later. But listen to this: Rodgers and his crew had stripped fabric from one of the lower wings, rigged it between the upper ones, and sailed over four hundred miles.

All for the Cause

I know you're an Army man, but just think about those sailors. In the face of what might have been certain death, they persevered. That's what it takes to survive.

And they did. They ran out of food after three days, and after three more, ran out of water. But it rained. That saved them.

Imagine being out there on the Pacific for that long. But these men used imagination to create a sail. By the time a very shocked navigator found them alive after nine days out in the elements, they had sailed four hundred miles!

This happened almost twenty years ago. Just think how far we've come since then. By the time you graduate from high school, what more might we have accomplished, and what new challenges will we face?

Tuning in to the rest of the conversation gave him the perfect ending for Benny.

"So what're we doing in the Army?"

"Well, here's the rest of the story. Two years later, the Army outdid the Navy when two pilots made it from California to Hawaii in twenty-six hours. So there you have it—that's why we're in the Army."

Picturing it all, Stan jotted another paragraph. Then he retreated into his own thoughts. Like Twila kept saying, everything had happened so fast. Yet even in the whirlwind of the past week, thinking of her brought a sense of calm.

A rough landing at Hickman Field shook him awake. Suddenly, the big plane shuddered as if the tail wheel had a mind of its own.

Tap... tap... tap... that must be the pilot's feet on the rudder pedals. For a full minute, it seemed the tail wheel might refuse to settle, but somehow, the pilot gained directional control.

Communal relief flooded the fuselage as they touched down and rolled in. The commander issued orders—stretch your legs, find something to eat, but stay close. They'd refuel here and undergo a routine engine check, that was all.

Feeling the earth beneath his feet, Stan glanced around. Still a few signs of the Japanese attack. The attack that hindered supplies from getting to Corregidor. The attack that changed everything.

"Take a quick whiff of Hawaii, men. We're almost halfway to paradise."

Ready for a night's sleep herself, Twila gathered the Alcott children around her. Sarah, Benjamin, and Susie snuggled on the couch, ready for a story.

"Maybe I'll tell you one that just came in a letter. A man named Stan wrote it and sent it to me all the way from Hawaii. Do you know where that is?"

"Where Daddy go?"

Six-year-old Benjamin frowned. "Naw. He isn't out in the ocean, sis. He's in France."

According to last night's news, father might well be stuck in a foxhole in Belgium. American forces were taking heavy losses in the heavily forested Ardennes region of Wallonia in eastern Belgium, northeast France, and Luxembourg.

Mrs. Alcott, who asked Twila to call her Adriane the first time they met, wanted this trio in bed with the chickens, so in the next two hours, Twila missed Benny. A checker game would do her good. She bet he missed her, too. Diana's behavior couldn't do anything to improve Aunt Margaret's outlook, but hopefully, Harry liked to play checkers.

Besides listening to the radio, tonight would be perfect for getting another letter ready for Benny. So far, he'd been a faithful correspondent, and she could imagine how much he'd have to say about Stan's Hawaii story.

After she told a brief version of it to the children, two of them fought back yawns. Even Benjamin offered no resistance, and twenty minutes later, she settled down to read several chapters and finish some worksheets.

But after the newscaster brought word of rising casualties in

All for the Cause

the Battle of the Bulge, he focused in on the German massacre of Americans at Malmedy. The horror of this story captivated her.

Picture yourself locked in the present life-and-death struggle in the Ardennes. What fires your morale? What tells you we will win regardless of our present sacrifices? One word.

Malmedy.

For it was here that on December seventeenth, a German tank force ruthlessly fired upon 150 Americans who had surrendered. The enemy herded these soldiers into a field during the opening hours of the Nazi counteroffensive.

In the words of a survivor, 'We had to lie there and listen to German noncoms use pistols on the wounded who groaned or tried to move.'

Another survivor says, 'They had 15 to 20 tanks. They disarmed us and took anything valuable. We lined up along the road for an hour, at least. Then they stood us all together in an open field. Then one German pulled out a pistol and shot down our fellows from less than 50 yards away.'

This soldier continues, 'We hadn't tried to run away—we had our hands up. Our only choice was to flop down and play dead.'

As we hear continuing reports from the Bulge, we grieve those we have lost. But through it all, we will re-

> member this vicious, unprovoked mur-
> der of 130 of our young men.
>   We can never forget this barbarous
> act, and rest assured that our troops
> over there will never forget it, ei-
> ther.
>   And we will win. No matter what.

Switching off the radio did nothing to remove the image, and studying became a struggle. Tendons and nerves, bones and ligaments, veins and arteries—they all swam in a field in Belgium.

When Adriane came home from her shift at the hospital, Twila hurried several blocks to her dormitory. A quiet night in Iowa City—most students were probably studying.

Inserting her key into the lock, she filled her lungs. That scene the newscaster described—one of those helpless soldiers might have been Butch or Paul. Or Stan.

A shiver took her as she climbed the stairs to her room. One day, the soldiers who survived would be coming home. They might be injured, and she would be proud to care for them.

This motivated every hour of study, every page she read, every lab she attended, every move she made.

Chapter Forty

Early January, 1945
Somewhere in the Northern Philippine Sea

Awaiting transfer to a Navy submarine once they reached the eighteenth parallel, Stan lay back on his narrow bunk. Another reason to be in the Army rather than the Navy—the wideness of the outdoors compared to these cramped quarters.

But he wasn't complaining—not at all—for the sub would take them north of where General Kruger's Sixth Army waited to land at Linguyan Bay. If General MacArthur's diversionary plan worked, the Japanese would stay focused on southern Luzon, where the Allies had been dropping dummy paratroopers.

Under that guise, the Sixth would debark and proceed north through San Fernando and Luma, clearing Japanese strongholds as they went. What Stan's patrol accomplished even farther north would embellish efforts.

Attached to a Sixth Infantry combat patrol, they would slip from the submarine to a PT boat and make way to a coastal point somewhere between Luma and Vigan. From there, they would reconnoiter with Filipino guerrilla units operating against enemy positions in the mountains north of Bontoc.

How long would they remain aboard this ship? Some of the others voiced this concern, but the timeline caused Stan no anxiety. His only task was to stay fit for the mission, and that involved walking up on deck as much as possible.

Urgency enervated him, but at the same time, the satisfaction of being where he needed to be enveloped him. Except for his last few days with Twila, this had been lacking at Camp Algona.

He closed his eyes as a guard's light swept the porthole opposite his bunk. Gentle waves lapped the ship's side, as they had the merchant mariner that transported him to the Philippines early in the war.

His contribution might be small, even minuscule compared to others' actions, but the Army had *allowed him to return*. The sense he'd had that he must come—guidance, some would call it—had proven trustworthy. He'd been given a great gift—the opportunity to contribute once again.

That was what mattered, and he relished the honor as he eased into grateful, dreamless sleep. Yes, dreamless—nearing his destination somehow kept those old nightmares at bay. He'd had a lot to learn, code words, radio lingo, and locations—mostly map work, which fed his passion and kept his mind busy.

It wasn't the maps so much, but the people in the locales he memorized that energized him. Each section of the island had been christened with a code name absolutely essential to every member of his unit.

Maybe those night terrors had plagued him because he'd been doing nothing—nothing in comparison to this, nothing to help those captives. Now, that had all changed.

If he dreamed at all these days, it was of a beautifully freckled face, a young woman full of vitality. One night, she stood on a platform receiving her nursing degree. In a crisp white uniform, she shook hands with the Director of Nursing and bowed her head as the Dean pinned a starched white cap on her shiny chestnut hair.

Then she spotted him in the crowd, sitting beside her parents and Rodney's family. Everyone was applauding, him so much his palms hurt. He caught Twila's eye as she took her place with the rest of her class, and the look she gave him held all the love in her warm Iowa heart.

In daylight, Cap still paid him visits at times. This morning as he woke, the image of Cap's twitching eyelid appeared. A few minutes later, up on deck in full sun, he gazed south, and Cap's voice rang inside his head.

I am a stranger here, within a foreign land; My home is far away, upon a golden strand, Ambassador to be of realms beyond the sea, I'm here on business for my King!

Now, so close to finding him and Carlos, every word from Cap sounded like a promise drifting on an ocean breeze, mild and harmless. Knowing that those words... *mild, harmless*... would have no place along the brutal trail ahead failed to stymie effect.

Without a doubt, this would be a bloody business. But even so, the prospect carried an undeniable thrill. To find Cap and Carlos, and who knew how many other men like them holed up on the heights of Bataan, would be worth whatever it took.

He wanted nothing more than to turn things around, to set the captives free and imprison captors. Bloody or not, this mission had the feel of a divine appointment.

On a bitter cold January day, Twila's mail brought her a smile. Not the kind of smile a letter from Stan would produce, but a smile, anyway.

January 23, 1945
Dear Twila,
Thanks for sending me the letter from Stan. Me and Dad figured out the clues he gave us. Sure was smart of him to think of doing that.
I been reading up on the Philippines, especially Mindoro. I know that isn't where he's headed, but I had to write a report about an important event that was quite complicated, so I picked the first part of the Luzon Campaign.
Wish I could have written about what Stan's doing, but that's classified. Believe me, I never breathe a word about it.

First I had to figure out what ovoid meant, why didn't they just say the island looked like an egg? Anyhow, the complications was easy.

The best airfield would've been up in the northeast part of the island, but that was too close to the Japs on Luzon and besides, it has bad flying weather.

So General MacArthur picked a beachhead near San Jose in the southwest. That way, they also could use Mangarin Bay, the best anchorage on the island.

Why did they even mess with Mindoro, you might ask? I mean, it's got bad humidity, lots of mountains, malaria, and it's only half the size of New Jersey. Well, here's the answer.

See, the Navy needed land-based air cover for convoys moving toward the Lingayen Gulf. When the Japs attacked from bases on Luzon, we could aim our guns on Mindoro at them and shoot them down.

So even though this was complicated, our commanders made the right decision to seize land for an air base on this little ovoid in the southern Philippine Islands.

I know you can't send this on to Stan, because it's got lots of military information in it. But Dad said you might like to read it, and I have a surprise for you, too.

I got a B for a grade. (Although I do have to admit Dad helped me a lot with this assignment.) He says if you and Stan can go to college, why can't I?

Hope you like your studies and that you know you will always be my favorite nurse.

Yours truly,
Benny Valentine

More than once, Twila laughed out loud, and when she finished, her roommate asked, "That couldn't be from Stan."

"Oh, no. But it's from his biggest fan, my cousin. He's 13, and Stan can do no wrong."

She reread the ending, and realized Benny had made no mention of his mom or Diana. Thank heavens for Harry.

All for the Cause

"Cap..." A diminutive Filipino nodded in response to Stan's question part way up a short rise. "He die. Last year this time." His eyes glinted. "Other GI—out with fighters." He patted Stan's shoulder.

"You come back. Eat. Carlos be here soon."

He retraced his steps, but Stan knelt beside a rude cross. When he touched the cross, it left a sliver in his forefinger.

Thanks, buddy.

The jungle encroached. Insects and birds paused evening occupation. Then, one of Cap's quotes intruded:

"There is a proper dignity and proportion to be observed in performance of every act of life. Marcus Aurelius."

A thick bamboo stalk offered Stan support, and for a second, he could have sworn Cap stood only a few yards away. Weaving in and out of thick foliage, he gave that familiar toss of his head. It seemed right to speak to him.

"You kept things lively for us, Cap—you gave us hope. Thank you, and may you rest in peace." The moon slid from behind a cloud, transforming the world to silver-gray.

"I have a quote for you now, my friend. *Earth to earth, dust to dust, ashes to ashes.*"

Gradually, like a mist in an early-morning Wisconsin forest, Cap retreated into the foliage.

Not much of a funeral service, but it would have to do.

The campfire's warmth declared that these guerillas had secured a considerable section of mountainside where they felt safe. From all accounts, Jap holdouts still existed, although considerable enemy forces had been moved southward.

The sizzle of dripping fat declared a successful hunt, and Stan's stomach growled. Thankfully, his commander had allowed him to bunk here tonight, with the rest of his patrol close by. It seemed fitting to stay near Cap's resting place this one last time—after, all he owed Cap his life.

After gnawing on meat down to the bone, his thin mat in a nipa hut offered no rest, but made a perfect spot to reflect. If it hadn't been for Cap, he'd have been on that trail to the prison camp, harassed by enemy guards. Maybe wouldn't even have made it all the way. Besides, he would never have met Carlos. Or Twila.

Rustle-rustle-rustle...

A Filipino whispered, "GI here."

Outside the doorway in wavering light from a slim moon, Stan waited. Half a minute later, Carlos slapped him on the back.

"I knew you'd be back. Just like MacArthur." Except for his American banter, Carlos might have passed for an abnormally tall, gaunt Filipino.

"That's me, just like the General. You're looking great, buddy."

"Even with my latest scars? Got 'em just the other day." Carlos turned his head to reveal rugged gashes on his cheek and neck.

"I've thought of you every day, every night... you and Cap."

"Glad to see that knee of yours healed—bet you met some pretty nurses." Carlos sobered and gestured in the general direction of the gravesite. "Before he passed, Cap said to tell you good-bye."

A sigh was all Stan could manage.

"Almost to the end, he kept singing that song: *I am a stranger here, within a foreign land... bum, bum, bum-bum-bum-bum.* When he got too weak to sing, he still hummed it."

"Singing his way out. So you were with him until...?"

"*Si.*" Carlos took his time. "It was early December. Seems longer ago than that."

"How was it for him?"

A shiver took Carlos in spite of the heat. "Bad. Really bad. He was delirious most of the time."

"I'm sorry—for him and for you."

"Like I said, he remembered you right up to the end. Remembered a lot. He was still teaching classes I'd never even heard of." A faint breeze through palm fronds matched the tenor of Carlos's sigh.

"Now, guess what? I sing Cap's song all over this mountain. If I ever leave, the hibiscus plants'll sing it for him."

He produced a weary grin. "Been out in my zoot suit tonight, lookin' for Nips, and I'm dead on my feet."

"You're taking care of those gashes?"

Carlos flipped his hand in the air. "The Filipinos pour some vile stuff on them a couple of times a day. Worked for your knee, didn't it?"

"Hard to argue with that." Stan motioned him into the hut and Carlos sank onto his mat. In an instant, his breathing slowed.

Immersed in the steady rise and fall of his chest, Stan kept watch. It was the least he could do... Exactly what he used to do, listen to Cap or Carlos—or both of them—sleep.

People back in the States would describe Carlos as *skin and bones*, but they'd be overlooking his heart. After all this time, he still homed in on his mission, searching out and destroying the enemy.

For an instant, Benny's innocent question strummed through Stan's consciousness. "Ever see any Japs? Ever kill any?"

There was no telling how many Carlos had sent into eternity, but if the scars and bruises on his body were any indication, it might be hundreds. Likely, no one would ever calculate his unseen contribution.

Outside, a Filipino maintained his night watch, though he must be exhausted, too. This was the time to sleep unhindered. But for Stan, too many questions arose.

Carlos had survived—that was all he could have hoped. When the patrol arrived in a few hours, would the commander ask him to join them? And if he did, would Carlos have a choice?

The next inquiry led him off into channels he and Cap might have bantered about. Given the choice, what would Carlos decide?

January 20, 1945

Before he left with his patrol, Stan visited Cap's grave one last time—a humble resting place for the captain who, back in California, had introduced them all to the Philippines. Stan knelt once more.

Only this simple cross marked Cap's resting place, but there was nothing simple about this American. He lived aware of the overall human story, and so many college literature students would miss out on his perspective.

Stan's gift arrived in a recollection from two years ago. Seeing the captives on the path to the prison camp left all three of them stunned and heartsick. They wanted to slash way up the mountain, descend on the Nip guards responsible for so many deaths, and slay them.

But that would have been suicidal. Not much later, the Filipinos discovered little band and led them to relative safety. For the next months, they scouted out small enemy patrols and made mark.

And so the time had passed, with Cap gradually succumbing to disease. But his heart had stayed true.

Off the trail, the patrol leader conferred with Carlos, and when they finished, Carlos joined Stan.

"So, off you go. Kill as many as you can for me."

"You're staying?"

"*Necesito.*" The look in his eyes underlined his meaning. "I must."

"They need you here more than with us?"

"*Si.* Our guerilla force has a radio now, and we'll be sending intel to General Kruger's units as they come closer." He flashed his grin. "It helps if somebody knows English."

"Doesn't get more important than that."

Carlos narrowed his eyes. "Maybe our paths will cross again."

"You'll probably be a respected businessman in L.A. some day. I'll read about you in the newspaper."

The sound of Carlos laughing became another parting gift. "And you'll be a lawyer, making things right."

"Let's head out, men." The patrol shuffled into place on the trail, and Carlos grasped Stan's shoulder.

"*Cuidate, mi amigo.*" He glanced toward the grave. "Take care. You and me—we'll never forget him."

Stan joined the men just in time to fall in line, and before they left, the leader shared the latest intelligence.

"Our Navy's crushing the Japs in the Gulf of Leyte. As we speak, a band of Rangers is heading toward Cabanatuan to free our prisoners. Whatever we do to decimate the enemy will only aid efforts. Keep your eyes open, your ears to the jungle."

With that, they were off. Somewhere along the trail, they'd take a break, and Stan might pull out the picture of Twila he carried in his helmet. Just yesterday, someone had looked over his shoulder at her.

"Got a girlfriend, eh? Me, too. They're what we're fightin' for."

Yes, and she was worth whatever it took to bring this war to an end. If he were in charge, he would help liberate these islands, be spared the fight on Japanese soil, and return home to marry Twila.

No doubt about it, she was the girl of his dreams. Even as he imagined this scenario, harsh facts taunted him.

This enemy would never surrender. What could possibly bring about such a change in the Emperor's heart?

Bowing to jungle foliage as he followed the GI ahead of him, he had no answer. Nothing to do but turn over his questions, and the future in its entirety, to a power far greater than his own.

Epilogue

April 21, 1946

The church in Halberton had seen its share of funerals over the past few years. Several of its young men, too young to die, had received last good-byes here in this sanctuary. But today people arrived for a happy gathering.

From a few blocks away, a young woman walked beside her father. Her brand-new tweed suit boasted flashes of daisy yellow that matched her hat, and her smile burst out every few seconds.

"I just can't believe it, Dad. Here we are on our way to my wedding."

"Well, I can. The first time I met Stan... actually, a few hours before that, when he nearly knocked Colonel Lobdell to the floor, I liked him. Your Mom and I couldn't be more pleased with your choice of a husband."

"And he hasn't changed. Not really. Even after all he's been through."

"Not where it counts—he sacrificed a lot for our freedom. But he came out of it all even more forthright and kind. We can't pretend his service in the Philippines and especially on Okinawa have had no effect on him, but he's the type to make the best of things. He stepped off the train determined to be a lawyer, and determined to love you the very best he can."

Twila reveled in the squeeze Dad gave her hand. "He'll be a wonderful husband and father, Tiger. What more could we ask?"

Up ahead, a horn beeped in front of the church, and sunshine dappled the spit-shined hood of Rodney's new car.

"Oh, there he is, just getting out." Twila gave Mr. Brunner a quick hug. "See you in a minute, Dad. I know it's supposed to be bad luck for Stan to see me before the wedding, but I don't really believe that old tale."

A few seconds later, Stan swung his good arm around her. His eyes sparkled as he gave her a solid kiss.

"You're sure about this?" He waved his empty left sleeve. "Certain sure? Remember, you're marrying somebody with a handicap."

"What handicap?" Twila leaned her head against him. "Of course I'm sure. Surer than sure. I'm marrying a hero, and the only man I'll ever love. How about you—are *you* sure? You're marrying a redhead whose nickname is *Tiger*."

"Mmm..." He angled his head and lifted her chin with his forefinger. "Absolutely."

Special Thanks

To Camp Algona POW Museum, Algona, Iowa—for providing excellent research resources.

www.pwcamp.algona.org

And to Linda Betsinger McCann, author of
Prisoners of War in Iowa

About the Author

Words have always been comfort food for **Gail Kittleson**. After instructing expository writing and English as a Second Language, she began writing seriously. Intrigued by the World War II era, Gail creates women's historical fiction from her northern Iowa home and also facilitates writing workshops/retreats.

She and her husband, a retired Army chaplain, enjoy grandchildren and in winter, Arizona's Mogollon Rim Country. You can count on Gail's heroines to ask honest questions, act with integrity, grow in faith, and face hardships with spunk.

Visit Gail online at: GailKittleson.com

Also available from

WordCrafts Press

House of Madness
   by Sara Harris

Angela's Treasures
   by Marian Rizzo

Pipe Dream
   by K.L. Collins

The Mirror Lies
   by Sandy Brownlee

You've Got It, Baby!
   By Mike Carmichael

www.WordCrafts.net

CPSIA information can be obtained
at www.ICGtesting.com
Printed in the USA
LVHW092242290419
615848LV00006BC/48/P